Critical Acclaim for *It Rhymes With Truth*

Named to the 2024 Notable 100 list by *Shelf Unbound*

Rated one of the top 50 literary/general fiction novels of 2024 in the *BookLife* Awards

"Miller's curveball coming-of-age tale lands in the strike zone." *–Publishers Weekly*

"The nature of memory is interrogated at every turn, and the possibility of love is never denied in *It Rhymes With Truth*, a poignant novel about a cross-generational friendship.... With equal parts wit and tenderness, Rich Miller's heartfelt novel looks for answers to the question of loneliness in the relationship between a young boy and an old woman. [The novel] burns with compassion and delights in all of the absurd, beautiful, and painful ways that people try to care for one another against the crushing weight of alienation." *–Clarion Reviews* [5 Star Rating]

"Miller's deeply felt tale illustrates how life's greatest challenges always arrive before we're ready for them, and how they shape us into the people we become.... A masterfully controlled tear-jerker of a novel about found family." *–Kirkus Reviews* [starred review]

"Miller's storytelling is charming and contemplative... subtly showcasing the defensive psyche of a child shaped by a rough childhood. A vital, moving novel." *–BookLife* [Editor's Choice]

"I lost count of how many times I laughed out loud while reading *It Rhymes With Truth*.... [The novel is] an absurd and unforgettable tour deforce." –Readers' Favorite [Unanimous 5-Star Reviews]

"Touching, humbling, and thought-provoking, *It Rhymes With Truth* is a beautifully written piece of fiction.... A homeless eight-(anda half)-year-old boy. A lonely retiree. A relationship borne from solitude and a future saved by compassion. It is the balance between light and dark, humor and introspection, loneliness and friendship, vulnerability and resilience that adds layers of authenticity and emotional depth through the story, inviting us to reflect on our own lives and relationships. *It Rhymes With Truth* by Rich Miller has something for everyone, and its message will remain with us long after we've reached the final page." –Reader Views [5 Star Review]

"A thoroughly engaging novel.... This book is wonderfully fresh, with a breezy style that incorporates song lyrics, drawings, and comical footnotes. Ruth is especially original and funny." –*Booklist* [Starred Review]

"The novel delves into themes of loneliness, friendship, healing, and self-discovery. It highlights the profound impact small interactions and gestures can have in shaping a person's identity and understanding of the world." –IndieReader [IR Approved rating]

"You made me cry. What a lovely book in ways that shouldn't be lovely. You made me feel deeply about these very flawed people, and that is what books are supposed to do." –Jenn Bailey, award-winning author of *Henry, Like Always* and co-author of the forthcoming *The Not So Quiet Life of Marcel Marceau*

"*It Rhymes With Truth* by Rich Miller is a truly original tale, masterfully rendered by a gifted storyteller clearly born to the craft." –Readers' Favorite [Unanimous 5-Star Reviews]

"[A] thoroughly engaging novel—by turns, funny, thoughtful, sweet, and sad.... This book is wonderfully fresh, thanks to the author's breezy style incorporating song lyrics, drawings, and funny footnotes.... The book's conclusion is heart-wrenching as the pieces of the story fall into place." –BlueInk Reviews [Starred Review]

For more critical acclaim for *It Rhymes With Truth*, visit www.richm illerbooks.com.

It Rhymes With Truth
By Rich Miller
Published by Lost Pictograph Publishing
Copyright 2023 by Rich Miller
All rights reserved. No portion of this book may be reproduced in any form without written permission from the publisher or author, except as permitted by U.S. copyright law.

Print Edition ISBN 979-8-9907709-04
E-book Edition ISBN 979-8-9907709-1-1

Cover by Caroline Teagle Johnson. Other artwork by Rich Miller.

For more information, visit www.richmillerbooks.com.

Special thanks to Heather Walsh Miller, Sela Miller, Owen Miller, Avery Burton, Kate Angelella, Jenn Bailey, Caroline Teagle Johnson, John Shors, Haley Stufflebean-Ortega, Bailey Goodell, Burlyn Birkemeier, Alexandra Gaunt, Aaron Sewall, Dan Lamberger, Jerry Chrisman, Jon Ellingson, Hank Sigmon, Noah Kolman. Elliot Geller, Michael Running, Urania Miller, Jennifer Miller, Valerie Miller and many others.

With gratitude to the following copyright holders:

PLEASE DON'T MAKE ME BE GOOD (from "Fifty Million Frenchmen")
Words and Music by COLE PORTER
© 1929 (Renewed) WC MUSIC CORP. All Rights Reserved. Used by Permission of ALFRED MUSIC.

THERE'S NO CURE LIKE TRAVEL (from "Anything Goes")
Words and Music by COLE PORTER
© 1934 (Renewed) WC MUSIC CORP. All Rights Reserved. Used by Permission of ALFRED MUSIC.

I'VE GOT MY EYES ON YOU (from "Broadway Melody of 1940")
Words and Music by COLE PORTER
© 1939 (Renewed) CHAPPELL & CO., INC. All Rights Reserved. Used by Permission of ALFRED MUSIC.

SO NEAR AND YET SO FAR (from "You'll Never Get Rich")
Words and Music by COLE PORTER
© 1941 (Renewed) CHAPPELL & CO., INC. All Rights Reserved. Used by Permission of ALFRED MUSIC.

I'VE STILL GOT MY HEALTH (from "Panama Hattie")
Words and Music by COLE PORTER
© 1940 (Renewed) CHAPPELL & CO., INC. All Rights Reserved. Used by Permission of ALFRED MUSIC.

INTER-DEPARTMENTAL MAIL

Cross out previous address. Use repeatedly until all spaces are utilized.

To: YOU

From: ME

Name
Dept.

Name
Dept.

Name
Dept.

Name
Dept.

Name
Dept.

Name
Dept.

Name
Dept.

Name
Dept.

Name
Dept.

Name
Dept.

Name
Dept.

until all spaces are utilized.
address. Use repeatedly
Name
Dept.
Name
Dept.
Name
Dept.
Name
Dept.
Name
Dept.
Name
Dept.
DON'T READ ME
HER SID
HER S

It Rhymes With Truth
oss out previous address. Use repeatedly
until all spaces are utilized.
Name
Dept.
Name
Dept.
Name
Dept.
Name
Dept.
Name
Dept.
Name
DON'T READ

D o you remember the day we met? I didn't know anyone had noticed me out there, but you were watching me from behind the curtain of your sliding door. Just like you do when a black-throated blue warbler has been lured in by your treats and you don't want to scare it off. It was the sound of the rock that did it, smacking down against the concrete to crack the sunflower seeds, but mostly scattering them and making a mess. That made you look outside, and there I was squatting down in my filthy green shirt with the stegosaurus on the front.

The dinosaur was saying "MEOW!" in letters carved out of enormous stones. The person who made the shirt thought that was funny. The stone letters. The talking dinosaur. The meow. The whole thing. They thought it was hilarious. I didn't think it was funny. I thought it was the opposite of funny. Back then, I was 137% certain the shirt would have been funnier if the stegosaurus was frowning and saying something like, "Cats smell like pee and people are dumb." That would have been a lot funnier to me. Way funnier. But you know how I was. Lemons would have said I was giving sour a bad name.

I'm not alone, though. A grumpy stegosaurus saying grumpy things[1] would be as funny as heck to you, too. Maybe that image is making you laugh hard and spray your tea right now. Right this very moment. Maybe.

I picked out the edible bits from the few seeds I had managed to break, and you told me later that I made a face when I chewed them. They tasted terrible without the mountain of salt that companies put on the seeds in bags at the store.

Ingredients: Salt, sodium chloride, sunflower seeds, more salt.

Salt makes everything better. These non-store seeds tasted like chewed newspaper. But I ate them. They were free.

I leaned over the metal railing along the edge of your mini patio and got another handful of seeds from your birdfeeder, but I didn't see you. I went

---

1. A grumposaurus. Meow! Woof! Oink!

over to the bushes and picked a different rock for breaking the new batch of seeds. It had a flat bottom and did a better job. I smashed seeds and picked out the bits until voices jolted me to attention. Some people were heading to the parking area down toward the end of the building where the dining hall is. They had been inside visiting their grandmother or great aunt or great-great aunt or great-great-great grandmother or somebody else super old, and now they were heading back to their car. I dropped the rock, pulled a not-very-yellow-any-more tennis ball out of my backpack, and bounced it like I was just a regular 8-year-old boy playing with a ball. Nothing to see here.

Nothing at all.

I continued to pretend to be normal. The stegosaurus on my shirt continued to lie about being a cat. Bounce, bounce, wait.

After those people drove away, I came back to the metal railing, got down on all 4s, put my arm through as far as I could, and barely reached the only piece of bread that wasn't pecked to death by the birds. I brushed off both sides, blew on a couple of spots that were still dirty, smelled it, broke off the crust, threw that away, and took a bite of the white part. Your curtain moved. I froze the way animals do when they want to be invisible and not get eaten. I tried not to breathe. But I did. I tried not to chew the bread. But I did. Then I saw the tall cup of milk on the carpet inside, leaning a little to 1 side like this \\\\\\ and threatening to tip over. Beside it was a plate with a cookie.

I saw your fingers 1st. They crept around the edge of the curtain and pulled it toward you so you could see whether I had noticed the treat. Then your hair. It came out slower than a glacier at a 90-degree angle to the curtain like you were being slid out horizontally on the world's slowest conveyor belt. Then your face, inch by wrinkly inch, trying to go slow enough for me not to notice. What you saw was me looking right back at you. Right into your eyeballs.

Your face and hair and fingers rushed back behind the curtain, but I could feel you wondering if I had seen you. I could feel it like heat. Your thoughts were like laser beams shooting through the curtain to my teeny, tiny speck of a hint of a long division remainder of a brain. My eyes went back and forth from the cookie to the curtain, back to the cookie, back to the curtain. Calculating. Calculating.

After hiding for a not-long-enough amount of time, you peeked around a different part of the curtain, hoping I wouldn't notice because you had used the amazing strategy of switching sides and waiting a bit. I was looking right at you again, still on all 4s, still chewing the terrible bread, digging in my shoes for traction just in case. You ducked back behind. It was a game of peek-a-boo neither of us wanted to play, but there we were playing it.

I watched to see what you would do next. Your hand came out from behind the curtain toward the handle of the sliding door. My muscles tensed like a cheetah[2] getting ready to run. The handle was too far, though. You flailed at it but were nowhere near close enough to grab it. To reach it you would have to step out into the open, but you didn't. Your hand went back behind the curtain and the curtain started to move. You pulled it along with you, blocking your body as you went. When you were close enough, your hand came back out and pulled on the door handle. It didn't budge, so your other hand came out of hiding and tried to help. They pulled. They pulled harder. Nothing.

A finger reached out and pressed the button to unlock it, then both hands pulled again, and the door zoomed open faster than you were expecting. You almost pulled the curtain down trying not to fall. Well, I assume that is what happened. All I could see was the curtain going crazy as the door slid open at 97 miles an hour. After the curtain commotion stopped, your hand came back out and opened the screen door, too, then went back into hiding. The curtain slid back to where it had started, and the cookie started shooting laser beams at me. Directly into my stomach. Zappety zap.[3]

You peeked out the back side of the curtain again and saw that I was still on all 4s and hadn't moved any closer to getting the milk and cookie. You waited and looked again. I still hadn't moved. You decided to stop the hiding game. You stepped out from behind the curtain, and I saw all of you.

You were wearing the blue pants and yellow shirt with flowers that you used to wear every day until the holes in the armpits were too big to hide. Your wig was not on right, but I didn't know it was a wig. I thought your hair just grew that way. You looked at me, tilted your head a little to the side—the same way the glass of milk was leaning \\\\\\—and smiled. I couldn't tell if your teeth were real or the fake kind old people get when all their non-fake teeth fall out. I stared at your "teeth." I couldn't stop staring at them until you leaned down.

You picked up the cookie and milk and brought them outside. I scurried back a body length for each step you took onto the mini patio. When you saw me do that, you stopped. I stopped, too. You took another step forward, and I crawled another body length backward. You took a step backward to see if I would move toward you, keeping the distance the same. I did. You took another step forward, and I moved back again. You took a step sideways and I did, too, in the same direction you took. Then I corrected myself and crawled sideways 2 body widths the other way so I was the opposite of you. My instinct was always

---

2. A cheetah wearing an un-funny t-shirt who was on highest-of-high alert because you were an extremely dangerous old lady armed with a cookie.

3. Yes, there are a lot of laser beams in this story. You know how much I liked laser beams.

to do the opposite of you, even on that very 1st day.[4]

You scratched your ear like you were thinking, then slowly spun yourself around until you were facing me again. You pointed at me to do the same and I shook my head. I was not going to spin. No way. You winked, set the dish and glass down on the concrete near the railing, making old person noises when you bent over, slid it underneath the bottom bar, stood back up, making more old person noises, went back inside onto the carpet, and turned around to watch me from the doorway.

I stayed where I was. You crinkled up your lips and looked confused. You went back out to the dish, made more noises bending down, and pushed it further out toward me, almost off the concrete and onto the grass. You went back into the doorway and waited.

I didn't do anything.

You crinkled your lips again, then went behind the curtain to see if that would help. That's when the cookie started zappety zapping me again.

I stared at the cookie and tried to decide if I could get the food before you could get me. You didn't seem very fast. I was pretty sure I could run faster than you if you jumped out and tried to grab me. Even if you managed to get a hand on my leg, you didn't look very strong. I could probably kick your hands off me, grab my backpack and get away. I was an excellent kicker. Kickety, kickety, kick.

My stomach decided to risk it. Stupid stomach, always making me make bad decisions. I crawled toward the cookie and milk, but my eyes watched you for a sneak attack. I reached for the milk, keeping my eyes on you, feeling for the glass with my fingers, grabbed it and guzzled half of it, most of it pouring down by chin and throat and chest. The grumposaurus was getting soaked, and so was the dinosaur on my shirt.[5] I felt for the cookie, eyes still on you, until my fingers found it. I took a bite, swallowed without chewing, braced for you to rush out and try to grab me, took another bite, and then ran like heck when a car horn went off to my left. The cookie broke. I dropped most of it on the grass, but I didn't stop to pick it up. I was goner than gone.

You picked up the cookie, though. After I fled, you wrapped it in plastic, put it on the plate, put the plate on top of the glass of milk to keep bugs out, and left it there for me when I came back.

You knew I would.

---

4. I'm sure you would call it Newton's 4th Law of Motion (aka Newton's 1st Law of Parenting Pain-in-the-Butt Kids).

5. Get it? I was the grumposaurus. Not the dinosaur. Is it funnier if I explain it? ...just like you always explained your jokes to me when I didn't laugh. Remember?

You checked every few minutes to see if the cookie and milk were still there. I saw you do that, but you didn't see me. I was doing a good job of hiding. If being invisible was a job that paid $1,000,000, I'd be so rich.

Then you checked only every hour or so. I didn't have a watch to keep track. I'm just good at time, and good at waiting. Very good at waiting. I can beat anyone at a waiting game. Even you.

Late that afternoon, you sat on the couch with your cup of cranberry juice, and you did your puzzle book for a while. You fell asleep with your head tilted back and your mouth wide open like the number 0. When you woke up, you saw the cookie was gone and the glass was empty except for the plastic wrap I had crumpled up and put inside so the wind wouldn't blow it away and make litter. Yes, I was a complete jerk, but I wasn't a litter monster.

On top of the plate, held down by the rock with the flat bottom, was a picture, drawn on the back of a bank envelope from the 1 down the street that used to have free donuts in the lobby every Friday. They don't have those anymore. That's dumb. Instead, they have lollipops in baskets every day. I'd rather have donuts once a week than lollipops every day because lollipops are 1 of the worst candies. But you already know I hate them. I told you that 37^{37} times, didn't I? There wasn't anything I liked more than talking about things I didn't like.

Here's another reason I didn't like lollipops: because they used to be called "suckers" and I knew that was what old people called stupid people. When you were my age 1,234,567,890 years ago, did all candies have nicknames that were insults? Was candy corn called "gibfaced imbeciles"? And did butterscotches used to be called "hedge-born good-for-nothings"? Were candy canes called "fusty flapdoodles"? And yes, I am definitely trying to make you spray your tea.

Here is the picture I left for you that day, held down by the seed-smashing rock. It's the 1st art I ever made for you.

It's been on the refrigerator for all these years, and now I am putting it into this memory book for you.

You put out another cookie the next day. A sugar cookie with sprinkles, wrapped in plastic on a plate, balanced on top of a glass of milk with a couple of ice cubes to keep it cold-ish. You watched me from the far side of the curtain while I ate. I don't like sugar cookies with sprinkles. I hate them, actually. But I was too hungry to be picky.

I left you a droopy dandelion flower. It was non-droopy for only about 10 seconds after I picked it, then it shriveled and looked sad. Things in the world don't stay nice for very long before they go bad, do they? I know you disagree, but your objection is overruled. That's a true thing about this shriveling, deflating, depressing, dehydrating world, and the droopy flower proves it. Court is adjourned! La la...I can't hear you.

On the 3rd day, there was a chocolate chip cookie on the plate, and the glass underneath it was filled to the very top with choco-milk. I watched to see if you were behind the curtain, but I didn't see you. I left you my Tony Armas card on the plate. Armas Sr., not Junior. He hit 43 home runs in 1984, but he struck out 156 times.

On the 4th day, there was a cookie but no milk. I didn't see you inside that day either.

On the 5th day, there wasn't anything there. I went up to the railing, squinted to look inside and could see the outline of you sitting on the couch watching TV. I waved—the kind of wave to get someone's attention. You waved back—the kind of wave to say hello—and went back to watching TV. I waved again to get your attention, but you didn't look over. You were focused on the TV. I looked around to see if anyone was watching me. There wasn't. I climbed over the top of the railing and went up to the screen door. It was darker inside than outside, so I had to press my nose against the screen door mesh to see. I cleared my throat to make some noise.

You looked over again and said, "Good afternoon, Dear. Nice weather we're having, aren't we?"

I nodded and the screen pushed my nose up and down, making it look like a pig snout, then a boxer's nose, then a pig snout.[6]

You looked back at the TV just long enough to make me antsy, then you looked back at me and said, "Silly me. You probably want a snack, don't you?"

---

6. Oink! Meow! Grumpety, grumpety grump.

I nodded again. Hog. Boxer. Hog boxer. Hoxer.

"Well, help yourself. The milk is in the fridge and there are cups on the shelf over the toaster. The box on the counter has some cookies." You went back to watching TV. I could see it was a baseball game. The Mariners were playing an early game against the Blue Jays. You had the whole thing planned out, didn't you?

T he 1st Blue Jays card I ever got was Pat Borders. His rookie stats were:

BA—G—AB—R—H—2B—3B—HR—RBI—SB
.273—56—154—15—42—6—3—5—21—0

I reached for the box of cookies but stopped. I turned my hand over and looked at the palm. I lifted my other hand and looked at that palm, then curled my fingers and looked under the nails. You were still watching TV, or at least pretending to. It was the commercials in between innings. I wiped my hands on my pants and looked at them again. That may have made them dirtier.[7] I looked back over at you, but you were facing the TV, as if that was the real show.

I went to the sink, but couldn't reach the soap container, so I opened the cupboard underneath the sink and stepped on to the shelf to lift myself up. I tried to squirt some of the dish soap onto my hands, but the cap was closed. I tried pulling it open, but it was too slippery, so I gripped it with my teeth and opened it that way. Some got in my mouth. I spat it into the sink as quietly as I could. I looked over at you and your lips were tied up in a knot hiding a laugh. I spat again, then lathered up my hands and washed the best I could.

I dried my hands on the towel draped through the refrigerator handle, but that made the towel dirty. I looked at my hands again and noticed the filth near

---

7. My pants were a grimy crime scene—a grime scene.

my wrists and around the outside of my thumbs. I washed again. This time the towel came away clean, except for the dirt I had wiped on it before. I hid the dirty towel under the sink, climbed up onto the counter to look in the upper cabinets for a plate. I found 1 that didn't look too fancy and breakable, and I put a cookie from the box on it. The cookie had M&Ms baked into it. M&Ms are 1 of the top 10 candies. The lower half of the top ten, but that's still pretty good.

I found the cabinet with glasses and got a plastic cup. I put it on the floor, got the milk from the refrigerator and most of what I poured went into the cup. I wiped up the spilled milk with the dirty towel from under the sink, hid it back under the sink, then picked up the cup and the plate and stood there on the edge of the linoleum. I wasn't looking at you or the TV. I was looking at the screen door. At the door's handle. It was looking back at me, too. It was staring at me with laser beam intensity.[8]

I wanted to run, to drop everything—or maybe to drop everything except the cookie—and bolt out the door and over the railing and onto the grass and through the gap in the shrubs, not looking back even once. Not looking back ever.

That is what I was thinking about when you reached forward, placed a coaster on the coffee table for my dripping glass of milk, and patted the cushion slowly and softly in a way that made it look like the comfiest stupid thing my stupid eyes had ever stupidly seen.

Y ou didn't say a word to me for 2 innings. It was probably 45 minutes altogether because of all the baserunners and the pitching changes.[9] I had finished my cookie and milk 4.7 seconds after my filthy butt hit your clean couch, then we just sat there and watched. You broke the silence by saying, "Good arm," when Ichiro held a Blue Jay to a single on a hit that could have been a double or more.

"He had—" I started to say, but my voice croaked like a frog that had become a hermit for 20 years because he hated other frogs so much that he went to live in a mountaintop cave to get away from all their endless dumbness. I cleared my throat and tried again, "He had 11 assists last season." I reached into my putrid

---

8. I told you there were a lot of lasers in this.

9. Will the Mariners ever fix their bullpen? Please, before I kick the bucket, give up the ghost, buy the farm.

backpack to find the most recent Ichiro card I owned to prove it.

"Well now. That sounds like a lot." The smell of my open backpack infected every molecule of air in the room. Luckily, you couldn't smell a thing.[10]

"He would have more, but people don't try to run on him very much. Not anymore."

"I should think not. That wouldn't be smart." Then you said, "Now, remind me again. What is an assist, Dear?" You asked the question while you were focused on the TV, not looking over at me.

I have to be honest. I thought that was the dumbest question I had ever heard. My face probably had that written all over it in the biggest font you can find, but I tried to be polite. "That's when an outfielder throws the ball in and gets a runner out. It's really hard to do. You have to have a super cannon for an arm."

"That makes sense," you said. "Would you like a lozenge?" You held out a small dish of them.

"I'm not sick."

"This isn't medicine. It's a lozenge." You shook the dish and the lozenges danced.

"What flavor is it?"

You looked at the wrapper and read, "Regular flavor." You moved a lozenge around in your mouth and it clicked against your fake teeth in a way that made my real teeth itchy.

"That flavor sounds terrible."

"Suit yourself," you said, then you looked at your watch. "Oh dear. I'm late! I mustn't be late." You got up, straightened out your pants, which had gotten twisted around in a way that made the front look closer to the back than it was to the front. You got your purse from the counter and went to the door—the front door, not the sliding 1.

"Where are you going?" I asked.

"Out."

"Out where?"

"It's bingo night. They hold it in the afternoon, but they still call it bingo night. I guess the afternoon is nighttime for old people. It starts in a few minutes. If I'm late, I'll get a bad seat and won't be able to hear the numbers they call, then I start guessing and call bingo when I don't have it, and Marcy will get mad at me. We don't want that. When Marcy is mad, it's a whole thing!" You rolled your eyes, turned your back to me and started to turn the doorknob, but you did it reeeeeeeeeeeeeeeeally slowly, giving me a chance to say something.

"But you can't go."

"Why, may I ask, not?"

---

10. "The nose is the 1st sense to go! Then the sense of decorum!" Remember when you said that?

"Because."

"Because why?"

"Because everyone knows you can't leave a kid at home alone." That was the best my brain could come up with.

"Don't be silly, Silly. You've got a bunch of grown men with bats to keep you safe," you said, motioning to the TV. You turned around and started turning the doorknob even more slowly.

"But I can't stay here. It's not my house. You're a stranger."

"We are definitely not strangers. We've been watching baseball all afternoon. In my book, that makes us practically family."

"If you're not a stranger, then why don't I know your name?"

"Because you never asked!"

"Oh," I mumbled, looking down at my grimy shoes. "What's your name?"

"Ruth. Rhymes with truth. And tooth. And John Wilkes Booth." You finished turning the knob, but you only opened it a couple of inches.

"Do I have to tell you my name now?"

"There's plenty of time for that later." You opened the door and scooted out before I could say anything else. You were a lot faster than I thought you were. Maybe you could have caught me that 1st day if you had wanted to. I guess you had a different plan.

I am adding this sticky note to your memory book:

I remember re-sticking and re-sticking it to the bathroom mirror, but it kept falling off because the stickiness was all used up. So I licked the back of it, pressed it hard against the glass, and left the bathroom before I could be disappointed.[11]

It's the 1st reminder note I put up for you. I thought I had lost it or thrown it out, but I just found it in a stack of books I am sorting through. These reminder notes never helped you remember things back then. Maybe they will now.

"I brought you some food," you said and held out the styrofoam plate with squares of American cheese, Ritz crackers and baby carrots. "They were late getting the dinner ready, so they put out snacks to keep us from starting a geriatric riot. That's the worst kind of riot, trust me. Don't ever mess with a bunch of hungry old ladies. It ain't pretty. I was able to sneak this out for you, though."

"I don't like those," I said, making a face and pointing vaguely at the plate.

"These? These are tasty," you said and bit into a cracker to prove it to me. You knew very well I wasn't talking about the crackers.

"No, not those. Those."

"Don't be silly. Those are delicious," you said and ate a piece of cheese to show me.

"No. The carrots."

You pulled the plate slowly back toward you and said, "Don't tell me you don't like carrots. That's the best part."

I made a face like the thought of them made me nauseous.

"Carrots are the dessert of the vegetable world, especially baby carrots like these," you said. "That's why they make cakes out of them. Don't you like carrot cake? Of course, you do," you answered before I had a chance to. "Everyone loves carrot cake."

"If you have cake, I will eat that."

"If you eat the carrots and the crackers together, it will turn into carrot cake in your stomach."

"That's gross."

"Gross is a state of mind," you said and set the plate down on the coffee table in front of me. "Everything is a state of mind. Gross. Not-gross. Happy. Not-happy. Alive. Dead." You took a loud bite of carrot. "It's all a state of mind, Munchkin." You waved grandly and took another crunching bite of carrot with your "teeth."

"That doesn't make any sense. You don't make any sense." There was some

---

11. A habit of mine—wanting to leave before the thing I am afraid will happen happens.

snarl in my voice, I'm sure. There was nothing I hated more than stuff that didn't make sense and was a waste of time, except for the 573[12] other things I hated even more.

You didn't say anything.

I looked at the sad plate on the coffee table. I looked at you. Even a dim bulb like me could tell I had hurt your feelings. Or maybe you just wanted me to think that. I took a bite of cheese and swallowed. Then I picked up a cracker and moved the carrots around so it looked like I had eaten 1 of those.

You went to the kitchen and puttered about.[13]

I tried to make peace. "Did you know baby carrots aren't really baby carrots?" I said with my mouth full of not-carrots. "It's a big lie. They are big carrots that are chopped up into pieces. Then big machines use sandpaper or something like that to make the pieces into this shape so it looks like a baby carrot. You can tell because they are all the same. Exactly." I held 2 up and measured them against each other. They were nowhere near the same length, width, shape or color.

"I didn't know you knew so much about carrots," you said, coming over to where I was.

"Of course, you didn't. We just met."

"Well, very nice to meet you, sir. My name is Ruth. Rhymes with youth. And uncouth. And phone booth. And sleuth." You held out your hand to shake.

"You said that already."

"Indeed I did. Now eat your dessert vegetables and let's check the paper for who the Mariners play tomorrow."

Out I went. As soon as I heard you lift the toilet seat cover in the bathroom to sit down, I put the crackers in my pocket, stuffed the cheese in my mouth, zoomed out the sliding door, climbed over the railing, ran across the grass, ducked through the gap in the bushes, and was gone.

But I did look back. I looked back as I opened the screen door, and when I reached the top of the railing, and just before I ducked through the gap in the branches and leaves.

I almost stopped. Almost. But everyone knows "almost" doesn't count for nothing.

Absolutely nothing.

---

12. Probably a low estimate for the number of things I hated. BTW, 573 to the 14th power equals approximately 411,305,680,497,081,700,000,000,000,000,000,000. Just slightly more than the number of hits that Ichiro got in Japan and the U.S. combined. Slightly.

13. Living with all of you for all those years makes me talk like an old person. Heavens! Mercy be!

T he next day, I tried to find a new you. A better you. A Ruth that would give me cookies without doing so many super-annoying things, like caring about me and trying to get me to stay.

1st, I went to all the other sliding doors with birdfeeders on the ground floor of your building, and I repeated all the things I had done the day you saw me. I cracked seeds as loud as I could with a rock. I nibbled on stale bird bread in front of old people's windows. I even pretended to cry to try to get someone's attention and sympathy and cookies. But life is full of disappointments.

1 of the old ladies acted like she didn't see me and kept reading her dumb magazine. 1 of them picked up the phone to call the cops, making a big show of it like the worst actor in the world. I left before she finished pressing the buttons in an exaggerated way like she was trying to help people on the moon see clearly that she was pressing 9 and then 1 and then 1.

1 of them opened the door with her hand behind her back holding something, and my mouth started watering so much it made me choke on my spit. But it wasn't a cookie. It was a small potato that she chucked at me, yelling for me to get out of there and stop stealing. That was you-know-who. The small red potato she threw hit the ground in front of me and rolled up against my crusty shoe. People think those potatoes are fancy. They are not fancy. They're just a potato. I thought about throwing it back at her. I should have. For everything she did to us later, she deserved a potato plunking. Then again, we deserved to be plunked by a planet-sized potato for everything we did back to her.

I tried the same thing at the old people's home down the street, but none of the rooms on the ground floor had bird food out. Some people on the 3rd and 4th floors had birdfeeders, but that didn't do me any good unless I found a way to grow wings. I was no angel, so wings weren't going to sprout any time soon.

I wanted a cookie so bad I almost bought 1. I went down to the Albertsons with the cash vouchers I had from returning cans earlier that week, and I stood in front of the bakery case. They didn't have any free sample cookies out, and there weren't any workers in the bakery to put out more, so I looked at the big cookies behind the glass that cost money. The sugar cookie had rainbow sprinkles, but those always look better than they taste.[14] The chocolate chip cookies looked good, but they were smaller than the molasses cookies with the big sugar crystals on top. The sugar crystals didn't taste like sand. They tasted like sugar bursts. I wasn't going to waste my money, though. Before I met you, I almost never wasted money on food. I only wasted money on important stuff.

I walked around the store, played with some of the bouncy balls in the toy section, went to the bathroom in the back through the double doors next to the milk and eggs, came back out and wandered around some more, looked at

---

14. It's like eating cookies with sand on top. They're 1 of the top 3 worst cookies in the world.

the videos in the "New Releases" display, then ended up where I always end up. I flipped through the packets of baseball cards at the Customer Service Desk, asked if they had more behind the counter, then picked out 2 packs. I also picked out a new sudoku puzzle book from the magazine section, paid for it all at the register and sat down at the picnic table near the loading dock where the store workers smoke.

I sorted the new cards and added them to the rubber-banded stacks in my backpack. I tried not to think about cookies. I flipped through the puzzle book to distract myself. I told myself I would never go back to see you. Never ever. Not even for $1,000,000 worth of donuts. I started working on a medium-hard puzzle, messed up right away, and ripped the page out of the book. I crumpled it, threw it on the ground and smashed it with my shoe, twisting my foot back and forth to grind it into a smudge. Back and forth and forth and back. All the way back to the sawdust they made it from. Ground down so hard into the concrete that an entire winter of rain wouldn't wash it away. 100 years of endless Oregon rain wouldn't change what my angry foot had done.

1 of the cards I got that day was for Rich Aurilia of the San Francisco Giants. I liked how he had the same number of walks in 2002, 2004 and 2005: 37. That is how old he was, too.

37 is not a number you see very often, on baseball cards or anywhere else. It's a prime number.

I did another sudoku puzzle after that. I stared at the numbers I had written down. They were all exactly where they should be, so I didn't tear it up and grind it into the ground with my shoe. Before I put it into my backpack, I stared at the shape of the 9s. I am starting at the shape of 9s now, too. If you stare at them for a while, 9s don't look like a number any more. They look like ancient symbols. Something in a pyramid tomb that scientists have never figured out the meaning of. 9. 9. 9999999. Don't you agree?

I put the sudoku book away and decided to never ever go back to you. Not now. Not in 379 years. Not ever. But my feet started walking back up the hill in that exact direction. I picked up a couple of cans along the way, shaking out any leftover drips of beer and soda, and putting them into the empty can section of my backpack, which smelled like garbage that had been sitting in the sun too long. I tried to de-stinkify it once. I washed it in the bathroom at McDonald's, but that made it smell worse. The water must have activated all the grossness in there. I'm sure you would try to tell me that is science in action.[15]

It's a good thing you are too old to smell anymore, otherwise you never would have tricked me into getting tangled up in all of this. You would have thrown "fancy" potatoes at me rather than luring me into your web with baked goods.

When I got back to the other old people's home, there was a lady with a walker. It looked like she was standing still unless you watched her for a while and didn't go crazy from being bored. I guessed it would take her a year to get back to the building 20 yards away. Maybe 2 years. She had a really bad stoop, and the hump of her back was the tallest point on her body. Her head drooped down against her chest like a deflated balloon, covered completely by a big straw hat.

A squirrel chattered at her. She was going so slow it seemed like she wasn't getting any closer to me and then, all of a sudden, she was right there. I didn't think she could see me because of the way the giant hat blocked all her vision—except for straight down at the ground. She went past me a few microscopic steps, but part of the concrete sidewalk was pushed up an inch by tree roots and blocked her way. She tried to lift the walker high enough, but only got 1 side over the edge. When she lifted the other side, the 1st side slipped down.

She tried again and again but couldn't get over. She started swaying forward and backward. I thought she might be passing out, but she was just building up momentum. She lifted the walker on her biggest backward sway, held it in the air as she swayed forward, and placed it exactly where she'd started. It was all for nothing, plus her hat had fallen off.

I should have left, but I was annoyed. Super annoyed. Stupid sidewalk. Stupid old lady. They were distracting me from being sour and finding a new you. That's why I went over to her. Not to help her. Definitely not to help her. Just to make her go away.[16]

I set down my repulsive backpack, lifted both sides of the walker over the edge of the concrete, and picked up her hat. When I looked up at her, her left hand was up in the air over my head. I flinched and covered my face, but her hand came down softly on my shoulder, squeezed it, and tried to pull me closer to her. I peeked out between my fingers and saw a pair of puckered, purple lips coming for me. I wriggled out of her grasp before she could plant a thank you smooch on my forehead, and I started to run.

---

15. $[(H^20 + H) + E^0 * MC^2]/3.14159 = PU^{1,000,000}$

16. Hush! Don't say a word. I am a selfish little turd. Don't you dare say otherwise.

After a few steps, I looked down at my hands and saw I was still holding her hat. I stopped and looked back. The old lady was watching me with her droopy head. She winked and nudged my backpack with her foot. My cards, cans and the smell of rotting reek—my whole world—were in there. I had to go back.

When I got close to her, I held the hat out as far as I could so she could take it without getting me.

She took it and shifted it to her other hand while I got down on all 4s to get my backpack.

I heard the smooch noise at the same time my fingers grabbed the strap.

Her hand swung down like a guillotine and transferred the kiss from her fingertips to the side of my face before I could scramble backward to safety.

She waved goodbye while I ran and wiped and ran and wiped and ran and wiped and ran and wiped and wiped some more.

I found that sudoku book in a box of my things you had stored up in the top of your closet. Everything in it smells like mothballs. You put 500 of those stinky things into the boxes to protect my stuff from bugs, plus a handful of cedar chips on top of that. You weren't taking any chances.

On page 17 was a puzzle I didn't grind into the ground that day. I know it was from that day because I had written at the top that it was 89 degrees Fahrenheit according to the gas station sign. That's 31 degrees Celsius. Celsius is stupid because it doesn't tell you how to dress. The same degree Celsius can mean shorts or pants, sweater or parka. It is a waste of time, just like everyone in the world saying "please" and "thank you" and "how was your day?" p.s. The only non-stupid Celsius is minus 273.15 °C.

I also wrote down that it took me 11 minutes to finish the puzzle. That's 11 minutes in both Fahrenheit and in Celsius.

How fast can you finish it?

I know you want to beat me.

Because winning is the best thing in the history of things.

What are you waiting for? 11 minutes goes by fast. Tick tick tick tick.

But I'm not going to make it easy for you. To make it extra hard, I cut it in half and put the bottom half of the puzzle on the top, and the top half on the bottom. I know you'll like it because you love to try solving impossible things...like me. You're welcome.

In the margin, I drew a not-nice picture of you with stink lines rising from a head that had almost no resemblance to your actual head. Looking at it now, the worst thing about it is that it was a terrible drawing. That's why I cut close to the edge of the puzzle and didn't include my "art" here. I'm embarrassed by how bad the drawing was. If I drew a mean picture of you now, it would be a much better drawing. I promise. I would put your head on a really detailed dragon body and give you scary hair made of 10 different species of terrifying snakes [the death adder, the Mexican jumping viper, the Philippine cobra, the jararaca, the Malayan blue krait, the Belcher's sea snake, the golden lancehead, the western green mamba, the Bothrops asper and the Dubois' sea snake (in order, left to right, on your head)] ready to kill whoever got close to you.

The snake-haired you would be hideous, and the wig-haired you would be proud of me. You would put it right up on the fridge. I know it.

When I got to the top of the hill where your building is, I slowed down to a walk, wiped my cheek again, took off a shoe, and shook it until a pebble fell out. On the far side of the building, I found a shady place to sit leaning up against a big, green metal box with electrical wires inside with warning stickers all over them telling you you'll die a horrible death if you get within a kilometer of them. It had been protected from the sun by a tree all day, and the metal was cooler than the air. I pulled out my tennis ball, but not to pretend to be normal. Nobody was around to watch me. I played with it for real, bouncing it in the triangle of dirt between my legs and catching it before the second bounce, trying to see how close I could let it come to hitting the dirt before my hand swooped in underneath. That's right. I was a daredevil living on the edge.

That spot was near the kitchen, and I could smell the roasted chicken they were making for everyone's dinner. After my nose got used to the chicken, I could smell the broccoli. I made a face and moved to the other side of the green metal box to try to get away from the stink.

I bounced the ball again until a sliding door on the ground floor opened. A man's face got very close to the screen and looked both ways before he opened it and stepped out. When he did, he walked on his tiptoes like someone pretending to be someone sneaking around in a game of charades. He looked up at the balconies above him to check if he was alone. I was only 20 feet away from him, but he didn't see me. My shirt wasn't the same green as the big metal cube, but I guess it was close enough to blend in. Or maybe I'm just invisible. When he was sure the coast was clear, he started setting down the armful of things he was carrying: 3 metal dishes, 2 cans, a spoon, a fork and a can opener. He opened the cans, set the can opener aside, scooped out the food with the spoon into the 3 metal bowls, used the fork to break up the bigger gross chunks into smaller gross chunks and clinked the edge of the metal bowls with the fork. Each bowl made a different note.

The 1st cat came from somewhere behind me, zoomed past, scooted through the bars of the metal railing around the man's patio, and curled around his leg. "Hello, Mabel," he said.[17]

The next cat that came was noisy. It meowed and meowed[18] even before it came out of the bushes. Then it took a detour to a tree to sniff something rather than head straight to the man and the food. When the cat got all the way there, the man said, "Did you smell something interesting over there, Tootsie? You did, didn't you?"

2 more cats came out through a gap in the wooden fence and raced each other to the man. "You won by a whisker, Hank," the man said. "Better luck next time, Trixie." I was 99.999% sure he was making the names up and would call them all completely different names the next time he saw them.

The man picked up the fork, clinked the bowls again, and looked around for a missing cat or cats. That's when he saw me sitting there watching him. He got a funny look on his face, like someone had accidentally walked in on him in a bathroom stall while he was going number 2. He stayed in his crouch but moved his body to the right to hide behind the thick corner post of the metal railing.

I leaned the same way until I could see his face again. 1 of the cats rubbed up against his leg. He leaned back the other way, putting the post back between him and me, but I leaned back to my original spot. Apparently, I play peekaboo with old people a lot.

He didn't try hiding again. He just looked at me. Then he lifted his hand

---

17. The cat didn't say that. The man did. As far as I could tell, it was not a talking cat.

18. Like a stegosaurus.

to his face and put his index finger in front of his mouth, making a shhhhhh gesture without making the sound. He stood up from his crouch and made the shhhhhh motion again with his other hand. He tiptoed backward into his room, and kept his finger pressed against his lips as he slid the screen door shut and backed up into the darkness of his apartment.

11 times out of 10, that would have spooked me and made me itchy to get moving, but I was tired from running away that morning, and going all the way down to the store, and wandering around the store for so long, and walking back up the hill to the 1st old people's home, and escaping from the old lady with the droopy head, and coming all the way up to the top of the hill to your building—all without any cookies to give me energy. So, I didn't get up and leave.

I just stayed there and tried to ignore the cat-man every time he peeked out to see if I was still there. I tried to ignore the cats, too. After they ate, a couple of them came over and started rubbing up against me. They smelled like pee. So did the broccoli from the kitchen. The smells hovered in a cloud around me like a cruddy mood. So did a cruddy mood.

I tried to block it all out. I flipped through my sudoku book for a puzzle to do, but I was tired of those. I put that away and pulled out my find-and-seek puzzle book—the 1 with number puzzles, which are harder than find-and-seeks with letters. I flipped through it, but I stopped when I found a blank page in the middle of the book. It was supposed to have a puzzle, but the printing machine had missed it somehow.

It was blank.

Blanker than blank.

It was the blankest.

I flipped to the back side. It was blank, too. It felt even blanker than the first side.

I flipped back to the first side. It was even blanker than before. It bothered me so much. No puzzle. No numbers. Looking at it made me fidget and squirm. It made me need to pee. Then it made me feel cold. Then it made me need to pee again.

I couldn't leave it blank. It would bug me more than anything else that had happened that entire day.

I fished around in my backpack and got a pen. It had a broken chain attached to the end. It said "Where Customers are #1" on the side. I wrote "1" in the center of the page.[19] That was boring, so I drew rings around it to make it look exciting. I did the same with other numbers surrounded by their own rings until

---

19. You always said 1 is the loneliest number, but you're wrong. 2 is the loneliest number. 2 makes your heart smash into 7,723 pieces way more than 1. You and I both know I'm right.

the page was filled up. I flipped it and did the same on the other side but made the rings more squarish than circlish. The circlish numbers look like they are reaching out from the page. Here is a piece of it I cut out.

I had forgotten all that. I had forgotten the green metal box in the shade. And the roasting chicken and steaming broccoli. And the man feeding the stray cats. And the blank page I needed to fill in so badly. But I remembered it all when I found these puzzle books in a box of my old junk that you had put in the hall for trash pickup after that bad fight we had. Sometimes little things can make people remember a lot they didn't even know they had forgotten.

The night of our big fight—after everything that happened in McMinnville—I dragged my boxes back into our room from the hall where you had shoved them. While you were in the bathroom, I put them in the corner behind the far end of the couch and draped my coat over the top to hide them as best I could. The next day I put them back in the closet. I am sifting through them now and remembering. I know you didn't mean the things you said and did. It was just a trick to make me stay, right?[20]

I don't want to remember that stuff, but I do remember it no matter what I try. It's a memory that smells like broccoli stew. I want to wash it out of my brain, but I can't. Even 100 years of Oregon rain won't wash it away.

Why is it so hard to make good memories stick in your brain, and why is it so hard to make the bad memories go away? Brains are the worst sometimes. The worst.

---

20. "The only psychology I believe in is reverse psychology." –A Ruthism

I also remember this:

The broccoli smell got so thick after a while that I finally got up off my butt and left the big, green metal box and the cat-man, but I wasn't thinking straight, and I almost went past your sliding door instead of around the other side of the building. I almost did, but I caught myself. I was close enough to see the glass of milk, though. It had a plate on top holding a cookie wrapped in plastic. My mouth watered so much, I had to spit.

Your lights were on, but I didn't see you. I made sure you didn't see me. I backed up several steps, got down on the ground and crawled over to the bushes, squeezing myself through a spot that looked like a gap. I got scraped up going through there, but you didn't see me and that was all that mattered. There was no way in heck I was going back to you. You weren't going to trap me.

I also remember this:

Sometime that day, I lost a baseball card. I realized it that night in my secret sleeping spot when I was going through all of my cards before I closed my eyes. It was my Rick Aguilera card from the Mets stack. It was an older card from back before he joined the Twins and became a closer. His ERAs the 1st 3 years were 3.24, 3.88 and 3.60. I looked through all the pockets in the backpack and my shorts to make sure, but it was definitely lost. I had trouble falling asleep after that.

I got another Aguilera card later, but it was a newer 1 with all his numbers as a relief pitcher. His beard was different in the new card, and you said you liked it. You called his beard "sharp," which didn't make any sense. No sense at all.

"Can I get your help with something?" you asked me the next day, when I was back in your room, sitting on the couch with you, watching TV, and eating a cookie. I was weak. So dumb and weak.[21]

I garbled, "What?" with my mouth full of chocolate chips and dough.

"I need help picking a good ending for a joke."

"You write jokes?" I asked with equal parts shock, disdain, dismissiveness, disbelief, sass, skepticism, incredulity, tactlessness, impertinence, obstreperousness and a general lack of any civility and diplomacy whatsoever. Pieces of cookie flew everywhere in a doughy spray. Thank goodness I wasn't born a fancy prince. They would have kicked me out of the castle for my lack of any manners, grace, class, propriety, decorum, decency, respectability, civilities, social skills, and delicacy.

"I write lots of things."

"But you're not funny...at all."

"I'm a hoot. They should put me on TV." You straightened your wig to get ready for your closeup.

"I would change the channel."

"That's not nice. I don't want to be on TV anyway. All that money would go to my head. I just want to write jokes for the greater good."

"That's dumb. People on TV are rich. They get so much money."

"Maybe so, but money isn't all it's cracked up to be. Then again, platitudes aren't all they're cracked up to be either." You laughed at what you had said. I did not laugh. I thought you might be making fun of me, but I wasn't sure.

"Here's the joke I need help with: What do you get when you cross an alligator with a duck?"

"You can't do that. They are not the same kind of animal."

"You can in a joke. You can cross anything with anything else. It's a rule. A rule of comedy, and those are the most important rules. Way more important than the Constitution and the Magna Carta," you said. "I have 2 punchlines, but I don't know which is better."

"What's a punchline?"

"The part at the end of a joke that makes it funny."

"Oh." I wiped my revolting nose with my nauseating sleeve.

"OK, here's number 1[22]: What do you get when you cross an alligator with a duck?" You paused   for   a   long   time. "A crocoduck." You looked at me expecting a laugh, but I just looked back at you like I was still waiting for you to start the joke.

"OK. Let's try number 2: What do you get when you cross an alligator with a duck?" You paused   even longer   than the first time. "A

---

21. Why, oh why, oh why, do we do the things we do, we do, we do.

22. The loneliest number, you told me approximately 999,999 times.

quackadile." You held your hand up to your mouth, muffling a laugh, and your feet did a little dance in front of the couch at the same time. After you settled back down, you asked, "So, which do you like better?"

"It can't be a crockoduck or a quackadile[23] because alligators are different than crocodiles.

"Yes, but it's funnier if I start by saying alligator and then the punchline has funny crocodile puns. The switch is part of what makes it funny."

"But it's wrong."

"Funny doesn't have to be all about facts. In fact, the best jokes use exaggerations and white lies to tell bigger truths."

"But it's wrong. Alligators and crocodiles are different."

You sighed. You did that a lot with me. "If you could set that aside, though, which of the jokes is funnier?"

"The 1 you laughed at."

"It doesn't matter what I think. I want an unvarnished opinion."

"What does that mean?"

"Unvarnished?" you asked.

I nodded.

"Without varnish," you answered flatly. "So which joke wins?"

I held up 2 fingers.

"Quackadile?"

I nodded quarter-heartedly.

"You're not just saying what you think I want to hear, are you?"

"Yes."

"Yes, you are? Or yes, you aren't?"

"I need to go to the bathroom."

"Okeydokey. Just a warning, though—I may or may not be here when you get back. I may just run for the hills, I reckon. Then down the river on a raft with Huck and Jim. You never know. I reckon I just might. I reckon."

You were still there when I came out. And somehow, I was still there, too. Neither of us had run away . . . yet. You were shuffling a deck of playing cards and you had a look in your eyes like you were thinking of a joke. It couldn't have been that crocodile joke. This was something funny.

"Do you know how to play Hearts?"

---

23. Spellcheck wants me to change quackadile to quesadilla. Maybe it is hungry.

"What's Hearts?"

"It's a card game."

"Is it like Slapjack?"

"No."

"Is it like Go Fish?"

"Not in the least."

"I don't know many games."

"Oh, that's a pity," you said. "We'll need to remedy that, won't we?"

"Is it hard to play?"

"It's easy for me. I know how. It might be a bit harder for you, though, since you don't."

I didn't say anything. I just looked at you like you had told me a terrible joke about crossing a starving hippo with a triangle[24] or crossing a raven with French fries[25] or something else crossed with something else.[26]

You winked at me, then you said, "First of all, we need 4 players." You looked around and tapped your lip with your pointer finger. "We seem to be short a couple people, but we'll make do. We'll pretend that players are sitting here and here." You started dealing out the cards on the coffee table to all 4 of us. "Everyone gets 13 cards. You should sort them into suits—hearts with hearts, diamonds with diamonds, and so forth. Then sort them lowest to highest within those."

"This is too many cards. I can't hold them. Can I lay them down?"

"No, you have to keep them a secret. If I see them, I will be able to beat you . . . more easily."

I tried to pick them up and organize them, but I kept dropping cards and it was a mess. "Can I put a blocker up on the table so you can't see my cards?"

"That's a great idea. I think I have just the thing." You got up and went to the bookshelf and pulled out the biggest book you had. It wasn't the thickest, but it had the tallest, widest, biggest pages, so it would be a great blocker. It didn't fit on the shelf standing up, so you had it down flat under other books. It was your picture book of the United States with photos of Yellowstone and Manhattan and the Grand Canyon and all the other amazingly boring things they put in books like that. You opened the book, set it up as a screen in front of me, and gave me time to organize my cards into rows behind it. A photo of trees changing color in Maine watched me.

We played 3 games and I got more confused the more you explained and

---

24. A hungry, hungry hippo-tenuse.

25. Edgar Allen Poe-tatos.

26. Insert dumb pun here.

re-explained the rules. The queen of spades seemed to be the key, but I kept not getting it in my cards until the 4th game. You groaned when I played it and I somehow won after that.

"You let me win." I was annoyed.

"No, no. You won this fair and square. You put down the queen of spades at the perfect time and I was stuck. Stuck like a duck in the muck who's lost its pluck."[27]

"Can we play something else? Something I already know?"

"Do you have something in mind?"

"Can we play Go Fish?"

"OK."

"Can I still use the book to block my cards?"

"Of course, but you should flip to a new page for a nice change of scenery. Travel broadens the mind, as they say. Although I have also heard people say it narrows the mind." You shrugged. "Either way, you might like a different picture. I am partial to the bald eagles. My favorite bird. I think you'll like it, too."

I started turning pages, but you pointed in the opposite direction, so I started going toward the back of the book and found it. There was a big eagle feeding baby eagles in a nest at the top of a dead tree. Another eagle was about to arrive. It was holding a snake in its claws.

"Gross. They're going to eat a snake," I said.

"To them, that's like a big, delicious cookie with lots of chocolate chips. If I wanted to catch an eagle, I would put a big pile of snakes out there. That would be perfect bait for luring it to join our game of Go Fish," you said, pointing outside to where you had put out cookies and milk for me. "We would be crawling with bald eagles just like that. Easy peasy, puddin' and pie." You snapped your fingers.

You saw my face change, and you knew you had made a mistake. A big mistake with all the talking about luring and trapping. You zipped your lips about eagles and snakes. You focused on shuffling, staring at the cards because you could feel me staring into your brain. I stared and stared, trying to get in. And then, suddenly, I was in. I could see what you were thinking. You were hoping I wouldn't get up and run—slipping off the hook like the big 1 that got away. You were afraid. I could see it so clearly. It made me feel like I was winning.

But I wasn't winning. It was a trap. You had let me in, and while I was distracted, you had marched right into my brain and start drilling away. I was horrified. You were drilling, drilling, drilling. I wanted you out. I made my hands into fists and pressed my teeth together, trying, trying, trying to kick you out. I

---

27. Stuckey, duckety, muckety pluck.

strained and strained to get you out. To de-Ruth my Ruthed-up brain.

You squeezed my arm softly and it jolted me. "Sweetie, I don't think you're an eagle." You said it so quietly I could barely make out what you were saying.[28]

I thought you were going to say more, so I waited, but you didn't. I kept waiting more, longer, more.

You didn't say anything else. Just that thing about me not being an eagle. You straightened the deck and dealt the cards.

I watched you. I had never really looked at an old person's face before, at least not up close. The makeup on the left side of your face didn't match up with the right side. The pinkish color on your left cheek was bigger and darker than on the other side. The lipstick on 1 side of your lips went up a little in the corner, but it went down a little on the other side of your mouth. The skin on your lips was cracked in a way that looked painful. I licked my lips trying to make yours less chapped. I looked up at your eyes. Your eyelids made little twitches and jumps in between each blink, never staying still. Your eyes were also crisscrossed with reddish and blueish veins like a road map, and the white part wasn't really white. It was 1 of those not-white colors that have names people never use unless they are going to paint a room on those fix-up-a-house shows on TV.[29] I hate those shows so much.

I picked up my cards and started organizing them. It was taking me forever to sort them because I was distracted thinking about hurdling the coffee table and hurtling toward the opposite of all of this—anything but this. This trap, this trick, this crushing-pain-waiting-to-happen, this catastrophic-hurt-lurking-around-the-corner, this fib, this mirage. This sugary, warm, comfy, smile-filled lie.

I looked up in the middle of fumbling with my cards, and you had the saddest look I had ever seen on a person's face. The kind of face like someone who's staring at an empty chair that didn't used to be empty and that will always be empty until the end of time, the universe and everything. That kind of face. You weren't expecting me to look up and see it. When I did, you hid what I had seen with an instant "smile" and cheerily said, "Youth before beauty. You go first."

The deepest insides of my bum felt like ice, but I managed to ask: "Do you have any 3s?"

I had no idea if I had any 3s.

No idea at all.

---

28. It sounded more like: "Sweetie, I don't think you're a beagle."

29. Tonight's lineup includes *The Property Plunderers*, *House Vampires*, *The Gentrifiers*, *Unpleasant Couples Buying Homes They Can't Afford*, and *Love It or Don't Love It. Who Cares!*

I found a poem in a box of my junk in your closet. It was on a piece of construction paper folded in half with the words, "To Ruth" on the front next to a drawing of a flower. That must have been on a day I wasn't completely annoyed with you.

> *Roses are red*
> *Violets are blue*
> *Oranges are orange*
> *And so are you.*
> *Orange you glad I made you this card?*

And this sticky note, too:

After we finished playing cards, we sat on the couch and watched TV, but all I could think about was the eagle stuff. What was I doing there? How dumb was I to let you lure me in? How dumber was I to stay? How dumbest was I that I didn't leave?

I could get free sample cookies from Albertsons—if there were ever workers around in the bakery—or free French fries from the dumpsters behind 3 different restaurants each night—mountains of them in nice clean trash bags. I could watch the Mariners at the Fred Meyer electronics department or through the window of house with the old guy with the huge tv that falls asleep by the 2nd inning every night.

But I didn't run. I stayed, and we watched the Mariners, and we ate cookies, and we played cards, and we slept and woke up and ate and peed and pooed. And then we did it all over again and again and again until I could barely remember what I had done before you lured me in like an eagle that was so, so hungry for snakes. The Mariners had said goodbye to Safeco Field and was on a road trip. But my butt stayed glued to the couch. That couch turned my brain to mush somehow. Complete mush.

The Mariners held on that night, barely, to beat the Astros in Houston.[30] You waited until the very end of the postgame show to turn off the TV. The pregame show, the game, and the post-game show added up to 6+ straight hours of sitting there like lumps. I was as sedated as a wild animal stung by 53 tranquilizer darts. You could have done zoo dentistry on me, and I would have barely blinked. Droolly, droolly, drool.

Do tigers in comfy cages just give up? Do they just shrug and stay inside even if someone leaves the door open? Maybe they would if Ichiro is on first and waiting for the right moment to steal 2nd base. "Yeah, yeah. I'll escape but give me a minute. The tying run will be in scoring position if he makes it. I can escape later during the commercials. Unless the game's tied up, then I'll escape after that, depending on the pitching matchup tomorrow. Felix might be pitching. If he is, I'll escape the day after. There's plenty of time to escape. Plenty of time."[31]

You looked at me, slouching there docilely, and saw an opportunity. "Before you go to sleep, we need to talk about some rules."

I shook off my grogginess and incredulously asked, "Rules?"

"I guess I shouldn't call them rules. Kids don't like that word, do they?"

My fuming eyes answered your question.

"Which other word can we use?" you asked yourself, tapping your pointer finger on the tip of your nose, then scrunching your face and scratching the itchy spot you had made there. "I know!" you said and got up. You went over to the shelf, squatted down to get something from the lowest shelf, pulled out a book with a blue cover, grunted when you stood back up, then came back, dusted it off, and opened it up on your lap. "This is called a thesaurus."

"I know," I said hostilely.

"I'm sorry. I keep forgetting how smart you are. You'll have to forgive me, since we just met, and I tend to underestimate people. It's a bad habit of mine, I'm not proud to say." You kept blabbering, loudly, "I also tend to over-estimate

---

30. I hate the Astros almost as much as I hate people who chew too loud.

31. My tiger speaks with a British accent for some reason, by the way. Don't they all?

people. Come to think of it, I don't think I've ever estimated anyone exactly. Hopefully, it averages out somehow. But that's neither here nor there.   Neither here nor there.   What were we doing, again?"

I pointed to the book in your lap.

You made a face like you had an epiphany, then flipped through the pages to the "R" section, found the word "rule," and ran your finger over the list of words. "Decree? No. Too authoritarian. Law? Too formal. Regulation? Too bureaucratic, especially since we're just 2 people. It takes more than that to make a bureaucracy. Imperative. The noun, of course. No, I don't like it. Axiom? No. Criterion? Uh-uh. Guideline? Too wishy-washy. Truism?" You stopped and thought about that word. "Truism," you said again and looked up at the TV screen. "I like it." You clapped the book closed and set it on the coffee table. Then you looked at me, smiled, and patted me on the knee. "Before you go to sleep, we need to talk about some truisms."

"What rules?" I asked, setting us back 5 minutes.

"The first truism is easy. When you go number 1 in the bathroom, please do it sitting down. That thing can be an out-of-control firehose," you said, pointing at my private parts and waving your arms like an out-of-control firehouse with 17 firemen bravely wrestling with it but unable to point it in the right direction. "I would prefer not to have pee all over the seat and floor and walls and ceiling and kitchen and living room and bedroom." You kept waving your arms in the air like a crazy person when you listed all the things I might pee on. "Deal?" you asked and held your hand out.

I reached out with the wrong hand—the hand on the same side as the 1 you held out. You grabbed my other hand, put it in yours, and shook it. Both hands, by the way, were likely covered in dried pee. You're welcome.

"The 2nd truism is about the remote control. Fights over the remote are the worst kinds of fights in the world. That's what led to World War II, you know." You winked, then shook your head and said, "Terrible war. That's why we need a system for who controls the clicker. So, here's what I propose: It will be mine on Sundays, Tuesdays and Thursdays. Every other day. You'll get custody on Mondays, Wednesdays and Fridays. We'll alternate Saturdays so it works out even for both of us. Deal?"

We shook again. I used the correct hand that time, but I had to think about it before I did.

"The third truism is the last, but not the least. It's the most important truism actually."

"Only 3 rules?"

"Truisms," you corrected me.

"Only 3?"

"Would you like more?"

"No."

"I can make up some more if you were expecting more. I don't want to disappoint you. I can add a rule about taking baths."

"No. 3 is fine."

"OK. As I was saying, the last rule—truism, I mean—is the most important. Do you promise to follow it?"

"I don't know what it is yet."

"Smart. Very smart. Always read the contract before you sign. OK, here it is: Under this roof," you said, motioning your arm toward the ceiling in a slow arc grandly presenting the ceiling that is a paper-thin barrier to the floor that Mrs. Clara upstairs walks loudly on because her sciatica problems force her to clomp, clomp, clomp on her heels like a sasquatch trying to salsa dance. "Under this roof," as you were saying, "there's no talking about the past. No asking me how I got here. No asking what happened to me the day before we met, or the week before, or a year ago, or 10 years ago, or 70 years ago. That goes for both of us, including you." You poked the tip of my nose and said, "Boop!"

"I can't give you the third degree either. It's none of my business, is it? Not in the least. Right? It doesn't matter how you got here, does it? No, it doesn't. It's none of my business why a kid your age is wandering around eating bird food and scurrying around in the bushes like some kind of rabid raccoon or an off-his-meds possum or something. None of my business at all. Right? So, you won't get any questions from me about that. Nope! No prying about why you have no better place to be than with a wrinkled old lady like me, about to curl up for sleep on a lumpy, farty couch in a complete stranger's home, because that's apparently 100 times better than what you ran away from. Nope! No-sir-ee!! Talking about that is a no-no. In fact, wondering out loud about it would be against the rules. The ugly past is the past. It's dirty water under the creaky bridge, down the polluted creek, into the poisoned tributary, through the trash-filled confluence, under another creakier bridge, into the giant dying river, and then out to the getting-hotter-and-hotter-every-day sea, never to be talked about again. Goodbye and good riddance. Yesterday is over. Today is what matters, and what matters is that you're here."

I just looked at you. My head hurt so much every time you talked like that, and you talked like that so, so much.

"Deal?" You held out your hand.

I started to reach out but stopped. My hand hovered there in the air. "What about baths?"

"What about them?"

"Do I need to take them?"

"If it's not on the list of house truisms, it's up to you."

"But what if I am really stinky."

"I can't smell much of anything anymore," you said knocking on your nose so hard I wondered if it would start to bleed and bleed. "So, you'll be smelling yourself a lot more than I will."

"What about bedtime?"

"For me? But I'm a grown-up."

"For me," I said with a voice that was so, so very tired of your joking around. "Do you want a bedtime?"

"No."

"It sure sounds like you want more rules—I mean, truisms. Aren't 3 enough for you? I didn't realize kids liked truisms so much."

"No. 3 is enough," I said and reached the rest of the way over to your hand. We had a deal, and I was sure I had won the negotiation. Kids are short-sighted. That will always be our downfall. I realize that now.

"**W**hat about a bedtime story?" I couldn't believe the words had come out of my mouth.

"Aren't you too grown-up for a story?"

"No. I'm a kid."

"Then what are you doing in a retirement home?"[32] You made quotation marks with your fingers when you said the word "retirement."

"I don't know." That was the truest thing I had ever said.

"You and me both, Kiddo. You and me both." You got up from the couch, which you had made up with sheets and blankets to prep for bedtime. You went over to the bookshelves next to the TV. "Let's see what I have that I can read to you." You ran your pointer finger over the bindings of the books, from left to right on the top shelf, then right to left on the next.

"I could read you the dictionary," you said, taking it off the shelf and waving it in my direction. I probably made a face. "OK, that will be our backup plan," you said and set it on the coffee table so it was out to tempt me. "Let's see what else I have." I scratched my rear end and you saw me out of the corner of your eye. You didn't tell me to cut it out, but I stopped. "Here's a good 1. It's long, though. We'll only be able to read part of it tonight."

I couldn't see the name of the book because your hand was in the way, but the cover had a drawing of a man with no shirt kissing a woman wearing very

---

32. At various times, you also referred to this place as: Purgatory, Heaven's Waiting Room, Hell's Waiting Room, Death's Door, Daycare for Octogenarians, Adult Diaper Town, Widowville and Chez Ruth.

fancy clothes.

"Chapter 1," you said after clearing your throat for 37 minutes.[33]

I looked through a bunch of your boxes today looking for the book because it would have been a funny addition to this memory book to balance out all the not-at-all-funny-in-the-least stuff that comes later, but I couldn't find it. Here's what I remember, though:

The story was about a woman who was lonely. I could tell because of how she endlessly talked about being lonely. She was the narrator in the story, and she talked a lot about how her husband was a jerk. She talked about how sad and lonely she was because he was always away on business trips. That part confused me because I thought she should be happy that a jerk isn't around much. "Why would she want him around more if he's rude?"

You said, "Some people want 2nds even if the food is terrible, otherwise they don't think they got their money's worth." I didn't understand what that had to do with the woman and her jerkface husband, but I kept my mouth shut. Sometimes questions just slow everything down to a painful, painful crawl with you.

You went back to reading and got to the part about the gardener. He did all the yardwork at the woman's big house and never wore a shirt. He had big muscles, but he didn't seem like a jerk even though most guys with muscles are awful. That's a truism. The woman talked more about how she was lonely and while she talked, she kept looking at the gardener through the window. When he looked back at her, she always looked away.

Then, after she finished talking about how lonely she was, she looked at the gardener again, and he looked at her. Neither of them looked away. They stared at each other, then he came to the door, asked for a glass of water, and she let him in. That's when you stopped reading out loud. Your face made a face as you kept reading it to yourself. You flipped to the next page and said, "Oh my." You flipped back to the page we were on. After that long delay, you abruptly said: "Then they lived happily ever after."

"Who did?"

"All of them."

"No, they didn't."

"Yes, they did."

"We're only at the beginning. There's a ton more pages left."

"They lived happily ever after," you insisted.

"Not everything has a happy ending," I said. "Only little kids and grown-ups who aren't smart think that."

"It's not respectful to call grown-ups dumb, even if they are. Even if most

---

33. The loneliest chapter.

of them are incredibly dumb and prove it nearly every minute of every day. Especially on voting day. Even though almost every single human on this planet is as dumb as a bag of broken hammers, it's not polite to talk about. It's nicer to let them go on thinking they are smart. And good looking. And interesting. Even though most people are none of those things. Excepting us, of course. You and I are smart and good looking and ought to be in movies." You patted me on the head, closed the book, put the book into your pocket (for later), turned off the light, and motioned for me to lie down.

When you pulled the blanket over me, I suddenly felt very little. "That wasn't a very long story. Can you tell me another 1?" I didn't know who was controlling what I was saying, but I didn't like him at all. At all.

"I don't have any kid books. Just grown-up stories like that."

"Can you make up a story?"

"I don't have a good imagination for that kind of thing. Making up stories is hard. Can you make up a story?"

"That's the grown-up's job. The kid is supposed to listen to the story."

"Oh, I'm new at this. You'll have to forgive me." You scratched underneath your wig, took it off, scratched your head harder, then put the wig back completely wrong. "I could sing a song to you instead. How about that?"

The shrug you gave was so half-hearted, it was quarter-hearted at best. "Great!" you said and cracked your knuckles like you were about to play piano. You slid off the couch onto your knees, inched over with great effort to where my head was, breathing all over me like a moose, and put your hand on my arm. You thought for a minute, then you sang this:

I so often dream we might make a team
But so wild a scheme I must banish
For each time I start to open my heart you vanish.

We might find some isle where lotuses smile
And our time beguile going native
But how can we go unless you are cooperative.

My dear, I've a feeling you are
So near and yet so far.
You appear like a radiant star
First so near, then again so far.

I just start getting you keen on clinches galore with me
When fate steps in on the scene and mops up the floor with me.
No wonder I'm a bit under par for you're so near and yet so far.

My condition is only so-so
'Cause whenever I feel you're close, oh
You turn out to be, oh, so far.

After you finished the song, you kissed me on the forehead and that was that. You turned out the light and I rolled onto my side, sinking into divots we had made in the lumpy couch over the past few days—my shoulders in the small meteorite-sized crater I had made, and my hips and legs curling up in the big comet-sized crater you had made. I wondered whether the dinosaurs saw the big rock of fire screaming through the sky and knew something big was about to happen. Or did they just go on about their day and wonder whether the Mariners could cut Oakland's division lead to 3 games by the end of the week?[34]

"**W**hat the heck are you doing out here?" You were mad. Your eyes were slits and your eyebrows looked like they were going to jump off your forehead, put me over their knees, and spank me into next Tuesday. You looked up and down the hallway, worried that someone might come out of their room and catch us. You looked back down at me, and your eyebrows demanded an explanation.

"I'm hungry," I said, but that clearly wasn't enough explanation for you, so I kept talking. "There's no food."

"Do you make all your decisions with your stomach?"

I looked down at my grimy feet. I could feel my ears and my cheeks burning.

You leaned down to my height, took a deep breath and said, "I'm sorry, Dear. I apologize." You put your hand on my shoulder, and I shook it off. "I shouldn't have spoken to you that way. You scared me. We could both get in a lot of trouble if somebody finds you out here. They could send you to a foster home or back to wherever you ran away from. And they could kick me out, or worse. They could put me on pills, so I don't make bad decisions anymore."

You put your hand back on my shoulder. I didn't shake it off this time.

"I promise I won't yell at you again. Cross my heart and hope to fry. Deal?" You reached your hand out, but I was looking over your shoulder at the person behind you. It was the potato-chucking lady. You stood up, turned around, and

---

34. Nope. The Mariners can't cut the A's lead. They never can. Never. Ever. Stupid bullpen.

stepped over to try to hide me. "Good morning, Millicent," you said to her with way more enunciation than normal.

She didn't say anything. I peeked out to see why she wasn't talking, and she was looking right at me. If you had asked me to describe her then, I would have said she had fangs and all-black eyeballs with no white parts. I would have said she was carrying a cane made from human bones and was wearing a fur scarf made from kittens and puppies that were still alive—barely—and making awful noises. I would have said she talked in a whisper as loud as a yell. I would say she coughed green stuff into her handkerchief that turned into insects that flew away. I looked to see if she was holding any little red potatoes, but her hands were behind her back. I ducked behind you just in case. Those potatoes are hard as heck and would leave a mark.

"Don't be impolite, Ruth. Introduce me to your handsome young guest," she said.

"He's not a guest."

"Oh, I didn't realize he was a new resident here." She looked at me and said: "I should have brought a housewarming present for you." She said the "house" in "housewarming" with a hiss that made my back sweat.

"Sarcasm is unbecoming for a woman of your very advanced age, Millie. This young man is from my church. He's volunteering his time to help some of the older parishioners. It's part of a youth program at the church."

"Which church is that, Ruth?"

"Down the road," you said, waving vaguely down the hall toward the "EXIT" with the burned-out bulbs that wouldn't help anyone in an emergency. You grabbed my hand and moved to go past her, but she blocked us.

"I didn't realize you go to church, Ruth. It's quite hard to believe. Impossible to believe actually."

"There's a lot you don't know about me. Some people prefer to have a bit of mystery about them rather than put everything on display like a billboard for laxatives."[35]

"What's the name of the church?" she asked me firmly, ignoring you.

I looked up at you, looked at her, at you, back at her and said, "Saint Patrick's."

You bit your lip to stifle a laugh. She leaned down toward me, pushed her glasses up higher on her nose, squinted her all-black eyes at me, and said, "Are you sure that's the name of it?"

"Yes, I'm sure. That would be bad if I didn't know the name of my own church. That would probably be a sin. I don't know for sure, though. I'm still learning all the sins."

---

35. Poopety poo.

"Millie, you could teach him a thing or 2 or 200 on that subject, couldn't you?" you said and led me the other way around her.

"Ruth, after you're done with him, I would love to have him do some volunteering for me. I have some chores that need tending to, including some potatoes scattered on the ground outside my patio that need cleaning up." She pulled an apple or a small animal out of her pocket, took a big, loud bite, and waved goodbye as slowly as a person can wave while you pulled me back into your room—our room.

Y ou got a pad of paper and a pen from a drawer in the kitchen and started writing down the plan. You refused to call it a list of more rules. It was "a plan." That was all. I knew better than to argue and zipped my lips as tight as they would zip. Here's what you wrote:

- *Going out in the hall is a no-no. You can come and go as you wish, but you must only use the sliding door.*

- *Whenever you come or go, always look to the left, to the right, and up at the balconies first to make sure no one is watching before you climb over the metal railing.*

- *If someone knocks on the door, do not answer it. Hide in the cupboard under the kitchen sink and let me answer the door. Also hide under the sink if someone knocks when I'm not here. It might be maintenance or someone else with a key.*

- *If the phone rings while I am out, do not answer it unless it rings with the secret code: one ring, then the ringing stops, then another ring, then the ringing stops again, then a whole bunch of rings. That code means it's me, and you should pick up.*

- *We will always have enough food for you.*

- *When I go to breakfast in the dining room each morning, I will bring my big purse with a Tupperware inside to sneak food out for you. That will be your breakfast.*

- *At lunchtime, I will ask for a boxed lunch from the kitchen staff to bring back to the room, plus I will make a peanut butter and jelly sandwich at the self-service station in the dining room. That will be our lunch.*

- *At dinnertime, I will bring my big purse again with more Tupperware and I will sit next to people who never eat much of their dinner. You'll have oodles of food to eat when I get back.*

- *At the end of dinner, I will also take three cookies from the tray they put out when they serve coffee and tea. Two will be for our dessert while we watch TV, and one will be a backup breakfast in case you are extra hungry or don't like the breakfast I bring back the next morning.*

- *I will go to the grocery store once a week when the van takes residents. I will buy milk, crackers, canned peaches and whatever else we put on the list during the week. I will pay for this with my money.*

- *If you want candy, baseball cards and whatnot, you will have to buy that with your own money.*

- *You will need to unmake the couch each morning and put the sheets and blankets in the corner so we can use the couch for watching TV.*

- *We will do your laundry in the kitchen sink and let it air dry on the counter so no one sees kid clothes mixed in with mine in the laundry room and gets suspicious.*

- *Whenever we have to make a family decision, we will take a vote. If the vote is a tie, we will flip a coin and the youngest person will call it in the air. There will be no reflipping.*

- *No reflipping!*

- *We will get some proper children's books as soon as possible for bedtime stories. Nothing with people doing smoochy stuff. Those are only for lonely old ladies, exclusively!*

You left space at the bottom for more things in case we thought of anything else, then we both signed it. I printed my name in letters small enough to require a magnifying glass. You signed with a giant swirl that swallowed up my signature like a megashark swallowing a tiny minnow. You put it on the refrigerator with a magnet and we both looked at it. You said, "It's a good plan, don't you think?"

I shrugged the same shrug I always shrugged.

"Someone might see it, though," you said while scratching under the edge of your wig. "It's not safe to leave it up. Let's put it somewhere for safekeeping."

You went in your bedroom and looked in your closet for something to put it in. You didn't find anything there, so you came back into the kitchen and looked in the cupboards. You picked up a recipe box but put it back down and grabbed the big oatmeal container instead. You shook it. It was almost empty. You opened it and dumped out the oats and oat dust into the garbage, whacking the bottom a couple of times to be sure it was empty, then you took the plan off the refrigerator, rolled it up into a tube, and put it in the oatmeal container. The roll unraveled inside the container and pushed out to the sides. You couldn't really see it unless you were looking for it. You put the top back on the container, then got out a marker from the kitchen drawer and wrote the word "NOT" in front of the words "Instant Oatmeal" on the label.

"There," you said and put it in the small cupboard over the stove. "Let's celebrate by seeing what's on the boob tube."[36]

I am putting a lot of things in this memory book, but I will take that plan with me. If I ever start to wonder if all this really happened, I can take it out, read your handwriting, smell the oatmeal smell, and know I'm not doing what comes so naturally: lying my lying little behind off.

This was all real, even the parts I don't want to remember.

I'm almost positive of it.

Y ou knew what you were doing.

Almost 10 years later, I'm looking at it now. The plan looks just like it did that day. Maybe people should make all time capsules out of oatmeal containers. Maybe if we made houses out of oatmeal containers, we would live forever.

There's also a nearly full container of actual oatmeal in your cupboard. Maybe I should make some raisin cookies before I go and leave them outside for the squirrels or birds or any kids that happen to be crawling by on all 4s.

It would be like a big juicy plate of snake snacks for the next sneaky snarky stinker you snare.

Don't you think?

---

36. 8008 = BOOB. 5318008 = BOOBIES. 55378008 = BOOBLESS. 376616 = GIGGLE

We put the plan to the test that day. You went to breakfast and brought bacon, a half a bagel and some scrambled eggs in your purse.

After I ate, you went to the lobby to call me from the guest phone. While I waited for the ring, I shoved my sheets and blankets behind the couch. The phone started ringing. It rang and rang, so I didn't pick it up. The 2nd time you called, you did the secret code and I picked it up. You said, "The raven flies at midnight," laughed, and hung up.

When you got back to your door—our door—you knocked and I ran to the sink, got into the cupboard, and closed the door behind me, leaving it a crack open so I didn't get scared in the dark. You opened the door and told me I was really noisy when I ran and we should try it again. I got out and went back to the couch, you went back out, knocked again, and I tiptoed into the kitchen and hid. You came in, squatted in front of the sink, opened the cupboard door, gave me a thumbs up, then tried to give me a high 5, but we mostly missed each other's hands.

You got some money from your purse and told me to go to the store and buy some kids books. I thought it would only be a dollar, because old people have no idea what anything costs. But it was $20.[37] "Only books, right?" you said.

"Right."

"No candy, right?"

"Uh-uh. I mean, uh-huh."

"OK, get going," you said, pushing me toward the door that led to the hallway. I took a couple of steps, staring at President Jackson who wouldn't look me in the eye, then stopped, looked at the doorknob, and took a step back. "Good boy," you said, spinning me around like a top, patting me on the behind and giving me a push toward the sliding door. I put the money in my pocket, opened the door, looked all around to make sure the coast was clear, scooted over the railing, and went through the bushes.

When I came back you were on the couch with lunch spread out on the coffee table. There was a meat and cheese sandwich in a box with a pickle and chips, and there was a peanut butter and jelly sandwich on a napkin. I put down the bag of books, sat down on the couch, looked at my hands, wiped them on my clothes a little, then reached for the peanut butter and jelly sandwich. My hand crashed into yours.

"I thought that was mine," I said.

"I thought it was mine," you said.

"That's a kid sandwich."

---

37. I smelled it and it didn't reek of feet and garbage like my money always did. For once, cashiers wouldn't take my money by trying to only hold the smallest bit of a corner, so they wouldn't catch whatever deadly diseases it was no doubt carrying.

"Grown-ups can eat PBJs, too."

"Nuh-uh."

"Looks like we need to put this up for a vote. All those in favor of me getting that delicious sandwich, raise your hand." You raised your hand, and I held my right arm down with my left hand just in case it wanted to jump up. "OK. That's 1 vote for me. All those in favor of you getting the gross sandwich made of nuts that grow in filthy dirt and berries that have been sitting in a jar for months and might have botulism that leads to a painful death, raise your hand." I raised my hand and waved it a little. You didn't. "That's 1 vote for you. That means we are tied. We will need to flip a coin." You reached into your pocket and pulled out a quarter. "I will flip it. You call it in the air. Whoever wins the flip wins the sandwich they want." You flipped it, I called heads, but it landed tails side up.

I said a bad word, but you ignored it, reached over the PBJ, and took the meat and cheese sandwich instead, leaving the PBJ for me.

That afternoon, we played cards and read books. I read a dragon book I had bought. You read the same parts of the book you had read before about the lonely woman and the gardener without a shirt. I also showed you some of my baseball cards. When it was dinner time, you put a fresh plastic container in your purse and went to the dining room. I fell asleep on the couch watching a nature show on PBS. When you came back, I woke up and you got a fork for me to eat straight out of the container. It was buttery rice with chicken pieces and green beans on top. I pushed aside the beans to get to the real food.

When the Mariners game came on, you got out the cookies from your purse. The Ms lost by 472 runs, but we watched the whole thing. It was after my bedtime when the game ended, but there was a good infomercial on after the game about a machine that dehydrates food, so we watched that too. I wanted to order it,[38] but you said no.

We put the sheets on the couch, and you went over to my bag of books to pick something to read. I asked you, "Can you sing to me again instead of reading a story?"

"OK. What would you like me to sing?"

"You pick."

"Should I sing about smooching and lovey-dovey stuff?"

"Gross. No."

"OK. That narrows it down," you said. "Hmmmm. Ooh. Got it. It's a song from back when I was young and dinosaurs roamed the earth."[39] You cleared your throat, straightened your wig, and sang:

---

38. I wondered what would happen if a person got stuck inside it.

39. "Meow!"

I've got my eyes on you,
So best beware where you roam.
I've got my eyes on you,
So don't stray too far from home.
Incidentally
I've set my spies on you,
I'm checking all you do
From a to zee.
So, darling, just be wise,
Keep your eyes on me.

We were looking at my collection of Montreal Expos, and I told you, "The Expos don't exist anymore."

You said, "I know that, Silly. Do you think I live under a rock or something? They moved to Florida."

"No, they moved to Washington. Where the president lives. Not the state."

"Are you sure?" you said.

"Yes."

"They didn't move to Florida?"

"No."

"Are you triple sure?"

"Yes, yes, yes," I said. That made you laugh.

"Which teams moved to Florida?"

"None did."

"Then where did those Florida teams come from?"

"They came from—. They just came from themselves," I said.

"Sounds fishy to me. Should we flip on it?"

"No."

"Why not?"

"Because you can't flip on that. It's not a vote. It just is."

"That makes sense...I guess." You looked up and off into the distance like you were thinking hard about it—thinking as hard as Einstein needed to think to come up with E=MC2. Then your lip snarled a little and you farted a fart as long as the national anthem when the singers want to be the main show at the

Mariners games. You stopped looking off into the distance and looked back at me like nothing had just happened. "Hey, I'll trade you this Pascual Perez."

"For who?"

"Him," you said pointing.

"Him?" I said pointing.

"Yes. Let's trade."

"But they're both mine," I said.

"What if I throw in this Hubie Brooks guy, too?"

The U-shaped part of the pipe was pressing against my ribs, and it didn't feel good at all. At first it was just uncomfortable, but then it started to hurt, and it was only going to get worse. I couldn't change position, though, because my legs would bump the cabinet doors and they would swing open.

I should have taken my time getting under the sink, but it was the first real knock on the door—not just a test—and I scrambled under there faster than I needed to. Now I was stuck. I couldn't do anything without taking a chance she would see me.

"Millie, what an unpleasant surprise," I heard you say over the sound of my ribs yelling at me.

"Aren't you going to invite me in?" she asked.

"No. I was just leaving."

"You can't go out wearing that and looking like that, so you can't be leaving immediately," she said. "I'm sure you have time for an old friend."

"Oh, is there a friend of mine standing behind you?" you said.

"Your hospitality is lacking."

"I wish I could let you in, but I really am in a rush," you said.

"Not a single person in this entire building is in a rush, Ruth. Now cut out this do-si-do and let me in."

I heard her heels march across the kitchen floor, then your bare feet followed her.

"It looks different in here," she said.

"I've been cleaning."

"No, it's not cleaner. It's the same mess it always is. I don't know how you live this way."

"What can I help you with, Millie? Do you need a cup of sugar or arsenic or something?"

She didn't answer, but I heard her footsteps leave the linoleum and head across the carpet over toward the sliding door.

"Aren't you going to offer me some tea, Ruth?"

"Sorry, but I don't have any," you fibbed. "Would you like some tap water? I can put a cup of sugar or arsenic in it for flavor."

"What's that smell?"

"What smell?"

"Do you smell it?"

"Smell what?"

I could hear a loud, exaggerated sniffing noise, then she took a few steps, then more sniffs, then more steps. She sniffed around the living room, then took a step onto the linoleum, then turned back and went into your bedroom. I heard her open the closet door. I heard your barefoot feet go over to the couch and it creaked when you sat down. She looked behind your bedroom door. I heard it squeak closed and then squeak back open. She walked around in your bedroom more, came out, walked onto the linoleum again, and tapped her foot as she stood there a few feet away from me.

I heard the couch un-creak as you stood up, and you asked her, "Are you done snooping yet?"

"What in the world are you talking about?" she said, dramatically offended.

You walked into the kitchen all the way up to the sink, bumping the cupboard door with your legs. I heard some glasses clink, and you ran the faucet. The noise was loud under the sink as the water went through the pipes and down the drain. I suddenly needed to pee a gallon of pee.

"I don't want to be a rude host, so here's a glass of water. You have 5 seconds to drink it and get your nosy nose out of my home. And be careful not to spill it on yourself. We wouldn't want you to melt, would we? Who would take care of your flying monkeys? Think of the monkeys, Millie."

"You better think about your little monkey, Ruth. You better think long and hard." Her shoes clacked toward the door. "That's some free advice. I would take it if I were you." The door slammed. Then the light flooded in and blinded me.

"**W**hat happens if she finds me?"

"She won't find you."

"What if she does?"

"What if ants grow as big as buses and take over the world?"

"That's not real."

"Well, it will take ants a zillion years to grow that big, and it will take 2 zillion years for her to find you. We'll both be dead by then, especially me,[40] so the joke would be on her."

"She's going to find me."

You tapped your fingers on your hip and said, "I wouldn't have guessed you would be scared of a sad old lady like her. What is she? 127 years old, at least."

"She's mean. Why is she so mean?"

"Why is anyone the way they are? It doesn't matter."

"Something made her mean."

"She probably just has gas. That's why old people look that way—like they hate the world. They wouldn't be so grumpy if they just let it out." You walked around in a small circle making fart noises with your mouth. I didn't laugh. You were avoiding my question. You always avoided my questions. You went to the door, mimicked how she stormed into the room, mouth-farting all the way. You pretended to smell something bad like she had, then started snooping in all the places she had looked, ripping mouth toots. I still didn't laugh. At best, my frown was 3.7 percent un-frowned.

You came back to the kitchen, completely out of breath, except for enough breath to give me a bunch of advice I didn't ask for. "If you worry about all the bad things that might happen, you're not going to be a very happy person." You were bent over, trying to catch your breath. "You wouldn't be much fun to be around, either, so I would have to replace you with a different kid who's more fun."

That sent a jolt through me, but I tried to hide it by folding my arms and shaking my head. "No, you wouldn't. You'll never kick me out."

Still bent over, you kept at it: "I'll upgrade to a kid who doesn't argue so much, all the time, always, at the drop of a hat. A kid who doesn't pee everywhere except in the toilet."

All I could muster in response was, "Nuh-uh!"

"Oooh, I know! I'll get a little girl!" You managed to stand up straight-ish and scratched your chin thinking about your boy-less future. "They're less trouble and less gassy, at least until they are 127." You put up your tickling fingers and aimed them right at my armpits, but I was quicker. I fled the kitchen and went into your room where I scooted across the bed over to the far side. You chased me into the room and flopped onto the mattress, completely out of breath again. For once, I was able to escape you.

Later that night, when the lights were off and I was laying down in the small divot and big divot in the couch, I wondered and wondered about what you said about getting a new kid. I didn't know why it was so stuck in my brain, since I was always either thinking about running away, threatening to run away, or

---

40. Until I started writing this memory book, I didn't realize how much you talked about being dead.

actually running away. But my brain went round and round that night thinking about it. My thoughts and worries and fears chased themselves in the same circle over and over again. Sometimes I wished there was a way for me to kick my brain out or, even better, to leave it behind and run, run, run.

W ally Westlake hit 127 home runs in his career. Willie Mays had 127 RBIs in 1955. I am sure I have seen that number other places, but those are the 2 I remember.

1 time that week, you weren't able to sneak any dinner food into your purse, so you just took as many brownies from the dessert table as you could fit in your purse. I ate the biggest as my main dish, made the 2 smaller brownies my side dishes, and put all the crumbs into a bowl, calling it my salad.

I was awake until after midnight because of all the sugar and chocolate. We watched a movie about a police detective until it ended. You covered my eyes whenever there were guns and you tried to mute the volume whenever they said bad words, but you were too slow. I would always see the shooting and hear the bad words, but we would miss everything else.

After the police movie, we flipped around for a while until we found a funny movie about kids in college who were throwing a big party that was against the rules for some reason that didn't seem real. They just needed the dumb rule so the movie would be 2 hours long instead of 5 minutes long.

You fell asleep on the couch right after it started so you didn't see me get the last brownie from the kitchen. You weren't awake to cover my eyes during the parts of the movie with naked ladies either. Ever since then, I can't help thinking about boobs whenever I eat brownies. It's all your fault. I was an innocent youth, and you corrupted me.[41]

"D o you know what today is?"

"Is it Saturday?" I asked.

"No."

"Is it Friday?"

"No, I don't mean what day of the week." You raised up your eyebrows waiting for me to put 2 and 2 together.

But I didn't. I shrugged and looked back at the TV.

"It's our month-iversary, Silly," you said. "We should celebrate!" I wasn't really tuned in to what you were saying, so you reached over, took the remote from the arm of the couch, and turned off the TV. That got my attention.

"Hey! I was watching that. You can't do that. It's my day to be the boss of the remote control."

"Anniversaries are exempt."

"You're making up a new rule. It's not on our list."

"Truism," you corrected.

"You can't just make up rules any time you want. That's not fair."

"I can make up rules because I'm the parent."

"No, you're not," I said and glared at you like I was trying to set your wig on fire with heat vision.

You could see where the conversation was heading, and you steered it in a different direction before it went flying off a cliff and exploded in a fireball. "You're right. It is your day for the remote." You placed it back on the arm of the sofa, and I wanted to grab it. "But it is our anniversary, and it is a special day regardless of whether it is officially on our list of truisms or not." You got a piece of paper in the kitchen and wrote down something silently. You folded

---

41. Actually, it wasn't just you who corrupted my "innocence." Later, everyone did. Mr. Will tried to get me to call boobs "knockers" because he thought that would be hilarious coming out of a little kid's mouth. He also educated me about all the types of scotch when I was 10 so I would grow up to be classy. Mrs. Beth explained "menses" in great detail to me "because young men should know about these things." Mr. Herman told me boobs should never be referred to as "knockers," but rather "bodacious ta-tas," because that's more respectful to women. And when Mrs. Bea (fancy Mrs. Bea with the fancy teapots and the doilies and the porcelain dolls) held her "tea parties" where all the old ladies drank schnapps instead of Lipton, they would giggle their buns off saying old-fashioned-sounding nicknames for men's private parts when they thought I wasn't listening: Admiral Winkie, The Fallopian Fiddler, Dr. Wang, M.D., The Impreg-a-nator, Hairy Houdini, The Ovarian Lancer and Pennis the Menace.

it in half, wrote something on the front and handed it to me. My name was on the outside. It said this inside:

You are cordially invited to a picnic
in celebration of our one-month-iversary.
Please RSVP by contacting Ruth in the kitchen.

It was in your fancy cursive writing with all the loop-de-loops that made the entire thing look like a bunch of circles crashing into other circles. The only word I could read was "You" and "picnic." When I looked up from the note, you were moving things around on the counter trying not to look like someone who was waiting for me to say something.

"Is it a picnic here on the floor like we did for dinner the other night?"

"No. It's a real picnic. At a picnic table. I'm too old for picnics on the floor. I can barely get up from the couch anymore, let alone the ground."

"Where will it be?"

"My, you're full of questions."

"Kids ask lots of questions. Everyone knows that."

"Well, it's 1 thing to read it in a book," you said and pushed your glasses up your nose. "It's another thing to hear the sheer volume of questions in person. It's impressively relentless."

I tried to set your wig on fire again with my stare. I did that a lot. I was impressively relentless with by angry laser beams, too.

"We'll have the picnic at a park," you said.

"Which park?"

"You can choose. It should have picnic tables, though. Does your favorite park have tables?"

"Yes, but there's bird poop all over them."

"A little bird poop never killed anyone."

"Yes, it does. It has all kinds of germs that kill people. I saw it on TV. Plus, it's gross. There's always the white watery part, then the weird chunky thing in the middle."

"Poop is poop."[42]

"Some poop is extra gross."

"Let's agree to disagree. Is there a park with tables without bird poop?"

"Yes, but the tables there have bad words all over them."

"What kind of bad words?"

"Really bad words."

---

42. Until I started writing this memory book, I didn't realize how much I talked about Number 2.

"Well, as long as they are poop free, then it's OK with me. Bad words don't bother me much. Some old people think curse words are the worst thing there is but they've got everything backward and inside out in their heads. There are plenty of things 1,000 times worse than curse words, but people don't like thinking about those things because it makes them feel helpless. So, they focus on being the bad word police because that's easy. Inspiring, huh? My generation is full of profiles in courage. Profiles in bleeping courage."

Your words sounded like a jet engine in my brain. I put my hands over my ears. You motioned for me to take my hands off my ears. I did, eventually, and you said, "Go ahead. Try me."

"What?"

"A bad word. Go ahead and say a bad word."

"Why?"

"To test me."

"Why?"

"To test me," you repeated, unhelpfully.

"Which bad word?"

"Whichever you want. Just cover your ears when you say it so you don't hear it. Kids shouldn't hear bad language like that, even though it's not in the top 8,000,000 worst things in the world. Our precious ears are safe, but nobody's doing a darn thing about kids dying of malaria and about human trafficking and wars and famine and plastic in the..."

I covered my ears to block out all your complaining so I could decide on which terrible, horrible, no good, very bad word I should say. You motioned for me to take my hands off my ears, which I did   eventually. You said, "Go ahead. Say it. I don't have all year. Have you noticed how old I am?"

I covered my ears again, decided what to say, and said it. It was really bad. Really, really bad. Every syllable of it was a sin I would have to fake repent for at the fake St. Patrick's church I had made up and would never, ever go to. Ever.[43]

I uncovered my ears, and you said, "Oh my. That *is* a bad word. Where did you learn that? Wait, don't tell me. I probably don't want to know." You straightened your shirt like it had been blown sideways by what I had said. "That was quite a test, but I think I passed. If Millie were here, she would have dropped dead on the spot. Maybe I should call her in and give it a try. That would solve some of our problems, don't you think?"

---

43. Amen!

We went down to the basement to get your bike out of storage. There was no shuttle today, so your hastily constructed plan was for us to take the bike to the store to get food for the anniversary picnic, which I was somehow a part of even though I hadn't said yes. I could have just walked to the store—which I told you multiple times—but you insisted on your plan. You had me go out the sliding door and wait in the bushes until you opened a door halfway down the building near the stairwell down to the basement. You motioned for me once you got there and opened the door. I scurried in like the cat-man's cats that all smell worse than broccoli-flavored pee.

Your bike had 3 wheels—1 in the front and 2 in the back—the kind old people use so they don't fall over and break their everything. It was chained up with an actual chain. I had never seen that before. People usually use spiral or U-shaped locks, but you had a really long, heavy chain like what dummies in movies use to try to control dinosaurs and monsters before those things easily escape and kill everyone. The chain was woven through the spokes of the front wheel, up over the handlebars, around the seat, through the big metal basket in the back, through the spokes in both back wheels, then back up to the front wheel. The bike wasn't chained to anything, just to itself. There's probably a joke I can make here about how most people are chained to themselves just like that bike, but all this clanking metal on my shoulders and arms is making it hard to type.

You unlocked the ridiculously large padlock with the world's smallest key, then we started unweaving the chain. It took both of us to drag it off to the side, and it made a big crashing noise when we dropped it onto the ground. You went back to the bike and were saying boring things I was paying no attention to. I was looking at the door we had come in through, wondering if it would lock us in if it closed by accident. How long would it be until someone else came down here? What if it wasn't for a week? Or a month? If we started to starve, would I eat you before you ate me?

You broke my cannibalistic trance. "Get your buns over here, Bub. Help me get this over to the stairs."

We managed to get it out to the stairs and up out of the basement before either of us had to consume the other person's gross body. We pushed it to the door I had come in through. You poked your head out, looked left, looked right, looked up, then said, "Green light." Outside in the sunlight, the bike looked like a wreck. It was rusty and dusty and covered in spider webs. When you got onto the seat, the tires got flatter than pancakes. Your bike had 3 wheels that didn't want to do the most basic thing wheels are supposed to do: roll. I guess everything in your life automatically wants to do the opposite of what you want.

You got off, put your hands on the handlebars, motioned for me to follow, and started to walk it. The wide double wheels in the back didn't leave much room for you to walk next to it, so you had to lean way over at an awkward angle that your back started hating within half a nanosecond. You stopped, tried rubbing spots on your back you couldn't reach, kicked the wheel of the bike, then walked away to say some bad words about how great your plan was going. You didn't go far enough away. I could hear all of them. You knew a lot more of them than I did then, but I'm catching up now.

I hopped onto the bike seat when you weren't looking. I put my feet on the pedals and wiggled the handlebars back and forth but wasn't pedaling. I looked down at the tires. They didn't turn into complete pancakes with my tiny butt on the seat. The bike started moving and I almost fell off. I rebalanced myself and tried to stop the bike by trying to squeeze the hand brakes, but there weren't any. The bike was picking up speed. I tried to guess how much it would hurt if I had to jump off. I started looking for a good spot to eject, then I heard your cackling cackle behind me. You were pushing and your legs were going way faster than I thought they could go—definitely fast enough to trap a snake-loving eagle or a snake-hating kid.

"That's not funny," I said.

"Yes, it is," you said.

"No, it's not. "

"Yes, it is. Objectively. In any culture. On any planet. In any galaxy."

"No, it's not."

"Trust me, I write jokes professionally, for free, for the greater good."

"No, you don't."

"For both of our sakes, you should focus on steering rather than debating my sense of humor. Otherwise, we're going to hit that tree and explode into a ball of fire people will see all the way over in Gresham."

I steered us away from danger and spent the next 11 minutes thinking of a way to get back at you with a prank while you pushed us to the store. The flat wheels got flatter as we went, trying their best to stop you or even just slow you down. But they didn't know what they were up against. Poor, dumb wheels.

My prank wasn't very good. That night I turned the toilet paper around in the holder so the paper came out the bottom of the roll rather than off the top. I knew you hated that. You didn't give me the satisfaction of saying anything, though. You would just fix it, then I would unfix it, then you would refix it, then I would re-unfix it, then.... I gave up after less than a day. Kids don't have a lot of stamina when it comes to revenge. That's another 1 of our many downfalls.[44]

At the park we ate ham-and-Swiss roll-ups. We got bread at the store, but we both skipped it. We got chips, too, but I didn't like them. They were the barbecue kind you like for some reason. The red barbecue dust on the chips tastes like metal to me. You were chomping them by the handful, and they made your hands look like they were covered in dried blood.

You were talking and talking, but I ignored you. I made grunts to make you think I was listening, but I was busy looking at the swings. There was a mom with a baby so small it did not look real. The baby was on the swing that looks like a big rubber diaper that goes up to the baby's armpits. You watched me watching them for a while then said, "Swings are fun, huh?"

I shrugged, looked down at the ground and kicked the bark chips with my shoes. Those chips were wood flavored and still probably tasted better than your barbecue chips. I waited until you looked up at the trees—because you always ended up looking for birds—then I went back to staring at the swings. The mom looked so happy pushing the baby. The baby looked so happy being pushed by the mom. Watching them made me feel sick to my stomach. I could taste the roll-ups in the back of my throat.

"That swing on the right looks like the perfect height for your legs."

I ignored you.

"I bet you can't go higher than that baby."

"I don't want to swing."

"I wasn't suggesting you do. I was just making an innocent observation about how high you could hypothetically go."

"I don't want to swing."

"I was just—."

"You're trying to get me to go."

"You keep looking at them, so I—."

"I can look at anything I want."

"That is true."

"I wasn't looking at them. I was looking at nothing." I turned to you and told you to shut up with my eyes.

"I just—."

---

44. Also, we can't reach anything put up on the second shelf or higher.

"It's none of your business!" I growled at you, then looked off to the left like I was looking at nothing, but I was still watching the swings out of the side of my eyes.

"You're being silly and overreacting."

I turned back to you and was blowing air out of my nose like an angry, snot-filled bull. "We. Shook. Hands," I said.

You looked confused.

I flared my nostrils and made myself as clear as I was capable of back then. "You—. You can't—." I had to stop and swallow a bunch of roll-up-flavored spit in my mouth. "You don't get. To ask me. About stuff. Ever."

You looked at the mom and baby, then back at me, then back at them, then back at me. The crinkles and wrinkles on your face looked different now. "You are absolutely right. No more questions." You zipped your lips with an imaginary zipper, locked the zipper with a complicated set of invisible locks, tossing each invisible key off to the side so your mouth could never be unzipped. Then you immediately started talking again. "I'm going to explore a bit." You got up and went over the climbing structure, which had at least a dozen ways kids could break their arms or snap their necks.

I watched the mom and baby on the swing again. The baby made a little squeal every time it went forward but made a concerned face on the way back. Happy, then scared to death, then happy. Back and forth, over and over. I didn't want to look at them, but I couldn't stop. I wanted to yell at them to go away until they were both crying and got in their Subaru and went away.

I was so focused on the mom and baby I didn't hear all the birds behind me. The table was covered with them, pecking away at our lunch. I started yelling at them to fly away, but I wasn't a very good scarecrow. They didn't budge. They continued their picnic until you came back and yelled, "Caw!" at them like you were the queen of the crows. The birds scattered and we surveyed the damage. It was a mess. The only thing they hadn't ruined was the bread.

You gathered up all the pecked food, said, "The mice are going to have a feast tonight," walked past the trash can, went to the trees behind the play structure, and started throwing meat, cheese and chips into the woods. A piece of Swiss cheese hit the trunk of a tree and stuck there about 7 feet up. You tried to reach it to get it off the tree and throw it in the bushes where it apparently belonged, but you couldn't reach it.

You went into the bushes and came out with a stick. You started hitting the cheese with the branch, but that just made it stick harder to the tree. You lifted up the stick to try again, but you saw something high up in the trees and got distracted from whacking the cheese. You dropped the stick, tiptoed to the back of the tree, looked up again, and tiptoed further into the woods.

The baby started crying and I stopped watching you. It was time to go, and the baby didn't want to leave the swing. The mom kissed and hushed the baby, and I felt my nausea tiptoeing back again. She put the baby in a baby-holder-thing on her chest, gathered the rest of their stuff, walked toward the table where I was, smiled at me, waved her baby's hand goodbye to me, went to the parking area, and took about 37 hours putting things into the car, strapping the baby into its seat, and driving away. I felt exhausted and empty once their dumb car turned onto the dumb street and was out of sight.

You trudged out of the bushes and trees looking exhausted and empty too. You sat down next to me and didn't say anything. You were looking up, searching for whatever had been in the trees.

"The cheese is still on the tree," I said unhelpfully.

"Did you see them?" Your voice was weird. Shaky and weird.

"Who?"

"The mourning doves."

I didn't know what a mourning dove looked like, so I reflexively did what I always reflexively did. I said, "No."

"The female comes to my feeder."

I looked up at you. Your eyes looked different. Not like when we are fighting and your eyes think they are going to win. This was the opposite of that.

"There is a male with her now." You reached for the bag of bread, opened it, and started crumbling the bread in your barbecue dust-stained hands. The chip dust made the bread pink. "She was alone for a long time. A long, long time." You scattered the crumbs and started making more. You handed me a piece.

I didn't crumble it. I just held it and looked at the swings.

"They mate for life." You made more pink crumbs. "But sometimes things happen." I looked at you. You spread more crumbs on the ground and kept looking in the trees. The skin under your eyes twitched in a way I didn't want to see ever again, so I looked down at my shoes.

We both sat there and stared at the missing parts of our Swiss cheese lives until I broke the terrible silence. "Anniversaries suck."

For once in your life, you didn't disagree with me. Not even a single tiny bit.

I threw the piece of bread down, stood up, and walked over to our wreck of a bike to go back to our wreck of a life.

Here they are. The mourning doves that made you cry without crying.

There were flashing lights when we got back to the building, and my feet got ready to run. But it was a fire truck, not a police car. "Someone must have kicked the bucket," you said and kicked a pebble on the sidewalk. "The fire station is right around the corner, and they get here faster than the ambulances do. Go around the back. I'll open the sliding door for you in a couple of minutes. Take the bike with you."

"It won't fit through the bushes."

"Well, we can't leave it here. Someone would steal it, for sure."

"That?"

"Of course. It's a valuable vehicle."

"That?"

"I guarantee you if you were a little hoodlum, you'd steal this bike in 2 seconds. But that's a silly example because you could never be a hoodlum."

"Yes, I could," I said with a level of indignation that it takes most people decades to build up.

"You? Ha!"

"That's mean. Telling a boy he wouldn't be a good bad guy is a big insult."

"But that's what I think, so I have to say it."

"No, you don't." I felt my ears getting hot.

"Yes, I do."

"No! Stop saying everything you think!"

You took a step back, probably because of my repulsive breath, made a calm-down motion with your hands, and then stepped closer and put your hand on my shoulder. "You have a point. I do tend to forget to edit what pops into my noggin. I always just say everything I'm thinking."

"No, you don't." My ears were even hotter now.

"Yes, I do. That's the entire point of our argument right now. The entire point!"

"That's 1,000,000% not true. Sometimes you look at me and I know you are thinking stuff, but you don't say anything."

You looked at me and didn't say anything.

"You're doing it right now," I said. "I can tell because of your eyebrows. They always look that way when you are not saying what you are thinking about me."

"Maybe you're right. Maybe you would make a good bad guy. Bad guys need to be able to read people like a book, even when they are not saying anything. So, I was wrong. I apologize."

I didn't know what to say. I wasn't used to winning arguments with you. That had me completely flustered. I changed the subject to something less uncomfortable. "When will they bring out the dead person?"

"Oh, it usually takes a while," you said after looking at your watch-less wrist to make that estimate. "The firemen won't do it themselves. An ambulance will if the person still has a bit of a pulse. If their ticker ain't still ticking though, a funeral home will send a car."

"What do they do while they wait?"

"The dead person just lies there."

"No. What do the other people do?"

"Oh, they probably say nice things about the person and stay with the body so it doesn't get lonely. That's a polite thing to do when a person dies, even though the dead person doesn't give a darn and even though the person may not have been very nice."

"Does it look like they are asleep?"

"No. People say that, but it's not true. You can tell when someone is asleep. When you see a dead person, they don't look like they are taking a nap. You can tell something is different."

"What's different?"

"They're dead."

I stared at you with dead eyes.

"Sorry for the jokes. It's how I cope with ever-approaching mortality."

I kept staring at you with dead eyes.

"You asked a serious question about how a dead person looks different, and you deserve a serious answer. It's hard to explain with words, though, so let's see with our own eyes. Soud good?"

That did not sound good, but you didn't give me a chance to answer. You grabbed my hand, pulled me toward the door in search of the first dead body I would see. It wouldn't be the last.

The front desk was empty, so you grabbed a visitor badge and clipped it to my shirt. We went through the lobby, past the elevators to the first-floor hallway. We looked down the north hallway and there weren't any people, so you took us to the right, past the rec room, to the south hallway. Nothing was happening there, so we went upstairs and saw a group of people standing outside a room near the end of the south hallway.

You put your finger to your lips and motioned for me to follow you. I started to taste roll-ups again. We weaved through the crowd until we got to the door where some firemen were blocking the way. You held a hand up to your face like you were overcome with emotion and leaned on a fireman with your other arm. He put his arm under yours to make sure you didn't collapse and guided you inside. You looked back at me through your fingers, winked, and pulled me into the apartment with you.[45]

Inside, there was a fireman filling out paperwork. The facility director was helping him. The nurse was organizing a rolling cart of medical stuff that she had brought to the room. Apparently, none of her gadgets and medicines was any good for making a dead person come back to life. Another fireman was packing things back into a medical bag. His stuff was useless, too. The dead person was on the couch lying down. The fireman holding your arm guided us there, made sure you were steady and weren't going to pass out, then let us have a moment with the dead guy.

You leaned down to me and whispered-asked, "Do you want to touch him?"

"Where?" I whispered-asked back, as if that were the right response.

"Anywhere."

"No." We looked at him. You fake-blew your nose on a tissue you had dug out of your pocket. I tugged on your shirt, and you leaned back down. "What's his name?"

"I don't know," you answered, wiping fake tears from your lying eyes. "There are a lot of people in this place, and they all look the same to me." You stood back up, fake-lamenting what's-his-name's death, then leaned back down and asked, "What do you think his name was?"

---

45. Maybe you should have been an actress instead of just a crazy old lady who fed wild birds and wilder boys.

I looked at him. I looked at his face. At the skin on his cheeks. At his lips. At his earlobes. I didn't look at his eyes at first. I avoided them even thought they were closed. I looked at the skin on his forehead. I looked at the hair in his nose. There was a lot of it. A lot. Then I looked at his closed eyes. They didn't look like a sleeping person's eyes, which are twitching and doing weird stuff all the time. I looked at his chest to see if he was breathing. I didn't see it moving. I looked at his hands. They were folded neatly on his stomach. The people must have done that after they found him. He probably didn't die on the couch either. I looked around to see where he fell. There was a remote control on the floor halfway under a chair near the window, but nothing else looked messed up. I looked back at him. He wasn't wearing any shoes. Just black socks. His toes were stiffly pointed down like a ballerina's. I looked at his hands again. His thumbs were tucked into the palms of his hands making it look like he only had 4 fingers. Cartoon characters on TV only have 4 fingers. It's too hard to draw 5 and not look weird. I wondered if people had 5 fingers because it was too hard for nature to make 6-fingered hands that don't look weird.

I tugged on your shirt, and you stopped fake-shaking your head at the injustice of the universe to lean down. I said, "He looks like a William."

"I think so, too," you said. "Does he look like he's sleeping?"

"No."

"What's different?"

"He looks like a doll. A creepy doll."

You put your hand on his forehead, said, "*Bon voyage*, Bill," then took my hand, and said, "*Vamanos*."

On the way out, I bumped up against someone and my visitor's badge fell off. I looked back at it but didn't tug on your hand to stop and go back for it.

You wanted to talk and talk that night after we looked at William's dead body. I was terrible company—too busy thinking about skin around eyes that no longer twitches and jumps—so you turned on the TV and found a channel playing a movie with talking animals that was supposed to be funny but wasn't. The computer lips didn't match the voices very well. You told me they made the lips move with computers, as if I didn't know that. You also told me they used to do it with peanut butter back in old movies and TV shows.[46] You said a lot of other things, too, but I didn't say anything back about any of

---

46. You said, "Helloooooooo, Wilbur." I had no idea what you were talking about.

it. When it was bedtime, you tucked me in, turned off the light, and went into your room whistling while you got ready for bed.

I snuck into the kitchen and got the flashlight from the drawer with 717 mixed-up things. I turned it on under my blanket and hoped the battery would last all night. I must have fallen asleep because I had a nightmare about a dead guy. Not William. A different dead guy, who was walking around even though he was dead. That's the worst kind of dead person, isn't it? The dream woke me up and I couldn't go back to sleep. I checked behind the curtain to make sure nobody was there, but the only dead thing in the room was the flashlight. I turned on the TV, tried to mute the sound before it came on, but I didn't press the button at the right time and the TV was super loud. I pressed the buttons like crazy to lower the volume and then listened to see if I had woken you up. I hadn't. It was still on when I got up the next morning and another terrible movie about talking animals was on.

I didn't tell you about the bad dream. I didn't want you to think I was a scaredy-cat who let something dumb like a bunch of dead people bother me.

Do you remember how sick I got right after that? People aren't supposed to get sick in the summer, but I did, and it was really bad. William must have given it to me. Maybe he was contagious.

You thought it was food poisoning at first because I was throwing up so much. But that didn't make sense because I don't think you can get food poisoning from a 100% sugar diet. The throwing up lasted for 2 days. When that stopped, the coughing and runs took over. That made my ribs hurt and made my butt burn like dragon fire. I had to blow my nose all the time, too. I went through tissues like crazy, and you kept asking me what color everything was that came out of me. We ran out of tissues and started using toilet paper. There was a roll of toilet paper on the couch next to me, 1 on the coffee table and 1 in the kitchen. You also put the trash can next to the couch in case I couldn't make it to the bathroom, plus another bucket halfway between the couch and the toilet even though they were only 6 feet apart. You didn't tell me whether those were for barfing my guts out or for pooping my guts out, but it was probably an all-of-the-above situation.

When you took my temperature with a thermometer, you didn't tell me what the numbers said. Even I knew that was a bad sign. You put icepacks on my neck and kept giving me drinks to drink. You took the building shuttle to the store and got grape-flavored kid's Tylenol to try to break the fever. You smuggled orange juice back from the dining room, but it tasted bad and I refused to drink it. You tried feeding me, but I refused to eat. I started refusing to let you take my temperature in my mouth, so you put it in my armpit until I started refusing that. I just wanted to watch TV. I barked at you when you tried to talk to me. I barked at you when you blocked the screen. I barked at the screen when there was no Mariners game because they had the day off. All that barking made my coughing 10 times worse.

The only time I wasn't mad was once when you finally left for dinner, but you came back in 1 minute and ruined my peace and quiet. You had an old man with you. Did you offer him cookies and milk too? Was he my replacement? I pulled the sheet over my head to hide. It wasn't hiding under the sink, but it was the best hiding spot I could come up with on short notice. You pulled the sheet down. Both of you were looking down at me.

"Hmmmm," the old man said, tilting his head and crinkling his giant eyebrows like he was trying to figure out a puzzle. "How do you feel, son?"

"Who are you?" I didn't know anything about him, but that didn't stop me from not liking him even a teeny, tiny bit.

"I'm Harry. Now, what seems to be the problem?" Maybe the fever was messing with my brain, but I thought he meant, "I'm hairy," so I looked at his un-hairy head and face and arms and hands and felt confused and annoyed. He charged ahead: "Sounds like you've been in a bit of a wrestling match with some germs over the past couple of days." He was wearing pajama pants with Rudolph and all his reindeer friends pulling Santa's sleigh on them. On his feet were fuzzy slippers with stuffed menorahs on the top that flopped around when he walked.[47]

"You're blocking the TV. Move, please," I said, but the please was not polite.

"Do you like candy?"

I looked at you, then back at him, and nodded.

"I thought so. I'm good at reading people. It's a talent I'm blessed with." He went back to the door—menorahs flopping—and picked up a black bag he had set down. He brought it over to the coffee table, opened it, and pulled out a lollipop. "Oh, my mistake. This has gum in the middle of it. You don't like those, do you?" and he moved his hand back into the bag.

"Uh-huh. I do." I didn't, but it was sugar. I wasn't going to say no to that.

"Are you sure? I wouldn't have guessed that. My instincts are rarely wrong about this kind of thing."

"Yes."

He started to hold it out to me, but then pulled it back, looked more closely at the wrapper and said, "Uh-oh. This is root beer flavor. That was a close call.

---

47. What he was wearing was ridiculous, but not as stupid as my t-shirt, which had a llama saying, "*Hola! Me llamo Llama. Como te llamas?*"

I almost gave beer to a kid."

"No. It isn't grown-up beer. Kids can have it."

"Are you sure?"

I nodded.

"You wouldn't fib to me, would you?"

I shook my head.

"You're not going to swallow the gum, are you?"

I shook my head even though I was definitely going to swallow it.

"OK. You can have it if you promise to be cooperative. Do you promise?" He held up a hand and put the other over his heart.

I put my hand over my heart and reached for the lollipop with my other hand. The non-hairy man handed it to me and started pulling things out of his bag. First was a stethoscope. He listened to my breathing and told me to cough a couple of times. The first was a fake cough because I didn't really have to cough, but the second was a real cough. If coughs had a color, that cough sounded puke green.

The next thing he took out of his bag was a thing for looking in people's ears and nose. He made me say, "Aaaah" in between licks of the lollipop and made me show my root-beer-brown tongue to you for a joke. He pulled out a thermometer, shook it, stuck it under my arm, and whistled while he waited. He said, "Hmmmm," when he read it. He made me lie down flat on my back, told me to try not to wiggle even if it tickled, and he felt my belly. "You don't have much poop in there. Good job. That makes it a lot easier to feel all the other parts of you. How do you like the grown-up beer lollipop?"

I nodded but didn't correct him again. He put his things back in the bag. Then I asked him, "Are you a doctor?"

"Why do you ask?" he said, handing me the remote control for the TV and another lollipop from his bag.[48]

I could hear you both. I had turned down the TV and was listening to you talk in your bedroom. The door was closed, but I didn't even need to squint my ears to hear. An open door would have been better soundproofing than that cheap door.

He said, "Ruth, what are you doing?"

And you said, "How is he?"

---

48. Clickety click and lickety lick.

"He's got bronchitis. He's got diarrhea, too, but that's unrelated. Probably from eating nothing but the all-candy diet you're feeding him."

"He eats salad, too," you said in defense of yourself.[49]

"Yes, yes, I'm sure you are both following the food pyramid like the fate of the world depends on it. Be that as it may, he should be on some meds and a nebulizer so his body can fight this off before it turns into something worse."

"Can you write the prescriptions?"

"Ruth, what are you doing?"

"I'm trying to get him antibiotics and a nebulizer, Harry."

"Not antibiotics. Bronchitis is viral, not—"

"You know what I mean."

He didn't say anything. He must have just been looking at you the way I do sometimes.

You kept badgering him. "You can write him the prescriptions, can't you? Yes, of course you can."

"I've been retired for more than 15 years, Ruth. I don't even have a script pad anymore."

"You could talk to the nurse."

"And tell her what? That there's a sick boy living in Ruth's room?"

"Tell her it's for me. I can act sick." You made a cough that didn't sound much like mine. It sounded more like when you are clearing your throat to remind me to use a coaster.

"Ruth. Who is he?"

You showed off your fake cough again.

"Ruth. You don't have any relatives around here. Who is he?"

"She'll trust you. She probably won't even make the doctor visit me. You can cut the pills to the right size for him."

"Ruth."

"He needs your help."

"He's not the only 1 that needs help."

"I will pay you back. How about if I make you a cherry pie?"

"You don't know how to bake. Those muffins you made me were only useful as paper weights."

"I'll learn, just for you."

"I'll bite my tongue and not say anything about old dogs and new tricks."

"Please, Harry. Please talk to the nurse."

There was quiet for the first time.

"OK, but only for his sake. I'll tell her I heard you coughing up a storm in here and checked you out. I'll tell her you have bronchitis and need the pills and

---

49. Recipe: crumble 1 brownie into a bowl. Voila! Enjoy your salad!

the puffer. I can't promise she won't still have the doctor visit you. If she does, don't pull me down with you. I get into enough trouble on my own around here without your help."

"Thank you, Harry. You're the best-looking guy in this place. That's the honest truth."

"All the men here look like hell, so that's not saying much. Is there anything you know of that he's allergic to?"

"Baths."

He didn't laugh. "Ruth, where is this going? What's your plan?"

"I don't have the foggiest notion why you are so worried."

"He can't stay here forever."

"Why not?"

"You need to have a plan."

"What makes you think I don't?"

"I'm not talking about a plan for hiding him."

"We have a great plan, and it's going to work out fine. Fine and dandy."

He didn't say anything in response to that.

"Thank you for helping us, Harry. You're a good man. I wish I had known you when I was younger, before we both became decrepit. I'm going to put in a good word for you with Jessica upstairs, though. I hear she's as easy as Sunday morning." The floor creaked and the doorknob turned. I pressed the clicker frantically to make the volume louder so it didn't seem like I was listening, but I pressed too many times and the TV was blasting when you came out of the bedroom. It was a commercial for medicine where everyone is smiling with every single tooth—even the teeth in the back—while the announcer lists all the terrible, terrible things that will go wrong.

"Gosh, that's loud. No wonder you have trouble hearing me when I ask you to clean up." You went over to the TV to turn down the volume by hand. While you did that, he looked at me and looked at me for what felt like 412 years.

He was right.

I couldn't stay forever.

This owl is looking at me and looking at me, too:

I want to joke that it's delivering an urgent letter to Harry Potter. But it's not a letter for Mr. Potter. I know the letter is for me. And I don't want to read it. I know what it says. And it's got nothing to do with me saving the world.

You were antsy after Dr. Harry left. He had given you a lot to chew on while I was busy swallowing the gum in those ancient lollipops. You aimlessly flipped channels on the TV. It was my day for the clicker, but I was too tired to argue. You flipped and flipped and then abruptly turned the TV off.

"Do you want to play with your baseball cards? Yes, of course you do." You often answered your own questions to me. It's like I didn't even need to be there. You reached over the side of the couch for my backpack and dragged it in front of us, making lots of straining noises like it weighed 139 pounds. "How many cards do you have in here anyway?"

"Not—" I coughed a juicy, green cough, then tried again. "Not enough."

You started pulling out stacks and stacks. "It's like a clown car. How do they all fit in there? Are there clowns in there, too?"[50]

You took off the rubber bands and spread them out on the coffee table, mixing them up so we could resort them. I was mostly a spectator. You wanted to sort them by team. I told you I liked it better when they were sorted by position. You flipped a coin. I won.

You started sorting them into piles. You were fast at it, like you had just had

---

50. Only Baltimore Oriole relievers.

a ton of candy and were all sugared up with energy. You handed me a stack of second basemen:

Nelson Liriano

Jim Gantner

Kelly Grubercrue

Gregg Jeffries

Wally Backman

Juan Samuel

Scott Fletcher

Jose Vidro

Billy Ripkin

Garth Iorg

Tom Lawless

Mickey Morandini

And a dozen more

I'm looking at the stack now. I found them with a rubber band around them in a box of my stuff you saved in the closet. Guess what I'm going to do? Alphabetize them.

Alphabetizing is the math of words.

You put your finger up to your lips when the phone rang later that day. You answered it. The call was really short. You said, "OK," and hung up. "The nurse is coming. Grab your pillow." You took me to the closet and moved some things to make space for me to sit. "Do your best not to cough, but if you have to, do it into the pillow. Go ahead and give it a try."

I shoved my face into the pillow and coughed as best I could on command.

"Perfect," you said. "She should be here for just a couple of minutes. She never stays long."

You closed the closet door and the bedroom door and turned the TV on loud. The nurse didn't come as quickly as we thought she would, so I was instantly the most bored any kid has ever been in the history of boredom. Light came in under the bottom of the closet, and some came through around the edges of the door. Once my eyes adjusted to the dark, I could snoop around. Up above me were dresses and other clothes on hangers. There were shoes on both sides of me on wire racks that kept them neatly organized in pairs. I put the shoes in the light coming under the door to see what color they were. In the dark, the first shoe looked black. It was black in the light too. The second shoe looked grey in the dark, but in the light, I could see it was bright yellow. I wondered what clothes would match it and wondered if someone would look like a banana if they wore it all together at the same time. The third shoe was red and sparkled when I moved it around in the light under the door. I found a shoe that was a lot heavier and bigger than the others. I felt the shape, then held it to the light. It was a man's shoe. I leaned over to see it better in the light. It was brown and the label inside said it was a size 11. I smelled it. It just smelled like leather, not like feet. I put it back. I picked up the red sparkly shoes again and tried them on my feet. They had heels. I didn't understand how anyone could walk in them without falling down 100 times a minute. I felt around in the shoe organizers and found a shoehorn. I didn't know what it was at the time. I tapped it against my leg like it was a drumstick and flicked a shoe box with my finger to make a different sound in between. You shushed me from the other room, and I stopped.

There was a knock at the front door. You turned the TV up even louder and started fake-coughing. Hearing you cough made me feel like I needed to cough, like someone yawning makes everyone else need to yawn. I grabbed the pillow, shoved it on my face, and waited. I could feel the itch in my throat. I tried swallowing. I tried to clear my throat quietly, but it kept coming. I pushed my face harder into the pillow and pulled the pillow harder onto my face. I fought the cough. I pushed it back down, deep, deep down.

There was another cough in there, though. This was much bigger. I swallowed a few times in a row to see if that would make it go away. My nose hurt because I was pressing my face so hard into the pillow. The swallowing seemed to be working, so I did it a few more times. My eyelids felt like they were closing, but they were already closed. I kept swallowing. My forehead got sweaty. My arms felt tingly. I wasn't going to lose. The cough was not going to win. My chest felt like I was standing in front of an open oven. That was the last thing I remember.

You told me you thought I was taking a nap when you opened the closet. I was slumped over with my head halfway on the pillow and halfway on a pile of shoes. You said I didn't wake up when you said my name and tapped me. You tried to lift me, but I weighed too much, so you dragged me out of the closet like a backpack full of cards and sat me up against the bed. You opened my eyes with your fingers, and I swatted your hand away clumsily, so I guess I wasn't dead. You said I made sounds that weren't words, but both my eyes were open, and I was really annoyed and grumpy. I remember my tongue felt weird. It felt big and dry and like it was covered in beach sand that I couldn't get off. You felt my forehead. I tried to push your hands away again but gave up. I tried to kick the stupid pillow in the stupid closet, but my legs couldn't reach.

You sat down on the floor and slid next to me. You pulled my head onto your chest and rocked us side to side, singing:

I'm always a flop at a top-notch affair,
but I've still got my health, so what do I care?
My best ring, alas, is a glass solitaire,
but I still got my health, so what do I care?
By fashion and foppery, I'm never discussed.
Attending the opry, my box would be a bust.
I never shall have that Park Avenue aire,
but I'm in such health, why should I care?
The hip that I shake doesn't make people stare,
but I got such health, what do I care?
The sight of my props never stops a thoroughfare,
but I still got my health, so what do I care?
Your face is your fortune, so some wise men spoke.
My face is my fortune, that's why I'm totally broke.
My ship ain't come in, but I grin while I bear,
'cause I got my vitamins:
A, B, C, D, E, F, G, H
I still have my.
Got no diamonds, got no wealth.
I got no men, but I got my health.

I didn't understand the song, because I never understood any of the old, boring songs you sang. But I knew this: I didn't cough when the nurse was there. And that meant I won.

T he medicine and puffer made my coughing stop, but my brain didn't feel better. It was tired and slow—too tired to even watch TV. You decided to celebrate my very incomplete recovery by having us do an impossible jigsaw puzzle. You were organizing pieces like a whirlwind. I was going in slo-mo, picking up blue pieces 1-by-1, staring at them with a confused look on my face, then dropping them back in the pile. The blue pieces were for the sky, which didn't have a cloud in it at all. Just the same shade of blue from across the entire puzzle.

"You already picked up that piece," you said.

"No, I didn't."

Your eyes lit up that my answer was somewhat hostile. "Yes, that's the same piece you picked up a second ago."

"No. It's different."

"How do you know?"

"Because I know," I said.

"But you don't have a system."[51]

"I know how to do this," I insisted.

"If you put the piece back in the same pile after you try it, you'll just take the same piece out again."

"I don't want to do the sky. The sky is stupid."

"I'll take care of the sky. You can work on this mountain. That should be easier. Here are the pieces I've found so far. It starts out white at the top and I have those pieces. But I don't have all the green pieces for this part," you said and pointed to the mountain on the box.

I spotted a piece that was the color of that mountain and picked it up.

"There you go. Mountains are clearly your strength. By the way, 2 more minutes until we need to take your next pill."

"No."

"You have to."

"5 more minutes," I said, not asking.

"That's what you said 3 minutes ago."

"I changed my mind."

"2 more minutes," you offered.

"I don't like them."

"You're not supposed to like them. You're supposed to swallow them."

"They taste bad."

"Wait until you get to be my age. The medicine tastes 16 times worse and they are 17 times as big."

"I'm never going to be that old."

"You definitely won't be if you don't take your pill. You'll die of pneumonia or something worse, like the plague. It would be a doozy to get the plague, all because you didn't take your medicine."

"That's from a long time ago."

"It's making a comeback. I saw it on the news. It's fashionable again, like jean shorts."

"I don't care. No more pills."

"You'll care when you're covered in black boils."

"No, I won't."

"Boils are bubbles that grows on your skin, filled with black goo. They get bigger and bigger, then they burst and leave big holes in your skin that hurt like

---

51. Or a strategy. Or a plan. Or a coherent set of guiding principles other than saying no and doing the opposite.

nobody's business."

"You're making that up."

"I wish I were. But I'm not. That the easy part of having the plague. The other stuff is worse. The boils are like a tropical vacation compared to the rest of it."

"I don't care. No pills."

"You shouldn't say that. Never say you don't care. It's unbecoming." You looked at me. "How about if I put the medicine inside a candy?"

"That would ruin the candy," I protested.

"How about if I give you a piece of candy after you swallow it?"

"2 pieces," I said.

"1 piece," you said.

"Only if you give me 2 pieces."

"OK, no candy."

"Wait."

"What?"

"I changed my mind."

"OK. You can have 1 piece. But you also have to have your next puff from the puffer."

"No fair. That wasn't part of the deal."

"You should have taken the earlier deal." You picked up a blue piece and said, "Ah-ha!" but it wasn't what you were looking for. You tossed it back in the same pile you had taken it from instead of into the pile of rejects. So much for systems. And so much for chapter endings that make sense because here is a tracing of my hand that I did way back when.

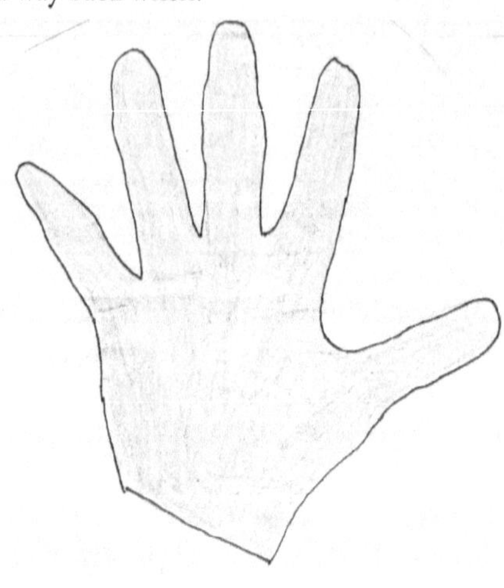

When I was feeling better enough that you stopped worrying about me kicking the bucket, that's when you shifted your focus to an anti-germ rampage. You were going to destroy whatever had tried to get me. That meant a trip to the big store to replace my germ-covered clothes, my crud-covered shoes, my hideous socks, and my truly dreadful underwear. Plus a toothbrush for my teeth, which somehow weren't rotting and falling out yet. You threatened to replace my backpack, too, but I fought you to the death and was convinced I had won the war when I agreed to only replace everything else under the sun. Do regular people think they've won when they've actually lost? Or just irregular people like me?

It was too far for you to walk, so you rode the shuttle. That wasn't an option for me, so I walked. Looking at a map now, it was only about 3 miles to Fred Meyer, but it felt like it took 17 hours to walk there. I can usually walk forever without getting tired, but my legs were slow. As slow as my brain. That made the walk extra-long and extra-boring. So boring, it made me mad. So mad I could spit. So I did. I spit a lot. I spit for distance, beating my record again and again until that got boring. I spit for accuracy, trying to hit specific spots on the sidewalk and trying to see how close I could spit to my shoes without hitting them. My shoes ended up absolutely plastered with spit. It didn't matter, though. They'd be in the trash soon, infecting all the garbage with their gross-ness. When the spitting got boring, I kicked pebbles and watched them skip along the concrete like stones bouncing across an ugly gray pond covered in gum and bird poop and kid spit. I picked up a few cans along the way and put them in my backpack. I brought it with me to make sure you couldn't throw it out. Every once in a while, kids are smarter than grown-ups.

I still got there faster than you did in the shuttle van. I waited inside in the sporting goods section like we planned. I bounced those little league baseballs that are coated with rubber so they don't kill a bunch of kids. Just a normal kid bouncing a ball. Nothing to see here. You crept up behind me and put your fingers into my armpits to surprise me. I clamped down my arms and tried to run, which didn't make sense, but that's what I did.

"It's me. It's me," you said.

I lifted my arms, released your fingers, and tumbled down onto the floor. "I knew it was you," I said unconvincingly.

"Sure you did," you said, helping me up.

"It's not nice to scare people."

"Did I scare you?"

"No."

"I'm sorry I scared you."

I made a face. "When did you get here?"

"Just now."

"When does the bus go back?"

You looked at your watch-less wrist and said, "We have 55 minutes. Just enough time." We got started, using the amazing plan you had made so nobody could possibly figure out we were together: I followed you around the store, but did it by staying 10 feet behind you. That was the whole plan.

When we got to the shoe section, you held up 2 choices. I ignored your choices and picked something else. You shrugged, made me try them on, pressed on my big toe to check they fit, and then motioned for me to put them in the cart. You put 3 packs of underwear in the cart without giving me a choice. I peeked in at them and they looked OK, so I didn't argue. You let me choose whatever shirts I wanted while you picked out shorts. You didn't veto any of the shirts I picked, and I didn't veto any of the shorts you held up.

The list you had made didn't have bed stuff on it, but you went to the sheets aisle and held up 2 choices for me. In your left hand was a set of princess sheets and in the right hand was a set of pony sheets. Both were pink. I frowned at the dumb joke. You held up 2 more. I pointed at the camouflage sheets with tanks[52] and fighter jets. You put it into the cart and pretended to cross it off the part of the list where it wasn't written.

In the aisle with bathroom stuff, you pointed at the grown-up toothbrushes. I pointed to the kid-sized Batman toothbrush. It had an on/off switch and a little motor inside for lazy kids like me. You shook your head and pointed to a kid toothbrush that didn't use batteries. The handle was in the shape of a car, but it didn't do anything battery powered. It was just a handle. I made a flipping-a-coin motion with my hands. You felt in your pockets for a coin but didn't find any. Only crumpled tissues. There weren't any coins in your purse either. You motioned rock-paper-scissors to me, and I nodded. You did rock. I did paper. I put the Batman toothbrush in the cart. You crossed that off your list. I also grabbed a tube of kid toothpaste and put it in the cart when you weren't looking. I didn't like your minty toothpaste. It tasted terrible every time I accidentally swallowed it, which was every time I brushed. It's 1 of the worst things in the world to swallow, other than broccoli.

When we were done shopping, you told me to go wait near the electronics section near the registers. I looked at the wall of TVs. They were all bigger and flatter than yours, and they were all showing a lion was chasing wildebeest in Africa. The 32 lions couldn't catch the 32 grown-up wildebeest, so they went after something easier. 32 big-screen lions snapped the necks of 32 baby

---

52. Knock knock. Who's there? Tank. Tank who? You're welcome.

wildebeest, then carried the limp lunches to 96 baby lions. They didn't know what to do with it. They climbed on top of it, then jumped off onto each other and wrestled. They must not make decisions with their stomachs yet.

I felt you come up behind me like a predator, so I clamped down my arms so you couldn't tickle me again. You put something in my front pocket and whispered, "See you at home." I reached in and pulled out a candy bar. I don't remember if it was a Three Musketeers bar or a Snickers bar, but it said, "GIANT SIZE," on the wrapper, which was all that mattered. I munched it while the lions munched the dead animal. I left the TVs when the vultures came for the leftovers.

I walked around toward the front of the store to see if the shuttle bus was still there. It was. I couldn't see inside it because the windows were tinted. I fussed with the straps on my backpack as I walked past it, wondering which darkened window was yours.

I kicked more rocks as I walked. I made honking noises at cars as they passed me. I made quacking noises at some birds in the sky, but they probably weren't ducks. I yelled some bad words, but nobody could hear them because of the car noise. I sang a couple of songs in a high-pitched voice that sounded like a girl. I stopped at a building that had a big dumpster in front for a construction project and unsuccessfully tried throwing rocks into it. I sang a song in a deep voice. It made my throat hurt. A bus pulled up next to me.

I thought it was a city bus, so I just kept walking. The driver whistled. It was the shuttle bus. Yours. I thought our little game was all over. They had caught us. I looked around for an escape route. There was an old, beat-up fence next to a building off to my right. It had some missing pieces of wood with gaps that might be big enough for me to squeeze through. But the driver interrupted my escape planning with another whistle. "Do you want a lift?" He motioned for me to get in. I pointed at myself, and he nodded at me. "Miss Ruth says you live right near our building." A window slid open and you waved your old lady hand at me. He said, "Hop in, but don't tell anyone. I'll get in a mess of trouble. Liability and whatnot."

I got in. The hydraulic doors made a sweesh noise and closed behind me. You were in the very first row, right behind the driver. You patted the seat next to you and said, "We go to the same church," in your loudest voice. I sat down next to you. "What are the chances I would run into you? God works in mysterious ways," you bellowed in an even louder voice.

A lady way in the back said, "Amen."

The driver, who looked even older than all the ancient people in the shuttle, turned around and looked me right in my eyeballs. "Remember, son..." he started to say before freezing like a video game with a glitch. He unfroze and finished by saying: "You were never here, OK?"

A lady way in the back said, "Amen."
I nodded. I was never there.

The next day, the news said it was going to be 98 degrees.

"We can't stay here. We'll roast in our own skins." You pulled at the skin on your arm for emphasis. It looked thin and rubbery and didn't go back right away after you let it go.

"But we have air conditioning," I said after I was finally able to stop staring at your arm skin.

"That doesn't count."

"It does count. It will be cool in here."

You made a fart noise with your lips to me. "We need to go swimming. That's what people do on hot days. People have done that for as long as people have been people, and, and we're going to do it today at the lake."

"I don't want to go anywhere. I'm tired. And I don't have a swimsuit." I thought that was the end of the discussion. Period. End of story. No need for more blabbering.[53]

"You can just wear your shorts. Or your underwear. Or you can go au naturel if you prefer." You winked at me to let me know that meant no clothes.

"Only little babies swim naked. I'm not a baby."

"Anyone can swim naked."

"No, they can't."

"Yes, they can."

"They would get arrested."

"Not here. This is a very open-minded state, thank goodness. I could go to the store without a stitch of clothes on if I wanted to and buy us a nice cantaloupe. As long as you're not doing anything rude, you can walk around as naked as a mole rat. It's perfectly legal. Plus, they might give me the cantaloupe free just to get my saggy buns and boobs out of there!"

"They would kick you out of the store and they wouldn't give you the melon. You have to wear a shirt and shoes. It says so on the door. Everyone knows that."

"Maybe so, but the police wouldn't arrest me. I would just walk down to the farmers market, all my parts flapping in the wind, and get a cantaloupe there. There aren't any signs there. I already checked! Or I would keep things simple

---

53. I always thought everything I said was the end of the conversation. I never learned.

and just make you go into the store to buy a melon while I waited outside with no clothes on. I would tell every living soul I was with you. How do you like them apples?"

"Apples are terrible and so are melons."

"Apples are overrated. I'll give you that. But what's not to like about cantaloupe?"

"I don't like it."

"Why not?"

"I just don't."

"That's odd."

"No, it's not. Everyone doesn't have to like every food."

"It is a free country...so they say."

"You don't like every food. What do you hate?"

"Hate is a strong word."

"I hate lots of things."

"So I've noticed. But back to the topic at hand. Which foods do I dislike?" You thought about it. "Well, I'm not the biggest fan of olives."

"Olives?"

"Kalamatas."

"What?"

"Kalamata olives. They come from Greece. I think they're too salty. I make a face when I eat them." You made the face. It looked like you had gas again.

"Olives taste good. And salt tastes good too."

"Some olives taste good," you corrected.

"Even kids like olives."

"I guess you're more worldly than me. More importantly, I got you a swimsuit yesterday when you weren't looking. It's in the bathroom. Go put it on and let's skedaddle."

For some reason, I did what you said even though I didn't want to. My body was still weak and so was my brain. Would it ever get back to normal again?

I didn't like the trip to the swim park. Not 1 bit. We took the bus, and it was 707 degrees inside it. That made me feel even more woozy than I was feeling already from being sick for so long. It stopped 7,007 times on the way there. All the stopping and starting made me feel 70,007 times woozier. It was 700,007 degrees at the park. There were 7,000,007 people swimming. All the floaty toys were taken by other kids. The lake water was too cold and there were slimy plants on the bottom growing in the sand. The snack bar wasn't open. There were 7,000,000,007 bugs biting me. It smelled like pee. Everyone was loud or stupid or both. We stayed too long. When we finally left to go back home, the bus was 7,000,000,000,007 degrees and made 7,000,000,000,000,007 stops. It smelled like someone had ripped 7,000,000,000,000,000,007 farts. It was probably you.

I fell asleep.

You woke me up when we got to our stop. You went into the building the front way. I waited in the back for you to open the sliding door. When I came in, the blast of cold air turned the sweat on my head into a glaze of ice and my breath made clouds that floated over to the couch and snowed onto my pillow. Cloudy with a 100% chance of snow flurries.

That's exactly how I remember it.

Exactly.

A nother sticky note:

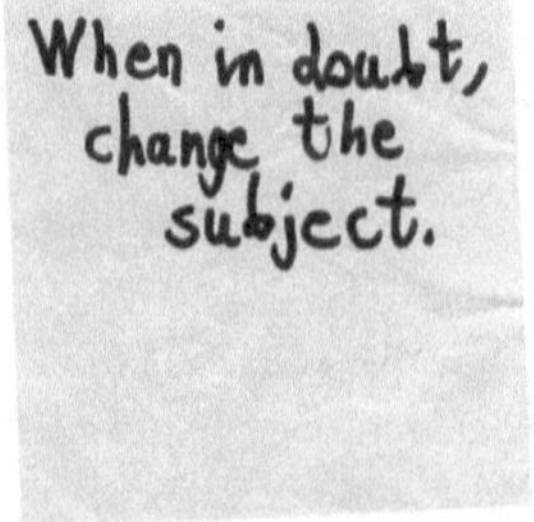

The swimming ordeal wore me out so much that I fell asleep early that night, slept straight through until the morning, and didn't wake up until after you had already gone to breakfast.

Somehow my bladder wasn't ready to explode when I woke up. Maybe my body had slurped all the pee back into my dying-of-thirst organs to survive after the 2,000,000-degree bus ride, after the long walk to the store, after being super sick for days and days, after seeing the first dead person I had ever seen.

The only thing in the fridge to drink was milk, which was way better than water, so I poured a glass and drank it while I walked back to the couch. It was a sloshing disaster. The milk splashed down all over my new shirt and dripped down onto my new underwear. Hopefully my new clothes were lactose tolerant.

I stood there, belly full of moo juice, looked up at the sliding door, and there she was, cupping her hands around her eyes, pressing her face against the sliding door glass.

She smiled and nodded. The glass made her nose into a hog, a boxer, a hoxer.

She looked at the couch with the army sheets.

She looked at my neatly folded piles of new clothes.

She looked back at me like she was going to make a coat out of me.

If I close my eyes, I can still see her teeth. I don't remember her face after all these years, but I remember that shark grin.

The hardest part about living in an old people's home is how noisy it gets at 5:30 in the morning. Everyone is up and whistling and boiling water in tea kettles and scratching the floor with their walkers and flushing toilets and . . . Everyone should go back to bed.

The second hardest thing is how quiet it is after 8:30 at night. Should I check everyone's breathing? Will the fire truck be coming again soon? Maybe I should open the sliding door so I can hear all the crickets and wolves and psycho killers and monsters.

None of those are as scary as the quiet.

And none of those are as scary as the scariest thing there is: someone who loves you.

Here is another owl:

Did you hypnotize it? Or is it hypnotizing you? Sometimes it's hard to tell who is hypnotizing whom. Sometimes that is the hardest thing in the world.

I should have had the curtains closed. I should have spotted her before she saw me. I should have done a lot of things. Yes, I know now it wouldn't have mattered. She was looking for me. If she didn't see me that day, it would have been the next or the next. But that little milk-soaked version of me was 172% certain I had messed everything up in a way that could never, ever be un-messed.

Maybe that lactose-drenched version of me was right, though. Maybe everything that came next would not have happened if I had just done the thing I had always been best at in the world: being invisible.

I didn't tell you she saw me. I kept it a secret. It was usually easy for me to keep secrets. Even the biggest secrets. But this secret made my chest hurt. That's why I was so distracted that afternoon at the park. A different park. Not the park with the cheese that was probably still on the tree (and may still be on the tree all these years later). You kept telling me to go play, but I just sat on the bench. You forced me to go on the slide—pulling me off the bench, dragging me over to it, and pushing me up the stairs. I reluctantly slid down at .0001 mph, frowning the whole time like you were making me brush my teeth. We cut the trip to the park short and went home.

I went out to the back of the building and waited for you to unlock the sliding door. A sliding door opened, but it wasn't ours. I scooted back even deeper into the bushes. It was 2 doors down from us. Arms reached out and set down a cat, then patted it on the bum to make it scoot. Then all heck broke loose, and animals were being pushed through sliding doors left and right. That's how I remember it. 1,000 animals coming out of 1,000 sliding doors. Don't try to use logic to tell me it was only a couple of animals and a couple of doors. Logic doesn't work with me. You know that.

None of the animals were making noises. The dogs didn't yelp and the cats didn't meow and the birds didn't squawk. It creeped me out. It makes sense now. The noisy pets would have been weeded out. Natural selection in action, I guess, but I didn't know that then. It was raining cats and dogs and cockatiels, and there wasn't a peep. It made me want to bark to fill the void. Or run away. Or run away barking.

Off to my right—your left—the last door slid open, and a lady tried to put her old, almost-dead, almost-hairless, guinea-pig-sized dog outside. I forget her name—the lady, not the dog. She died a long time ago. That dog might still be alive somewhere, though. Little dogs live as long as giant tortoises. The dog would only go as far as the railing. It refused to go further. Its front paws were out on the grass, but its back paws were still on the concrete patio and its belly barely cleared the horizontal bar at the bottom of the railing. She tried to nudge it with her foot to make it take the last step onto the grass, but the nudge didn't make it budge. It just stared straight ahead at something that wasn't 6 inches in front of its face.

The lady saw me because I wasn't hiding in the bushes anymore. I was standing right out in the open like a magnet had pulled me out against my will.[54] The old lady motioned for me to come over. My feet disobeyed my brain because they walked right over to her. "I've got a little job for you," she said. "I'll give you a dollar if you keep an eye on her until they're done with the pet check."

I didn't say anything. I looked down at the dog. Up close I could see it was doing more than staring at nothing. It was also very busy shivering for no reason. The temperature outside was as hot as lava, but the dog was shaking like it was stranded at the North Pole of Pluto.

"2 dollars. My final offer." I didn't realize I was in the middle of a financial negotiation, but apparently I was. She tossed the end of the leash to me and motioned for me to go. She shut the door and closed the curtains inside. I looked down at the dog. It stared at my shin with the same devoid-of-any-brain-activity expression I have when I watch TV. I put my hand down for the dog to sniff. It checked my hand to see if I was offering a treat. If it was disappointed, its disappointed face was the same as its regular face. Maybe it was just perpetually disappointed. Maybe I was projecting.

---

54. A dimwit magnet clearly. Was I trying to get caught?

I looked over at your apartment but didn't have a clear view inside. I told myself not to go look, but my feet ignored me again. Your apartment—our apartment—was empty. Then it wasn't. A parade of people came in. You were in the middle. Ms. Millie was in the back. There was a guy wearing maintenance-style blue coveralls in front. The person behind him was the director lady, dressed in a suit-looking thing. I recognized her from William's room where she had been talking to the firefighters and filling out paperwork. She was wearing a different suit-looking thing this time, so I guess she had 2 of them. Ms. Millie went from the back of the group to the front and started looking around in the living room, then in your bedroom, then back in the living room. She pointed around and the other folks looked where she pointed.

My stuff was put away. I may have been too stupid to not be spotted by her that morning, but I wasn't an idiot. I hid all my stuff afterwards. It was like I was never there.

Ms. Millie kept pointing around, but the rest of the group was losing interest. The director lady motioned with her arm and the group of people headed toward the door to leave. The director lady said something to you while her hand was on your arm. Then she said something to Ms. Millie without her hand on her arm. Then she left. It was just the 2 of you. Millie looked around the room again, then came to the sliding door to see if I was hiding on the patio. That's when she saw me outside, standing there holding the leash of a 100-year-old shivering dog. You saw me, too. You made a little wave in front of your chest to say hello. She did not wave hello. She kept looking at me, mouthing words I couldn't hear—words that probably would have blown your skirt sideways. She turned back to you, pointed at you while she said something, then left.

You went to the fridge, then the cupboard, and then came back to the sliding door. You set something down on the carpet. It was a tall cup of milk, leaning a little to the side and threatening to tip. Beside it was a plate with a cookie.

You love making lists of your favorite things. You had 76,000 of them. The 5 best cheeseburgers you ever had (including the 1 you ate in France). Your 10 favorite birds (which was a completely different list every time). The first 8 things you would do if you won the lottery (all boring). The 6 best presidents (Truman was #3 on the list). The 7 best cheeses (string cheese wasn't on the list). The 20 best sunsets you'd seen (even more boring). The 3 best cups of coffee you'd had (all in Portland). The 3 best places to skinny-dip (gross). The 4 best kissers in your life (grosser). And the definitive list of best pizza toppings (which you were completely wrong about).[55]

I didn't like doing best-of lists. I specialized in worst-of lists. The 7 worst days of the week. The 12 worst months of the year. The 100 worst chores. The 8,000,000,000 worst people in the world. The worst smells. The worst-tasting foods. The worst places to find soda cans. The most annoying old ladies I've ever secretly lived with. The worst rules (truisms) you made me follow. The worst best-of lists you ever made me listen to you talk about. I was a fun kid, huh? It's like a hug and a smile made a baby and I popped out.

Do you remember my list of the 6 worst cookies? I do. I put it on sticky notes so you would please, please stop bringing them to me. But I was never any good at making you do what I wanted you to do, was I? Here they are from almost-worst to completely-worst:

6. Peanut butter cookies (A waste of perfectly good peanut butter.)

5. Fake Oreos (I would rather eat a bowl of mayo with a straw than store brand Oreos.)

4. Sugar cookies with sprinkles on the top (See earlier complaint about how the sprinkles turn to sand.)

3. Fancy cookies from France and England, which don't even taste sweet, so they should not be called cookies.)

2. Chocolate chip cookies with sea salt (Sea salt is dried whale pee and dolphin poo, so these cookies should be called Ocean #1s and #2s.)

1. Ginger snap cookies (They taste like fire and cause fiery diarrhea—fire-rrhea. Winner!)

By the way, is it obvious that I'm writing about cookies because I'm avoiding writing about what comes next?

You were whistling cheerily when I came back inside after giving the shivering-for-no-reason dog back to the lady. I had stepped over the milk and cookie, leaving it where you had set it, un-munched and un-gulped. You ignored my shocking protest.

I sat sternly on the couch with my arms folded, waiting for you to apologize for the building-wide childhunt even though the whole thing was my fault. All of this felt like it was your fault, so it was. Facts could go straight to jail without passing Go and without collecting $200. Thinking back on this now, it made

---

55. Too many vegetables.

no sense why I was angry. Not just that I was angry at you, but that I was angry at all. I didn't want to be there with you, but somehow I was mad that I was on the verge of being discovered and kicked out. I should have been the annoying person cheerily whistling a Cole Porter song while I gleefully shoved everything into my backpack and disappeared into the bushes. I'm sure he wrote a song or 12 about hobos about to hit the road or the rails. I would whistle it and you'd know exactly what it meant. Adios! Sayonara! See you later, crocoduck! In a while, quackadile!

But I wasn't packing my junk and taking a hike. Not even close. I was sitting there stewing. You had the Mariners game on, which would ordinarily put me in a not-hostile mood, but not this time because there was a rain delay, which only made me more upset. The grounds crew looked upset too. They had just pulled the tarp off the infield, but now they were rolling it back out to re-cover it. I wondered if a grounds crew worker ever tripped and got the tarp rolled over him. Would he have air to breathe? Would it crush him? Would he be able to crawl out from under it? Would everyone watching on TV see a lump wriggling under the tarp until it didn't move anymore? Would I be able to crawl out in time if it was me? Or would I just sit there and let the tarp crush me without putting up a fight?

"Penny for your thoughts?" you said as you dropped your butt on the couch, making my cushion jump and knock me sideways. I sat back up and ignored you. "Oops, I forgot about inflation. 25 cents for your thoughts?"

I debated whether to give you the silent treatment. I bet I could give you the silent treatment for a long time. Maybe for days and weeks and months. Maybe for years and years if I really tried. I bet I could for sure. I stared at the tarp and wasn't thinking about a ground crew worker being trapped under there anymore. I was thinking about you being trapped under there. I thought it, and then I said it out loud—just like you say stuff out loud that should stay in your head. I asked you if you thought you would run out of air or just be crushed. I asked you if you would be embarrassed about dying on TV and having people watch it again and again on the internet. I asked you a lot of questions about your hilariously tragic tarp-related demise. I thought that would shock you, but you laughed and shook your head and laughed some more.

"Don't be a silly goose, Silly Goose! I would be completely fine. The crew members all have pocketknives and would cut a hole in 2 seconds. Like a C-section!" You laugh-snorted and held your belly. "I would pop out, someone would towel me off, smack me on the bum, and say, 'Mazel tov!' Then they would sew the tarp back up lickety-split! It would be like it never happened . . . except for the stretch marks. Ha!" You shook your head at how funny you thought you were, then you shook your head at me. "You worry too much."

I looked at you and could feel myself starting to shake. My hands were in fists and they pressed into my thighs deep enough I thought I felt the bones inside.

"She was trying to get me."

"Who, Dear?"

"You know who."

"Oh, her? Don't worry about her."

"She wants to eat me."

"I doubt that. She's a vegetarian and won't shut up about it. There's a picture of her in the dictionary next to the word 'insufferable'."[56]

"Why is she so mean?"

"She's just bored. I should give her that jigsaw puzzle we never finished because the sky was too hard. Let's throw a few pieces in the trash first, though. All that work and she wouldn't be able to finish it. Nothing's funnier than when something refuses to end the way you want it to end. Absolutely nothing. That's true with puzzles and with life if you stop to think about it." You scratched your chin like you were a philosopher, and it made the hairs there jump and dance. You needed tweezers as badly as I needed a bath—maybe more. "Are you in on this dastardly plan to drive her batty?" You held up your knuckles for me to bump them.

"You're not funny." I stopped staring at your chin hairs, looked at your fist and left your knuckles hovering there, un-bumped. You let your hand drop, then you made a face, reached underneath you, and pulled your romance novel out from under your butt—the same boring story with the 3 people who "live happily ever after." Why didn't you get any other lovey-dovey books? You just read that over and over. The guy on the cover holding the rake even seemed bored with the book. You set it on the coffee table, looked at me, looked back at the book, turned it face-down so the shirtless gardener wasn't looking at us, then looked back at me.

"What were we talking about?" you asked. "Oh yes. You were saying I'm un-funny after I made an ill-timed joke rather than answering your serious question. I have a bad habit of trying to be funny at very inappropriate times. I would tell you I'm working on it, but that ship has sailed, and even Magellan couldn't find it. So, I'll just apologize. I'm very sorry. I shouldn't have done that." You paused long enough that I thought this was over, but then you put on a very serious face I had never seen before and said, "You asked a serious question—a very serious question—and you deserve a serious answer, Sweetness."

I suddenly felt worried. I looked back at the grounds crew, who was also fighting a futile battle against a force it couldn't control. You put your hand on my arm—a hand that always quivered and shook the way chihuahuas quiver

---

56. There was no picture of Millie. I checked in your dictionary just to prove you wrong. But I did draw a picture of you there never answering my questions. It's there. You should check.

and shake—except for right now. Right now it was as steady as a rock attached to a bigger rock attached to a granite peak. That made me look up at you, and I couldn't look back at the TV no matter how much I wanted to.

"Do you really want to know why she is mean? . . . why bad people are the way they are?"

You had never done that before. You had never doublechecked with me first. You usually just blurted stuff out like someone with no control of their mouth due to a brain injury caused by a tragic accident everyone talks about only in whispers. These questions you asked me felt like warnings rather than questions, like when someone says, "Are you sure you want to put sunblock on my super-hairy back?" or "Are you sure you want to see my surgery scars?" The answer is always no when someone ask-warns you, but I just looked at you with my mouth open. You took that as a yes, because that's when you told me things that adults never tell children.

"You're a big boy and you deserve the truth. So, I will tell you." You squeezed my arm the lightest squeeze that could be squeezed. "The world is not what people tell kids it is." You blinked so slowly I could feel it in my eyes. "We want to protect you sweet little things, so we put rainbows and teddy bears at the front of the stage for as long as we can. We hope you don't see what's behind all that, back in the darkness, out of the spotlights. We hope you don't ever see it . . . but this world makes it so hard. So very hard."

I wanted to look at the handle of the sliding door, but I couldn't not look at your eyes. The skin around them wasn't twitching or jumping even a little bit, just like on William's face.

"You and I made an agreement to never talk about what happened before we ended up here on this couch together watching the Mariners. And I won't break our agreement, but I will say this: I know you know the world isn't all cookies and milk. And you know I know the world isn't all smooches and living happily ever after. You are a smartie, for sure. You've already seen what's behind the rainbows and teddy bears, haven't you? You know what the world is, don't you?" You let the question hang there like a noose, gently swaying from side to side between us, then answered. "Of course, you do."

Your voice was gentle, but that somehow made it all 37,000,000 times worse. I wished you were screaming all of this at me instead, spraying me with spit and anger about all the unacceptable things in this unacceptable world.

"Now back to your very smart, very important question. Yes, there are very bad people in this world. People who are so bad they don't seem real. They can't possibly be real. But they are. They aren't 3-dimensional. They aren't even 2-dimensional. And they do things that are so terrible, you wish it wasn't real. But it is. It's as real as a pinch on the arm." You pinched the skin on your arm really hard, and the spot you pinched turned to the color of a creepy doll's skin for a long time. I kept staring at it until you picked up the remote and pointed it at the TV.

"If I press this down-button 6 times, we can see some of the terrible things terrible people have done today. Just today. In a single day. Here's the worst part. What they show you is only .01 percent of .001 percent of .000001 percent of all the bad things thoughtless, cruel people have done today. There's too much for even the TV to keep up with, and there are 500 channels for goodness sake. Don't worry, though. I'm going to leave it here on the game." You tried to hand the remote to me, but I didn't want to take it. You put it next to my leg and the corner of it touched my skin. It felt cold enough to burn.

"But I know you know all that. You're not like other kids. I knew the moment I saw you outside that door." You pointed at the door, but I didn't look at it. I looked at your finger, which wasn't shaking even a teeny, tiny, microscopic bit. "Which brings me back to your question, which I was futilely trying to distract from with my dumb jokes. Why are bad people so bad? And why do they do the bad stuff they do to all of us non-bad people? Why is Millie trying to do terrible things to us?" You paused and put your hand on my arm. "Why is she the way she is? Why does she exist? Why hasn't some higher power edited her out with a big eraser that comes down from the sky?" You paused to give me a chance to think about it, but my brain wasn't working.

"I have to be honest, Dear. Why doesn't matter." You let it hover there for a moment like an un-bumped fist. "I used to ask why. I wasted a lot of tears and angst and heartache and more tears asking why. But then a light bulb went off. I realized it doesn't matter. We could spend all our anxious days and sleepless nights trying to figure out why that eraser doesn't come down from the sky. We could spend all our anxious days and sleepless nights trying to figure out why this broken world is so, so broken."

My mouth was dry, and I had to pee. All the moisture in my body had gone to my bladder.

"We could ask a lots of well-thought-out questions about why a sad old lady in this building is meaner than Cruella de Vil. What happened to her in her childhood? Who hurt her so badly? What created the hole in her heart? Why does she like ruining things like a bully smashing sandcastles at the beach? We could spend our days asking ourselves those questions and spend our nights trying fruitlessly to answer them. Questions like why she gets to live so long when people we love die so young. Too, too young. We could ask why bad people end up at the top of the pyramid so often. Why does evil exist? Why does evil win? Why does it win so often? So, so often."

You took your hand off my arm and my guts felt like I had to poop. All the atoms in my body had gone straight to my bowels and wanted to escape as quickly as possible.

"We *could* ask those questions. We could ask them and ask them. And we could try to figure it out like a jigsaw puzzle. We *could* do that. But we shouldn't be trying to piece together that puzzle. That's because asking why is asking the wrong question."

You put your hand on my shoulder and ran your fingers up the side of my neck until you cradled my jaw and gently pressed a spot behind my ear that made my eyes want to close.

"Once I figured that out, I was a much happier person. And that's why I'm telling you these hard things. I'm telling you because I love you."

You unpressed the spot behind my ear and asked me, "Do you want to know what the right question is?"

I couldn't answer you, so you answered yourself. "Of course, you do. The right question isn't, 'why?' The right question is, 'What are we going to do about it?'" You brought your hands together in front of you like the slowest clap ever. "That's the right question. What are we going to do about all the bad people and bad things in the world? The right question was right there in front of our noses all along." You playfully poked my nose with your finger and said, "Boop!" then stood up.

"That question suits me better, anyway, because I've always been a woman of action. Psychology isn't my thing unless it's reverse psychology. Ha!" You slapped your leg. "I am a hoot, aren't I? Hoot rhymes with newt...playing a flute...in Beirut."

My bladder and butthole were in crisis mode.

"Speaking of action, I'm going to shuffle a deck of cards. How about if we play hearts and then go get fro-yo?" It was a statement rather than a question. "No limit on toppings tonight! We deserve to be happy. And we're going to be, gosh darn it!"

I knew that face you were making. It was the same face you made when you started your anti-germ crusade. That ended with all my junk in the trash. So that must the face you make before you start crusades that end very, very badly for me.

There are a lot of things I don't like. I don't like lemonade mixed with iced tea. That's just a way to ruin lemonade. I don't like when people say to stop and smell the roses. Most roses smell like nothing or have a bad smell, so those people have no idea what they are talking about. I also don't like when people are too busy talking on their phones to notice the line has moved. What you are talking about is not interesting—even less interesting than smelling roses. Pay attention to the line! I don't like all those things, just like I don't like that last chapter of this memory book.

I wish some giant eraser would come down from the sky and make it disappear. I have tried to delete it. My finger hovers over the button, but I can't press it. Maybe I'm the eraser you talked about that won't do its job.

It's hard to read, but it wasn't hard to write. The opposite. That was the only chapter that wrote itself. Everything else in this book has been like digging for dinosaur bones, trying to put together bits and pieces from eons ago into something that resembles the living, breathing, eating, farting, pooping, meowing dinosaur it was at 1 time. Luckily, I've spent years and years going over and over all those bits and pieces, so I had some practice before writing all these pages for you. But at a certain point, I am filling in blanks.

How do I know? Because the words I've put into your mouth in this memory book include words no little kid knows. None. Not even a smartass like me. I only know those words now.

How else do I know? There's no way an 8-and-a-half-year-old's brain could remember all the stuff you said and keep remembering it for years and years until I am writing this now. Remembering even a minute of what you said is hard because you talked nonstop, nonstop, nonstop until I couldn't take it anymore. Sometimes I would put my fingers in my ears to try to block out your never-ending stories and requests and jokes and advice and questions and reverse psychology and on and on. And even those parts with my fingers in my ears are here just like I had a tape recorder on the whole time.

I have reconstructed a dinosaur from bits of rock that might be bones, but is it the right dinosaur? Is it even a dinosaur? Meow? Woof? Ribbit? Moo?

Maybe what I have pieced together in those other chapters is what really happened. *Maybe* I'm building the right dinosaur. Maybe this book is the truth. At the very least, I hope it rhymes with truth. Maybe.

But all this assembling-of-dinosaur-bits process is about the other chapters. Not about the chapter above. I am certain the chapter above happened exactly as I've written it because it was burned into my brain. There are no blanks to be filled in here. It's like a dinosaur hunter digging a hole hoping for a leg bone and having a hungry velociraptor jump out and rip open his belly. Chompety chomp.

So, what do I do if I can't un-remember it? What do I do if I can't erase it? That leaves only 1 option . . . Hey, what's that over there? Is that a black-throated blue warbler?

Maybe it will sing to us and make us forget all about how lousy this crummy world is. This little bird has the power to do that. You taught me that.

We took a taxi to get fro-yo that night because it was too late for the shuttle. The taxi got a flat tire, and they needed to send another car to pick us up and take us the rest of the way. I was in a daze the entire time. I took forever picking which flavor to get and which toppings to get. My hands eventually filled my cup with way more than any human can eat, but my brain wasn't controlling any of that. It felt like I was watching me get fro-yo from up in the air, like it was the boringest TV show of all time. I still felt that way when we came back, and I still felt that way in the morning. I woke up and went in to take an enormous pee like usual, but my brain watched it all from up near the ceiling. Watching myself pee was way more boring than watching me get fro-yo. People are incredible boring, and life is incredibly boring. Anyone who would want to watch someone's dumb life and hear their dumber thoughts is crazy.

I was also watching myself from ceiling height when you started dressing us up for the war you were about to start. You rubbed eyeliner onto your fingers and smeared it under each of my eyes, across my cheekbones, and along my jaw line. The war paint didn't look scary in the least. I would have looked less ridiculous trying to walk like a fancy lady in a dress and the sparkly shoes from your closet. You sang:

And when they ask us how dangerous it was
We never will tell them,

We never will tell them.
How we fought in some café
With wild women night and day—
'Twas the wonderfulest war you ever knew.
And when they ask us, and they're certainly going to ask us,
Why on our chest we do not wear the Croix de Guerre,
We never will tell them,
We never will tell them.
There was a front, but damned if we knew where.

You had me get up on the stepstool to look at myself in the bathroom mirror. The camouflage pants you had gotten me were too loose and the camouflage shirt was too tight. It made me look kind of like a triangle. I had no idea where you had gotten the army clothes. You hadn't gotten them on our clothes-sheets-toothbrush-shopping trip to the store, so you must have gotten them a different way. Maybe there was an infomercial for ill-fitting kid camo in the middle of the night while I was asleep, and you ordered it delivered by FedEx for a bazillion dollars in shipping fees. I pulled on the neckline of the shirt to stretch it out, but it went right back to being tight again. I tried to tighten the camouflage belt so the pants wouldn't fall down, but it refused to tighten. I looked at myself in the mirror. The camouflage on the belt didn't match the style of camouflage on the pants, and neither of them matched the camouflage on the shirt.

"I hate this." I was talking about the war makeup, and I was talking about my life, the universe, and everything. I touched a black smear on my cheek and looked at my finger. It was as black as the black I saw when I made myself pass out in your closet. You wiped my finger off with a piece of toilet paper, but it stayed black.

"You are my handsome soldier!"

"I look stupid. And the shirt is tight and annoying."

"It'll stretch out quickly as you carry out your missions."

"If I have to look stupid, you should, too."

"That sounds fair, but it's not very practical. If I dressed up like you, she'd figure out we're up to tricks. Luckily, you look scary enough for the 2 of us."

"It's not fair." Again, I was talking about the makeup and clothes, and I was talking about everything.

"OK, Dear. I'll put some on too. Hold on a sec." You went out to the kitchen, came back with your purse, and pulled out a tube of lipstick. The color would have made a vampire hungry. You puckered, put it on your lips, then put some on your 2 pointy teeth. "How about this? Am I scary now?" You showed your fangs.

"No."

"Good! I was aiming for silly rather than scary." You pulled your wig down over your eyes and said, "Boo!"

I gave you stink eyes, but you couldn't see it. "Does that taste bad?"

"My 'hair'?" you said with air quotes. You pulled the wig back up, but it was all wrong.

"The lipstick."

"It tastes like lipstick." You straightened your wig in the mirror.

"Does it have a flavor?"

"No flavor. Just a color."

"Some have berry or cherry flavor."

"Those are probably lip balm. Lipstick doesn't have flavors."

"They should add flavor to it. More people would buy it. The company would make so much money."

"I bet you're right! You're full of good ideas. Maybe you'll grow up to be an inventor."

I didn't know what to say, so I just looked at us in the mirror. A child soldier with clashing camouflage and a vampire who soaks her teeth at night.

"OK," you said. "Grab the breadcrumbs. Remember to wait a minute and a half before you go over. That's like counting to 90."

"I know that."

"Show me how quickly you will count."

"12345." I rattled the numbers off like I had just eaten ginger snaps and had fire coming out of my rear end.

"Too fast! Too fast! I won't even be at her door when you finish and barge over there. Say 'Mississippi' in between each number."

"Why?"

"To slow you down."

"That's dumb."

"Everyone says Mississippi when they count seconds."[57]

"I don't want to."

"Why? Do you have something against Mississippi?"

I folded my arms.

"If you do have something against Mississippi, that's fine with me. I knew a boy from there once. He was a jerk. A jerk and a half."

"You always change the subject."

"Do I?"

"Yes."

"That may well be, but I don't do it nearly as much as you do," you said.

---

57. No, they don't.

"Nuh-uh," I said.

"Yuh-huh," you said.

"Nuh-uh."

"Wow, look at that bird," you said and pointed. I did. "Ha! Made you look."

"I was going to look over there anyway."

"Nuh-uh," you said in a terrible impression of the way I talked.

"This is boring. People doing secret missions don't spend so much time talking and talking and talking."[58]

"You're probably right about that."[59]

I didn't want to count Mississippis. I didn't want to count anything you suggested. "I'll count apples. 1 apple. 2 apples." I thought that would settle it. It didn't.

"You need something with more syllables, otherwise your seconds will be too short."

"Ok. Orange."

"That's still only 2 syllables. But if you smushed them together to make a whole new fruit, that would work. Appleorange. 1 appleorange. 2 appleoranges. 3 appleoranges. See? That works great."

It was the dumbest thing I had ever heard since the last dumbest thing you said. "Can I just use a watch?" I asked, defeated.

"Yes, Dear. That works fine." You went to the junk drawer and got an old kitchen timer out. You twisted the spinny part to the right time, handed it to me, pressing my hand against the dial so it wouldn't start the countdown yet. The timer had a picture of a chicken chasing an egg chasing a chicken chasing an egg. Someone thought that was hilariously funny, but it wasn't funny at all. You broke my trance staring at the chickens and eggs by saying, "When I leave, go ahead and let go of that spinny thing. That will count out 90 seconds, and then you start your mission. I will keep her occupied as long as I can. If anything goes wrong, I'll give you the signal. Good luck, Soldier." You saluted me. I didn't salute back.

You left out the hallway door. I went to the sliding door, flipped the lock, and got a good grip on the handle so I was ready. I let go of the spinny thing and it started ticking louder than a time bomb in a lame movie. I decided to test my counting against the timer without using use apples, oranges, appleoranges, or Mississippis. When I got to 90, the timer still had 43 seconds to go. I waited and waited. When the timer finally got down to 0, the ringing was so loud, I dropped the timer, and it rolled over under the coffee table. I grabbed it, tried to make it

---

58. Actually, they probably do.

59. I probably wasn't.

stop ringing, couldn't make it shut up, and tried smothering it with pillows on the couch. Remind me never to babysit a crying baby.

The pillows didn't do a thing. The ringing was still super loud, but I had to go. I held the bag of breadcrumbs with my teeth, went out the sliding door, poked my head outside, looked left, right and upstairs, hopped over the railing, crawled over to Ms. Millie's patio, peeked around the wall, and looked in through her sliding doors. She was at her hallway door talking to you. Her back was to me. I stood up and hopped over the railing, careful not to kick the metal and make a clanging noise. I opened the bag of breadcrumbs, scooped out a handful, and spread them over the little side table. I spread a second handful on the bigger table, spreading out the crumbs evenly on the top like mozzarella on a pizza crust. I looked up and she was still talking to you. I put a handful on the left chair, but I put 2 handfuls on the chair to the right, her favorite place to sit. I made sure I didn't leave any piles because she would notice that from inside. I took the rest of the crumbs and spread them on the ground around the table and chairs. I did a good job. You couldn't tell there was anything there unless you were looking right at it on purpose. The birds would have no trouble seeing it though.

I looked up and you were pointing straight up. The alarm signal. I hopped over the railing and scrambled over past the dividing wall between her and her neighbor. I crawled back to your patio and went inside. You were there waiting. "Did you do it?"

I nodded.

"Did you get both chairs?"

I nodded.

"No piles, right?"

I shook my head, then corrected myself and nodded my head. You saluted me. All I could think about was getting back to watching TV.

The next morning, Ms. Millie microwaved a mug of water, put in a tea bag to steep, got the newspaper from outside her hallway door, tossed the classifieds directly in the trash, stood at the counter reading the front page while she waited for the tea, took out the teabag, added milk and sugar, mixed it up, tested it, added more sugar, mixed it again, carried the mug and paper to the sliding door, pulled it open, came outside, sat down in her poop-covered chair, and placed her mug down on the poop-covered table. That's when she noticed. Everywhere she looked, there was the white watery part, then the weird chunky thing in the middle.

The bait was gone. It was the perfect crime.

Y ou also sent her an anonymous birthday card wishing her a happy 128th.

Y ou ordered a pizza to be delivered to her room every day for 3 days. You paid for them, so she wasn't stuck with a bill. That wasn't the trick. You did it so the delivery person would say,

"Hi, I've got a pizza for Inneedova Bath. Are you Inneedova Bath?"

"Hi, I've got a pizza for Drew P. Cups. Is there a Drew. P Cups here?"

"Hi, I've got a pizza for Mrs. Leekbottom. Do you need napkins, too, Mrs. Leekbottom?"

To be honest, I was shocked you didn't do that for an entire month. Especially since you had made a list of about 759 of those insult names.

Y ou made a donation in her name to the ACLU and the Sierra Club. You couldn't decide which she would hate more, so you did both. They sent her hand-signed thank you cards, which no doubt ended up torn into 345 pieces and thrown in the trash.

Y ou submitted an obituary about her to the newspaper. It claimed she fought in the Civil War and famously booed Lincoln during his Gettysburg Address. It said she threw Citizen Kane's sled in the fire. It said she convinced Ken Griffey Jr. to leave Seattle and go play for the Reds.[60] It said she created a line of treats that were exact copies of Girl Scout Cookies but purposefully only cost half the price so she could put them out of business. It said she was a medical marvel who had survived decades without a human heart. It said her favorite hobby was taking packages from people's front porch. It said a lot. It was long.

The factcheckers must have been on vacation because they published it. And

---

60. Boo! Double boo! Triple boo!

you cut it out of the paper and pinned it up on the bulletin board in the dining room so nobody would miss it.[61]

Y ou put Crisco on the hallway knob of her door, and she had trouble getting back into her room after dinner.

Y ou made cocoa and put it into thermoses to keep us warm for the night-time stakeout out behind the bushes near her room.

It was still at least 80 degrees, and we were both wearing shorts. Drinking the cocoa made me sweaty. Bugs buzzed around me, loving my stink.

When her lights went off, you pulled a Casio watch out of your pocket and pressed tiny buttons with your big fingers to set a timer for 9 minutes. I asked why you set it for 9 minutes instead of 10, and you told me 9 was scientifically better than 10 minutes for maximum annoyance.[62] Waiting 9 minutes took forever. The bugs had told all of their best friend bugs about the stinky kid. And they had told their best friends.

When the watch beeped, you pulled the cordless phone out of your other pocket and dialed. Her light turned on, she picked up her phone, and you pressed the hang-up button. Caller ID wasn't a thing, so she had no idea it was us.

Her lights went back off. You pulled out the Casio and set it for 9 minutes. Beep. Dial. Lights. She picked up. You hung up.

You did it a third time, but you didn't hang up right away. You held your thumb over the talking part and listened. She yelled. She was mad. I could hear her through her closed windows as well as through the phone. In stereo. She hung up before you did.

I had a queasy feeling in my stomach. Was I starting to feel bad for her? Was I starting to worry about us?

---

61. Instead of a good picture of her, the obituary had a picture of an old man. You told me it was a guy named Abe Vigoda. "He was on Barney Miller, Dear. That's an all-time great show. In a way, we're complimenting her . . . in a way."

62. Science?

You had other plans, too. You had talked about putting hot sauce into her sundae on ice cream night. The color would have matched the strawberry topping and she wouldn't know it was there until she took a big bite and smoke came out her ears. But you couldn't figure out how to distract her and get the hot sauce into her dessert without her or anyone else seeing. You scrapped that idea.

You tried to think of a good prank involving a very public delivery of a box of extra-large adult diapers.

You thought about having her win a fake contest where the prize was a 1-way ticket to the missile test range in New Mexico.

Your most complicated plan was to put a black cat painted like a skunk in her room. The only problems were that you didn't have a black cat, you didn't have any paint that would be OK to put on a cat, you didn't know how to go about painting a cat that probably would not enjoy the process, plus you couldn't figure out how we would get the cat-skunk into her room (if we somehow managed to overcome all the other obstacles).

So, you left that prank on the drawing board—the literal drawing board. I don't know where you got it, but it was big and took up most of our living room. It fit a lot of plans on it. It also blocked the TV, which I had strong opinions about.

The prank you spent the most time planning was the water balloon prank. You drew complicated pictures of how it might work, including using a PVC tube powered by compressed air that would shoot the balloons at her from a hiding place in the bushes while she read the newspaper. You drew all kinds of ideas for it, laughing at every single scribble louder and longer than the last. I didn't think you were actually going to do any of them, though.

But then she said the things she said.

You looked out the peephole and said, "Don't hide, Dear." You pointed for me to stand out in the open over by the counter. I was halfway under the sink but did what you said. You opened the door.

"Ruuuuth—" she started to snarl, but then she saw me and stopped dead.

You opened the door wider and beckoned her in with a graceful wave of your arm like a hostess at a fancy restaurant you and I would never, ever be allowed into. She came in and stood in the middle of the kitchen like she owned the place and was getting ready to sell it. She looked at me, then you, then back at me.

"You 2 have been having a bit of fun at my expense, haven't you?" she asked, but didn't wait for an answer. "Juvenile. Infantile. Have they all been your ideas?" She was looking at me.

I didn't say anything. I looked at you.

"We don't know what you're talking about, Millie," you said. "Are you sure you have the right room? Fred down the hall is quite the cut-up. Maybe he's been doing whatever hilarious pranks you're talking about."

"I've had enough of your fun and games, Ruth. Everything comes at a price, and your bill is about to come due."

"I'm a churchgoing woman, Millie, and I believe deeply that people deserve what they get and get what they deserve."

"If you're a churchgoing woman, I'm the Prince of Siam." I didn't know what Siam was. I had never heard of it before, and I couldn't find it in your atlas that night.

You did a curtsy and said, "Pleased to meet you, Your Highness." You winked at me.

It was a dumb joke, but it made her even madder. Really, really madder. She started breathing loudly through her nose while she stared at you. I could see the grey hair inside her nose going in and out, in and out. You made a let's-all-calm-down motion with your hands, not meaning it at all.

"Ruth, you're not going to be grinning and having a laugh when they bring in the doctor. They'll have the diagnosis written before they even walk through the door: Crazy old cat lady, except worse because you're collecting stray kids." She hissed when she said the word stray. "They'll give you your first dose of meds before the ink is even dry on the paperwork. You'll be so doped up you'll soil yourself and not even know you're sitting in your own shit."

You looked bored and mimed a yawn. She looked at me. I wanted to hide under the sink.

"Your bill is about to come due, too, little man. There are lovely stories in the paper every week about what happens in foster homes, which is where you'll go. Take your pick. Would you rather be locked in a closet without food? Or would you rather get the belt from the tattooed boyfriend who doesn't like having a snot-nosed kid running around under his feet? Maybe you'll be lucky and get both."

I was distracted from everything she was saying. The only thing I could focus on was you smiling confidently behind her. The more vicious her words got, the bigger your smile got. The most horrifying thing happening in that room wasn't Ms. Millie's prediction that my future was going to be full of foster home knuckles and belts. That was just ambient noise compared to you starting to whistle "Somewhere Over the Rainbow," strolling to the sink, casually getting out a glass, and taking your time filling it with water.

Ms. Millie continued her threats. "Maybe I should have a bit of fun myself. For good measure, I'll tell them you haven't just been living here against the rules. I'll tell them the 2 of you have been fornicating. A regular Harold and Maude right here in our own building. I'll tell them I walked in and saw you doing disgusting things. Sinful things. It'll be in all the papers. They'll triple your meds, Ruth, and they'll have him in a psych ward until he's old enough to collect Social Security."

You threw the water at her face. You didn't miss. Even Ichiro wouldn't have had better aim.

I felt like I was melting.

We could hear her scream curse words all the way down the hallway until she slammed her door. I was shaking. I got my baseball cards. I started sorting them. I tried to make my hands stop shaking by shooting laser beams at them with my eyes, but they didn't stop.

"Do we still have the balloons we bought?" you asked calmly like you were asking if it was cloudy outside.

I pretended like I didn't hear you.

"Nevermind. Here they are," you said and hummed a song. Was it "Yellow Brick Road"? Was it "Ding, Dong, the Witch is Dead"?

I decided to make a stack of players with interesting names. I picked Chili Davis first. Then Rance Mullinicks.

You started filling the balloons. You set the full balloons next to the sink. 1 slipped from your grip and squirted water on the counter. It looked like a baby boy taking a whiz when someone changes his diaper. I watched it pee and I shivered. I looked back at my cards and put Argenis Salazar in the pile along with Don August and Ron Oester.

You got twine out of the junk drawer, put all the balloons into a colander with the swollen sides down and knotted sides up, gathered the ends, and tied them together with the string. You slowly lifted them up with the string to see if it would hold, and all the jiggling orbs of revenge rose and hovered like a bad idea nobody was saying no to.

I put Mookie Wilson and Eric Plunk in the pile.

You measured out a few arm-lengths of the twine and cut it with scissors.

I put Goose Gozzo in the pile, and you said, "Let's go."

I put the cards in my back pocket and followed you out the sliding door. "Check if her drapes are closed."

My brain told my body not to go, but there I was scurrying over there on all 4s. The curtains were mostly closed, but I could see she wasn't in her living room. I scurried back, gave you my report, and you lumbered over your metal railing and headed toward her patio, hiding behind the dividing wall at the empty apartment next to hers. You picked up a small rock, looped the end of the twine around it, and knotted it. You swung it around a couple of times to make sure it was secure.

You handed me the end of the twine with the rock. "You remember the plan, right?" You pointed at the lamp thing attached to the wall over her sliding door. You patted me on the butt, and I climbed over the railing. "Don't forget this," you said and handed me the colander of water balloons jiggling and jiggling, waiting to burst, ready to change everything.

It took a couple of throws, but I got the rock over the arm of the light. I kept looking inside but didn't see her. There was a light on in the bedroom/bathroom area, so she was probably in there. You made a pulling motion with your arms, so I grabbed the rock-end of the string and took in the slack. I backed up so I was hidden by the part of the wall next to the sliding door, then I started pulling the balloons up. You made a slow-down motion with your hands when the balloons were a few inches up, and I did. They lifted out of the colander, swayed in the air, bumped against the sliding door, but didn't break. I waited for the swaying to stop, then I raised them the rest of the way up above the doorway. I looked at you. You gave me a thumbs up, then whispered, "Wait for my signal."

You came out of hiding, walked to the part of the railing right across from where her sliding door opens, picked up a pebble from the ground, and chucked it at the door. It didn't make a very loud noise so you threw the next rock harder. That didn't work, so you threw a handful of them. I heard footsteps inside and almost let go of the string. The latch on the door unlocked and the door slid open a few inches.

"Unless you're going to offer me a towel and a groveling apology, I have nothing to say to you, Ruth. Not that it would make a difference. There's nothing you can do to stop me from making that call."

"We have something for you, Millie," you said in a voice purposefully too quiet to understand.

"What?" she asked.

"We have something for you, Millie," you said, even more quietly.

"You're mumbling, Ruth. That's a sign of bad breeding and low self-esteem. And your cheap wig is on crooked."

"What?" you said loudly, pretending to have trouble hearing her.

She opened the door wider and took a step through the door onto the patio to say it again. "Low self-esteem. And a cheap wig," she said cupping her hand around her mouth to project. "Those will be carved on your gravestone, if I have any say in the matter."

Then she saw me out of the corner of her eyes. She looked at my face. She didn't see I was holding the string, at least not at first. Her expression looked like she had just smelled burning hair. She looked at you, then back at me. That's when she noticed the string in my hand. Her eyes followed it up to the light over her head and looked straight at the balloons, but I don't think she understood. She didn't move out of the way. She just looked up at them.

You pointed up toward the sky. My hands let go. I didn't see them hit her. I heard the splash and felt splatters on me. They felt hot. I waited for a scream. I don't remember it, though. I also don't remember us rushing back to our room. I just remember feeling the hot drips running down my cheek and arms and legs so slowly. So slowly.

I can still feel it now.

While you were at dinner that night, I tried to watch TV, but I kept changing the channel, not watching anything, just flipping through them, over and over and over. When you came back, I nervously asked you if she had yelled and screamed at you in the dining room even before you had a chance to finish closing the door behind you.

You took your time answering me. You took off your sweater and hung it up. You put your keys in your purse and put your purse on the counter. You switched from your dinner shoes to your slippers. You sat down heavily on the couch, making my cushion jump up and tip me over. "Nope."

"She wasn't mad?"

"What are you watching?"

"You never answer my questions."

"That's true. I almost never do. You are very observant," you said. "But if you must know, Millie wasn't at dinner."

My stomach got tight. "Did she eat in her room?"

"That's a very sensible explanation."

"Maybe she just went to bed early because she was mad?"

"That is also a sensible explanation. What's on TV?"

I just looked at you, so you took the clicker from me and switched the channel to the home improvement shows I hate. I didn't squawk about the clicker or the channel, though. I watched without really watching. 2 episodes went by and then there was a scream, but not from the TV. Footsteps rushed past our room. There were a bunch of them. You didn't get up. There were more rushing footsteps. Then it was quiet, and I could hear the siren coming from far away. Then the siren was close enough it sounded like it was in the hallway right outside our door. The siren screamed and screamed while the men ran down the hall in their loud boots.

You didn't get up to check on the commotion. Instead, you pointed to the TV, shook your head, and said, "This poor designer is going to be driven crazy by this couple. How can you combine country living décor with contemporary modern in a ranch-style split-level?"

I got up from the couch and broke 1 of our most important truisms. I went out into the hallway, and you didn't stop me. More people were "rushing" down the hall, mostly in slippers, going .000000001 mph. I got low, weaved around their legs, reached her door, and looked inside. At first, all I could see was a wall of legs and feet. Then they all moved like a curtain parting at the beginning of a show. She was face-down on the floor. The firefighters weren't even taking out their equipment. They would put her on the couch soon and fold her hands so her thumbs were hidden. I stared and stared at her hair. It was still soaking wet.

T he Mariners played the White Sox that night. You watched Ichiro get 3 hits. I tried not to think of dripping wet hair.

I'm trying not to think of dripping hair right now, too. So here is a crow looking over there.

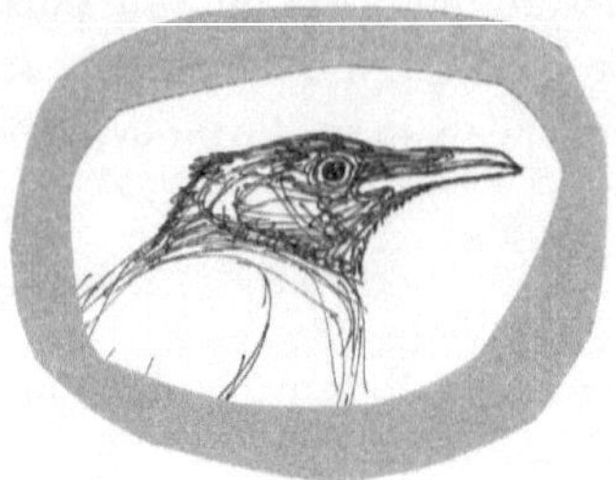

He doesn't want to think about dripping hair either.

On the day of the funeral, I looked at myself scratching under my shirt from my viewpoint up near the ceiling. The picture of the monster truck was itching my chest like crazy. You gave me a look telling me to stop fidgeting. When you looked away, I snuck my hand under the shirt and scratched more.

The me up near the ceiling and the me standing down there both didn't think we would fool anyone with my shirt inside out, but you had your mind set. You had gone through all my clothes that morning and picked out the most appropriate outfit. You picked the t-shirt with a monster truck smashing 3 junker cars. The word "CRUNCH!" was above the truck. The letters were smashed like the truck had run over them, too, but the truck couldn't have because the word was floating over the truck, looking down at the truck like it had done bad, bad things. You had turned the shirt inside out so it just looked like a plain black shirt. Before you put it on me, you took it into the bathroom and snipped loose threads with your little scissors—the pair I am not allowed to use for anything because I would ruin the sharpness. Once you were done dressing me, you fixed your hair and put on the same red lipstick you had worn in prep for the war. Then you grabbed your purse and my hand, took me out the sliding door, over the railing, through the bushes and down the street to the other old people's home where a taxi was waiting for us. You pulled me in and told the driver where to go.

"You look very handsome, Sweetie," you said (to me, not the driver).

I didn't say anything back to you. I looked out the window and everything zooming past made my stomach churn. I don't remember getting out of the taxi when we got there. I don't remember you paying the driver. But I remember how dark it was when we went through the big doors. My eyes tried to adjust, but everything stayed dark like it was permanently nighttime inside the building. You led me to the room where the funeral would be and patted me on the shoulder before we went in.

There was quiet music playing. The brightest lights in the room were over the podium and over the coffin. From the back of the room, I couldn't see her. I was too short, and she was down inside it. All I could see was a ring of flowers around the edge of the opening. You guided us into the second row of seats on the left. That is when I saw her. Her face was looking up at the ceiling. I looked up, but there wasn't anything above her worth looking at. I looked back at her face. They had tried to make her pretty with makeup and clothes, but I thought she looked mad. Not crazy mad, like in England. Just angry mad, like in our country.

There weren't many people at the service. Only 9 or 10, counting us and the guy in religious clothes that looked really hot to wear. I scratched underneath my shirt again. The music got quieter, and the priest/rabbi/pastor/reverend guy went up to the podium. He stopped at the coffin, leaned down and said something to her. I was worried he was going be clumsy and knock the whole thing over, making her fall out and roll, roll, roll up to my feet and point her bony finger at me.

He said, "Family and friends, today is not a day of sorrow. It is a day of celebration for a life well lived."

I felt even more sick to my stomach than in the taxi. I leaned forward and closed my eyes. You put your hand on my back. "Remember to breathe," you whispered.

I stayed doubled over. I only heard bits and pieces of what the man in black was saying. Something about how all her sins would be forgiven. Something about how all our sins would be forgiven. Something about how she would receive her reward in heaven. Something about how we were all going to get what was coming to us.

He finally finished and called up her niece, who lived somewhere else. She was wearing sunglasses and started sobbing. She said she didn't know Aunt Millie very well but wished she had spent more time with her. She started crying harder and her words became a blubbering mess nobody could understand.[63] The guy in the way-too-hot-for-summer clothes led her away, then came back, looked at his notes and called you up. I sat back up like the seat was electrified and tried to grab your skirt to stop you from going up. You patted me on the back, escaped my grasp, walked up to the coffin, leaned down, said something to her, went to the microphone, and cleared your throat. I tried to swallow the spit in my mouth, but it felt like I was drowning in dust.

"Most of you probably knew Millie longer than I did, but even in the short time I was her neighbor I feel like I got to know who she was deep down inside. The true Millie."

My throat hurt. I was so thirsty; I could have swallowed a lake and all the fish in it.

"Most people her age and my age have given up or given in. They get tired of fighting their failing bodies or fighting the changes in the world or fighting the ghosts all around them. But most of all, they get weighed down by the loneliness. Millie was different. She didn't give in. She was full of vinegar, as many of you know. Full of fight. She would never walk away from a battle. Wouldn't even think of it. That's a rare thing in this world."

I wanted a pillow to shove my face into until I passed out.

"She also had a way with words, as many of you know. You always knew exactly where she stood. A lot of people make you read their minds or their

---

63. When someone cries about someone else, aren't they mostly crying about themselves? Don't answer because I already know. That's totally true. True enough for it to be a truism. Or maybe an axiom? A regulation? A decree? What's the right word for something that's as true as it is sad as it is true as it is sad?

hearts. They are wishy-washy with their words. They don't say what they mean or mean what they say. Not Millie. If you talked with her for 30 seconds, you knew exactly who she was and what she believed in. There was no mistaking what kind of person she was inside."

I stood up and ran out. Out in the hallway, all the doors looked alike, and I couldn't tell which was the bathroom and which was the exit. The first 1 I tried was locked. The second 1 was locked, too. The next was open. It was a small room not much bigger than a closet with 2 benches facing each other, a box of tissues, and a small trash bin half full of crumpled tissues. I got on my knees, put my face over the bin and expected my stomach to empty. It didn't. Barely eating meant there wasn't anything to barf up. I sat down on the floor with my back against a bench and put the bin between my legs. I closed my eyes and kept them closed for a long time. That started to help, until you came in and made everything worse, worser, worsest.

"Are you feeling any better?" you asked.

I didn't answer you.

"Do you want me to help you find the bathroom?"

I didn't answer you.

"Funerals are hard for everyone. I'm proud of you that you came."

I didn't answer you.

"Did you hear my speech? Could you tell I was nervous?"

I didn't answer you.

"I promised myself I wouldn't say anything untrue about her. I didn't, right? It's important to tell the truth...but there's a way to do it that doesn't make you a Negative Nellie. Too many people forget that." You were talking about me, weren't you? But I had no clue because my nose was suddenly running like a gazelle—a gazelle with a disgusting runny nose. I took a tissue from the box and blew my nose. I was terrible at it. I sprayed slime all over my fingers.

You cleaned my fingers with a tissue and asked, "Do you want to go back in with me or wait here? There are a couple more speeches before they wrap up."

I looked up at you. I didn't answer your question. Instead, I asked the question I had been pushing down as far as I could—down into the tips of my toes—for days. "Don't you feel bad about what we did? We—. We—. She's dead because of us."

Part of me was sure you were going to pat me on the arm and tell me we shouldn't feel guilty because her dying that day was just a coincidence. That part of me was sure you were going to say our little water balloon prank had nothing to do with her dropping dead. You were going to say I was a silly goose, weren't you? You would tell me to put it out of my mind because she was very, very old, and dying is what very, very old people do all on their own without needing any help from people getting them a bit soggy. Wouldn't you?

But you didn't say any of that. What you said was this: "That's not the right question, Dear." You put your hand under my chin and gently tilted my face up to look at you. "We deserve our happily ever after, and we're going to get it, gosh darn it." You leaned down, kissed me on the forehead, then went back to hear the rest of the eulogies. I sat there and stared at something that wasn't 6 inches in front of my face.

By the time we got back, the dining room was closed, so we just had cereal for dinner. I didn't eat any of mine. I had to run the disposal to make the mushy bowl of mush go down the drain. After that, you turned on a movie about an all-girls baseball team.[64] At the end of that movie, you turned the TV off, kissed me on the forehead, said, "Don't forget to brush your teeth," then went to bed.

I stared at the dark screen of the TV. I felt so tired inside and my brain felt like mashed potatoes. You turned off your light and started snoring within 3.14159265358 seconds. I sat there and could see my reflection in the TV screen. I could see tears on my cheeks. They felt like hot splatters. I was too worn out to wipe them off.

My stomach was rumbling like crazy because I had rejected food all day. I thought about smashing sunflower seeds outside and eating those. I got up, quietly pulled your door almost closed, and went to the kitchen, but I didn't get food. I got a piece of paper and a pen from the junk drawer and wrote you a note. It said I was leaving and never coming back. I signed my name at the bottom so there wasn't any confusion about who was bailing out of this sinking ship. I folded the note, wrote your name on the outside, and put it in my backpack so you didn't accidentally see it in the middle of the night before I left.

I tried not to sleep. Every second took a year and a half, but it finally started getting light outside. I went to the kitchen, got milk and a donut, and ate next to the sink staring at the drain. I wasn't hungry and couldn't taste the food, but I made myself eat so I had enough energy to walk as far as my little feet could take me. Hopefully as far as West Timbuktu.

I got the note out of my backpack, put it on the counter, and then packed my stuff. I took my sheets, blankets, and pillow off the couch and stacked them off to the side, like I had never been there. I went over to the sliding door, then turned around to check if I was forgetting anything.

---

64. Too much talking. Not enough baseball.

You came out of your bedroom, yawned like a cartoon character yawns, and calmly asked, "Are you leaving?"

"None of your business."

"Where are you going?" you asked, without a hint of concern in your voice.

"Somewhere you can't find me."

You put your hand on your back and stretched a little to the left, then a little to the right. You sat down on the couch and folded your hands on your lap. "If I asked you to stay, would you? Hypothetically, of course."

I shook my head.

"You probably wouldn't be swayed by a cookie, would you?"

"No. I ate a donut."

"I can't compete with that. A donut beats a cookie any day. That's just science.[65] Is there anything I can do to change your mind?"

"I want to be alone."

"Nobody truly wants to be by themselves. Loneliness is a cruel friend."

"I don't need any friends."

"Everyone needs friends."

"Not me."

"Everyone needs someone. Someone to love. And someone to love them."

"Not me."

"Well, you may not, but I do. I need you."

"No, you don't," I said as quickly as I could spit the words out, but I changed my mind and said, "Even if you do, I don't care." You wouldn't be able to argue with that.

You looked at me, then down at your lap. You smoothed the cloth on your pajama pants, which had penguins dressed up in tuxedos wearing top hats. I thought your silence meant I had won. I turned around to grab the sliding door handle.

"Before you do, let me get my purse."

"I don't need money. I will find cans."

"I'm not getting you money. I'm coming with you."

I spat out, "Nuh-uh!" It was the best I could do on short notice.

"It's a free country. You can leave if you want to. That's true. And I can come with you if I want to. That is also true. Those are both truisms."

My ears felt bright red. You were ruining everything. You always ruined everything. I started to shake, but then I stopped. My shoulders slumped. My face slumped. My ears went from lava to ice cold. They probably slumped too. I felt weak and my voice was weak. "Why won't you leave me alone?"

"Because I love you, Silly. I'll pack us a snack." You threw on some non-pen-

---

65. Einstein's General Theory of Baked Goods Relativity

guin-covered clothes, got pretzels from the cupboard, and put the purse strap over your head so it went diagonally across your body like a beauty pageant sash.[66] "Let's go," you said, stepping in front of me and pulling the sliding door open. "You can drive," you said and held out keys.

I needed to take a break after writing that last section. I didn't write anything for 2 or 3 weeks after I typed the word "keys" and put a period after it. My fingers didn't want to type any more, and my brain didn't want to remember any more.

So I stopped and thought about throwing all of these pages in the trash. Not just the regular trash, but the trash behind the dining hall that's full of food scraps. All that goop and gunk would soak into the pages and really ruin them so even if I changed my mind and tried to take them out it wouldn't matter. This would be over.

But I didn't. I just put the pages in my desk and tried not to think about it.

Today I pulled out a sheet of paper and what came out of me was this drawing of a sunflower. There is no real sunflower that has this shape and these colors. So it's not a real sunflower.

But it rhymes with it.

And maybe that's OK.

Because it's the best we can do.

And because it's what we need.

After drawing that sunflower that wasn't a sunflower, I pulled out the pages and was able to put more memories in this book. I might still put all of this in the soupy, slimy dining hall garbage, but for today, at least, I will keep doing this. At least for today.

You had held the keys out to me, then we went out to the car. I didn't want to get in, but my butt ended up in the driver's seat, and your butt was in the passenger seat, and I was screaming, "I won't! I won't!"

You didn't say anything back to me. You weren't even looking at me. You just stared at the key I refused to turn.

"Stop it!"

"I know you want to," you finally said after the moon had revolved around the earth 17 times. "Every kid under the sun wants to turn the key in the ignition."

I folded my arms and stared straight ahead.

"I'm too old to drive any more. My vision is terrible, plus I take too many risks. It's in my nature. There's nothing more dangerous than an old lady with nothing to lose." You looked around in the car. "Maybe we can tie something to the bottom of your shoe so you can reach the pedals."

I was tired of talking to you. I wanted this to be over, even if it meant we both drove off a cliff. I reached down and turned the key violently. Nothing happened. I turned it again, twisting it so hard I thought it would snap. Nothing.

"The battery must be dead," you said, scratching your chin. You got out of the car, came around to my side, opened my door, pulled a knob, and the hood popped up an inch. You fussed with the hood for a long time until there was a click. You lifted the hood partway up, but it came crashing down and locked shut. You had to start over: pull the knob near the driver's seat, reach in to press the invisible thing, lift the hood. This time you got the metal rod in place, and it stayed open.

You said "Hmm" and "Interesting" and "Wow" and other things trying to lure me out of the driver's seat to look. It worked. I had never seen an engine in real life before. It was a chaotic jumble of metal and hoses. You pointed at the battery. It had mounds of white crusty stuff where wires connected to the top. The crusty stuff had oozed down the sides and had dried there. I wondered what it would taste like.

"That's not good," you said insightfully. "That must be what happens to batteries when you don't drive a car for a while."

"Is this car older than you?"

"It's a classic, like me. Plus, new cars are expensive. This works fine."

"No, it doesn't."

"It just needs a new battery. I should have come down once a month to run it and keep it charged. I guess I was too busy living it up to remember. As the old saying goes, 'Life is what happens when your car battery goes dead.' Ha!"

"It's ugly."

"Don't listen to him, Daisy!" you said and patted the hood. "They don't make cars like this anymore. Now everything is plastic, plastic, plastic. Look. This is all metal." You knocked on the grill of the car, and it sounded like hitting cardboard.

"It looks really slow."

"Speed isn't everything, you know. It's not about how fast you get there, but about the motion of the ocean . . . or something. This was built to be reliable rather than just fast."

We both looked at the engine of the reliable car that didn't run. I walked around the side and looked at all the rusty spots. I pressed my foot against the fender and a piece of metal crackled and fell off. I picked it up and handed it to you.

"Thanks. We probably both need a tetanus shot now. Aside from the battery and a bit of rust, Daisy is a very good car. Aren't you, Daisy?"

"The tires are all flat," I said helpfully. "And bees are coming out of the back." I pointed to the trunk, which was buzzing ominously.

"Daisy, you're being reclaimed by nature," you said to the car. "This is the circle of life in action!" you said way-too-excitedly to me. You unpropped the rod holding up the hood and let it all slam down. That made the bees buzz louder. "Nature is getting angry. Let's get out of here before the circle of life gets us."

You led me down the road to the other old people's home. You went inside to the reception desk while I waited outside. I don't know why I didn't run. I could have. Maybe I thought it was no use. No matter where I went, you'd be standing there annoying me. It was useless to try to get away, and that made me feel sad all the way into the deepest, grossest part of my guts.

I stood there deflated, right near where the old lady with the droopy head had held my backpack hostage in exchange for smearing a kiss on my cheek with her guillotine hand. I reflexively rubbed my filthy cheek with my grimy sleeve. Then I looked up at the birds eating from the bird feeders up on the second and third floors. I watched them and wished I could fly away. A bird pooped and it fell down, down, down to the ground, which was spackled white with droppings from day after day of birds getting their breakfast, lunch and dinner up above. In 2,000,000,037 years all that poop would be a foot high, I guessed. Would I be free of you in 2,000,000,037 years?

You came out whistling, stood next to me, and started singing the words:

> *I'm so awfully weary*
> *Doing just what I should.*
> *I'm getting so bored*
> *With virtue's reward,*
> *So please don't make me be good.*
>
> *Gee, but life can be dreary*
> *When you're misunderstood.*
> *In spite of my rep,*
> *I'm all full of pep,*
> *So please don't make me be good.*
>
> *Though heaven may be OK,*
> *When life's long journey ends*
> *I'd rather go down below*
> *And be with my intimate friends (God bless 'em)*
> *I could love you, my dearie,*
> *More than anyone could*
> *You can make me, sweetheart,*
> *But please don't make me be good.*

We didn't start walking anywhere. We just stood there. I had no idea if we were waiting for something or just standing there. "It'll be here soon," you said confusingly. "In fact, that might be it." A car drove past and kept going. "False alarm. But it'll be here soon." You whistled the song again. A Radio Cab pulled up. The driver lowered his window and asked, "Are you Ruth?"

"Yes, we are," you said. You nudged me in and then scooted in next to me. Terrible things happened every time we took a taxi. I don't know why I kept getting into them with you.

"You're going over to the medical center across from Meridian Park Hospital, right?" he asked over his shoulder.

"No, actually. We would like to go to McMinnville."

"What?" He half-turned around to look at you. His grumpy face matched the grumpy picture on the certificate that said, "Your Driver Is: FRANK."

"McMinnville, please."

"Is this a joke, lady?"

"No. I have the money." You fanned out a lot of 20-dollar bills and then fanned me with them like I was a pharaoh on a hot day alongside the Nile River.[67]

"I guess you're serious."

"I guess I am serious! Think of that! There's a first time for everything, I suppose!" You bumped me with your elbow and then fanned me some more.

"I'll have to charge extra after we leave the metro area to cover my gas coming back."

"Of course. That would only be fair. So, we have a deal?" You put your hand through the teeny, tiny window in the glass to shake on it.

He looked at your hand, then he shook it awkwardly by reaching his hand backward over his shoulder. "Sorry I snapped at you. People love pranking drivers. Last week someone asked me to drive them to Margaritaville. They almost peed themselves laughing. Drunk a-holes, pardon my French."

"I wouldn't mind going to Margaritaville," you said, licking your lips. He didn't hear you, though.

"Another time, someone asked me to drive them to Sesame Street. People think they're hilarious when they have a couple of drinks in them."

"Hilarious and attractive," you added.

"What?" he asked, confused.

"People think they are attractive after they've had a couple. Hilarious and attractive." You made a motion with your hand like you were drinking a glass of something, put your hands on what used to be your hips, and made a face that was probably an attempt at what was sexy 200 years ago. "You're lucky they didn't try to kiss you, Frank."

"Ha! Very true. This is a no-kissing cab. I should make a sign just to be safe." He motioned to the 75 other signs on the dashboard, the ceiling, and the glass barrier between him and us.

"You should make that for him," you said to me. "You have very good penmanship when you write notes and whatnot." You patted your pocket, and I could hear the paper of my adios note crinkle inside. I ignored you. I pulled up the door lock in case I decided to jump out at a stoplight . . . or while we were on the highway going 50. I would cross that bridge when we got to it, and probably take a flying leap off and try to swim away.

He pushed a button on the fare meter. "What kind of music do you guys like?"

---

67. Please tell a giant Nile quackadile to leap out of the river, swallow me whole, and put me out of my misery.

"Show tunes," you said unhelpfully.

"I don't think there's a station for that," he said, pressing the preset buttons on the radio to look around. "Is NPR OK?"

You gave him a thumbs up and smiled at me. I thought running away was supposed to involve fewer people, less chit-chat, and no singing. I must have been doing it all wrong.

All of it.

Completely wrong.

I s this a bunch of birds fleeing from what's about to happen? Or is it the seam of a baseball?

"G osh, this is fun. Isn't this fun?" you asked but didn't wait for me to answer. "Isn't this fun?" you asked the driver. He nodded in the rearview mirror to be polite. "Can I ask you a question?" you said to him.

"Sure."

"It's a bit of an odd question."

"That's OK."

"It's not personal or anything. I'm not going to ask about your love life or anything of that sort."

"It wouldn't be the first time if you did," he said. "Ask away."

"If you had any trip in your life to do again before you die, which would it be?"[68]

"To do again?"

"Yes. To do again. Not a wishlist trip you haven't taken. It has to be something you did in the past and would do again if you were running out of time." You were talking loud enough for people in other cars to hear you.

"Am I healthy enough to travel?"

"Yes. You're not ill or feeble or anything. You'll just drop dead suddenly once you're there."

"Do I know I'm going to die?"

"Does it matter?"

"Maybe."

"Let's say yes, then."

"That's a toughie."

"It is, isn't it?"

"Where would you go?" he turned the question around at you.

You scratched your chin, as if you didn't already know what you would say. "Who knows? I might just pick McMinnville." You scratched your chin some more. "Well, Paris would be nice, too. But McMinnville ain't half bad."

Frank[69] drummed his fingers on the steering wheel while he tried to think of a place. The sound was so annoying. Both of you were so annoying. I wished you'd both get married and forget all about me.

"I'd go back home to Idaho."

"Where in Idaho?" you asked. I didn't ask because I didn't care. I just wanted complete, utter silence.

"Pocatello." Then he added, "And I'd walk."

"Walk?"

"Yes."

"Why?"

"That would take longer. That way I'd stay alive a few extra days. I would probably take the scenic route, too. Add a few more days before I cash in my final hurrah, so to speak. Head up to Coeur d'Alene or something. Maybe over to Bozeman before circling back."

"That's a good strategy, but I think it breaks the rules." You leaned over to me and whispered, "Truisms." Then you went back to chattering with him. "It's supposed to be a trip you've made before. You haven't walked to Pocatello before, have you?"

---

68. You talked more about death than a funeral director at a funeral director convention receiving a lifetime achievement award for excellence in burying stuff.

69. Actually: FRANK in all capital letters according to the "Your Driver Is" sign.

"No, but you should bend the rules a bit. I'm dying, for Pete's sake." He laughed. "Can't you grant me a final wish?"

"No, I'm sorry. Rules are rules. I don't make 'em. I just enforce 'em . . . and put 'em in oatmeal containers." You bumped me again with your elbow.

I stared out the window and tried to ignore both of you. I counted things. I counted red lights. There were lots of them. 9 so far, and we had barely started driving. I didn't know how far it was to McMinnville, but I knew it was going to take forever to get there. I counted dump trucks. I counted fruit stands. I counted how many times you laughed. You laughed more times than there were hazelnut farms, which is a number larger than 23 and slightly smaller than 923.

I asked you for a tissue and you gave me 1 from your purse without even pausing your conversation. I ripped it in half, crumpled a piece up, put it in my mouth, chewed it, then shoved it in my left ear. I did the same with the other ear. I could hear my pulse and the sound of the ocean. I could still hear you, though. I think you started talking even louder to be sure I could still hear you. I pushed the tissue plugs in harder and tried to focus on the sound of the blood in my arteries, but I still heard you. You were talking about how to make a cake or how to hold a rake. You were talking about flying to Japan or frying some ham. Doing your taxes or booing at Texas. Who knows. You talked and talked, and the driver nodded and nodded. It went on and on.

I noticed a fly on the ceiling of the taxi, upside down, clinging to the fabric and looking down at me with at least some of its eyes. It was moving its front legs together like it was cleaning itself or plotting a scheme. I pushed the tissue harder into my ears until it hurt. The fly stopped moving its front legs. It waited. It waited. Then it made a run for it. It flew over to the window, bumped into the glass, bumped again, slid to the left, down to the bottom of the window, then back up again. It buzzed, cursing up a storm of bad, bad words in its insect language.

It went to the front passenger window and tried there. The driver pulled the papers off his clipboard, rolled them up, and swatted at it. The fly cursed louder,[70] tried the windshield, got swatted at again, then disappeared. The driver held the papers up, ready for it if it wasn't dead, but he didn't see it again. I didn't see it either. Then it was there on the ceiling of the car above me again, looking down at me judgmentally with at least some of its eyes.

I looked over at you. You were still talking. Something about east Nevada or an empanada. I looked back at the fly, then pressed the button on the door and lowered the window a couple of inches. The fly stayed put, just working its legs. I lowered the window a couple more inches. I reached up and waved my arm to try to steer it toward the window, but I couldn't reach very high because of

---

70. Mother-buzzing son of a buzz.

the seat belt. I pulled the belt down off my shoulder and loosened the lap belt. I waved at it with my left hand to try to get it to escape. It didn't move an inch. I lowered the window more.

You tapped me on the shoulder. I looked at you. You motioned for me to roll up the window like it was an old-fashioned car with handles for that. "I can't hear myself think with all the wind. Plus, you'll let the rain in." There wasn't a cloud in the sky. I pressed the button and the window went up. I left a crack open, though. You weren't the boss of me.

I looked at the fly again. You looked up at him with all 2 of your eyes. I showed you what I was trying to do. I reached up again and waved at it again to try to get him to go toward the window. It didn't budge.

"Maybe it wants to stay."

"No, he wants to go."

"Actions speak louder than words," you said to me and looked at me longer than you needed to.

You lifted yourself up a bit and blew a lungful of air at it. It didn't move. You looked at me. You adjusted your bra strap, then reached over and pressed the button. The window closed the rest of the way. You patted me on the leg and left your hand there. I shook my leg but couldn't buck you off. I gave up. "Flies can't talk," I mumbled, but you were already talking about who knows what. Who knows what.

2 3 red lights. Plus 4 other times when we stopped for no reason. The traffic just came to a halt. "People going to the wineries," the driver said. "They have no clue where to turn. Not a clue in the world." He honked.

3 other times we were slowing down for a red light, but the light turned green, and we didn't come to a complete stop. We almost stopped and our bodies leaned forward from the brakes, then our bodies went back into the seats when the driver pressed the gas.

There were 2 Dairy Queens. Their signs advertised grasshopper shakes. I didn't know what that was. You said it was yummy. I didn't believe you. Nothing with grasshoppers in it could taste good. At least not to a human.

You said, "Well, isn't that interesting," to the driver at least 5,000 times.

There were 3 billboards for a museum with the Spruce Goose.

There were 2 police cars. I should have screamed I was being kidnapped. "Help! I can't escape my geriatric, arthritic, largely-immobile captor!"

And a partridge in a hazelnut tree.

It takes a long time to go through 23 red lights. David Justice was number 23. Ryne Sandberg had 23 doubles in 1988. Bill Swift pitched in 23 games the first year he played for the Mariners. Rance Mulliniks had 23 walks his first year and 23 strikeouts his second.

I closed my eyes and pressed the crumpled tissue in my ears again. I started to hum. I tried to match the vibration of the engine with my humming. It was hard. My humming was pretty high compared to the low hum of the engine. I got my hum down as low as I could go. The engine and I were matched up. I couldn't hear you and the driver anymore. I was asleep and you told me later I was drooling like a faucet and snoring like your husband used to do. It was the only time you ever mentioned him. You weren't supposed to talk about the past. You broke a truism.

Ryne Sandberg had 23 doubles in 1998, but his best year was 2 years later. He had 7 more doubles than that. And he had 40 homeruns, 100 RBIs, and 344 total bases. A lot of people ignore total bases, but that's an important number.

I had no idea where I was when I opened my eyes. We were stopped outside a brick building that was really old. Maybe even as old as you. I looked at you and tried to remember your name. All my brain could think was that it rhymed somehow with Ruth.

You had a lot of money in your hands. "Plus your tip," you said and handed it to him. The machine on the dashboard said $95.75. "Thank you for the lovely conversation. It's a lost art. Give my best to your wife, and I hope your aunt gets well soon. Tell her to listen to her doctor. The world doesn't need another paranoid old lady who doesn't take her meds."

We got out. I didn't know what to do with myself so I just stood next to you and kept trying to wake up. "Drive safely," you said, closing the door and hitting the side of the taxi with your hand like they do in movies in New York City. He drove off, and we looked around. It wasn't Manhattan, for sure.[71] A girl rode

---

71. Not even Manhattan, Kansas.

by me on her bike. The tassels on her handlebars were sparkly. A dog came up and sniffed my shoes. It had a limp.

"Oh dear. You're hurt, aren't you? Come here, you poor little thing." You made a kissing noise. You took a step toward it. It took a step back. You made another kissing noise. It took another step back. "It's OK. I'm going to help you."

It bolted. You followed it making more kissing noises, but it was too fast. You stopped the chase, watched it escape, then came back to me.

I was still in a daze and blurted out, "What's the Spruce Goose?"

"What's that, Dear?"

"The Spruce Goose."

"Yes?"

"What is it?"

"It's a plane."

"Does it look like a goose?"

"No."

"Why do they call it a goose?"

"Because it rhymes with spruce."

"What is a spruce?"

"It's a kind of tree."

I shook my head. I had never heard of that kind of tree.

"They called it that because the plane is made of wood rather than metal," you explained.

"That's dumb. Wood would break."

"And it's a pun. Spruce also means trim and neat, like a button. Not exactly the first word you would think of looking at a plane that large, but that's the point. It's ironic."

I looked blankly at you.

"Ironic means it's the opposite of what it means."

"So, it's the opposite of a goose."

"It's the opposite of spruce."

"The opposite of a tree?"

"I guess you could say that. A tree can't fly, can it?"

"No."

"I can't fly either, so I guess I'm 'spruce' too," you said looking down at your belly.

"There's a squirrel that can fly." I wanted my sleepy brain to shut up, but it kept saying stuff to make this conversation drag on.

"That's very interesting. Does it lay eggs like a bird?" you asked.

"No. It's a squirrel."[72]

"Well, isn't that clever of them? And very clever of you to know about them."

"Everyone knows about flying squirrels," I said.

"I didn't know about them."

"Yes, you did."

"No, I didn't."

"You're just pretending you didn't know about them."

"Sometimes you're too smart for your own good."

"No, I'm not."[73]

"Let's not argue. Let's talk about the rest of the day. What would you like to do?"

"Run away."

"We *are* running away."

I was fully awake and shaking mad again, just like that. Like you had pressed a red button and I went from 0 to 100. "You are so—" I swallowed the words but stamped my foot. I was going to say something nasty and hurtful. Something that would change the way you looked at me. Something that would make you not want to be with me anymore.

You waited to see if I would say what I wanted to say. Then you stopped waiting and asked me, "Have you ever stayed at a hotel?"

I ignored you.

"Well, there's a first time for everything. You're in for a treat."

"I don't want to be here."

"Don't be so contrarian. This is a special hotel. Not your run-of-the-mill place. You'll love it."

"No, I won't."

"It's very old and lovable. Like me." You smiled and posed for a picture nobody was taking.

"It's probably full of rats."

"That's just part of its character. But more importantly, it's haunted."

"No, it's not."

"How do you know? You've never been in it."

"Ghosts aren't real."

"I guess we'll find out."

You had tricked me again. Now I wanted to prove you wrong. Wrong about ghosts in the hotel. Wrong about it having rats. Wrong about it being fun. There's nothing kids love more than proving a grown-up wrong.

---

72. Meow! Oink! Buzz!

73. No, I wasn't.

The lady at the front desk told you 1,000,000 boring things about the hotel. I looked for rats behind the furniture in the lobby but didn't see any. Hopefully, they were up in the rooms. But I shouldn't get my hopes up, right?

I looked at the old photos on the walls from when the hotel was built 100 years ago. All the people in them were wearing old-style clothes. A lot of the men had big moustaches. Everyone in the photos was dead by now, I guessed. You were probably going to tell me some of them were still around, haunting the hotel. You were probably going to tell me there were ghost rats, too. And ghost flying squirrels. You were going to tell me anything you thought would make me un-unhappy. I wasn't going to fall for it.

You whistled at me. "We're on the third floor. Number 311. I'll race you! You take the elevator. I'll take the stairs." You didn't wait for me to agree. You zoomed toward the stairs.

"I don't want to race."

"I can't hear you," you said. "And I'm winning."

I said a bad word, then ran to the elevator and pressed the up button. It took forever to come down and open. It was an old elevator and it moved like an old snail—a snail that wanted me to lose because you had paid it a dollar to sabotage me. I got in and tried to press "3," but my hand went to "2" and pressed it by mistake. I said another bad word. I tried to un-press number "2," but it stayed lit. I pressed the "3" button too. The elevator door was still open. I pressed the button to make it close. Nothing happened. I pressed it again. It closed and the elevator took me up 1 floor and opened. It took forever to close again. By the time I got up to the third floor, I was sure you had beat me. I was expecting you to be right there smirking at me when the door opened, but you weren't.

I went to room 311 and tried to open the door. It was locked. I knocked. No answer.

I walked down the hall and looked around the corner for you. Nope.

I came back to the room, but you still weren't there. I got a bad feeling in my chest.

I went to the stairs and walked down to the second floor. I looked around, didn't see you and started down the next set of stairs. That's where you were. You were sitting down with your back to me. You were hunched over with your face pointing down at your feet.

"Did you fall?"

You lifted your head a little and said, "No, I'm just old."

I sat down next to you. I wasn't going to say it, then I did. "I thought you were dead."

You pulled me closer to you and kissed the top of my head. "No such luck. You're still stuck with me."

The kiss felt like a timer going off inside me. Now that I knew you were OK, I was furious. I was furious at you for scaring me . . . for possibly being dead . . . and for still being alive. But mostly, I was furious at myself for caring.

"You're sweet for worrying about me," you said.

"I'm not sweet. And I wasn't worried."

"It sure seemed like you were worried."

My body temperature went to 1000 in a nanosecond. "I. Was. Not. Worried. About. You."

You looked at me and didn't say a word, which made me madder.

"I. Don't. Love. You."

You looked at me and didn't say a word. I stormed off, wishing 100s of hungry ghost rats would emerge from the walls and eat every part of you so there wasn't anything left except your wig and your fake teeth sitting on those stairs.

I gave you the silent treatment when we got into our room. I refused to look at you, too. Since you wouldn't let me run away, I was going to pretend you were invisible. I was sure the "you're invisible" act would totally get your goat.[74]

But you yawned, told me you were going to going to close your eyes for a few minutes, got onto the bed and fell all the way asleep in 2.0000002 seconds. All the way and then some. A couple of times I got really close to your face to check if you were breathing. I was pretty sure you were, but what did I know. I had

---

74. Baaa! Meow! I talk like I'm 128 years old.

only seen a couple of corpses at that point in my life.[75]

Once you were asleep, all my furiousness from earlier went on hold, but it was just waiting for me to un-pause it. Until then, I would be completely, utterly bored to deathly death. I looked around at our completely, utterly boring room. There was the bed you were on, a small table with a lamp, a wooden chair against the way next to a sink, 2 cups on a shelf, some towels, and not much else.

I looked for a TV, but there was a problem. There wasn't 1. I checked everywhere on the walls to see if there was a secret button to make a TV pop up or drop down or appear in some way. No luck. Just dumb murals painted on the walls showing people from the town who died 1,000,000 years ago. How were we going to watch baseball? That's all I could think about until all I could think about was needing to pee. The room didn't have a toilet. I remembered hearing the lady at the front desk tell you the bathroom was somewhere else for everyone to share, but I couldn't remember where she said it was. It didn't seem important at the time, but it was suddenly really, really important.

Opening the door would wake you up, so I held it. I tried to ignore it, but it got worse. I stood up and walked around to see if that would help. That made it worser. I tried turning the door handle quietly, but it sounded like the earth was ripping open to swallow up the hotel, so I stopped. I paced back and forth and held my pants away from my stomach so they wouldn't press on my bladder. I tried taking slow, deep breaths. I tried taking fast, shallow breaths. All of that made it even worser than worse.

That's when the little sink started staring at me.

It was the perfect height. I felt like I was going to explode, so I pulled out my wiener and whizzed in there. It made a loud spraying noise, and I looked back over my shoulder to make sure I wasn't waking you up. I almost lost control of the firehose 3 times, but most of the yellow gusher made it into the sink. I ran the water to wash the yellow down the drain, but the room smelled like 500 gallons of pee. I took the hand towel and flapped it back and forth like a fan to try to make the smell go away. That just made the smell worse. It still reeked like 100 urinals in there.

I looked at you sleeping and wanted to get close enough to see if the blankets were moving up and down. But I stopped myself. I knew they were moving. I didn't need to check. I knew I was too cursed to ever be free from you.

---

75. Here's what I imagined you saying just now: "Couple of Corpses would be a great band name! Clara and I could do show tunes wearing hospital gowns with tags on our toes. 'We'll meet again. Don't know where. Don't know—.' Bam! Boom!! That's the sound of our bodies hitting the stage. Always leave the audience wanting more!"

After the excitement of taking the biggest pee of my life, I almost died of boredom 57 times while you just kept sleeping. It got dark outside and you kept sleeping. I peed in the sink 2 more times, making the entire room smell like the wettest diaper in the history of diapers, and you kept sleeping. You kept snoring away, until suddenly you stopped and there was the loudest silence I've ever not heard. I thought that was it. You had kicked the farm, bought the bucket, gone to the big dirt nap in the sky. I got close closer closest to your face to check. The hairs in your nose weren't moving in and out like they usually do. I didn't hear any breathing. I touched your skin and it was cold. Then you snorted the loudest snore you've ever snored right into my eyeballs. You weren't dead even .001%. Messing with my emotions is what you were born to do, apparently. You were the Mozart of tormenting my brain and with my life. And I was the Beethoven of getting played like a piano.

I watched you from the chair, with my un-meaty buns aching from the hard wood, smelling the reek of my own urine in that sink and on the wall, listening to you snore like a bear, and I could feel myself start to cry. I hated it. I pushed on my eyes to make it stop. I pushed harder to make the tears go back in. I pressed my fists halfway into my brain to think about something else other than being sad. I wanted to howl at the moon to get my paw out of the trap. But the moon didn't care. The moon didn't give a flying fudge. I was the loneliest boy that had ever walked the surface of this crappy, crappy planet, all because you wouldn't leave me alone.

That night, I slept at the bottom of the bed near your feet, like I was your obedient pet.[76]

In my dreams, I ran away. You tried to follow me, so I threw down marbles as an obstacle to you. You were able to jump over them, so I rolled boulders behind me. You were able to jump over those, too. So I ran across a highway,[77] dodged cars zooming 99 miles an hour from the left, hopped over the median, dodged cars zooming 199 miles an hour from the right, and avoided certain death by millimeters at least 299 times. When I got to the grass on the other side, I could

---

76. "Sit! Stay! Don't run away! Who's a good boy?"

77. Why? To get to the other side, of course.

feel your eyeballs like laser beams on the back of my head. I could feel your brain trying to get into mine across 8 lanes of traffic.

My body wanted to turn around to look back, but I wouldn't let it. I put my hand on the handle of the sliding door, pulled it open, climbed over the railing, ran across the grass, ducked through the gap in the bushes, and was gone. I didn't look back even once. Not when I went through the door. Not when I reached the top of the railing. Not before I ducked through the gap in the branches and leaves. Not even once.

In my dream, I got away. But that doesn't count for nothing. Absolutely nothing.

When we woke up, it was the next day. I had never slept that much in my life. I felt like I was in a daze. Where was the sliding door? Where were the 8 lanes of traffic? Why were we still together? Nothing made sense.

Sleeping for 87 hours had made you as fresh as a daisy. You were talking up a storm and getting ready for the day. You straightened my clothes and brushed my teeth for me, making me spit my foamy, minty spit into the toilet-sink. I was an undead zombie. You were like Mary Poppins after 37 coffees. I was in a brand new circle of heck. You marched us downstairs for the next inevitably terrible thing that was about to happen.

When we got outside, I could tell it wasn't even morning. It looked like afternoon. I felt completely lost.

"You choose," you said once we were outside near where the taxi dropped us off.

I shook my head.

"What would be fun?"

"Nothing."

"Don't be silly. If you could choose anything fun, what would you want to do?"

"Watch TV."

"We can't watch TV, Dear. We're on vacation."

"We're not on vacation. I'm running away."

"Running away is dreary stuff, so we should distract ourselves with something fun."

I looked at my relatively new shoes. They were already gross and disgusting, like I was a tap-dancer at a pig farm.

"No need to decide now. We'll just head out and see what happens. Life is best when it's got a bit of improvisation to it. It's the sprinkles on the cookie of life."

"I hate sprinkles. And I hate this."

"Then we'll just stand here. That's fine with me. It's a nice spot." You folded your arms through the handles of your purse and looked up at the old building next to the hotel. The building had a faded painting of an ad for some laundry soap that doesn't exist anymore—probably because it was terrible at making stuff cleaner.[78]

"This is dumb."

"Then you should do something about it. Lead the way."

"But then you'll win."

"It's not about winning and losing."

"Everything is about winning and losing."

"I don't think that's true at all. Not at all."

"Yes, it is," I said.

"I think that's just something people tell themselves to justify bad behavior," you said.

"You're trying to win right now. You're always trying to win when we talk. So you just proved yourself wrong."

"Are you calling me a hypocrite?"

"You are a faker and a liar."

"Are you saying the lady with fake hair and fake teeth is a liar? I'm outraged," you said without an ounce of outrage.

"You keep proving yourself wrong."

"OK. I admit I'm trying to win this debate, but that doesn't mean everything is about winning and losing. There are lots of things in the world that aren't about that."

"No there aren't."

"What about love?"

"I knew you would say that."

"Did you?"

"Yes, and that's the dumbest thing you could have said. Love is all about winning and losing. Everyone knows that."

"Do they?"

"Yes. The only people who don't know are people who still believe in kid stuff like Santa Claus and the Easter Bunny." Then I added, "And ghosts."

"You've got me there. I very much believe in ghosts. Don't forget I'm planning to haunt you after I'm gone," You wiggled your fingers at me while saying, "SpoooOOOOOooooky!"

---

78. It only had 1 job and couldn't even do that right. I could relate. My only job was to run away, and I
    was failing spectacularly.

I ignored you. "I'm winning."

"It appears you are. Can I try again, though?"

"You're not going to win."

"OK. You can do this, Ruth," you said to yourself. "You just need to think of anything at all that isn't about winning and losing. I can't believe I wasted my turn with that first answer. What was I thinking saying love? OK, no time to dwell on the past. I still have a chance to win."

"You're not going to win."

"Pride before the fall, Dear."

"I'm not going to fall. You're going to fall."

"Well, you have me there. Falling is what old ladies do like it's going out of style."

I started to think about wet hair but stopped myself. "You're not going to win."

"Now you're just egging me on."

I didn't know what to say, so I said what made sense. "Egg. Egg. Egg."

"That's not nice at all," you said, pretending your feelings were hurt. "It's not nice to egg someone on."

"Egg. Egg. Egg."

"That's it. I'm going to say it."

"Say it."

"I will."

"Say it!"

"It's more dramatic if I wait a bit longer and really   stretch   this out."

"This is getting boring."

"OK. Here it is! I'm about to say it! It's—. It's—. 7 puppies taking a nap on your lap."

I looked at you. My brain spun its gears 1,000,000 miles an hour looking for an answer, but all I could think of was puppies with their tongues sticking half out while they all slept in a pile of fuzziness. You had me, and that made me mad. Mad at puppies. Mad at their dumb little tongues. Mad at them taking dumb naps. But I could still win. I pointed across the street. You turned that way to look. I ran the other way down the block and around the corner. I didn't look back. I wanted to get to the next corner before you got to the 1 I had just gone around. I looked back when I got there and didn't see you. I went around that corner and ran for the third corner, then turned right again and headed back to where we started. There was a door to the restaurant on the first floor of the hotel. I went in. A sign said, "Please Seat Yourself." I did. I got into a window booth so I could watch for you. I picked up a section of the newspaper someone had left on the table and held it up in front of me, high enough to block most of my face but low enough so I could peek over the top. I waited and watched.

The waitress came over. She looked at me funny but held up her pad ready to write down my order.

"Would you like a cup of coffee to start?"

"I'm a kid." She was joking, but I didn't get it.[79]

"I can make it a decaf."

"That's coffee, too," I said, still not looking up at her. I leaned toward the window and looked for you again.

"Silly mistake. Can I get you something else, sweetie?"

"I don't have any money," I lied. I had lots of stinky money in my socks.

"I could get you an ice water with a slice of lemon in it. You could put some sugar packets in it to make it lemonade. That's free."

It sounded gross, but I shrugged a shrug that meant yes. I leaned again to take another look.

The waitress slid into the other side of the booth, sifted through the newspaper sections, pulled a page out, and handed it to me. "You'll like this better. It's the funnies. You're a little young to be reading the obituaries." She put that section back in the stack. "I'll be right back with your drink."

It took you forever to finally come around the building. You must have taken a side trip through Coeur d'Alene or Bozeman. When you got closer, I lifted the paper higher so they completely blocked my face. You walked right past my window without seeing me. You turned the corner and went back down that first sidewalk we were on when I started running. You went out of view. I got up from the booth and tried to see where you were going. The booths on that row of windows were full of people so I couldn't get a good view. There was a big potted plant behind the last booth, though, and I was able to press my face against the glass there. I could see pretty far down the sidewalk, but you weren't there. I almost tipped over the plant when I got up. A sharp stem poked me in the cheek and it hurt. I touched the spot and looked at my finger to see if I was bleeding. I rubbed the spot and went back to the booth. You were sitting there sipping my lemonade. It wasn't the fake lemonade I'd have to make myself. The waitress had given me the real stuff.

"I knew you were here," I lied, convincing only myself.

"You did, did you?"

"I won the race."

"I didn't realize we were racing."

"The prize was this lemonade." I held out my hand. You slid it over to me. I took a sip through the straw. It was too sour for me, but I didn't wince. I

---

79. I rarely got jokes. That's charming in a young person. So charming.

pretended that victory was way sweeter than it was.[80]

Y ou got a lemonade, too, and we sat there not talking to each other. I was giving you the invisible treatment again, but you didn't notice because you were reading the obituaries and shaking your head at all the horrible ways people had died.

The limping dog was outside looking in at us. I shot laser beams at it with my eyes to make it go away before you noticed it. My laser beams were apparently becoming more useless by the day because it just stood there waiting to cause trouble. I waved to make it shoo, but that caught your attention. You looked at what I was waving at, and your eyes lit up. You pulled a $5 bill out of your purse, put it on the table, slid out of the booth and left me there. It was the first time in days you hadn't pulled me along to wherever you were going. I didn't know what to do, so I just sat there.

Through the window, I saw you making kissing noises to the dog and talking to it. It took a step back for every step you took toward it. You took a step back, but it didn't take a step toward you. You took a step to the left, and it didn't take a step to its left. You scratched your un-tweezered chin and tried to think of a strategy. You looked up at the sky, started to walk away like you had lost interest, then spun around and lunged toward the dog. It escaped easily, trotted down the street, then across the street, down a block, and around a corner. You chased after it as fast as you could, but 2 veiny legs were no match for 4 furry 1s. After you went around the corner following the dog, I watched and waited. The dog didn't come back, and neither did you. I don't know how much time passed, and I tried my best not to get my hopes up. But then you sat down at the booth holding a bag of candy and taffy and other sugary things.

"I lost him. But I found an old-timey candy shop. This town is the bee's knees! Want some sweets?"

"No." I was mad you were back and even madder you were bribing me with sugar again. "Kids shouldn't take candy from strangers." I thought that would sting.

"Oh, I'm a stranger, huh?"

"Stranger danger!" I said quarter-heartedly, knowing nobody was going to save me by taking you away in cuffs.

"Well, if that's the way it is, then that just means more candy for me." You

---

put the bag of candy in your purse.

"Wait."

"What?" you asked, as if you didn't know what I wanted.

"What kind of candy did you get?"

"My, how the tables have turned! If you want any of this candy, you'll have to come down to the creepy cellar with me." You got up from the booth, shook the bag of candy at me, walked over to a cellar door out in the lobby, shook the bag of candy at me again, and then descended into the darkness. My stupid stomach wanted candy, so I followed you. The long, narrow, dark stairs led to a long, narrow, dark room with small tables on the left and a bar with spinny round stools on the right.

You were already sitting down on a stool placing an order. "He will have a Shirley Temple with 2 cherries. But what should I get? I wonder." You tapped your lips while you looked at the shelves of bottles behind him. "Do people still order Old Fashioneds?"

You had placed candy on the bar in front of the stool next to you. I grabbed it but went to a stool 3 seats down from you to punish you. I popped the candy in my desperately-in-need-of-brushing mouth and spun around on the stool, but unfortunately not fast enough to go flying off into outer space.[81]

"Yes, ma'am," the guy behind the bar said. "They are very popular nowadays, actually. Everything retro is cool. Would you like 2 cherries as well?"

"That would be lovely. I haven't had 1 in years and years, but this is a special occasion."

"What are you celebrating?" This was the taxi driver situation all over again with FRANK. You both would never, ever, ever, ever shut up, would you? I looked for a napkin to chew up and shove into my eardrums so I didn't have to listen.

"This is our first trip together, just he and I. We're running away from our regular lives, at least for a little while." You winked at me about the running away part.

"It's good to get away sometimes," said FRANK II. "It makes you appreciate home more, that's for sure." He patted the edge of the bar for emphasis. "I will be right back with your drinks"

I started getting dizzy, so I stopped spinning and looked around. The room wobbled. The spinning made me forget how mad I was at you and at everything. When the room slowed down, there was another distraction. I noticed a pile of bags and cords against the wall at the far end of the bar.

"What's that?" I said pointing to it.

You looked where I was pointing. "Bags and cords," you answered. "Here's a

---

81. In space, I wouldn't be able to hear you talk and talk and talk.

menu. Pick something. You're wasting away because of your hunger strike. You need to eat."

I wanted to ask FRANK II about the bags and cords, but he was busy putting 19 things into your complicated drink.

I ignored the menu and kept at it. "Maybe it's a bomb."

"It's not a bomb."[82]

"You don't know."

"I am deeply offended. I know plenty about bombs. I know lots of things about lots of things because I've been around the block a few times. I'm no spring chicken. I didn't just fall off the turnip truck. There are quite a few rings in this tree. And so on and so forth. I've seen plenty of bombs, and that, Munchkin, is not a bomb. It's not ticking."

"Not all bombs tick. That's only in movies."

FRANK II brought over our drinks. He set down the kid drink in front of me and the grown-up drink in front of you.

"Is that a bomb?" I asked.

"The drink?"

"No, that stuff." I pointed at the bomb.

"Oh, those. No. They belong to the musicians that are playing tonight."

"Will it be terrible music like that?" I was pointing to the speakers in the ceiling. The music they were playing made me want to tie rocks to my feet and leap in the deep, dark ocean.

"Ha! No. That's Steely Dan," he explained.

"He's terrible."[83]

You jumped in. "Ooh! Live music. My favorite. What do they play?"

"Celtic harp and fiddle," he said, and you bit your lip. You bit it hard, like people do when they want to keep themselves from saying something. FRANK Jr. pointed to your drink and said, "Let me know if it's to your liking."

You took a sip. Your eyebrows went up. You nodded.

"It's not too strong, is it?"

"I guess we'll see, won't we?"

You moved over to the stool next to me, sliding your drink down the bar like it was a slip-n-slide. You sat down and slowly spun around 360 degrees until you were facing me again. You leaned down to me until our noses touched and looked me in the eyes, first in 1 eye then in the other then the first 1 again. Your breath smelled like lozenges because that's what it always smelled like. I waited for you to say whatever you were going to say, but you didn't say a word.

---

82. Tick, tick, tick, tick, tickety, tickety tick.

83. Correction: *They* are terrible.

Instead, you put your hands on my knees and spun me around. When I came back around, you were spinning, too. We were going around in circles, circles, circles while the bomb in the corner just sat there refusing to put us out of our misery.

"W hat do you think you'll have?" you asked.

"Nothing."

You had moved us over to the table right next to where the musicians would be. Someone had come in and the bartender quietly apologized that he had to enforce the rule about no kids at the bar. The chair I was in now didn't spin. Everything was getting worse by the nanosecond.

"You need to eat something."

"I'm not hungry."

"You're probably over-hungry. Food will do you good. How is your Shirley Temple?"

I shrugged. I had eaten the 2 cherries floating on top but hadn't sipped any of it. It was a girl drink, and I thought that was dumb.

You made your thinking face while you looked at the menu, like it was the most important decision you would ever make in your life. You looked up from the menu and said to me, "I think I am going to have the fish and chips." You looked over at the bartender and asked him, "Are the fish and chips good here?" He gave you a thumbs up. You looked back at the menu, then said to me, "But the burgers sound delicious." You looked over at him again and asked, "Are the burgers good here?" He gave you another thumbs up. You looked back at me and said, "It's been so long since I've had a good burger. They are always dry in the dining room because they cook them to death to make sure nobody gets sick. After all, we wouldn't want people there dropping like flies, huh?" I was too far away for you to nudge me with your elbow, so you just nudged the air so the air knew you were being sarcastic.

He came over carrying a tray. "On the house." He put a beer next to your drink. "In honor of your special occasion. Our stout goes great with Old Fashioneds and with the fish and chips."

"I will definitely get that, then. Fish and chips for me, please."

He nodded and turned to me. "These are for you. He put down a stack of the cardboard beer coasters. It was a teetering tower of at least 20 of them. Then he pulled a black marker out of his apron pocket and drew on a coaster. On it there was a picture of a man holding a mug and smiling like he just won the lottery. He drew a huge moustache on him, spiky hair, and a prom gown. Then he handed me the marker, took the barely touched Shirley Temple, and replaced it with a glass of Sprite and a separate glass full of maraschino cherries. "The tater tots here are excellent. I highly recommend them." He placed his pen against the little pad awaiting my momentous decision.

I shrugged.

He took that as a yes. He picked up both menus but didn't walk away. He leaned down and whispered in my ear, "I know it's no fun when you're stuck doing what other people want to do. Your grandmother loves you and wants you to have fun. Hang in there." He patted me on the shoulder, then went over to the computer screen to type in our orders.

You looked at me and smiled. I fiddled with a coaster. You kept looking at me, waiting for something. "You want to know what he said. Don't you?"

"No, that's none of my business . . . unless you want to tell me."

"He said I should try to have fun."

"Oh, he did, did he?" You nodded your head like someone had just told you the most profound thing in the history of things. "What's fun for you?" you asked.

"Watching TV," I said without looking up. "And eating candy." I held out my hand.

You pulled a treat from your purse, put it in my grubby little hand and asked, "What else?"

"Nothing."

You gave me a chance to say more, but I didn't, so you talked. "I like dancing, but I can't anymore. I haven't danced in years and years. I would probably break a hip if I tried, so my dancing days are over."

"I don't want to be old."

"You and me both."

"Being a kid is worse."

"Worse than being old and decrepit and almost a ghost?"

"Way worse."

"How so?"

"Being a grown-up is way better. Even if you're super old and gross and things are falling off your body every day, you can still do whatever you want."

"I can, huh?"

"Yes. You're a grown-up." I gave you a look like you were an idiot.

"If that's true, why is this the first time I've left the home in who knows how long?"

I shrugged.

"I don't know either."

"You can do anything you want."

"I never looked at it that way. You've given me a lot to think about. But more importantly, I need to congratulate you. I think you won this conversation." You reached over and offered your hand.

I thought it was some kind of trick, but you waited and waited until I finally held out my hand. It was the wrong hand. You reached for my other hand and shook it firmly. I was worried that was all a setup for a trap or a trick, so I squinted at you waiting for what you would do next. You tapped on the table while you hummed something. You watched FRANK dry some glasses. You took a sip of the beer. It gave you a foam moustache. You pointed at your lips, then down at the big moustache the bartender had drawn on the man on the coaster. You wiped it off. You smiled at me and tapped a bit more. Then you did it. You took the Queen of Spades out of your cards and laid it down—you reached across the table, put your hand on mine, and said, "I've been meaning to tell you. Thank you for letting me come with you. You could have escaped 100 times today if you wanted to. You could have disappeared out the sliding door 1,001 times over the past few weeks, months, however long it's been. But you don't really want to. We both know that." You winked, made a kissing noise at me, and turned to watch the musicians set up.

What you said made me lose control of my body. I burped and farted and my arm spasmed away from my body and knocked over the glass of cherries—all while I stared at you with horror-soaked confusion.

I was deathly afraid you were right.

I wanted to stop thinking about what you had said, so I started making baseball cards while you put the cherries back in the glass. I flipped over a coaster to the blank side, drew a rectangle in the center, and then drew the best picture I could of Kenji Johjima. He was wearing his catcher's mask and pads and was about to throw the ball. It wasn't a great picture, but I had never tried to draw a baseball player before. I wrote his name in block letters underneath the picture. Since there wasn't room on the other side of the coaster to put his statistics there, I wrote them in a ring around the drawing. I wrote that he bats and throws right-handed. I wrote that he was born in Sasebo, Japan. I wrote that he hit 18 home runs and batted .291 his first year.[84] I squeezed a few more numbers into the empty space, then picked it up and blew on it to help it dry.

A musician came in the door next to the bags and wires that weren't a bomb

---

84. Kenji only hit 1 triple in his career. That is only interesting to me.

and started unpacking the equipment. He was tall and had a long beard like he had been living in the woods since Griffey's rookie year. I slid the wire basket with the salt and pepper and ketchup and malt vinegar and real sugar and fake sugar over to the wall, took out a sugar packet, folded 2 of the corners down so it looked a little like a home plate, and placed that on the table. I put Kenji behind it ready to throw out anyone who tried to steal second.

I decided I would draw a pitcher next. The man unpacking the bags was making a lot of noise and it was hard to think. I had looked at Rafael Novoa's rookie prospect card that week, so that popped into my head. I couldn't think of anyone else, so I drew a picture of him standing on the mound ready to go into his windup. First, I drew the ball in his right hand, but that was a mistake, so I drew a ball in his left hand and covered up the original ball with a drawing of his glove. I could still see the outline of the ball underneath the glove, so I darkened the glove with more marker ink until that part of the cardboard was saturated and mushy. I wrote his name under the picture, then put his stats in the margins. I wrote he was 6 feet tall and born in New York City. I wrote he pitched in 7 games after he came up to the Giants in 1990 and struck out 14 people.[85] The food came, but I stayed focused on the card. I wrote down he got 1 save that year and had an ERA of 6.75. I tasted blood. I was chewing on my tongue while I was concentrating and broke the skin. I ate a tater tot to change the taste in my mouth, and the salt burned.

When I was done, I blew on the coaster and put Rafael a few inches away from home plate facing Kenji.[86] I looked over and there were 2 musicians now. I hadn't noticed the other musician come in. It was a lady, not another beard guy. She was setting up her harp. It was huge. It was taller than her and looked heavier than her. It looked impossible that someone as small as her could carry something that big. Maybe she was as strong as ants. I read they were so strong it would be like a person carrying a car or a truck (or a harp).

I set down 3 unfolded sugar packets for the bases, flipped over another coaster, and started drawing Carlos Baerga. He would play third base.[87] I got half-way through the drawing but messed it up and decided to start over. I ate another tater tot. It was cold by then. Your plate was empty, and your beer glass was too. The musicians were all set up. The harp lady was tuning the harp, and you were turned sideways toward her, leaning forward so far you could have reached out and touched the harp if you wanted to. The beard guy was sitting

---

85. Rafael only threw 1 wild pitch in his career. That is also only interesting to me.

86. They never played together in the majors, but I could do what I wanted. I could make Babe Ruth play third base if I wanted to.

87. Not the ghost of Babe Ruth.

down on a stool holding a fiddle and sipping a drink. I looked over at the bar and almost all the seats were taken now. The tables along the wall behind us were mostly full too. When I saw how full the place had gotten, I noticed the noise. It was loud. Everyone was talking loudly trying to be heard over the rest of the noise.

My brain tuned out the noise so I could draw the rest of my team. Tony Phillips would play shortstop. I drew a picture of him in his A's uniform scooping up a groundball. I spent a while drawing the edge of the grass behind him and putting texture in the infield dirt around his feet where his cleats would dig in. I wrote he was from Arizona, but I couldn't remember the city, so I left that out. I wrote down he had 4 homeruns in 1983 and 1984 and 1985 and 1989. I wrote he had 76 walks in 1986 and 76 strikeouts in 1987. I set Phillips down in between Baerga and second base.

I noticed all the noise again. I picked up another coaster to make it go away, but someone started hitting their glass with a fork and it quieted down. The harp lady said who they were, but her mouth was very close to the microphone. I couldn't understand what she said. Beardface waved when she said whatever his name was, then finished his drink in a giant gulp. The next thing she said started with, "This first song . . . " but all I could make out after that were words like "ship" and "drown" and "grave." She stopped talking, put her hands on the strings, and nodded to the guy. He counted a few beats with his foot and they started. The song was about a man who was on a ship that was hit by a cannonball and sunk. He drowned but they couldn't find his body, so his family made a grave for him but left it empty. It sounded like an old song from back when everyone went everywhere by ship and drowned in the ocean left and right. I was hoping it would get scary with the dead man coming back as a ghost or zombie and seeking revenge, but it didn't. Lame.

The song must have activated my hunger because I suddenly wanted a grilled cheese sandwich more than any food I've ever wanted. You were sitting there hypnotized by the music, so I went to the bar, waved at FRANK II, and asked for a grilled cheese sandwich. He gave me a thumbs up and started pressing buttons on his computer screen. I turned around to go back to our table and what I saw was you leaning back away from the harp, frozen, your head half-turned away from it like it was a light that was too bright to look at directly. Your hands were clasped on your lap like you were at church, but pressing down hard, and a shiny wet line ran down your cheek to the wrinkly loose skin on your neck. It looked like someone had pressed pause on you, but the music was still playing.

W hen the song ended, you unclasped your hands and clapped the loudest claps in the bar. The harp lady nodded to you and said something about the next song into the microphone, but I didn't understand what she said. I could only focus on the wetness in your eyes and on your cheeks and on your neck. I wanted it to go away. I never, ever, ever wanted to see that again. I didn't know why I felt that way. I just did.

You leaned forward, close enough to help pluck the strings. The violin guy tapped his foot a few times and they started a new song where everyone would probably be dead by the end. I couldn't watch any more. I turned my chair sideways so my back was to the musicians and you. I pressed the chewed wads of napkin deeper into my ears, closed my eyes, and my brain pressed play on the last 3 innings of the Mariners game we had watched before this terrible trip started. It was working. I was at SafeCo field, not at a hotel with no TVs. I was 210 miles away, and Ichiro was in the batter's circle. But then you tapped on my shoulder.

I gave you a dirty look, but then noticed the music was over. I pulled the napkin wads out of my ears. "Are they finally done?"

"Intermission. How's your food?"

The grilled cheese sandwich was sitting there. I didn't know they had brought it. I ripped off a bit of the cheese oozing out of the side. It was cold.

You asked me, "Do you like the music?"

"It's boring songs about boring dead people."

"Yes, it's that kind of music. You stay here and keep up the good work on your art. I'm going to go talk to the musicians for a bit."

I re-chewed the napkin wads to get them wet again and shoved them back in my ears. But I didn't go back to drawing right away. I watched you go over to where the musicians were standing. You held out your hand to introduce yourself. I tried to read your lips but didn't know how to do that. It looks easy in movies, but it isn't in real life.[88]

The musicians went back to the area behind the microphones where their bags and cases that possibly contained a bomb were. You followed them. The man picked up his violin and showed it to you. He showed you the front, then flipped it over and showed you the back. You pointed to the bow and said something. He handed it to you, and you ran your fingers along the part that rubs against the strings. The man reached down and got something out of the bags. It was a small piece of cloth. He held the fiddle out to you. You shook your head no, then waved your hands no. The lady put her hand on your shoulder and said something to you. The man placed the instrument in your hand and placed the cloth on the spot where your chin goes. You looked over your shoulder at me, looked back at them, and started playing. I pulled a wad out to hear. It was

---

88. Nothing's easy in real life. Not a single thing.

"Twinkle, Twinkle, Little Star," but you stopped after only playing a little bit, shook your head, and tried to hand the violin back to the man. He put his hands up refusing to take it.

You put the fiddle back up under your chin, put the bow on the strings, took it off, put it back on the strings in a different position, and started playing again. It took me a few notes to figure out it was "Silent Night." The bar got quieter. You went through half the song, and the harp lady put her hand on your bowing arm and whispered something in your ear. She sat down at the harp and got ready. The violin guy clinked his glass with a fork, and the bar got even quieter. You started to play, and everyone was focused on you and listening—everyone except for 1 table of people who were still making noise. They were blabbering about stupid stuff and thumb-typing on their phones and making a racket with their dishes and their forks and their glasses and their stupid-ness.

I stared at them, trying to send laser beams into their tiny brains to shut up, but it didn't work. I started to shake. I shook more. I got up, walked back to their table, and stood in front of them. I waited for them to see me. My lips were pressed together so hard the muscles in my face shook. My arms vibrated. My hands vibrated. I tasted blood. 1 of the women was the first to notice me. She looked at me and saw what was in my hands. Her face changed. She tapped the shoulder of the man next to her and pointed. He looked up from his phone and down at my hands, full of tater tots, dripping with ketchup. He tapped the other 2. All of them were looking at me now, at my vibrating face and then at my vibrating hands. I whisper-hissed at them: "Be. Quiet." I raised my tater-filled hands a couple of inches to make it clear I wasn't just holding all that food for the heck of it. I was squeezing the tots so tightly, blood-red ropes of potato-and-tomato goop were extruding from between my fingers like they were a furious Play-Doh Fun Factory.

I turned and watched you play the rest of the song. Everyone did.

After you finished your song, everyone clapped. Even the terrible people. I unclenched my fists and felt like I was going to pass out. I ran out of the room and found the bathrooms behind the stairs. The walls were filled with more old photos of people who were all dead by now. I went into the bathroom, was confused there weren't any urinals, left, and went into the other 1. That 1 had urinals and it smelled like 1000 men had taken the biggest pees of their lives. I went into the stall and latched the door. Someone had forgotten to flush. I pushed the handle to flush, but it didn't work. I tried again and then gave up. I sat on the seat, with the smell of poop and ketchup all around me. I pressed my hands into the sides of my head to try to squeeze all the thoughts and feelings out of my tiny head. I couldn't. I kept thinking about what you had said about how I could have gotten away 1,000,000 times if I really wanted to. I thought about how you said I didn't really want to run away. I thought about how I worried you were dead when you raced me up the stairs. I almost threw tater tots at those jerks because they were rude to you. Why did I keep doing that when I hated you so much? Why couldn't I run away? Why did I keep doing the opposite of what I really wanted to do? I wanted my brain to turn off in the worst way. Pressing on the sides of my head wasn't working, so I pressed on my eyes like the night before. Maybe I could get all the way into my brain this time. The ketchup stung. I pressed and strained. The ketchup burned. It was working. It was working.

Hot.
Sweat.
Stars.
Black.
Blacker.
Blackest.

I don't have any of the coasters I turned into baseball players that night, but here's a cartoon bird on a cartoon tree.

Maybe this is where I went when I pressed my eyeballs back into my brain to try to not feel what I was feeling.

"You're awake! You slept a long time, Dear."

I was confused about where I was, who you were, and who I was. I looked around as slowly as a head could turn. My eyes were blurry, but I could see we were in the hotel room. It was bright outside, so bright a sharp pain went to the center of my brain. I closed my eyes, which made it worse.

"You put quite a scare into me last night," you said. "I couldn't find you, but then a man went into the bathroom and there you were. You passed out from being too hungry! I told you you weren't eating enough. You had me worried sick. You look much better today, though. Much better."

I needed to pee more than I've ever had to pee. I scrambled off the bed, almost fell over, staggered to the sink, and started peeing a colossal stream of fire. The hot splatters hit my feet, my arms and my face. "Wait! That's a sink, Sweetie. Not a—" But it was too late. You let me finish, then ran water in the sink. "You're clearly in a daze. We need to get you 100 CCs of food, stat. This is a blood sugar emergency. Put on some pants and shoes, and let's head downstairs."

I followed you like a zombie. You asked the lady at the restaurant if they were still serving breakfast. She said they had just switched over to lunch. "Time flies when you're having fun!" you said to the boy next to you who could barely focus his eyes. The lady told you they didn't have any open tables, so you ordered burgers and fries and sodas to go and told her we would wait outside on the sidewalk bench.

Outside, you talked and talked while we were waiting for the food, but I stared straight ahead like I had a head injury and had lost the ability to speak. Everything was blurry. Even the waitress was blurry when she brought out our blurry food in blurry plastic containers filled with steam.

You took a big bite of your cheeseburger like you hadn't eaten in a week. I just stared at the street. You put a fry in my mouth, but it just hung from between my lips for a second like a cigarette before falling onto my lap. You took another big bite like you hadn't eaten in 9 years. You chewed and chewed, making the grossest noises in the history of noises. Then you stopped. It was back. That stupid dog.

It was sitting 10 feet from you on the sidewalk, looking at your food, then your face, then your food. It was drooling like a faucet. You ripped off a piece of the burger and lowered it down toward the ground, hiding it in your hand. The dog took a couple of steps toward you. You opened your hand and showed it the food. It took 2 more steps forward and sat down. You made a kissing noise and lowered your food hand a little more. The dog took the last couple of steps, sniffed the food, and started reaching for it. You grabbed for its collar with your nonfood hand as quickly as you could, but the dog was faster. It swiped the cheeseburger chunk from your hand and then lunged to the left. You saw the patch of red.

"It's bleeding," you said. "Near its back leg on that side."

I didn't say anything.

"I think it's blood."

I didn't say anything.

"It's definitely blood."

The dog backed up to its original distance, sat down and waited for you to give it more food. You got up from the bench, put a piece of cheeseburger down near your feet, and got ready. The dog crept closer but stopped. It was looking up at you. You were looking down at it. You nudged the food with your toe. The dog was too fast. It swiped the food and lunged to the right. You tried to grab where it had been rather than where it was going.

"I'm going to get him this time," you said, then ripped off another piece of your cheeseburger. You stretched your legs and rotated your arms in circles like you were warming up for a track meet. You put the cheeseburger chunk on the ground and squatted down ready to grab the dog whether it went left or right. It took 2 small steps forward, sat down, then took 2 smaller steps forward, but it didn't come any closer.

"Here you go, boy. Yummy, yummy meat and cheese," you said and made a kissing noise.

The dog wouldn't budge.

"Yummy, yummy," you said and leaned forward to try to grab it where it was. That spooked the dog, and it started trotting away from you.

"No, no. We won't hurt you. We're going to help you." You reached for me and grabbed my arm to come with you. The container of food fell off my lap and spilled all over the sidewalk. The dog had stopped up ahead and was looking back over its shoulder at us. I blinked and blinked. When we got within 20 feet of it, the dog started going again. It went all the way to the railroad tracks, turned onto them and walked down the middle of the rails keeping its paws on the wooden ties rather than the rocks in between.

You kept making kissing noises and promising it food whenever it turned to look, but it kept going right down the middle of the tracks to where it was all industrial buildings. You weren't pulling my hand anymore, and my legs weren't doing the walking. I was floating behind you, tied by a wire I didn't know how to cut.

You were slowing down from the long walk. The dog didn't slow down. It got farther ahead of us, 50 feet, 100 feet, more, until it was around the bend and out of sight. You stopped to rub your calves. I rubbed my eyes. 1 of them was starting to see better, maybe. The other was seeing worse.

"He's right up there," you said motioning toward where the dog went. I followed you. And I watched myself follow you. I could see it all from behind myself. And I could see myself watching myself from above that.

"He's right around this bend," you said. And you were right. I closed my bad eye to see better. The dog was there, waiting patiently for us next to a boy who was sitting on the rails. He looked a little older than me, or maybe the same age. He was bigger, or maybe the same size. He was throwing rocks at nothing in particular. I wish we had never met him. Stupid kid. Stupid dog.

"**M**y name is Ruth." Both of my eyes were suddenly clear. Your hand reaching out to him was sharper than the sharpest 3D. "Rhymes with truth. And tooth. And John Wilkes Booth."

He ignored your hand and threw another rock. I could see the air vibrate as the rock sailed through it. The dog sniffed your purse, smelling the candy. I saw every whisker on its nose wiggle as it sniffed. Everything was so clear that it hurt to look at it. I backed up from where you and the boy were. Then I backed up some more.

You leaned down, put your hand on the rail and eased yourself down into a sitting position. "Oh my, this is cold," you said and adjusted how you were sitting.

He didn't say anything. You looked at me and raised an eyebrow. You tapped your fingers on your leg like you were playing piano, then held a finger in the air and made a face like you had an idea. You fussed around inside your purse, pulled a piece of candy out of the bag, and offered it to him. He shoved it into his face hole. He may not have taken the wrapper off first.

You tossed 1 to me, but my hands were in my pockets, and I couldn't get them out in time. It bounced off me and landed on the ground. I didn't pick it up. He put his piece inside his toothy mouth and looked at me. I looked away.

"What's your dog's name?" you asked.

He shook his head and grunted something.

"Bob?" you asked.

He pushed the wad of taffy to the side of his mouth so it was a lump in his cheek. "Not my dog."

"He sure acts like your dog."

The boy shrugged and picked at a glob of candy stuck in his greasy teeth with his greasier finger.

"What is a boy like you doing out here in a place like this?" you asked him.

"Throwing rocks," he said, and did.

"Can I throw some too?"

He shrugged again.

"What are you aiming for?" you asked him.

He pointed to a piece of twisted metal against a fence. You picked up a rock, threw it, and didn't come close. You looked at me and smiled, then rotated your arm in a circle to warm it up for the next throw. He picked up another rock and hit it. The sound of the metal echoed off the wall of the warehouse behind us.

"I always wanted a dog when I was a little girl."

"Take it," he said. "It's not mine."

"Thank you, but I can't. The place where I live doesn't allow pets. Only people. Usually only really old people." You winked at me.

"That place sounds terrible." He threw another rock but missed.

"Do they allow pets where you live?"

He shrugged.

"Do you live around here?"

He shrugged.

"Did you ride here on your bike?"

He looked around. "What bike?"

"Any bike."

"I don't have a bike."

"That's a shame. Every kid should have a bike. I got my first 1 when I was 5. It was a hand-me-down from my cousin. I wanted a shiny new, red bike with tassels on the handlebars and a bell that went ding-ding-ding, but I got a beat-up blue wreck of a bike with a missing back fender so it always threw mud up the back of my clothes."[89]

He dug around in his ear with his finger for a long time and then smelled his fingertip. He didn't answer you.

"Hey, I just had an idea," you said, but didn't say what it was. You paused for him to look at you, but he didn't. "You should join us for a very late lunch slash very early dinner. Our food has probably been gobbled up by an enterprising pup, so we need to get something else to eat. Do you like pizza? Or hot dogs?"

"Nuggets."

"What?"

"Nuggets."

You looked at me for a translation.

"Chicken nuggets," I explained. My voice croaked like I hadn't spoken since the hotel was built.

"Oh, those are delicious. That's a great idea for lunch." You groaned as you stood up from the track. "Where's your favorite place to get those?"

He shrugged and threw a rock. I didn't hear it hit anything. Maybe it floated away. Maybe I was floating away.

He grunted, "McDonald's," without looking at you.

"Of course! They have the best nuggets for sure." You picked up a small,

---

89. Maybe this memory book should have a subtitle about how life can be full of disappointments. "It Also Rhymes with Disillusioned."

round rock the color of a dried dog turd that'd been sitting in the sun so long the flies don't even bother with it anymore. "I was having a craving for chicken nuggets before you even mentioned them. What a coincidence! It's like we were meant to meet. It's like this was all meant to happen." I was too busy hating every atom in his body to debate your view of fate, fortune, destiny and whether any of the broken people in the world truly have free will or just the self-delusion that they aren't on a set of immovable tracks with a predetermined destination.

He looked at me, chewing with his mouth hole. I looked away again.

"Before we go, I'm going to try 1 more time. I have a good feeling about this," you said and threw the turd-colored rock at the target.

You were off by a mile.

Off by 37,000,000 miles.

If you stare at this baby bird long enough, will it get the worm?

If I stare at the Mariners long enough, will they not collapse in September?

Also: Do you like my drawing of wiggly squiggles? The baby bird sure doesn't. It hates those squiggles as much as I hate the Yankees and Angels.

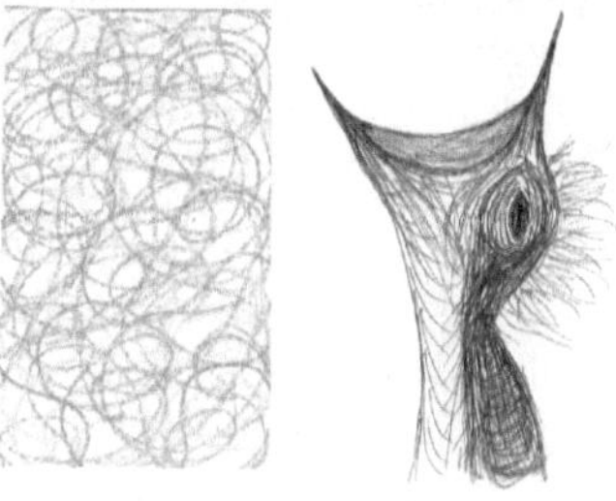

We walked back to the hotel and the person at the front desk called someone on a walkie talkie to drive us to the McDonald's. It was apparently too far for an old lady with a huge smile and 2 identically-annoyed-looking boys to go by foot.

You stared up at the menu and asked me what I wanted. I said I wasn't hungry, so you ordered the same for all of us: 3 boxes of chicken nuggets, 3 orders of fries and 3 milks. At the table, I pushed my food away. Within 6.66 seconds, he had finished his and started grabbing at mine.

"Why don't you show him your baseball cards?" you said to me, then asked him, "Do you like baseball?"

I didn't want to get them out, but you made a face at me to be friendlier to our charming guest. I pulled a rubber-banded stack out of my pocket, held it down below the table, and flipped through it to check if any of my favorites were in it. I pulled out my new Ichiro card, put that back in my pocket, put the rest on the table, looked at you, and slid it over toward the boy.

"You should look at some of the older cards. People had funny haircuts back then," you said to him.[90]

He picked up the top card with his greasy hand, looked at the front, turned it over and looked at the back. He put it down next to the pile. He picked up the next card and looked at it. "Do you have any Pokémon cards?"

I shook my head.

"Do you have any Yu-Gi-Oh! cards?"

I shook my head.

"You should get some," he said and didn't look at more baseball cards.

You mouthed something at me, but I didn't even try to read your lips. I was too busy trying to imagine how many nuggets it would take to make him choke. Maybe just 1 if I pushed it down, down, down his throat far enough. I don't remember picking up a nugget, but there it was in my hand ready to go. I put it down, though, and picked up my cards instead. I wiped ketchup and oily fingerprints off the 2 cards he had picked up, put the rubber band back around them, and slid them back in my pocket. I thought about kicking him in the crotch. He was right across from me, and my leg could probably reach perfectly to really nail him. To be polite, I would say it was an accident. You always like it when I'm polite.[91]

I didn't kick him, though. I kept my feet and my hands to myself and just asked, "Can I go look at the video machine?" I pointed back toward the red vending machine. You nodded. I got up out of the booth, went to the machine, and started pressing the screen. I scrolled through the list of movies to rent. There were a few kid movies, but not many. I finished the list, went back to the main menu, and started looking through the list of movies again without really looking at what was on the screen.

---

90. And funny beards and moustaches and more beards and more moustaches.

91. Which is as infrequent as a comet that hits the Earth and puts an end to everything. Stupid comets, always missing this planet.

I felt your hand on my shoulder and looked at it. "Thank you for being so patient, Dear. He needs help, and we're just the people to help him, aren't we?" Were we? I looked back at him. He was dipping his finger into the ketchup and licking it off. I felt nauseous. "When you're ready, come on back and we'll head to the hotel."[92]

You went back to the booth and offered him a napkin for his hands. I looked through the list of movies again. I was amazed at how many horror movies there were, but maybe I shouldn't have been. People love them. They love being scared of things that could never ever happen because it distracts them from the even-worse things that will definitely, without-a-doubt happen to them.

Back at the hotel we sat in a room off the lobby. You shuffled cards and asked him, "What about Crazy 8s?"

He didn't answer.

"What about Hearts?"

He didn't answer.

"What card games do you know?"

He shrugged. I wanted this to be over, so I announced we would play Go Fish.

"Okie-fenokee-dokey," you said and dealt the cards. I couldn't hold them all in my hands, so I turned around in my chair and laid my cards down, blocking them with my body so you both couldn't see. He picked up his cards but didn't organize them at all.

2 people came into the lobby near where we were sitting. The husband talked to the person at the front desk, and the wife looked at us. Moms always looked at me. I was a magnet for their eyeballs. It made me want to be invisible. I looked back at my cards, but I knew she was still looking at me.

"You go first," you said to him.

"Kings," he said like he was in a hostage video.

"Are you asking me or him?"

He shrugged.

"No, I don't have any kings. Go fish."

He picked up a card from the pile.

I looked at you. Your wig had slid up a little and I could see the edge of your

---

92. To quote a smart man with a bag full of ancient lollipops: "Ruth, where is this going? What's your plan?"

real hair, which looked grey, white and brown at the same time. I looked at the
jagged edge of your eyeliner. I looked at the mole on your neck with the 2 hairs
growing out of it. Your fake pearl necklace pressed into the thin skin along your
collarbone. It looked like it would rip if anybody or anything tugged at it. The
necklace. And your skin. Both. Even the littlest thing would tear either of them
to pieces.

You were looking at him and looking at him.

"Your turn," I said to snap you out of it.

"Ummmmmm," you said slowly as if there were 100 cards to pick from
instead of 7. "Do you have any 3s?"

I asked: "Who? Me or him?"

With a steady pace of candy as lures, you got us from the lobby area up
into the room.

"Home sweet home," you said after you closed the door behind us.

"Is that where people pee?" he asked, pointing at the sink.

"No, that's just a sink," you answered while looking at me and raising an eyebrow. "There are shared bathrooms out there. It's old fashioned and charming.
Follow me." You led him out of the room. The door closed behind you and it
was silent. I closed my eyes and felt my belly go in and out as I breathed. It was
too, too fast. I tried to imagine a world with none of this. None of it.

You knocked on the door to get back in. I waited a couple of seconds to open
it to give you something to think about. Maybe I had split. Bolted. Skedaddled.
Hopped on a raft to float down river. But I hadn't. When I opened the door, it
was just you. I was confused. You said, "He'll be back in a sec," and sat down at
the edge of the bed. "Good deeds," you said. "Good deeds in someone's time of
need." You smiled like you had just won bingo.

He knocked. You pointed to the door. I opened it. He stepped into the
doorway, stood next to me, and said, "I want to go back." He wasn't talking

about the bathroom. It hung there in the air like a poisonous fart. Your bingo grin was gone. You stared at him like he was speaking whatever they speak on Neptune.

"What? Where?" you asked.

"Back."

"Did you forget something there?" It didn't make any sense to you at all. Not a bit of sense.

He blinked twice and then left. You followed him down the stairs, through the lobby, and out onto the sidewalk, talking a mile a minute.

You said, "There's a really good movie on TV tonight with robots and aliens. I saw the commercial for it. You don't want to miss it. Let's go back."

And you said, "Have you ever had room service? They bring ice cream right to your room. We should do that."

And you said, "It's getting chilly out here. We should go back to the hotel where it's warm."

I floated behind you. You said 100 things to turn him around, but he just kept walking, up the street, then onto the railroad tracks, only stepping on the wooden ties. You were right behind him, pleading your case. I was right behind you.

We went around the bend to the place where the warehouses were. Then he stopped and sat down on the tracks. He looked down at the rocks and fiddled with them. You were breathing heavily and pressing your right hand into your hip, digging in where something didn't feel right after walking so far so quickly.

"Come back to the hotel with us, dear."

He picked up a rock and threw it against the fence running alongside the tracks. I reached down and picked up a rock, too. It was disc-shaped and as big as my palm. I squeezed it in my hand, then loosened my grip, then squeezed it again. The sharp edges pressed into my skin and made dents that hurt.

"This is silly. There's a comfy bed and hot food for you there."

He picked at the rocks between his feet. You braced your hand on your left knee and kneeled to get down closer to him.

"I know it's probably hard for you to trust anyone. I understand. Believe me. I'm just asking you to come back for a while. Just for tonight. That's all. What do you say?"

He threw another rock. It hit the fence, but it made a sickly cracking noise like it had hit bone. He said, "More candy."

Your face changed like you had another eureka. "Of course, dear." You stood up, pulled your purse off your shoulder, and started digging through the 37,000,000 things in there. "A piece of candy is a great idea. A spoonful of sugar, as they say." You pulled the candy bag out of your purse and took out 2 pieces. You gestured to me that 1 would be mine. You held the second candy out to him. He put his fingers on it, but you didn't let go of it right away. "Let's head back while we enjoy the treat."

He looked at you with his hand on the candy. He didn't say anything, and I didn't see him nod or even blink, but you let go of the candy and let him have it. He unwrapped it and put it in his mouth. He said something, but it was garbled because of the mouthful of taffy. He held out his hand.

"What?" you asked.

He swallowed the cheekful of candy in an exaggerated gulp and wiped the drool off the corners of his mouth with his sleeve. "More."

"They are delicious, aren't they? That's a down payment. You can have another when we get back to the room, OK?"

"More."

"When we get back at the hotel, dear."

He reached into your purse and took hold of the candy bag with both hands. You grabbed the bag to stop him.

"No need to be rough. You can have another piece shortly." You tried pulling the candy bag closer to you, but he was stronger than you expected. I gripped and regripped the rock in my hand. You dislodged 1 of his hands, but he grabbed a different part of the bag and pulled harder, making you lean way forward before you rebalanced yourself. He took 1 of his hands off the bag, swung, and slapped your mouth. You let go of the bag. You ran your fingers along your lips and then inside your mouth. Your teeth were pink.

He pulled a piece of candy out of the bag, unwrapped it, and swallowed it without chewing. He held the bag in his arms like it was a football. I gripped and regripped the rock in my hand.

"That, too," he said, pointing at the only piece of candy he didn't have. The piece in your hand. The piece for me. He reached for it and locked his hand with yours, trying to pry open your fingers. You squeezed the candy tighter. He tried harder to get it. You tried harder to not let him get it. The 2 of you leaned back and forth like it was a tug of war. He lifted his right arm, fist near his ear. You didn't do anything to block it. You looked at me instead. You were staring deep into my brain when he did it. Deep into the center of my broken little brain.

The last piece of candy fell and disappeared into the rocks. You bent down, but not to look for it. You covered your face with your hands. He fished the candy out from where it had fallen. You staggered backward, still bent forward. He unwrapped the taffy, started to chew it, made a face, then spit it out. He pulled a different piece out of the bag, put that in his mouth, and walked away down the tracks. You reached down for the ground, trying to find it with your shaking hand. You lowered yourself onto all 4s and bled.

I just stood there.

I could hear the ocean, like I had seashells up against both of my ears. You were probably making noises, but everything was waves and wind and seagulls looking for gross things to eat. The rock dropped out of my hand and the ocean noises stopped. I had forgotten I was holding it. I should have thrown it at him after he hit you the first time, when he had just bloodied your lip. I could have done it then. Or I could have done it before he put his fist up beside his ear. Or I could have done it after his fist was up but before it started zooming toward you. I have good aim and I throw fast. Not Ichiro-fast, but fast enough. The rock would have cut through the air like a rocket going 777 miles an hour and hit him right in his dumb, nugget-loving face. But I didn't.

It was just the 2 of us. He was gone with his stolen candy. The ketchup-covered dog was still nowhere to be seen—probably off scamming some other dummies for burgers and fries. I came around to the front of you. I said your name. You didn't say anything or even move. You were still looking down. I pushed on your forehead to lift your head and see your face. It was a mess. You were bloody from the top of your nose down to your chest. It was oozing out of your nostrils, collecting around your lips, and turning into a bright red spray every time you breathed out. 1 appleorange. Bloody misty mess. 2 appleoranges. Bloody misty mess. It did that over and over again. I couldn't stop looking at it. I heard seagulls and waves again. I felt dizzy and hot. The spray was painting the fronts of my sneakers red. It was on the backs of my hands. The seagulls screamed. Were they judging me? The waves crashed all around me. Would they wash away the red?

I wanted to run. I wanted to run through the nearest sliding door, not stopping to open it, just crashing through the glass, stepping on the shards, toppling over the metal railing, stumbling through the bushes, and hoping I would never hear the ocean or see the color red ever again. But there was no way out now. There was no running away from this. And that made me want to smash everything I could see.

I walked in a circle around you, kicking rocks as hard as I could. I kicked a piece of metal and it felt like my toe had shattered into 498 pieces. I picked it up with my bloody hands and felt the weight of it. It was the length of a baseball bat. I squeezed it as hard as I could until my knuckles were so white I thought I could see the bones underneath. I walked over to where you were slumped, still making a bloody, misty mess. I pressed my teeth together so hard my eyes ached. I lifted the metal bat up over my head and swung it down as hard as my scrawny little body could make it swing. When it hit the track, the bang went up my skinny arms, into my neck, to the back of my head, then down my legs.

It rang like a church bell. It blurred my vision. There were 3 of you. 6 of you. 3 of you. 1 of you. I raised it up over my head again and brought it down again on the track. Again and again. It felt like my arms were going to rip right off my shoulders. Again and again. My teeth felt looser. My eyes felt like they were pressing out of my skull. I did it until I couldn't lift it up anymore. I dropped it, sat down on the track next to you, and closed my eyes.

When the vibrations in my body finally stopped, I knew what we had to do.

"Wait here."

I went to the fence where some newspaper had blown against it. I ripped off a piece and shoved it in my mouth. It was hard to chew. It was scratchy and tasted like dirt. It took forever for my spit to soften it. I chewed and chewed while I made you sit down in front of me. I used other pieces of newspaper to wipe the blood off you. I wiped your hands first because the blood there was scarier to look at than on your face. I don't know why, but it was. I worked upwards from there. Your chin next. Then the mess under your nose.

"Hold still."

I took the newspaper wad out of my mouth and shoved it into your nose. That nostril bulged. I tore off another piece of newspaper and started chewing it. I cleaned around your nose and up to between your eyes. There was a cut there, but it had stopped bleeding. I cleaned that, then had to re-clean under your nose because it was still oozing. I put the second wad in. I twisted the wads and pressed on the bulges to try to make them less noticeable. You made faces and noises and your feet kicked, but you let me do it. I reshaped it until you looked semi-normal. I wiped under your nose and looked to see if it leaked. It didn't. I gathered up all the bloody paper from the ground, carried it over to a spot near the fence where it was dirt rather than rocks. I dug a shallow hole with the heel of my shoe. I put the paper into it and pushed the dirt over it. I put a rock over the top.

"Hold my hand."

I braced my foot against the metal track and leaned back as hard as I could. When you were up, I could see the front of your shirt. It wasn't anything I could wipe off, and anyone who saw it would be dialing 911 in half a second. That would be bad. I was convinced of it.

I peeked under your shirt to see if you had a t-shirt or something underneath that would look OK, but you just had a giant bra on. I tried pulling your sweater closed so I could button it and cover the blood, but it didn't reach. Your tummy and boobs were too big. I took your sweater off and put it on you backward—with the back of the sweater on your front and with the unbuttonable front on your back. You looked weird but your blood-soaked shirt was hidden. I took a couple of steps back and looked at you. I pulled your sleeves down longer so nobody could see the red stains on the arm of the shirt underneath. I stepped back again and looked at you. I pushed the 2 wads of newspaper a little further up your nose so they weren't so easy to see. That was as good as it was going to get.

"Come on."

You still weren't talking, but you did what I said. You were pretty slow and stayed a step behind. I kept hold of your hand to make sure you didn't stop and sit back down. I looked back at you, looking down at your feet to see if you were getting wobbly and looking up at your face to make sure you weren't going to pass out or something. I didn't have a plan for what to do if you sat down or fell. I was just hoping you wouldn't.

You didn't. You kept following me, past the warehouses, onto the main street, past all the shops, and all the way to the hotel. I didn't take you inside, though. I turned us onto the street before the hotel because there weren't any stores and nobody would be walking there. Halfway down, there was a bench with a view of nothing. I sat you down.

"Give me your purse."

I dug inside it, found the hotel key card, and held it with my teeth. I pulled out your wallet and looked inside to see how much money was in it. There was a bunch of $20 bills. I looked around to see if anyone was looking, then put all the money into my sock. I shoved your wallet back in your purse and snapped it shut.

"Don't talk to anyone."

You blinked slowly. I walked quickly back to the main street, looked back at you before I went around the corner, down the street, to the next corner, and into the hotel lobby. I went past the front desk and up the stairs to the third floor, eyes down the whole way so I wouldn't make eye contact with anyone. I swiped the room key. It didn't turn green. I wondered if I could bust the door open by throwing myself against it. I tried the card again. It made the unlocking sound. I collected the few things we had brought, squeezed them into my backpack, and turned to leave. But I needed something else. I took a small towel, ran it under the water to get it wet, and shoved it into my backpack. I turned off the light, closed the door and took the stairs, jumping down the last few steps of each flight.

In the lobby, I got in line at the registration desk. There were 3 people in front of me. I tapped my foot, wanting it to go faster. I could see into the restaurant from where I was standing, and the booth closest to me had a big lady's hat hung on the hook where people usually put their coats. A hat like that would make it hard for anyone to see your face. The person at the front of the line finished up and went to the elevator. I looked at the hat on the hook again. The man and woman in the booth were sitting on the same side and were facing away from the hook. I reached down and patted my sock to make sure the money was still there. I shifted the backpack to my other shoulder. The people in front of me finished and left.

"How can I help you, big guy?" the woman at the desk asked.

"We're all done," I said. "My grandma and I are going home. She asked me to come tell you."

"Which room is it?"

"311."

She typed that into her computer. "Does your grandmother want to keep the charges on that card?"

I didn't know what the right answer was, but I said yes. I put the key card on the counter.

"Did you enjoy your stay?"

I nodded.

"The weather has been great. I hope you had a chance to get outside and enjoy it."

I nodded.

"OK. Here is your receipt. Be sure to give that to your grandmother. You're all set."

"OK," I said, but I didn't go out the doors to the street. I went toward the restaurant instead. I looked at the hat on the hook again. The people weren't looking. I shifted the backpack back to my other shoulder. But I didn't steal it. I went back to the registration desk. I cleared my throat to get her attention.

"Can I help you with anything else?"

"We need a taxi."

"Sure. I will call them for you." She dialed the phone. "Hi John, this is Stephanie over at the Hotel Or—."

"No, that's the wrong 1. We need Radio Cab."

"Hold on," she said into the phone, then said to me, "They don't operate down here, sweetie. Only up in Portland."

"Ask for Frank. He drove us here yesterday."

She looked at me for a second, then talked into the phone. "My mistake, John. False alarm. No need to send a car over." She hung up, typed something into her computer, dialed a number, and asked the dispatcher if Frank was working. I could hear the person say he was.

I whispered, "Tell him to have Frank come pick up the old lady and kid. But don't say where we are. The boss will get mad."

She said it the way I asked, then pressed the speaker button so I could hear. The dispatcher said he would check. There was silence. Then he said Frank would come after he dropped off his passenger. The lady said thank you to the dispatcher and hung up. "All set. Is there anything else I can help with?"

"A hat?"

"Oh, you lost a hat? Let's see if we have it in the lost and found box." She turned around and pulled a cardboard box out from under the far side of the counter. "Is this it?" She showed me a small hat that would only fit a kid head.

"No, it's a grown-up hat."

"Is this it?"

It looked like it would fit. "Yes." It was orange and said 'Beavers' across the front. "Sunglasses?"

She moved things around in the box and asked, "Are these the right pair?"

They looked like they would fit. "Yes."

"Did you lose any toys?" She smiled and moved some things around to show me the free toys. "There are a couple of bouncy balls. A glow-in-the-dark stick that still glows a little. A toy car." I looked at them rattling around in the box. A week ago, or even an hour ago I would have claimed those in a second, but I just said, "No thanks."

I scooted out of the lobby through the big doors. I ran down the sidewalk to the far corner of the hotel and looked. You were still there. When I got to you, I pulled the wet towel out of my backpack and cleaned your face and hands more. I undid the strap on the hat and made it bigger so it could fit around your wig. I tried it on you but needed to make it bigger. 1 more notch was right. I pushed down the bill so it covered your face a little, then I put the sunglasses on you. You made a noise when I first set them on your nose, but then you didn't fuss, so it seemed OK. I took a couple of steps back and looked at you. You looked ridiculous. You would have laughed and snorted and snort-laughed if you had seen yourself. I did math in my head about how long it would take for FRANK to get there. We waited there on the bench with a view of nothing until it was time to go out in front of the hotel.

I took your hand and led you to the bench where you had tried to capture the dog. 1 of your nose plugs slipped out a little, so I pushed it back in. I counted cars. I got to 29 when the taxi got there.

"Let's go home."

We did. I didn't know it then, but I know it now. You knew. You knew what I would do. And you knew everything that would happen after that.

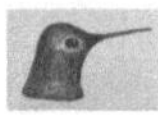

Ichiro had 12 triples in 2005, almost all of which would have only been doubles for regular players. He made things happen.

Here are all the triples he had every season in the Majors:

8

8
8
5
12
9
7
7
4
3
3
1
5
3
2
6
5
0
0
0

He also had 23 triples in Japan. He made things happen on 2 continents.

Here is something you said to me a lot. And here is some construction paper art I made way back who knows when. I was trying to make a flower. I am sure you would call me Georgia O'Keefe and laugh, laugh, laugh.

F RANK was expecting a lot of conversation like the day before, but he
     didn't get it. I didn't say a peep after he picked us up, and my face probably
made it clear I didn't want to talk. I saw him look at you in the rear-mirror mirror
a bunch of times, but he probably thought you had way too much to drink the
night before, so he kept quiet, turned on NPR, and drove. We still had to stop
at 1,000 red lights, but it felt a lot faster than on the way there.

He dropped us off at the other old people's home—not ours—and I gave him
all the money from my sock. He gave me some back, then looked at you, back
at me, and then back at you. I pulled you out of the taxi before he could say
whatever he was starting to think, closed the door, and slapped the fender like
you had done. After the taxi was out of sight, I grabbed your hand and steered
you up the hill toward our building. We went around the back and I tried to take
us through the usual gap in the bushes, but you couldn't bend down very well,
so we went further down to a bigger opening. That meant we would have to
walk past a few people's sliding doors, but luckily nobody was looking outside.
I helped you over our metal railing, pulled the door open and led you inside. I
sat you down on the couch, turned on the TV for you, picked up the phone
and the list of extensions for the building, carried them into the bedroom, and
dialed Dr. Harry. It rang 3 times, but he answered.

"Is this Dr. Harry? This is Ruth's little friend. Do you know who I'm talking
about?"

"Of course. How could I forget?"

"Can you help us? She got hurt."

His voice changed. "Did she fall down?"

"No. She got hit in the head, but it wasn't me."

"Does she need an ambulance?"

"I didn't do it."

"I'll be right over. Just give me a minute to get my pants on."

When he knocked, I pulled a chair over and looked through the keyhole to
make sure it was him. He had probably heard furniture dragging because when
I looked out, he was looking right back at me. He put his hand up telling me
to wait, looked both ways, then gave me a thumbs up. I slid the chair out of
the way and opened the door just wide enough for him to squeeze in. He had
his black bag. He patted me on the shoulder as he walked over to where you
were. He leaned down and tilted his head sideways to see under the bill of your
lost-and-found Beavers hat. You stared at the TV.

"Hello, Ruth," he said. You didn't say anything. "How are you feeling?"

"She's not talking. At all."

"Not a word?"

I shook my head.

"Hmmmmm." He took off your hat. "It's not like her to not be talking up a storm, that's for certain." He carefully slid the sunglasses off your face. Your eye sockets were a color that's not in a crayon box. They had puffed up like an angry blowfish. Dr. Harry tilted his head left and right and moved around you in a semi-circle to look at you from all angles.

"Ruth, can you follow my finger? Go ahead and watch my finger." He put it in front of your face and then moved it slowly from 1 side to the other. Then up and down. Then back to the middle. "Hmmmmmm." He straightened up and his back made 47 sounds.

"I didn't do it."

He looked at me. I thought he was trying to figure out if I was lying, which is the only thing that occurred to me back then because I had the brains of a bag of hard-boiled eggs. That wasn't why he was looking at me. He was asking himself why I would even think I had to say that. I'm sure of it now.

I didn't give him a chance to think I was lying. I told him the whole story in a flood of words and very few breaths. I told him about how we "ran away" to McMinnville, and how you played violin, and how I passed out on the bathroom floor, and how we chased each other around the block, and the stupid dog, and how we met the boy, and the chicken nuggets, and how you tried to help him, and how it ended with blood on the tracks. Dr. Harry nodded his head like every bit of it made sense, even though none of it did. I pulled the taxi receipt out of my pocket to show him I wasn't lying. He whistled when he saw how much the taxi ride cost. He patted me on the shoulder and said words I wasn't expecting him to say. "Let's do some surgery."

He opened his bag, took out some tweezers and reached millimeter by millimeter into your nose like we were playing Operation and he didn't want to set off the buzzer. He got a good grip on a plug of chewed up newspaper and started to pull it out. He stopped and had me get the trash bin from the kitchen, which I shoved between your legs in case a gusher came out. He pulled out the plug. It had a long, dark clot attached to it, but there was no gusher. He dropped it in the trash and pulled the other plug out. The clot on that 1 was even darker and longer. I closed the bag after he put it in the trash so I wouldn't have to look at it. He shined the light inside your nose. He touched the top of your nose where the cut was, and you made a face. He felt the bones in your eyebrows and around your eyes, then held the bridge of your nose and put pressure on 1 side, then the other. Your hands came up off your lap but hovered halfway between there and your face.

"Is she hurt anywhere else?"

"In the mouth. Her lip was bleeding, but she was still normal after that. She didn't get like this until the second hit."

He pulled up your upper lip and pulled down your lower lip. You kept staring at the TV. It was an infomercial. He felt along your jawline, around to the back of your head, down the back of your neck, and down the top of your spine feeling each of the bones down to between your shoulder blades. When he finished, he shined a light into your eyes and watched to see what happened. He did it a couple of times. It made you really blinky and annoyed.

"Is she going to die?"

"If she were going to die from that kind of trauma, something pretty significant probably would have happened by now."

I looked at you and your messed-up blowfish eyes and your wonky nose that looked more crooked the longer I stared at. It all looked pretty significant to me, but he was the doctor.

"It's probably just a concussion, but it's better to be safe than sorry," he said. "You should go out for a while. I'm going to tell them she fell and hit her head and I found her when I came over to visit. They'll take her to the hospital and do some tests I can't do with these old-fashioned things in my bag." He shook his bag to demonstrate, and everything inside clanked and clanged.

I looked at him. Then at you. Then back at him.

"It's good you called me. Now, skedaddle and go see a movie or something so you're not here when they come in." He reached into his pocket and gave me 2 dollars, which must have been what movie tickets cost the last time he went.

I picked up my backpack and went to the sliding door but came back to tie up a loose end. I reached behind you and unbuttoned the sweater. I took it off so you just had the shirt with the blood down the front. Someone would have started to wonder how you had put a sweater on backward and buttoned it in the middle of your back where no human being can reach. Even if they hadn't noticed they definitely would have noticed how you had somehow bled through the sweater onto your shirt without getting a drop on the sweater itself. He told me that was good thinking, then motioned for me to get going.

I went out, climbed over the rail, found a spot in the bushes with a good view into the room, and watched. He turned off the TV, turned over a stool to make it look like the scene of an accident, took some paper towels from near the sink, got them red from the clots in the trash, and set them on the coffee table like he had cleaned you off. He looked around the apartment to make sure he had made everything look like a convincing lie. He arranged some more things to make it look right, then opened the front door a few inches to get it ready for everyone who would come running. The last thing he did was hide his medical bag under the sink, then he dialed someone on the phone, said a few things, hung up, and sat down next to you to wait. I was impressed. I guess everyone has a little criminal inside them. They just need a good reason to let it out.

I could hear the siren. It was probably a fire truck from the station just down the street, just like when people fall down dead, dripping wet or otherwise. A building employee came into the room and talked to Dr. Harry. He motioned with his hand pointing to a spot on the floor, then acted out like a game of charades where he helped get you from the floor up to the couch. The employee said something to you, but you just looked at the turned-off TV. Another employee came in and the first employee repeated the same hand motions Dr. Harry had just made to explain what had happened.

The fire engine's brakes made that air sound when it stopped on the other side of the building, and its flashing red and white lights were visible against the tree leaves over the top of the roof. 2 firefighters came into the room with equipment. They said some things to you, checked your pulse and your breathing, and pointed a light in your eyes. A second siren came down the street and pulled up in front of the building. I could see its blue and red lights over the roof. An ambulance person came into the room, talked to a firefighter, and left. He came back with a gurney and a second ambulance worker. They put something around your neck and then guided you into a lying position on the couch, facing up toward the ceiling. They slid a board under your back, lifted you over to the gurney, and slid the board out. The ambulance people strapped you in and took you away. The firefighters shook Dr. Harry's hand and left with a building employee. The ambulance siren started up again and it drove away. The other building employee stayed behind and talked with Dr. Harry for a couple of minutes. After that, they walked to the door, turned out the light, and left.

I waited a while to make sure no other people were going to come in. When it seemed safe, I left my spot in the bushes, climbed over the metal railing, went into the room, and sat down on the couch in the spot where you had sat. It was still warm from your butt heat. It was dark in the room with the lights off and with that outside light bulb burned out. I turned on 1 of the small lamps next to the couch, but it was too bright—someone would notice it. I turned it off. I went to the junk drawer in the kitchen and got the flashlight, some paper, and a pencil. I went back to the warm spot on the couch, held the flashlight in my mouth, and did math.

7x3 = 21
3x3x1 = 9
7x5x2 = 70
8x30 = 240
9x0 = 0
112x1 = 112
2x6x0 = 0
2x10x1 = 20

S itting there in the dark with the flashlight in my mouth, I noticed how quiet the apartment was without you there. I didn't like it at all, but it was nothing compared to how quiet it was about to get. That would be after we had our biggest, noisiest fight—the last 1 we would ever have.

T here wasn't anything for breakfast the next morning. We were supposed to go to the store on the day we ended up running away to McMinnville, so the only stuff in the refrigerator was ketchup and mustard and that sort of thing. In the cupboard, there was only flour and sugar and not much else beyond an empty canister of oatmeal with a bunch of rules in it.[93] I tried to eat a spoonful of sugar, but it didn't taste the way kids dream it would. I spit it out.

I got my dirty socks from the day before and pulled out the few remaining dollars that were left in them. Almost all that money had gone to pay for the taxi. I got the baseball card money from my backpack and found some spare change in the junk drawer and on your nightstand. It was enough to get some food, so I walked down to the store, returned a few cans to help boost my budget, and started shopping.

I looked at the baseball cards at the customer service counter but didn't get any. I got a quart of milk, some of the cheap no-brand cereal, some old bread that was on the discount rack, raisins and some cheese. I added up all the prices in my head and recounted the money. I would have enough if I put back the raisins, so I did. Raisins are more expensive than a bunch of old grapes should cost. It was enough to get me through a couple of days if you were in the hospital that long.

I paid, took everything out to the picnic table behind the store, shoved everything into my backpack, struggled to close the zipper, took everything out, rearranged it, tried the zipper again, got it even less closed than the first time, and gave up. I put it on backward so the backpack was on my front and tried to keep things from falling out with my arms. It was pointless. I had to stop and pick something up every 13 feet.

When I got back home, I closed the curtains and kept the lights off so it didn't look like anyone was there. I ate cereal for a really late breakfast/really early lunch. I watched TV but turned it off pretty quickly because I was so distracted. I did some math, then I drew pictures. Some of the pictures were of birds at your feeder. I would peek out from behind the curtain to watch the birds, like you

---

93. Cough. Truisms. Cough cough.

did to watch me. Then I would draw them in my notebook and tape them to the refrigerator.

Dr. Harry called that afternoon to check on me and to tell me you were going to be at the hospital again that night. He said they hadn't found anything wrong with you, but the doctors were keeping you there for observation.

I had a cheese sandwich and a glass of milk for dinner. I picked a book from the shelf. It was about sailors. It didn't have any pictures in it. Just words because it was a grown-up book. I brought it and my pillow and my sheets and the flashlight into your room, went around to the far side of your bed, and arranged it all on the floor there. That way, I could roll under the bed and hide if anyone came in.

I read until the batteries in the flashlight got weak and the light was so dim I couldn't make out the letters anym....

Dr. Harry called during breakfast the next morning. I had forgotten all our truisms and picked it up right away, then remembered the truisms, freaked out, and hung up before I even said hello.

He called back and this time I actually said hello. He told me you were being discharged, but he remembered he was talking to a kid and explained that that meant they were sending you home. I finished my cereal, hid my stuff, opened the curtains, and went out for a long walk. When I came back, I looked through the bushes and you were sitting on the couch. Nobody was there with you. I scooted across the grass, climbed over the fence, and pulled on the door handle. It didn't budge. The little lever was pushed down instead of up. I had never seen it pushed down.

I knocked. You looked over at me, but you didn't get up. I pointed toward the handle to unlock it. You got up, came over, and pushed down on the lever, like you were trying to lock it even better. I pointed up for you to push it up rather than down. You did. I slid the door open and blew in like a tornado.

"Hi," I said, not sure if you were talking again yet.

"Hello," you said like I was a guy trying to sell you something.

I looked at you and squinted to see if you were back to normal. You stood there with your hand on the sliding door handle and looked out at the cruddy view. The look on your face gave me a cold feeling. I tried to make some conversation. "Dr. Harry told me you were coming back, so I went out. That way they wouldn't see me when they brought you back."

I sat down on the couch. You were still standing over near the sliding door. You looked at me, at the door, back at me, back at the door, then slid it sort-of closed, but not all the way. You sat back down on the couch.

"Dr. Harry said they checked your head and nothing is messed up. Did they put you in the big donut-shaped machine to see inside you?"

You shrugged. You looked straight ahead at the TV. It wasn't on.

"What did they do?"

"Tests."

"Are you OK?"

"I'm fine." You were still looking at the TV.

I looked around for the remote and turned it on so my skin would hopefully stop crawling. I tried to make a joke. "Did they have to shave off your hair? I saw that on a movie once."

"No." You didn't lift up your wig to prove it.

"Did you have to get any shots?"

You shook your head.

"What did you get to eat?"

"Where?" You were paying more attention to the TV than me.

"At the hospital." It was an infomercial.

"Chicken."

"Did you get to eat a lot of ice cream?"

"No."

I tried to make another joke. "Did you have to wear a gown that was open in the back and showed your bum?"

"Yes."

I thought mentioning bums would "crack" the code with you, but it didn't. "It must have been funny with everyone's bum poking out."

You shrugged and watched more of the infomercial.

"Are you OK?"

"Fine," you said, but you didn't look it.

I didn't want to ask more questions and get the kind of answers I was getting. I got up and went to the kitchen. I got a glass of water but didn't drink it. I sat at the counter and watched you watch TV. The infomercial was for the food dehydrator we had seen advertised a while back. You didn't blink much. You blinked so little; I started counting the blinks.

You reached for your purse on the end table and pulled out your wallet. The announcer said, "Call now to order." You did.

Y ou didn't go to dinner that night. You didn't decide not to go. You didn't say, "I am going to eat here tonight instead of going to the dining room."

You just didn't go.

I watched the clock turn to 7:00 and knew they were closing the doors and it was too late. That meant you wouldn't bring food back from dinner, plus you would make a big dent in the little bit of food we had left from my last trip to the store. I looked in the refrigerator to do an inventory. It didn't take long.

"I'm hungry," you said when you saw the light of the fridge out of the corner of your eye. I made you a cheese sandwich, poured you some milk, and brought it to you. I watched you eat, staring at your mouth. I had never seen you eat without saying 923,567 things. All you did was chew and swallow and chew and swallow. I couldn't look away.

I started to worry about the next day. I was hoping you would go to sleep early so you didn't get hungry and eat more that night. You flipped to a movie that was full of talking and looked like it would last 3 hours. You were definitely going to get hungry again. I would have to get some more food really soon. I needed a plan.

M aybe this owl has a message for me. Maybe he doesn't care. Maybe he's looking at something behind me and this isn't about me.

T he next morning when I was getting breakfast ready for us, I found the almost-empty milk carton. You had finished all of it the night before except for a teeny bit splashing around at the bottom. When I had gone to sleep it was still half full, but now there was just a mouthful or 2 left. I don't know what you did with it. Maybe you guzzled it down. Maybe you flushed it down the toilet. I don't know, but it didn't matter. The only thing that mattered was that we had to eat cereal with 2 tablespoons of milk mixed into 2 bowls of water. It tasted like a soggy bowl of sadness.

We had enough bread and cheese for lunch, but that would be pretty much it. We would be out of food after that. I thought about asking Dr. Harry for help, but if he knew you were having this much trouble he would probably intervene, and it would all be over. He kept our secret before, but that was when you were normal. I worried he wouldn't do it again.

I put on my shoes and told you I was going out. You blinked. You were watching the shopping channel when I left. Your purse and the phone were next to you, ready to call now. I went to a place near the park where teenagers drink beer. Usually there was a good haul there, but not that day. I looked in recycle bins out on the street for trash day and found some cans people were too lazy to return. I didn't take the bottles. They were too heavy to carry after I got more than 20. I knocked on a few doors and said I was collecting for charity. I made up something about kids in need, so technically it wasn't a complete lie. I searched until my feet were sore, but I only got 61 cans. A miserable $3.05.

I had heard that stores were going to start paying 10 cents for cans, but not soon enough to help me. I had to make the best of it, so I bought 2 things: a loaf of the bread they bake at the store (only $1.49) and cheap ham at the deli (that was on sale for even cheaper than usual). I asked the lady to cut 4 thin slices of the ham for me. She was probably annoyed about slicing such a small amount, but she did it. I checked the price tag she stuck on the ham to make sure I could afford it. I could.

You were still watching TV when I got back. Your wallet was out on the end table with a credit card laying on top. The phone was in your lap.

After I made us lunch, I went back out to look for more cans. I wasn't having much luck, so I tried knocking on doors again with that story about raising money for kids in need. I didn't get far with that, though, because a lady asked me why I wasn't in school. I told her it was a school project I was working on, so it was OK I was out of school. She clearly didn't believe me, and I was sure she was going to call the cops or maybe throw fancy small potatoes at me, so I got out of there in a hurry.

I didn't have enough cans to make it worthwhile to go turn them in at the store, so I came back home and washed the breakfast and lunch dishes. I was hot from all the can hunting and dish washing, so I splashed some water on my face and then told you I was going to lie down for a nap. You blinked. I went to the spot next to your bed where I had been sleeping the past couple of days. I tried and tried to sleep.

I guess I eventually did because I woke up covered with sweat. The sun was coming in the window and baking the spot on the floor where I was sleeping. I went to the bathroom and then came out to where you were. You had the clicker and were watching a show about sewing. There was a loud knock on the door. I hid under the sink, scraping my knee badly on the way in. I didn't hear your footsteps go over to the door, though, and there wasn't a second knock. I peeked out. There was a paper slid under the door. It was a delivery slip. I pulled a chair over to the door and looked out the peephole. Nobody. I opened the door a crack. There were 2 boxes. I opened the door enough to look around and make sure nobody was watching. I pulled them inside. The heavy box was a food dehydrator. The not-heavy box was a set of bowls in ugly colors.

"Why did you order these?" I asked with quite an attitude.

You looked over, then back at the screen.

"Can we return them?"

"No." The word shot out of your mouth and jolted me.

"We haven't opened them yet, so we can still return them."

"No!" you said again, in the loudest voice you had used since getting home.

"What are you going to do with them?"

"Mind your own business!" You got up off the couch, picked up the not-heavy box and carried it into your bedroom. You set it on your bed. You came back, tried to lift the heavy box, couldn't, and slid it into your room by kicking it along .000000000009 inch at a time like the heaviest soccer ball in the world. You kick-pushed it into the corner on the far side of your bed where I had been sleeping and put the light box on top of it. You sat back down on the couch. That was that, for the moment.

I stayed away from you until my stomach started to grumble. It was past 5:00. I came back into the room where you were and said, "It's roast beef night, isn't it? You should go tonight."

"I'm watching TV."

"Ok. You'll go later," I said.

At 5:45, I brought it up again. "You should go to dinner before they run out of the roast beef. I bet they have that really good gravy."

"I'm still watching this."

At 6:30, I brought it up again. "The dining room will be closing soon. You should go before they shut the doors."

"I'm not hungry."

"Some of your friends are probably there. I bet they would like to see you."

You pressed on the remote control to make the TV louder and drown me out.

After 7:00, I looked through my backpack to see if there was more money or recycling credit slips I had hidden in the little pockets and forgotten about.

There weren't any. I looked through the junk drawer to see if there was any there, maybe way in the back, but there wasn't. I went over to you and stood there until you looked over from the TV. "Do you have any money?"

You pointed to your purse without looking at me.

I looked through it. No cash. Just your credit card. There was no way a kid could use a grown-up's credit card without getting attention that I didn't want. I imagined sirens and cops and me being shoved into the back of a police car. "I don't see any money."

You shrugged.

"But we need to get food."

You put your finger up to your lips and said, "Shhhhhh," in a way that made your eyebrows into the shape of knives. I took a step back so I wasn't in front of the screen. You looked back at the TV and your eyebrows went back to normal.

I didn't know what to do. I sat down at the kitchen counter and drew criss-crossing lines on a piece of scrap paper. I don't know why I did that. I just did. I hated it and crumpled the paper. I tried drawing something else, but it just ended up being criss-crossing lines again.

That night after you went to bed, I ate sunflower seeds outside under a moon that wanted to look away but couldn't. I broke them with the heels of the man shoes that were in your closet, barely keeping them on my puny feet as I stomped and stomped to get my dinner. I squatted down and picked out the edible stuff. I looked up and saw myself in the reflection of the sliding door. I turned and faced the other way. The moon couldn't stop staring at me, but I didn't have to watch.

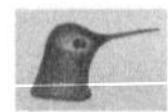

I slept terribly. Then as soon as I got up, I had to rush under the sink again. It was the nurse.

"How are you feeling?" I heard the nurse say through the cabinet doors.

"Fine," you said.

"How is your head?"

"Fine."

"That's wonderful," she said. "We haven't seen you at dinner, Ruth."

"I eat here."

While you talked to the nurse, I ate extra sunflower seeds I had stuffed into my pockets the night before. I shouldn't have been munching anything under there because it made noise, but I was starving. I chewed the way I usually do with my mouth wide open like an animal, and that made noise. I slapped my hand over my mouth to cover the sound of my chewing, and the slap made noise. It must have sounded like 2 badgers fighting under the sink, but somehow the nurse didn't hear it.

"Are you going to join us for lunch or dinner today?"

"I will eat here."

"Well, maybe tomorrow night," she said. "We're so glad to have you back and so glad you're on the mend."

Since you weren't planning to go to the dining room, that meant I definitely needed to get some money. After the nurse left, I crawled out from under the sink, got my backpack, and went to the sliding door. Before I left, I said, "Bye." You didn't say anything back.

It was too soon to go back to my best places for cans or even my second-best places, so I went to my sometimes-worth-a-try places. Behind the Thai restaurant where they sometimes leave a recycling bin with cans. The alley near the 7-11 where people throw stuff out because they're too lazy to go to the trash can feet away. The dish cart at the Starbucks where people put their iced tea bottles. Not much luck, though. I only got a few, so I went to the school to check the bin where people donate cans for the PTA. I only went there in an emergency. I may have been a jerk, but I had principles sometimes. There were too many people around for me to get close to that bin, so I went around the side, sat in the bushes, and watched kids out at recess.

The kids were littler than me. They swung on the monkey bars and went down the twisty slide and picked at bugs in the dirt. 1 of them fell and cried. Some were chasing each other. 1 picked her nose. 1 held his crotch like he had to pee, then he ran off and kept playing. They screamed and ran around and screamed. I felt like I was looking at animals at the zoo. They weren't like me, and I wasn't like them. I picked up a pebble and threw it at another pebble. I left.

It was still too dangerous to go check the PTA bin, so I went to the grocery store thinking people may have left cans there rather than wait in line to use the recycling machines. No luck. I put my scrawny harvest into the machines, pressed the button to print the slips, and went inside. If anyone wondered why I was there during the day, I had 17 lies ready to go.

I wanted to get us as much food energy as possible for the money I had. I looked at the cheap frozen pizzas, both at the price and the number of calories. They would give us a lot of energy, but they were too expensive. I looked at day-old bread and donuts on the reduced-price rack. They were my 1st choice for a while until I looked at the candy bars. There was no contest. Those were the most calories I could get for the least money. I got 3 bars that were on sale and put them in my basket. They looked sad and small in there. I did the math in my head and still had some money left over, so I went to the fruit department and got us a lemon so we wouldn't get scurvy like sailors and pilgrims and pirates.

I had read about scurvy in books and it sounded terrible. The lemons all cost the same, so I went through the entire display, picked 5 and weighed them all to make sure I had the biggest, juiciest, scurvy-fightingest 1.

I took my time getting home. I was in no rush to see you. I went to the tennis courts and searched in the bushes around the fence until I found a tennis ball. School was out by then, so I could go anywhere without worrying. I checked the PTA bins. Empty. I walked and bounced the ball. I went to the park and rode the swing for a while. I watched older kids hitting balls off a tee at the baseball field. Most of them hit line drives but the biggest kid pulled the tee up as high as it would go and swung up at the ball, launching them to the warning track. Off the bat, every ball looked like it would clear the fence, but they would stall over the outfield, drop onto the far edge of the grass, and roll onto the clay track. The other kids were annoyed because it took longer to go get those and the warning track was muddy. The biggest kid asked if I wanted to hit, too. I shook my head. Saying no is my superpower. I just bounced my tennis ball.

It was a little before 7:00 when I got home, but you were on the couch. You hadn't gone to dinner and clearly had no plan to. I waited until the dining room was officially closed, then I cut the candy bars in half, split them on 2 plates and served them with a fork and knife for each of us. I cut the lemon into wedges and put them on a separate plate between our glasses of water. I waited for you to say thank you, but you didn't. You scarfed down your food without hardly chewing. I was too upset to eat mine right away. I just stared at the tendons and muscles, straining just underneath the thin skin of your throat, fighting and struggling to shove the chocolate and peanuts and nougat down into the bottomless pit of your stomach. You motioned to mine since I wasn't eating it. I didn't have an appetite. I didn't say anything, so you took it and scarfed it down. Your throat went back to work, and I couldn't look away until the anger snapped me out of it. I stopped staring at your throat and I looked at you with tiny daggers in my tiny, beady eyes, but you were oblivious so I opened my big fat mouth. "It was a lot of work to get that, you know."

You looked over at me with a confused look on your face, but you didn't say anything. You had chocolate smeared on both sides of your mouth.

"You should say thank you," I explained, to make sure you didn't miss my point.

"For what?"

"For the dinner I got us."

"The candy bars? That's dinner?"

"That's all I could get."

"Let me get this straight," you said, with your eyebrows carving deep into your forehead and the words firing out like a machine gun. "I let you live under my roof and protected you from a woman who wanted to do you harm and I gave you all the food you could possibly eat and now I owe you something when you bring me a single measly candy bar?"

My beady little eyes weren't beady anymore. They were as big as scurvy-fighting lemons, and my mouth hung open like a ventriloquist dummy whose inside levers are broken.

You got going again with your voice louder and higher than before, so fast and high it felt like it was cutting deep inside where my eardrums and brains connected. "DoIunderstandthatcorrectly, Mr.I-Owe-You-Something? DoI? Well,I'mnotgoingtosaythankyou. I'llbedamnedifIsaythattoyou." You stood up, but you were wobbly. I held your arm to balance you. "Let. Go. Of. Me. I. Don't. Need. Your. Help."

You stopped wobbling and your voice got very calm and steady and quiet. It scared me more than when you were talking infinity words a minute. "Don't hold your breath if you're expecting a thank you from me. And if you don't like it, you can leave." Your finger pointed to the door—the hall door, not the sliding door. It hung there and hung there for 1,723,000,000 years—longer than it took for the mountains to get tall, longer than it took for fish to grow legs, longer than it took for dinosaurs to all die like a bunch of idiots. Your finger hung there, and then it dropped like it was chopping off a stupid king's stupid head. "In fact, that's exactly what you should do. You should get your tiny behind out of here. Not tomorrow. Not in an hour. Not in 10 minutes. Now."

You shuffled over to where my backpack was and went around the apartment stuffing things into it, some of which was actually my stuff and some of which was just stuff. You ran out of room in there, so you got a box from your closet, dumped it out onto your floor and shoved my backpack and more things into it. You picked it up, but it was awkward to carry, so you dropped it on the floor loudly, kicked it toward the front door a centimeter at a time, opened the door, kicked the box out into the hall, bent down, lifted the box a few inches off the ground for no reason, and dropped it loudly onto the hallway floor exactly where it had been. You closed the door, said, "Good riddance. Now I'll have some peace," walked past me, and slammed the bathroom door behind you.

I stared at the bathroom door with my un-beady eyes and my open mouth and I couldn't think. I tried to think, but it didn't work. I tried to think of a baseball player. Any baseball player. I couldn't. Not even Ichiro. I tried to think of numbers. I couldn't. Not even 0, which would have been something, even though it's nothing. My brain was completely broken, except for the part that tells my lungs to breathe . . . and tells my heart to beat . . . and tells every other part of me to always do the opposite. If you wanted me to leave, I needed to do the opposite. If you were kicking me out forever, I needed to move right back in—forever. The opposite was all that was left. It was the only thing that still made sense.

I opened the front door, looked both ways to make sure nobody was looking, and pulled my stuff back inside. It was too heavy to lift, so I pushed it along the carpet behind the sliding door on the far end of the couch and covered it the best I could with a blanket. I took my pillow off the couch, went into your room while you were still holed up in the bathroom, pushed the food dehydrator box out of the way, got down on the floor next to the bed, crawled underneath, and pulled the pillow behind me to block me in. Nobody was making me go anywhere with me bunkered in under there. Good luck trying. Good clucking luck. Cluckety cluck.

I didn't know it at the time, but that night you tried to kick me out was the last time you spoke to me.

I spent so much time before then wishing you would shut up, and I've spent years and years and years since then trying to get you to open your mouth. I can't make up my mind, can I?

After that big fight, I vibrated under your bed like I was plugged in and cranked up to 11. My brain buzzed and crackled for 823 hours when I should have been sleeping. It was buzzing and crackling so loud, I was able to ignore the grumbling in my stomach. And then the buzzing and the crackling and stomach-grumbling stopped just like that. And there was the idea: You were so different. You were too different. Suspiciously different. You were faking.

A whack on the head couldn't change you that much, at least not a whack from a brat barely bigger than me (or maybe the same size) who was trying to take candy from a lady.

I couldn't believe it, so I didn't believe it. You weren't really hurt. This was an act. I was sure of it. Why? You were trapping me. You were betting I wouldn't leave if you couldn't take care of yourself. And you were betting I would try twice as hard to stay if you wanted me to leave. It was all part of your plan to get me to stay. It all made sense. This was a game, and you were trying to win. Any idiot could see that.

If you were faking, then it didn't matter that I didn't stop nuggetface from knocking your brain for a loop, right? If this was all an act, I would stop feeling the marks in my hands where I squeezed that disc-shaped rock while I just stood there like a big bag of stupid, right? This was my "Get Out of Jail Free" card. I needed that card bad. I just needed to catch you faking.

When I finally woke up the day after our fight, I forgot where I was, tried to sit up, and hit my head on the underneath part of the bed. I pushed my pillow barrier wall out of the way and scooted out. You were still sleeping. I waited until I saw your chest move a little just to make sure, then went into the bathroom and peed for about 7 weeks. After my bladder was empty, I noticed my stomach. It wasn't grumbling. It was beyond that. It had given up and gone to a faraway place.[94]

I started to go toward the kitchen, but it was pointless. There wasn't anything in there. I had tried everything and failed. We were going to starve to death. I was sure of it. That is what was going on in my teeny-tiny brain while I stood there in my racecar underwear, which were covered in cars driving in every direction trailed by sparks and smoke and words like "WOOSH!" and "ZOOM!" I didn't know what to do. 2 birds started fighting at the birdfeeder, which you hadn't filled with seeds since before we "ran away." Settle down, guys. There's plenty of nothing to go around.

A man holding a ladder walked past our patio, then came back because he had gone too far. He looked up at the outside light above our patio, straightened up his ladder, and propped it up against the wall. I tried not to move so he wouldn't notice me. Freezing had never worked before, so why stop now? He steadied the ladder, took off his hat, scratched his head, put it back on, leaned down to his toolbox, took out a light bulb, went up to the third rung, removed the cover of the light, removed the dead bulb, put the dead bulb in his chest pocket, reached up with the fresh light bulb, and looked over at me. He stood there on the ladder, bulb in mid-air, frozen except for his eyes that squinted and adjusted and re-squinted trying to figure out why there was a kid standing there. Then his eyes got big. He knew.

I turned around so he couldn't see my face. I counted to 10 appleoranges. I turned around and he was still staring at me, holding the bulb in midair. I closed my eyes and tried to figure out what to do. Doing the opposite was no help in this situation. There was no opposite to do in this case. I was stuck. I didn't know what to do . . .

. . . but Ichiro knew. I saw him on the insides of my eyelids, warming up in

---

94. Vancouver, Washington?

the batting circle with the heavy donuts he always used so that the bat would feel like it was a feather when he got to the plate. He took practice swings as the pitches came into the batter at home plate, getting the pitcher's timing down right, then he knocked the donuts off his bat, strolled to the plate, and called time. He looked straight at me.

He dug his back foot into the clay, rotated the bat in a giant circle from in front of him, down past his feet, all the way back, over his head, and then into that vertical position between him and the pitcher, holding it, holding it, holding it there. But he looked at me while he did it. He pulled his right sleeve up like he always does, brought the bat back until it was nearly horizontal behind him, with his hands up as high as his ears, and tapped his front foot. I waited for the swing, but he didn't.

There was this: a nod to me.

I opened my eyes and let everything come into focus. I walked to the sliding door, put my hand on the handle, pulled it open, pulled open the screen, walked out across the sea of broken seed shells, looked up at him and said, "I need help."

He looked past me at the couch again. He looked at me, standing there half-naked in filthy racecar underwear.

He looked at me, and I stood there, not running away.

He took a step back, looked to the far end of the building on my left—his right—and counted from the far end of the building to your patio. He stepped forward to where he started. He pointed inside and asked, "*¿Señora Ruth?*"

"Yes." It was a word I wasn't used to saying much. "I mean, *sí.*" Another word I wasn't used to saying much.

He pointed at his head, meaning your head. "*¿Señora es OK?*"

"Yes, but she is different now."

"*Señora* must rest. Rest *es muy bueno.*"

"I need your help," I said again. It was easier than the first time I said it. I tried to remember some Spanish from the Dora show. "I need *ayuda*. I need to *trabajo* for money."

"*¿Trabajo?*"

"Yes, *trabajo*. Can I *trabajo* for you?" I said pointing at his tool belt.

"*¿Trabajas para Jesús?*"

"I am good at fixing things. I fix...*muy bueno*. And I am...*pequeño*, so I can fit places a grown-up can't. And look. I have my own tools for *trabajo*." I went over to my backpack and got out my multitool knife. I slid open the screwdriver and showed him.

"*Lo siento. Las reglas*," he said, shaking his head and motioning in the direction of where the front office was on the other side of the building.

"We can make it a secret," I said and put my finger on my lips and made a shhhh noise.

"*Lo siento, Mijo. Lo siento mucho.*"

I nodded and looked down at my feet. I was certain the bottoms of my feet were bleeding from the seed shells.

I had another idea. "Do you have friends who need *ayuda*? *Trabajo* for your amigos?"

Jesús scratched his chin, looked at me, looked at the light bulb, scratched his chin some more, adjusted his tool belt, spun the bulb in his hand, raised his eyebrows, nodded at me, climbed the ladder, screwed in the new light bulb—which flickered on—came back down the ladder, looked both ways and up above to make sure nobody was watching, stepped toward the metal railing, kneeled down to my height, and did some fix-it work on my problems.

"*Las Señoras y Señores aquí,*" he whispered while motioning his arm in a grand way that started at 1 end of the building and went to the other end. "Many, many jobs *para las Señoras y Señores. Trabajos pequeños.* Limpieza. Clean." He acted out dusting and wiping. "*Leer libros.* Read the books." He acted out turning pages and running his fingers over each sentence. "*Otros trabajos pequeños. Yo? Ayudo las Señoras y Señores, pero nunca para dinero.*" He touched his chest over his heart and held it there like he was looking at the flag, then he motioned slowly toward me and said, "*¿Pero tú? Mucho dinero. Comprendes, Mijo?*"

I didn't understand, but I nodded. He saw right through that and knew I wasn't *comprende*-ing any of it.

"*¿Yo? No. No dinero para mí.*" He put up his hands and waved away the imaginary offer of money from all the imaginary old people. "*Ayudo los solo para ayudar. ¿Pero tú?*" He pointed at me and let the question hang there.

My brain was slow, and I just stood there like an empty bucket not realizing what he was suggesting.

"You, *Mijo.* You say yes. Yes *a las Señoras y Señores.* Yes *a los trabajos pequeños.* Yes *al dinero.*"

"I say yes," I echoed.

"*Sí.*"

"I do work for the old people."

"*Sí.*"

"And they give me money."

"*Sí.*"

"To buy food."

"*Sí, Sí. Muchos, muchos trabajos pequeños aquí,*" he said and waved his arm grandly again.

"OK," I said, although I was only 10% convinced.

"OK," he said, way more convinced than me.

"OK," I said, only 13% convinced after his reassurance.

He reached his hand out. I shook it. He patted me on the head, looked at me for another second, smiled, adjusted his tool belt, grabbed the ladder, patted me on the head again, and walked back from where he had come, whistling something I didn't know. Pretty sure it wasn't a Cole Porter song, but you never know.

I stood there staring at the light Jesús had fixed, trying to think of reasons why his plan couldn't possibly work. It couldn't, right? Never in 1,000,000 years, right?

I sat down on the couch and thought and thought. I decided to let Jesús take the wheel. I needed those *trabajos pequeños*. I needed them bad. I couldn't support us on 5-cent cans anymore, not with how much you ate. You were a giant stomach on legs, topped by a wig that wasn't fooling anyone. I needed the big money those little jobs would give me.

But I couldn't walk around the building knocking on doors offering to be everyone's helper. They would figure out I was living there in a half a second, and our game would be all over. And I couldn't go knocking on people's patio doors. People would throw potatoes at me or call the cops. So that was out.

I could feel an answer on the edge of my peripheral vision, just out of sight, but I couldn't bring it into focus even if I turned my head really fast to try to see it. Or maybe I was kidding myself. Maybe there was no way to make this work. It was a conundrum. A conundrum stuffed inside a duck that was stuck in the muck.

I didn't know what I was going to do, but what I did know is that nobody would hire a half-naked, filthy kid with bleeding feet. First things first; I needed to look respectable. I would figure out the rest later.

I slid off my racecar underwear and kicked it in the air, flipping it up high enough to catch it. They were beyond repair, not worth washing ever again, so I put it into the kitchen trash. Every part of me stunk, even the inside of my nose. I went into the bathroom and turned on the shower to the hottest temperature. I would cook off the nastiness. I would boil and steam myself until I could fool people that I was an upright citizen worth inviting into their room for those *trabajos pequeños*. I would need to scrub hard. So hard it would feel like I was losing every last bit of me. Scrubbety scrub.

While I waited for the water to get too hot for any human to stand, I looked at myself in the mirror over the sink and practiced everything I would say if I found a way to knock on people's front doors. I watched my lips while I mouthed the words so I could remember them. The mirror fogged up from the steam, so I wiped it with my hand. I noticed how bad my fingernails looked, and that made me look at my toenails. I found the clipper and clipped all 20 of them while I practiced my speech again. The clippings flew everywhere, setting new world records for distance. I picked up as many of the nail clippings as I could find, which was probably 11 percent of them. Then I got in the shower and cauterized off the old me. Burned it off until every inch of me was red and raw. Until my brain was too hot, too full of burning, to remember anything except   for   right now   .

After I was clean, I went back to the mirror, wiped off more steam, and practiced a nice friendly face. A face that wasn't always angry. A face that didn't seem ready to say "no" as soon as anyone opened their mouth. I needed to look like a regular kid if this was going to work. A stupid, brainless, regular dummy with a stupid smile. Those are the kids that good things happen to. Those are the kids that people say yes to.

I tried and tried to look friendly. But mostly I looked sneaky . . . or like I was hiding a deep dark secret . . . or like I had been hit really hard on the head. I gave up. Friendly was overrated. I would focus on looking clean. I got dressed in my cleanest, least-ripped-up, least-stinkiest clothes, combed my hair the way moms and grandmas love little boys to comb it, checked to make sure you were still breathing, then grabbed my backpack and went out with no plan, no strategy, and no nothing. I went out onto the patio, looked to the left, to the right and then up to make sure nobody was watching. I went through the bushes, circled around the block, crossed the street to the side opposite the old people's home, found a shady spot, and sat down. I stared at the building. I squinted and stared harder, trying to think of a strategy. I stared so hard I kept forgetting to breathe.

I reached into my backpack and searched for my sudoku pencil. I dug for a scrap of paper but couldn't find any. I put the pencil back, looked around for a rock with sharp edges that would fit well in my hand. I found 1 along the fence. I came back to my spot, got down on all 4s and leaned forward to write on the sidewalk. I squeezed and un-squeezed the rock in my hand just like that day at the railroad tracks. I stared at the sidewalk waiting for something to happen. I couldn't wait for a smart plan so I just started scraping the rock on the concrete to draw a map.

I drew the old people's home with as much detail as I could. I drew it like I was flying above the building with x-ray vision to see through the roof, mapping out the layout. I had only been in the front door once when you took me in to see the dead guy, but I tried my best to recreate what I remembered. The sharp edges of the rock pressed into my hand and made deep marks as I drew. I scratched the left wing of the building where you lived. I scratched what I remembered about the other wing. I drew the area in the back where I scurry to and from your patio. Then I drew a little version of me across the street from the building. I looked at the picture. It was terrible, but it was good enough. I looked at the little version of me. I looked at the building. I looked at the little version of me again. I regripped the rock in my hand. I could feel Jesús standing next to me. I drew a line from the miniature me to the lobby, putting a big arrow on the end of the line. I drew another line from that arrow through the lobby into 1 of the halls and down to the end. I put an X at the end of that line. X was where I needed to go.

I stared at the drawing. I followed the arrow with my eyes. I stared at the X. I looked across the street at the building. I stood up. I dropped the rock but didn't hear it hit the ground. Maybe it hung there staring at me, seeing if I would screw things up again. I ran as fast as I could across the street, not looking either way for traffic, not remembering my backpack back next to the drawing, zoomed right up to the double doors, which opened with a shoooooosh just in time for me to not crash through the glass, tripped on the rubber rug where you're supposed to wipe your feet, breathing heavily and half-expecting security to tackle me and throw me in to a small dog kennel as a temporary jail until the cops came. It would be the kind of kennel for a wiener dog or a chihuahua. I was pretty small.

"Who are you here to visit, sweetie?"

I didn't see who said it. I looked up in the air like the voice came from the sky. God sounded really cheery, which didn't seem right. It didn't seem right at all. Not in this universe.

"Over here. The desk is too tall. Nobody can ever see me." She stood up and smiled at me. "Who are you visiting, lovebug?"

I was still breathing heavily but managed to spit out, "Ruth" reflexively.

"Oh, we love Ruth. Everyone loves Ruth. Such a sweetheart. Are you her grandson?"

"Huh?"

"Lucky you. I'm sure she's the best grandma in the world."

"Who?" I had no idea what was happening. None.

I was bent over, pressing a cramp with my hand, like I had just run a marathon up a mountain. How could a kid be out of shape? Did that building turn everyone into an old person?

"Here you go, cupcake. No need for you to sign in." She reached out and handed me a visitor badge to clip to my shirt. I couldn't get it to clip on, so she came around the desk and did it for me. "What a lovely surprise for Ruth. She will be tickled, I'm sure." She sat back down at the desk. She clicked some keys on the computer and said, "Ruth's apartment is number 129. Do you see that sign on the left that says 120-139? Follow that arrow and you won't miss it."

I took a step but stopped, looking back at her to see if it was a trick.

"Go on. She'll be so excited to see you. Have fun, pumpkin, and tell her I said hello!"

I did as I was told . . . sort of . . . which is more than I usually do when I'm told to do something. I walked toward the sign, followed the arrow to the left, which pointed the same direction as the arrow I had scratched into the sidewalk across the street. I walked down the hall, saw 129 on your door, went past it, went to the very end of the hall, knocked on the door and tried to fix my hair with my hands because it was already a mess somehow. When the old lady opened it, I said, "I know truth. I mean Ruth. Do you have small jobs? I'm a good worker."

She let me right in. They all did.

I chiro pitched once. Because his team needed it. He threw 18 pitches. 11 were strikes. He gave up 2 doubles and a run. Sometimes you gotta do what you gotta do.

I was planning to knock on more doors, but it just took 6 to fill up my pockets with chore money. I went back out to the lobby trying to think of how to get back in the next time. I needed a plan, but a voice from behind the tall counter said, "Come back any time, sweetie! No need to grab a tag! I'll tell the other desk girls who you are. Was Ruth tickled to see you?"

"When?"

"You're such a nice grandson! Would you like some candy?" A hand reached over the counter with a bowl like it was Halloween or something. "Take hand-fuls, please! Lord knows I don't need this sitting here tempting me all day! You're doing me a favor, really!" Everything she said sounded like it had an exclamation mark at the end. I looked at the candy, but it made me feel nauseous. There was really good stuff in the bowl. Even a Kit Kat bar. No taffy at all, but it still made me feel sick. I shook my head.

"Well, take some any time you want! I'll leave the bowl right here! I'll see you tomorrow, right? Can't wait! Have a peachy day!" she said like she wasn't a real person. Like she peed puppies and pooped kittens. Like rainbows came out when she blew her nose. Every atom in me needed to get away, but I kept acting like a normal kid. I waved, walked outside, and didn't start to run until I was all the way down the block.

I kept on running all the way to the store. Not Albertson's. I was too hungry to go that far. I went to the corner store. I got some premade sandwiches and stuff from the cooler section where they have real food instead of just snacks. I didn't even glance at the candy aisle. When I came back with the bag of food, you were awake, sitting up, not doing anything.

"Hi," I said.

You didn't say anything back. I told you I was going to make lunch, which involved unwrapping stuff from plastic. I called you out to the kitchen, but you didn't budge, so I brought a plate in to the bedroom. You ate like you had been stuck on an island for a month with only coconuts to eat. I couldn't watch. I turned away. Even animals would have turned away. I went out to the kitchen.

You ate 5 doors worth of food, money-wise, including the extra sandwiches I was going to have us eat for dinner. You came out and sat down on the couch after lunch to watch TV. That's what you were doing when I left to go knock on more doors, and it's what you were doing when I came back with fresh pockets-full of dollars and coins. I looked at your face. You had gone to bed with your makeup on the night before, and your face looked like Picasso was having a bad day. I tried to think of when your last shower was, but I had no idea. Kids don't pay attention to that sort of thing, so I got a washcloth and washed your face. You blinked a lot and made noises when I cleaned the top of your nose and between your eyes, but you stayed still enough for me to do it. The washcloth wasn't getting all of it off, so I went into the bathroom and got some of the little cloths I had seen you use at night sometimes. They were magic somehow and removed even the dark makeup around your eyes. When I was done, your face looked like a tired ghost—a ghost with bruises who must have been beaten up by a ghost bully with anger problems.

I didn't like it. Made me feel sick again. I went back to the bathroom and got your makeup bag from under the sink, took out all the stuff, set it on the coffee table, and started putting stuff on you. I started with the little jar of skin-colored stuff because I thought that would hide the bruises. I smeared it on like I was finger painting, and at best hid 28 percent of it. I gave up and got out the lipstick. Lips are designed all wrong. It would be way easier if they had straight lines, but none of them are straight. I did my best, which wasn't very good at all. I thought I was done, but I stood back and looked at you. You looked creepy enough to murder everyone, starting with me. I did some more work and got you to only look mildly crazy. I declared success, put the makeup away, turned the TV on for you, and left you alone for a bit in hopes you would be slightly less disagreeable when I did what I was going to do next.

I waited until 5:15 to give you extra time to relax and forget about all my pestering, then I said, "I'll be right back." I unlocked your hall door, went out through the sliding door, came in through the front doors of the building, barely acknowledged the way-too-upbeat woman at the desk, got 1 of the 49 wheelchairs they had parked in the lobby, pushed it down the hall, came into your room, pushed it right up to your feet, and told you, "We're going for a ride." I didn't say anything about dinner, and I sure as heck didn't turn off the TV. That might have made you mad. I pulled on your arm and you did the rest. You stood up, pivoted, and sat down on the wheelchair, all without taking your eyes off the TV.

I spun the wheelchair around, clicked the TV off after you couldn't see it anymore, tossed the remote onto the couch, and pushed you out into the hallway. I took you through the lobby, past the front desk, waved at the girl there, wheeled you outside, did 1 lap up to the corner of the property and back to make you think we were just on a way, then steered you back inside, through the lobby, and straight to the dining room. I had no idea where you usually sat, so I waited until someone waved and said your name. I took you to that table. I slid the regular chair out of the way and slid you in. The ladies at the table said a lot of stuff to you and to me, but they were all talking at the same time, and I had no idea what they said, so I told them you were my grandmother. I said I was visiting and would be coming to see you a lot. I said it loud so everyone would hear. They oohed and aahed and told me I looked exactly like you and that I was such a big boy, even though none of what they were saying was even remotely true.

The food hadn't come yet, so I gave everyone at the table my sales pitch. I added in something about saving up for a trip that sounded really good, and they buzzed and buzzed like bees that were going to come out of the trunk of your car and sting me to death 3 times over. They told me they had a zillion *trabajos pequeños* for me, and 1 of them pulled a pen and paper out of a purse as big as her torso to write down their names and room numbers.

I put the paper in my pocket and said I would come get Ruth later, but they made faces like I had ripped a rancid burp in front of them. They told me I shouldn't think of leaving. They scooted their chairs to make room for me. I sat down and braced for a waiter to tell me to get out, but the ladies asked them to set a place for me, and they did. Dinner was meatloaf and mashed potatoes. I couldn't remember the last time I ate either of those foods. I cleared my plate in about 3.33333 seconds and the other ladies at the table gave me their leftovers, smiling at me while they watched me swallow and swallow, barely chewing at all, like a sad animal that needed to choke it all down before the food could be stolen away by something bigger and stronger with huge teeth.

It felt like everyone in the dining room was looking at me. While I was stuffing my face with food, the ladies at my table had informed people at other tables that I was a little businessman and that I was saving up for a trip to Kalamazoo or West Timbuktu. I had forgotten already what my lie was. I had probably knocked on their doors earlier that day, but I didn't recognize them. All the old people looked the same to me. Almost everyone was an old lady. There were only a couple of old guys. Neither of them was Dr. Harry. Did they all die in wars and stuff? I didn't get a chance to come up with a better theory because a lady at the table closest to the kitchen got up, came over to me, leaned down, cupped her hand to her mouth, and whispered into my ear. I had a date the next morning. She would give me $5 dollars to get the cat fur out of her sofa with scotch tape wrapped around my fingers. $10 if I got every last hair. She told me her room number, but I almost missed it because I was looking at you. It looked like you were grinning. Not just a regular smile. It was a smile like when you win an argument. I leaned to the right to see your face better, but the grin wasn't there. I was sure you had done it. 3,000% sure of it.

Back when you were still talking, you said you were planning to write a book with all the things you say. Actually, that's not right. What you said was, "You should write a book with all the brilliant things I say." I looked at you like you had snot dripping out of your nose and you weren't doing anything to clean it up.

That reaction was all you needed to keep going. "I'm what this country needs, but people just don't know it yet. It's our little secret right now, but luckily, we are terrible at keeping secrets. So let's spill the beans and let the cat out of the bag. Let's sink some ships with loose lips. You get the picture. Let's get a pad and pen. Not pencil. This needs to be in ink so it lasts forever—for all posteriors. Ha!"

You started blabbering stuff at me to write down, but I folded my arms and sat there like it was some kind of protest. Eventually, you just grabbed the pad and pen and started writing down pages and pages and pages—laughing way too hard in between each 1, slapping the counter, dropping the pen, wiping your eyes, catching your breath, searching for the dropped pen, finally finding it, writing down more, and then doing the whole thing again. 1 of us was having a heckuva fun time. 1 of us.

I found those pages this week in a box in your closet. They were all crumpled because I had torn them out of the pad later, made them into balls, and thrown them into the trash. You must have fished them out and saved them for when I inevitably, inevitably, inevitably did exactly what you wanted—put them into a book. You must have put a chip in my brain that has a remote control. There's no other explanation. I just wish I controlled the clicker sometimes. You are monopolizing it. When is it going to be my turn? It's never going to be my turn, is it?

Here are some of the things you wrote. I will save the rest for the sequel.[95]

> *If you don't have anything nice to say,*
> *at least use good grammar.*

> *Nothing hurts more than unrequited love,*
> *except for a zit inside your nostril. That hurts way worse.*

> *If I kept all my opinions to myself,*
> *how would everyone know what to do?*
> *It's a risk I'm not willing to take.*

> *Love is magic.*
> *It can make your brain disappear (poof!).*
> *And it can saw you in half.*

> *Why do girls dress like sexy nurses for Halloween? There's nothing*
> *sexy about having to clean up barf, blood and poop for a 12-hour*
> *shift in uncomfortable shoes.*

> *The difference between humans and other animals is that we live*
> *with the burden of knowing we are mortal.*
> *Also: we invented s'mores. So that balances out the whole death*
> *thing.*

> *What's the meaning of life? That's easy.*
> *It's . . . It's . . . Oh, gosh. Senior moment.*
> *What was the question?*

> *I went to Ashland and laughed during Hamlet.*

---

95. "2 Many Ruths; 2 Many Truths"

People gave me the dirtiest looks, but he deserved it.
Hamlet is a schmuck. A real schmuck.

Death isn't something you should fear.
It's a natural part of life.
What you should really fear is dying in a ridiculous, hilarious
way.

The worst part of getting old is going to friends' funerals. Constant
constipation is no picnic either.

If you gave me $1,000,000, I would give half to charity, half to
my family, and half to the college where I got my degree in math.

Some people still argue that the Civil War wasn't about slavery.
They say it was about states' rights and federalism. Those people
are assholes.

People like to say that nothing good comes from war. Those people
have not read anything Kurt Vonnegut wrote.

My boobs used to be way up here and made all the boys love me.
Now my boobs are way down here, and all of those boys are in the
ground. I don't have anything smart to say about that. Life can
be cruel.

Some people say the most important thing you need in life is an
open mind. Others say it's a willingness to live in the moment.
They are all wrong. The most important thing is keeping a bottle
of hot sauce in your purse. There's a lot of bland food out there,
folks. A lot!

If I opened up a wig store, I would call it "I'm Wiggin' Out"
because the world needs more puns.

Scientists say that there is an infinite number of parallel universes
where there could be other versions of ourselves living other versions
of our lives. One thing I know for sure, though, is that in none of
those universes does my hair look good when it is humid out.

There are 3 kinds of people in the world:

People who think of themselves first.
People who think of others first.
And people who oversimplify everything.

On my gravestone, keep it simple:
"Good Tipper"

I had a full schedule of jobs right away, but it was all easy stuff that didn't use my brain at all. So I spent all of my time wondering more about whether you were faking. I wavered between being only 87 percent sure and being 98 percent sure. The average amount of sureness was probably 94 percent. My hands would be doing the job that was going to get me a dollar or 50 cents or whatever the amount was, but my head was back in the room wondering if you were acting normal while I wasn't there.

In between jobs, I would scoot out through the lobby, head around the building, and hide in the bushes to watch you. I wanted to see if you were up singing and talking to the birds and doing other Ruth stuff while I was out, having a grand old time until I came back, when you would flip the switch before I walked in and put the blank look back on your face.

I didn't catch you doing that, but that didn't mean anything. You probably expected me to be out in the bushes spying on you to catch you, so you didn't do anything normal. You were too smart to make that mistake.

So I tried other ways of catching you. I would announce that I was heading out to do my jobs or go for a really long walk to look for cans, then I would burst back in after 60 appleoranges—just long enough to make you think I was really gone. That didn't work the umpteen times I tried it.

I pretended to cut my hand once by smearing ketchup all over my arm and the floor and hiding my thumb in my palm. I jumped around in pain and pretended to pass out on the floor from loss of blood, but you didn't buy it. I gave up and licked the fake gory mess off my arm. Sugar by itself is gross, but ketchup by itself is still ketchup. It's still good stuff. I did my best to clean it off the floor, too, but the bottoms of my socks kept turning red for 3 days afterwards.

I tried crying in the middle of the night like I had a terrible nightmare. I really put some effort into the fake sobbing and felt pretty proud of it, but you didn't come out to the couch and comfort me. I even went into your room and cried 1.111 inch from your face, mumbling something impossible to understand about the bad dream just like kids do. No luck.

Another time I said your name over and over again like I needed something—Ruth, Ruth, Ruth, Ruth, Ruth, Ruth, Ruth—to drive you so crazy you would have to tell me to shut the heck up. I must have said your name 500 times in a row until it started driving me crazy. I had to stop to save my own sanity.

I thought I saw you watching me with a twinkle in your eye when Miss Elsa came over that first time to talk about school stuff. She didn't call it schoolwork, though. She called it exercise for my brain, but I wasn't a dummy. It was easy schoolwork I already knew how to do, so I didn't make a fuss. My hands did the schoolwork, but my eyes and my brain were reading your face to see if you were fighting to hide a grin. A "win grin" because you thought you had beaten me, but you hadn't. I was going to win, then I would grin and grin and point and grin. Just wait. You just wait.

There was no way I was going to stick with the school stuff, but my cricket-sized brain figured it was the best way I was going to catch you in this big lie. It was just a matter of time. You wouldn't be able to keep a straight face. You'd crack. I just had to be patient. You were stubborn. Almost as stubborn as me. But I was more stubborn. You thought you were more, but that would be your downfall. You could keep this up for a week if you needed to. Maybe even a month. But I could keep it up longer. Some day when your guard was finally down, you would let a snort slip out while I was concentrating on some hard math problems with my tongue poking out of my mouth the way it does. You couldn't help it when my tongue was out. It was the funniest thing to you. I would hear the snort, see the life in your eyes, hop up from the couch, point at you, yell "I caught you!" and do a victory dance like I had just hit a home run. Then this would all be over.

I was sure of it.

I was 163% sure of it . . .

. . . but just in case, I also tried to undo what had happened to you. That's what made me buy the cucumbers and squashes. If I hit you in just the right way, it might undo what that boy had done, and you'd go back to normal again. Plus, if you were faking, there was no way you'd be able to just let me hit you with semi-hard vegetables. So, it would work whether you were lying or not. It was a foolproof plan. There was no reason not to do it, if you think about it.

I spent a lot of time in the produce section picking out what I would use. Usually when I shopped, I would spend 30 seconds at the most in the fruit and vegetable section, just grabbing a few bananas or apples and then getting the heck out of that area to focus on real food. But veggies were my number 1 priority that day. I could have picked lots of things to hit you with, but it seemed like vegetables were the best idea. My thinking was, they would break before I broke your head, so they had built-in safety. That's just science.

I checked the cucumbers first. The regular 1s seemed too soft on the inside, like they would burst when I whacked you, but the English cucumbers were great. They felt firm all the way through. Plus, the plastic wrap around them made them feel extra good for head-whacking. I got 2 of them in case I broke the first 1. I looked at squashes after that. I picked up all the butternut squashes to see how they felt, but they were all too big and hard to hold. The spaghetti squashes were even bigger, so I didn't even try those. The acorn squash felt way too hard, plus they were the wrong shape unless I was going to throw it at you like King Felix throwing a fastball. I decided against that, but only after thinking about it for at least 30 Mississippis.

I almost got a yellow striped squashes that was way in the back of the display. I didn't know what they were until the sticker label told me they were delicata squash. They were a good shape to hold and swing. Plus their name was really close to "delicate," so that meant it couldn't possibly hurt you. I pressed my fingernail into it. It didn't give way at all. It was way too hard. I would have knocked you out, so I put it back and went over to the zucchinis. They were all small, so I asked the worker if they had any bigger 1s in the back. He went back to check and came back with 1 that looked as long as my leg. He handed it to me and said it was free because nobody ever bought the giant zucchinis. I looked around like security was going to get me, but he told me just to tell the cashier that Brent said it was free. I barely paid attention to what he was saying because I was pressing my thumbnail into it to check if it would knock your head off by accident. I swung it in the air like a stick to see how it felt. He gave me a funny look. I gave him a thumbs up and put it in my basket. I left the produce section. I grabbed 2 rolls of paper towels on the way to the register. I was assuming there would need to be a cleanup on aisle you.

At home, you were sitting on the couch watching TV. I went into the kitchen and washed all the vegetables. I must have thought that was important somehow. I carried them over to the coffee table, sat down next to you and told you what I was going to do. I waited to see if you argued back. You didn't, so I did it, using each vegetable, 1 by 1, from the softest to the hardest. That was a scientific approach, but it didn't work.

I looked at the pile of bruised and broken vegetables on the coffee table. I scratched my head and decided to put them outside for the birds. They didn't touch them. After 2 days I was sick of looking at them, so I chucked them into the bushes as hard as I could. They would turn back into dirt. It was the circle of life in action.

Here are some of the jobs I had:

Mrs. Grace had me help her with her bills and write letters for her because her arthritis was too bad to do those things herself. I didn't know what arthritis was, so she showed me how twisted her hands and fingers were getting. They looked a little bad, but not terrible bad, and I just sort of shrugged. She went into a stack of stuff in her closet and pulled out an X-ray picture from the doctor that showed the bones turning into pretzels inside of her hands. That was the grossest, coolest thing I ever saw. Getting old is stupid and crazy and disgusting.

Once, Mr. Will's only job for me was to tie his shoes. The laces had come undone, but his back was acting up. He gave me a dollar just for that. But once a month he gave me a lot more to get him a bottle of Glenmorangie. I would ride down to the liquor store on the bus with a pair of 50-dollar bills in my pocket and then wait outside—not too close to get noticed by the workers and not too far to miss the customers going in. I would wait for a friendly-looking man and ask him to help me get it as a present for my grandfather. I would tell the guy how old the scotch needed to be, and they would always nod solemnly like I was making a wise, wise choice. Usually the first guy I asked would do it for me. The longest it ever took was 3 guys. I guess it's safe to assume a kid wouldn't buy expensive scotch for himself. Mr. Will always let me keep the change, which was a lot.

Once a month, Mrs. Beth had me walk down to the Albertsons and buy all the "dirty magazines" she didn't like receiving in the mail so she wouldn't be judged: *Cosmopolitan, Glamour*, the latest *Enquirer, Allure, Muscle & Fitness*, and the latest issue of *The New York Times*. She gave me a special reusable bag to carry it in because everyone can see right through the cheap plastic bags the store gives. What she read was nobody's business but hers (and mine).

Mrs. Iveta had me kill spiders for her and collect dead flies from the windowsills. They scared her silly. They didn't bother me, though. I had seen way worse things. Way worse.

After the vegetable experiment didn't work, I started to worry more that you weren't faking. I was still 138% sure you were, but a very small part of me was worried you weren't. I know that math doesn't add up, but math doesn't always add up when it comes to people's feelings. Actually, I'm pretty sure it never adds up when it comes to feelings. Every person in the world has at least 184% percent of feelings in them. That means they can feel a certain feeling 100%, but still have plenty of percent left over to be feel a completely contrary, inconsistent, opposite, reverse, upside-down feeling. You can't argue with facts.

All of those more-than-100% feelings made me feel mixed up. I thought Dr. Harry could help, so I asked him to meet me down the street at the coffee place. That would be a neutral location where you wouldn't be able to hear what we were talking about.

I saved the 2 comfy, cushioned seats that were away from everyone else. When he came in, he waved to me and pointed to the register area to tell me he would get us drinks. He ordered, came over to set down his jacket on the empty chair, went back to wait for our drinks, and talked and talked to the girl making drinks, who was clearly sick and tired and more sick and more tired of talking and smiling at strangers all day. When she was done, he brought over our hot chocolates. Mine had whipped cream. His didn't. We had sips, then he asked me how you were.

I shrugged.

"Has she gotten worse?"

"She's the same." I scratched between my legs like there was a centipede loose in there.

He nodded.

"She doesn't say anything and doesn't look at me."

"She had a serious injury."

"She does everything else, but not talking. When it's time to wake up, she gets up. She works the TV with the remote. She goes to the bathroom. She never pees her pants. She gets in the wheelchair when it's time to go to dinner. She goes to bed when it's time to sleep. She is like a robot." I let the robot word hang there because I thought it was the perfect word. Then I got to the important part. "I don't like it."

"I understand how upsetting that would be." He took a deep breath and let it out really slowly. "There's no blueprint for these kinds of things. No single way it affects a person. This may just be a temporary thing. The good news is that she's able to do all the basics. She doesn't need 24-hour care, which we should be grateful for. We just need to be patient."

I bit a fingernail, then said, "I thought she was faking."

He stopped mid-sip and looked at me. "Faking?"

"Yes. She wants to win."

"I don't think she's faking." He said it with the voice doctors use when they tell someone the lump on their neck is just a disgusting zit rather than a tumor, but the patient insists it's a tumor, even though it's just a disgusting zit.

"She's always trying to win. She's the same as me."

He put his hand on my arm. "You may be giving her too much credit. This kind of head injury can change a person, especially someone at her age."

"I just stood there," I said really quietly.

"It's important to her you are with her and helping her. Even if you're just there next to her, that is a valuable thing. There are studies that prove it."

I put the hot chocolate on the table in front of us and pushed it away.

"This is very early in the process, so things may change. The human brain is an amazing organ, and any time you think you have it figured out, it outsmarts you." He shook his head for what was probably 18 minutes, then said, "All those years as a doctor made me very humble because of how many ways you can be wrong about what the human body can or can't do. The only thing you can be certain of is that you're probably wrong."

"You sound like her."

"Well, she is a smart lady."

"Was."

"We need to be patient. Just keep doing what you're doing because it's working. She's eating. She's alert. I've been checking in with the nurse every day. Thank goodness she doesn't give 3 cents about privacy rules. She keeps me up to date, plus I've stopped by to check on Ruth while you've been off making a mint with your chores."

"Did she talk to you?"

"That's not the most important thing. It could be much worse, and we should appreciate that."

"Grown-ups always say it could be worse."[96]

"We do tend to say that."

"It's dumb."

"Well, it happens to be true."

I pressed my lips together hard and looked at my shoes.

"I need to tell you something," he said to me. He looked at me with a serious look. It made me want to get out of there. "I didn't agree with Ruth about all this," he said, motioning his hand in a circle in my direction. "But she made her decision, and the least I can do is support it until things are back to normal. That way you won't be on your own, and I can sleep at night." He cleared his throat and took another sip of cocoa. "I need to ask you something, and I would appreciate an honest answer." He moved to the edge of the chair, turned toward

---

96. Some kids say that, too. [cough cough]

me, and leaned toward me like he wanted me to open wide and say, "Aaaaaah!" "Do you have a good reason for being here rather than where you came from?"

My eyebrows got very mad. "Ruth said I never had to talk about that. We signed a paper. It's in the oatmeal."

"That sound very official."

"It is."

"You know, legally speaking, that doesn't apply to me."

"I'm a kid, so I don't care."

"I guess not." He took a sip.

I thought about what he would do if he knew I had hit you in the head with vegetables to try to make your memory come back. He would probably freak out and call the police, the army, and the fake priests at fake St. Patrick's. I wouldn't blame him.

He was looking out the window now, looking at the trees or the sky or nothing. "If someone had asked me if I would let this kind of thing carry on, I would have told them they were crazy. I'm not an irresponsible person, but that's neither here nor there to you. Here's what you will care about. I've organized a group of ladies to help look after you until—. Until things change."

"I'm staying with Ruth."

"Yes, yes. You can stay put. That won't change. The ladies will just help out a bit."

"I can take care of myself."

"I know you can."

"I don't need anyone's help."

"You're a very capable young man, that's clear."

"I don't need—." You motioned your hands in a "calm down" way, so I shut up. My face was mad, but I kept my lips zipped.

"Look. You could walk out of here right now, and there's nothing I could do. I don't even know your last name, so I couldn't even track you down after your feet went across that threshold." I couldn't tell if he was pointing at the door of the coffee shop or toward the old people's home. "Nobody is forcing anything on you. I'm just trying to work out something that is the least-worst thing for you. Sometimes the least-worst thing is the best thing." He shook his head like that was deeply disappointing to him about this cruddy world. "I wanted to tell you man-to-man, so you weren't surprised. Miss Elsa and the others promised me they won't scare you off. So please don't prove me a liar. My final years will be hell if these ladies are mad at me. God help me."

"You should move to a place with all boys."

"That's a thought," he said. "There aren't that many men my age, though."

"Is it the wars and stuff?" I asked.

"Mostly the 'and stuff.'"

"I hope I never get old."

"My job is to make sure you do. My apologies in advance. It stinks. It really stinks." He took a last sip, but the cup was empty. He made a face of disappointment, then shrugged and made a face like he was used to disappointment, so what the heck. He struggled to get up from the comfy chair and said, "Hang in there. I know you will."

I watched him walk out to the parking lot. It took him approximately 17 hours of shuffling and waddling to do it. He got into a car that was way nicer than I thought an old person could afford. It was red like blood fresh from a deep cut, and the engine roared like a lion that had just snapped the neck of a baby wildebeest.

I didn't want to go back yet. All those ladies would be so excited to boss me around, or even worse, ask about my day. My hot chocolate wasn't hot anymore and it tasted gross. I looked around and saw coloring books in a basket for kids who were bored. It probably helps the place make more money because the coloring books calm the kids down and the parents can stay longer and spend more money. I thought about how smart that was and how much money it made them. Dollars and dollars, I bet.

Mrs. Stephanie always had the most chores for me, even from that very first week. I made stacks and stacks of money from her. She had me do her dishes because she said the soapy water aggravated her eczema.[97] She asked me to come by every afternoon to help her with that even if there was just a mug and a small spoon to wash and dry. She also had me dust things that didn't need dusting and clean windows that didn't need cleaning and do 100 other things that didn't need to be done.

Mr. Wilfred paid me to get fancy cat food for Percy that wasn't at the regular grocery store. I had to take the bus to get to a store that sold it. It took forever, but he paid me for all my time, telling me, "Always make people pay you for your time, no matter what. That way you get paid even if things don't turn out. And if you get good results, make them pay you double for that. That way you get paid coming and going. It's good business." I took his advice and asked him if I could get paid extra for getting the right cat food for him. He laughed and laughed but didn't pay me extra.

Mrs. Nadia was the first person that didn't want me to do any chores. She

---

97. Thank you, spellcheck.

just wanted me to read to her. I did that 3 times a week until she died a few years ago. She paid me in cookies she made herself. Mr. Wilfred would have shaken his head and called me a bad businessman if he knew. But it was none of his beeswax.

Jeez, that place makes me talk like such an old person.

There was a knock on the door 1 day, and I hid under the sink out of habit. I didn't need to because I was "just visiting," but I zoomed under before they let themselves in. I could tell it was the nurse and the director woman because they said it in a loud voice like they were trying to be heard on the moon. They asked how you were. You didn't say anything. They asked about what you were watching on TV. You didn't say anything. They said some things to each other that were too quiet to hear. I opened the cupboard a couple of inches to try to hear better. I could see the backs of them near you on the couch. The director woman unfolded a paper and read something in a voice that sounded like a robot. The nurse leaned toward you and did something I couldn't see.

The nurse said, "Have a good afternoon, Ruth," in a voice loud enough to be heard on Neptune, and I closed the cupboard door when they turned to leave. When they were gone, I came out from under the sink, locked the door, came over to you and saw the plastic bracelet on your wrist with the thick part that sends out signals. I knew what it was. I knew who they made wear those. I tried to slide it off your arm. It was too tight. I tried to cut it off, but the plastic was too hard and thick for our stupid scissors. You watched TV while I tried to hack it off with everything we had in the kitchen. I even tried to chew it off with my teeth like a wolf caught in a trap. I gnawed and gnawed but no escape.

I bet you could have gotten it off with a knife, but you didn't try. You just sat there. We both just sat there. Both of us could have escaped, but neither of us could or would.

I picked up a couch pillow, pressed it against my face as hard as I could, and yelled until my lungs burned like dragon fire.

I won't be there for your next birthday, so I am going to give you your present before I leave. I am flipping through it now reading the lyrics, careful not to bend any of the pages or leave fingerprints. It has all his songs. The songs when he was as young as me now. The 1s when his legs were broken from the horse. And the 1s when he was as old as he was ever going to get.

I could have paid for it with other money, but I only used empty-can money for this, which I think you will like. I don't remember you singing this:

> *When the poor brain is cracking*
> *There's nothing like packing*
> *A suitcase and sailing away.*
> *Take a run 'round Vienna,*
> *Granada, Ravenna, Sienna*
> *And then a-'round Rome.*
> *Have as high time, a low time,*
> *And in no time*
> *You'll be singing "Home, Sweet Home."*

Here's something I remember from back when you still talked:

I set a prank-trap for you and waited. It was a dish of room temperature revenge for whatever prank you had done to me before that. Or maybe just payback for turning my life upside down.

The lights were off, and I had put both stools from the counter in the middle of the kitchen right where you would be tip-toeing, trying not to wake me up. I had closed the drapes to make our place as black as the inside of my eyelids, so you would never see the trap until your toes rammed into the legs. I was 197% certain you would say a world record amount of bad words.

I waited on the couch in the darkness and tried to think of nothing. But things were always bouncing around in my dumb brain like ping pong balls. Why couldn't I make them shut up? It was a curse. It is a curse. Stupid ping pong balls. When I try to not think about you now—3,248 miles away from you—all I can do is think about you twice as much. When I try to not think about coming back to see you, all I can do is think about it 17 times as much.

While I waited in that pitch-black room, the biggest ping pong ball was about a 10 pound pinecone you told me about that morning when you were reading the newspaper. It had fallen out of a tree and bonked a man on the head. He was going to sue for a bazillion dollars.

"What is the world coming to?" you had said. "Who sues someone over pinecones?"

"A pinecone doesn't have money."

"He's not suing the pinecone, Silly!"

"Trees don't have money."

You shook your head. "He's suing the property owner."

"Maybe a squirrel threw it."

"Squirrels can't throw a pinecone that big," you gently corrected.

"What if they were really mad? They get really mad."

"Even the world's maddest, strongest squirrel couldn't throw that."

"Maybe did it with a catapult."

"But how would they buy a catapult. They don't have money."

"They could buy it with acorns."

"You're right! Acorns are their money. Someone could sue them for all the acorns they have...but you'd be nuts to do that. Nuts to sue for acorns." You held your hand up to your mouth, muffling a laugh, and your feet did a little dance in front of the couch at the same time. It was the quackadile joke all over again. "Get it? Acorns. Nuts." You stared at me waiting for me to laugh. I was certain you were the most unfunny person in the world.

"Acorns aren't nuts," I corrected.

"Are too!" you countered.

"Are not!"

"Are nut!" Your feet did a little dance again, and I made a not-amused-in-the-least face at you. "Seems like we are at loggerheads, My Dear. So we will need to put this up for a vote. All those in favor of acorns being nuts, raise your hand." You raised your hand, and I held my right arm down with my left hand just in case it wanted to jump up. "OK. That's 1 vote for nuts. All those in favor of acorns not being completely, utterly nuts, raise your hand." I raised my hand and waved it a little. You didn't. "That means we are tied. We will need to flip a coin." You reached into your pocket and pulled out a quarter. "I will flip it. You call it in the air. Whoever wins the flip wins the great acorn debate." You flipped it, I called heads, but the coin spun and spun in mid-air....

Sitting there in the darkness, I didn't let it land. I wanted all of those ping pong balls out of my head, so I pinched the skin on my arm as hard as I could. I could still see the coin spinning mid-air, so I twisted my pinching hand to make it hurt even worse—giving myself a purple nurple on an armple narmple. The pain went to the center of my brain, and the coin went away. No coin. No acorns. No nothing.

I stopped the pinching, and my arm pulsed with pain each time my heart beat. I focused on the pulse. I stared into the darkness. I had forgotten where I was. I had forgotten about you. I wanted it to last forever, but....

Ping. Where were you?

Pong. Were you having fun without me?

Ping. Were you sick of me?

Pong. Were you coming back?

It went like that for about 13 hours until you rescued me. You fiddled with the key and the lock and the doorknob, opened the door a few inches, tried to squeeze through without letting a lot of light in, couldn't get your belly and boobs through the opening, opened the door more, made it through the opening, closed the door, knocked over the stools, and said a world record amount of bad words. You turned on the light, blinding me, and looked at the scene of the crime.

"You boobytrapped me, Mr. Shenanigans!"[98]

"You boobytrapped yourself," I said back. That didn't make any sense, but it was the best I could do.

You picked up the stools and put them back where they belonged. You came over to me and did that dumb joke you always do: you slowly started to sit down in the spot I was sitting in, with your giant butt threatening to crush me, but did it slowly enough for me to scoot out of the way at the last second. Well, this time I wasn't budging. I didn't scoot. And you sat on me, pressing me into the couch so hard it felt like I was going to disappear into the cushions just like the remote control always does.

You squealed and said more bad words, but I couldn't understand any of it because my face was swallowed up by your back. You rocked back and forth to get enough momentum to get back up and finally freed me. I took a big gulp of air. You checked if I was still alive,[99] felt my arms and legs to make sure you hadn't snapped me like a twig, then sat down next to me, let out a big blast of wine-smelling breath, and said, "Do you want to know a secret?"

"No."

"I'm a little tipsy."

I didn't say anything.

"Actually, I'm a lot tipsy."

"Where were you?"

"Getting tipsy."

"The Mariners lost."

"That team could drive a person to drink."

"You were supposed to be here."

"Agnes had a little get-together. We were celebrating her new hip. It's a miracle what doctors can do today. She's up and about right away. She was doing

---

98. 8008YTRAPP30

99. Hey, that's my move!

the Watusi, but I don't think we can call it that anymore. It's not PC."

I just looked at you.

You put your hand on my arm and asked, "Were you lonely?"

"I'm only lonely with you."

You raised an eyebrow at my attempt to hurt your feelings. "I think you missed me. That's sweet."

"I didn't miss you."

You reached over and tapped my nose with each word you said. "You. Did. Miss. Me. Didn't. You."

I stared at the blackness of the TV screen and fumed and said, "I. Did. Not. Miss. You." I looked into your drunk eyes and tried to think of something to say that would make you hate me forever.

You knew exactly what I was thinking. I could tell. You looked over at the sliding door, said, "Holy cannoli, what's that?" When I looked over there, you leaned down and kissed me on the head.

I was stunned. Stunned that I fell for that mega-dumb trick. And stunned that I had allowed another old lady to land a smooch on me. But this time I didn't wipe and run and wipe and run and wipe some more. I just said, "No kissing! That is a new rule."

"Truism," you corrected.

"We need to shake on it." I held out my hand.

You shook it, then booped my nose again and said, "I love you, too, Sweetie Pie."

E gg. Egg. Egg.

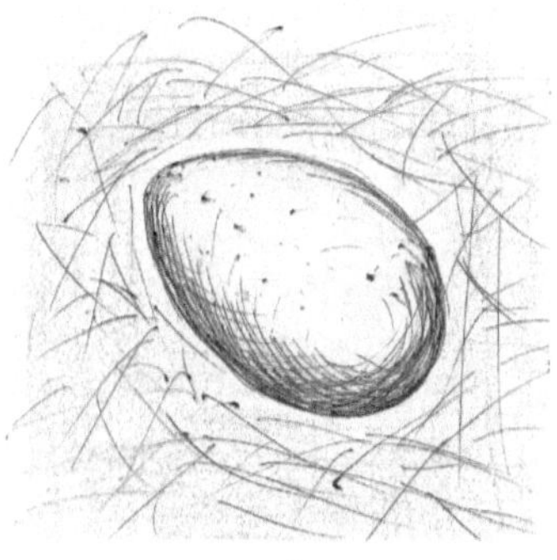

A lso from when you still talked:

"Ok. Next, we need a plural noun. Plural means more than 1."

"I know that," I said with needless attitude.

"Pardon me for assuming incorrectly. I'm still getting the hang of what you know and don't know. Now, what should I write down?"

I just looked at you.

"A person, place or things, Dear."

I just looked at you.

"Take your time."

I just looked at you.

"No need to rush."

I just looked at you.

"No rush at all. You have plenty of time to think of a great plural noun. No rush at all."

I just looked at you.

"I'm shutting up. I won't say another word.   Promise.   Cross my fart. And hope to cry.   Stick a beetle.   In my thigh.   Catch a tiger.   By its toe.   Larry, Curly, Shemp.   And Moe."

I sighed.

"I know, Dear. I am very annoying."

"Sticks."

"Sticks?"

"Yeah."

"Sticks aren't funny. You should say something funny."

"I don't want to do this."

"Clearly, because you're undermining it with answers like sticks. There are only 3 more to fill in. Let's put some effort into it so it's good and funny."

"Rocks."

"Rocks are even less funny than sticks. You're heading in the wrong direction. Let's turn this car around and head back toward Chuckletown."

"I can't think of anything. I won't."

"Farts. Butts. Burps. Boobs. Wieners. Poops. Did I mention farts? Those are all plural nouns."

"Fine. Wieners."

"That's the spirit. Wieners are hilarious. OK, now I need an adjective—a describing word."

"Stupid."

"You don't need to be rude."

"That's my word."

"Oh! Good." You wrote that down. "OK, we need a kind of liquid. Goodness, that is a softball pitch. So many funny liquids, like pee. Isn't pee funny? Go ahead and tell me the funniest liquid you can think of, Dear."

I pretended like I was thinking for a long time, then I said, "Water."

"Oh for goodness sake, why do I even bother?" You dropped the book and pen, left in a huff, and closed the bathroom door behind you.

I picked it up, flipped back to the right page, and wrote down a liquid: "greenish brown diarea pee mixed with blood and boogers and fingernails." Misspellings and all. I set it down and reread it. It was and may still be the funniest thing ever written. And you missed out. I think that means I won at Mad Libs.

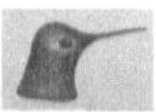

N ow all the way back to now:

When I try to remember that boy's face, I only see a blank. A flesh-colored, face-shaped blank where there ought to be a face. That's what I see if I try 25%. If I try 50% as hard as I can try, I start to see some blurry parts, but that's all. Just a blur of a face. But when I try 100% to see his chicken nugget-loving face, what I see scares the crud out of me. I see my own face. I'm looking back at me. I'm holding a bag of taffy and chewing and chewing and staring right into my own eyes. It makes my eyes want to pee their pants just thinking about it.

When I wrote the parts of this memory book that are about that boy, I tried to remember his voice, but I only heard my voice saying what was supposed to come out of his mouth. It was my face and my voice. That's what I saw and what I heard. This isn't a dumb dream I'm talking about. It's when I'm wide awake.

It happens right now if I try it right this very moment.

I bet if I think about it long enough, the clothes he wore will actually be my clothes. And I bet his shoes will be my shoes. And I bet he'll stare at the ground a lot just like I do, almost never looking anyone in the eye. And I bet he won't be able to pass a can on the ground without wanting to pick it up for the 5 cents. I bet I can't think of anything about him that is different than me.

Maybe he was never real. Maybe there were never 2 boys in McMinnville. Maybe my brain made him up because I did something so terrible that even a boy (me) who had no problem breaking rules (me) and laws (me) and truisms (me) left and right, willy nilly, couldn't deal with something that big. People do that all the time when terrible things happen to them or when they do terrible things to other people, right? They block it out or make up something that makes it easier to live with themselves so they don't go to the top of a tall building and jump off to splat their stupid heads on the stupid ground.

Why would some kid be standing there on the tracks?

Why would that stupid dog lead us right to him when it didn't even belong to that kid?

Why would any of it happen?

There are too many things that don't make sense. Maybe the only thing that makes sense is that none of it happened, and it was just you and me, and you took me on that annoying trip, and you made me do 777 annoying things I didn't want to do, and you kept trying to make me learn things that I didn't want to learn, and you kept trying to expand my horizons when I wanted them to stay exactly how unexpanded they were, and it built up and built up and built up and built up until it was too much. It was too much, and something happened.

If he never existed, then it's no wonder I spent almost 10 years working my skinny butt off, doing everything the old ladies tell me to do, trying to snap you out of it so everything would go back to the way it was, and never once trying to run away.

If he never existed, then all this has been about trying to not be that boy.

I know what you would say. You would listen to me say all those things about how he was me and I was him and what happened to you is my fault blah blah blah, and you would tilt your head and your eyebrows would look like they were trying to crawl up under your wig, and you would say:

"That is a big, steaming crock of baloney, My Dearest. Not even real baloney. Completely phony baloney. You think too much. Way too much! Now stop yapping and get the cards. I'm going to beat the pants off you. I hope you have clean drawers on because you will be pants-less in mere moments. Utterly devoid of trousers. Sans slacks. Plum out of pantaloons. Your mortal corduroys will be shuffled off...."

You always have the final word, don't you. Even when you refuse to speak.

Mrs. Bea would call me whenever she needed a good dish from the top of the cupboards. I would climb up like a monkey and try to pick the right piece based on how she described it. I would never pick the right 1 until at least the 5th try. They all looked the same to me.

Mr. Edgar hired me to wash and wax his car every other week. It was a white Cadillac his wife had bought him as an anniversary present when she was still alive. He wasn't allowed to drive anymore, but he kept it parked under the carport and had me rub it like it was a bottle with a genie in it. He would watch me sometimes from his window with sunglasses on to hide all the crying. That's when I would switch to the other side of the car, so I couldn't see.

Mrs. Sylvia paid me to set up the computer her daughter had sent her, then she paid me to do email for her so she could get photos of her grandkids. I told her we could do it much easier on her phone, but she wasn't ready for that. 1 step at a time. 1 step at a time.

Mr. Tim called me up to his room after he came back from the hospital from his stroke. I brought my cleaning stuff because I figured he needed help with that until his arm started working again, but that's not what he wanted. He had me do the knot in his tie so he could go to dinner looking the way he always did before. I did my best, which was pretty terrible. The front part was way too short, but his vest covered up my mistake. After that, I stopped by every afternoon to help him with his tie unless he beat me to the punch and did the secret knock on our door.

Mrs. Maria paid me to dust her Virgin Mary candles.

Mrs. Marta paid me to gather moss outside for her terrariums.

Mrs. Marla paid me to get fresh flowers from Albertsons. Sunflowers, if they had them.

Mr. Herman paid me to figure out how to go onto the Internet and order him catalogs from women's shoe stores. I didn't ask questions. I just did it. His coffee table was always full of them.

Mrs. Patricia had me come by every Friday afternoon to be her model. She would pose me however she wanted and then would turn on the TV so I didn't get bored while she practiced her sketches. When she passed away, she left me $2,000 for my college fund, plus she left me a sealed letter of recommendation to the Admissions Department of Middlebury College in case I decided to go there like she told me to every 11 minutes.

Mr. John had me get him food from Riccardo's every weekend, usually the sausage sandwich with marinara. When I was old enough, he asked me to go downtown on the bus and get him cigars from the place that has all the fancy kinds. I asked him what kind to get, and he just told me to tell the person at the counter that John D sent me. I did, and the worker gave me a bag with some boxes inside. He told me not to open the bag and not to show it to anyone. I didn't listen. I looked inside. It was cigars. I was hoping it was something exciting. No such luck.

Mrs. Mary was the easiest. I didn't have to do anything, not even pose or read. Her chore for me was coming by a couple of times a week and bringing my schoolwork. She had me sit with her while I did my homework. She just drank tea and watched me. I may be the only kid in the world who was paid to do schoolwork.

I carried boxes.

I opened jars.

I swept.

I turned sheet music.

I got books from the library.

I returned books to the library.

I took packages to the post office.

I gave advice about presents that grandchildren and great-grandchildren wouldn't hate.

I opened medicine bottles.

I bought cat food.

I brought secret cats to the vet.

I cleaned carpets with a handheld cleaner thing when secret cats peed on the carpet. I bought the cleaner myself and it has been the best investment I have ever made. I made a ton of money with that thing.

I shined people's shoes and helped them tie them too.

I helped button stubborn buttons.

I applied Bengay to hard-to-reach places. I did that so much, it stopped smelling terrible.

I bought better toilet paper for people who didn't like what the building provided.

I unclogged toilets.

I listened to people talk about things they wanted to tell anyone who would listen.

Those were my *trabajos pequeños*.

The ladies bought me a small safe for me to store my money. When it got too full, they gave me twenties in exchange for the dollar bills and coins to help me make more room. Then they gave me 50s and 100s to replace the 20s later on. I never counted it, though. I didn't even look at it. I would just shove the money in and close it back up a half second later because it made me sad. A kind of sad that doesn't have a word for it in the thesaurus. I know because I looked.

I had no idea back then why it made me feel that way, but I'm a little smarter now and I have a theory. But you can go first. Why do you think I felt that way?

I know you know.

I was a liar.

A fake.

A fraud.

I made such a fuss about never ever wanting to go to school while you were still you, but there I was sitting at the counter and doing exactly what an army of little old ladies told me to do, never putting up much of a fight, never threatening to run away.

I was an imposter.

A poser.

A sham.

While they were giving me a way too many assignments, I would listen to them with my ears, but I would look at you on the couch. For old time's sake, I wished 1 of them would use some reverse psychology on me to make things more interesting. Or get in a debate with me about the answer to a question to trick me into doing a ton of reading and research to prove them wrong. Or use a complicated scheme that would lure me into an activity that would eventually involve math or science, forcing me to do stuff with my brain before I even realized I was doing it. I wished they would pull a Ruth, but I guess there's only 1 you.

There were no mind games and tricks with my army of little old ladies. They were going to help me achieve my potential even if it killed them. Some of them have died, but I had nothing to do with it. I swear. I haven't touched a water balloon since that day.

Dr. Harry told me I was keeping them around longer. He told me that fussing over me so much I could barely stand it helped keep them alive a lot longer than they would have otherwise. He didn't even let me give him a nasty, dismissive look because he jumped right in and buried me under 6 feet of medical detail about the horrible medical problems each of them had—dire medical prognoses that somehow went into remission or faded away after they started coming in every day to torture me with lessons, and homework, and posture corrections, and critiques of my hygiene, and advice about how to be successful, and pointers about how to not be an idiot, and tips about how to find nice girls, and point-by-point instructions on how to treat nice girls nicely, and on and on.

Apparently, I was the cure for cancer, lupus, high blood pressure-related complications, wounds that hadn't healed in years, minor strokes, major strokes, unexplained numbness, blurred vision, irregular heartbeats, intermittent heartbeats, kidney failure, incontinence, cardiomyopathy, hypochondria, and clinical boredom. Dr. Harry told me someone ought to bottle me and sell me as an elixir.

But I was a placebo.

Sugar water.

Snake oil.

The power Dr. Harry claimed I had didn't do squat. They all keep dying.

The latest funeral was for Mrs. Childress. She didn't think young people should call adults by their first name, even if it has a Mrs. in front, so I always called her Mrs. Childress. Everyone did, so I have no idea what her first name was. The subject she bossed me around on was science. Dr. Harry told me she lived 4 years longer than her doctors told her she would. He told me a long list of problems she had. They all had long names and were terrible things that God (if there is 1) and Mother Nature (if there is 1) should be ashamed to have invented. When I got home from the service, I went through some of the assignments she had graded. The paper on top had a C-minus written on the top in the green ink she always used. I had done a half-assed job on it and didn't even deserve that high of a grade. Next to the grade she had written, "What would Ruth think?"

That's a very good question. Do I even know anymore?

And even if I did, should I believe a fraud like me?

Should you?

I did everything the army of little old ladies told me to do . . . except for 1 thing. But you know that, don't you? I bet it made you grin and grin on the side of your face I couldn't see when I finally put my foot down. I told them:

No girls.

No granddaughters.

No great-granddaughters.

No grandnieces.

No cute neighbor girl from down the street.

Not the darling girl who has the dog-walking business.

Not the cook's hot daughter.

Not the girl who works at La Provence who the ladies say smiles at me when they take me to brunch. Every time we go there, the ladies look back and forth between me and her and me and her like it's a tennis match. No!

Not the girl who does the bagging at Albertsons.

Not the girl in the newspaper who is student of the month.

Not the girl who made the huckleberry pie at the church bake sale I got dragged to.

I had to do something. It was out of control. I would show up to do my jobs, but there was no *trabajo* to be done. Just the little old lady sitting on the edge of the couch, scooted dangerously forward, imminently in danger of crashing to the floor, and vibrating with excitement to introduce me to the girl sitting next to her. I was too dumb to realize what was happening the first few times. I would just keep asking what chores needed to be done while the conversation kept getting steered back to things I had in common with the girl.

I could never look at the girls. They were too pretty. Too clean. So clean. The ends of their hair had curls that probably took 3 hours to make with 10 different machines in the bathroom. They smelled like flowers and sunshine and clear consciences. They smiled like it wasn't weird to smile. Their eyelashes made my brain hurt. I couldn't not think about how they were naked under all their clothes.

They had polite things to say and acted like I was worth talking to. I mumbled and wanted to flee. Because of the skin on their necks. Because of the shape of their ears. Because of the peach fuzz hair on their forearms. Because of the tiny socks peeking out of the tops of their sneakers. I couldn't look and I couldn't not look.

When they were quiet and wanted me to say something, that was the worst. I wanted to die and then run away and then die again. They were too everything, too everything for me. I didn't deserve them. They weren't real. I wasn't real. This was a dream.

I would tell them I have another job in another apartment, and I would escape. But it would be the same thing there. An even more excited old lady sitting next to an even prettier girl with eyes that cut me like a samurai sword through my baloney heart. Right through my chest and out the other side, while my heart pumped a few final beats at the end of the sword.

Escaping was no use, because there would be another girl in another room as soon as I got out of the room I was in.

I had to do something, so I made a list and refused to go to the rooms of ladies who had had girls waiting for me there. They still wanted my help with chores, so they stopped that scheme. But that just meant they shifted to other tactics. They started bringing the girls to dinner and arranging for us to sit next to each other. They scheduled movie nights in the dining room, and the only seat open was next to a girl who was too pure for this terrible world. For the trip out to Cannon Beach, every other seat in the bus was filled with old butts before I ever got on, and the only open spot was in the back row where I would have to squeeze between 6 long legs wearing capris pants that led down to 6 flip-flopped feet with 30 toenails painted 3 shades of pink. The driver slammed the door shut and started driving before I could turn around and escape. He was in on it too.

I threw out the list and made a new rule . . . decree . . . axiom . . . truism. No more girls. No more set-ups. No more coincidences. No more grand schemes. No more.

I must have sounded serious because the army of little old ladies stopped. They were peeved. I could tell when I went over to their rooms for *trabajos* and when they came over to our room for classes. I'm sure you noticed.

Was that all part of your master plan, or for once did I go off script?

I wrote a bunch of chapters for this memory book about what happened during all the years after the army of old ladies started teaching me, but it's as boring as staring into a fogged-up mirror. So I cut all of that out. My goal is to snap you out of it, not put you into a coma. I deleted all 27 boring-as-mud pages:

- All the stuff about the pet snake I got as a new ploy to get you to stop pretending. How I draped it over you, and hid it in your bed, and 369 other things that didn't work. Then how it got lost and is probably still somewhere in the building. Delete.

- All the stuff about how you-know-who arranged for me to get an ID, Social Security card, and everything else from someone shady, so I could go legit like a gangster in a movie trying to get out of the mob. Don't those always end in a storm of bullets? Maybe it's best not to ask. Delete.

- The time someone put a lot of alcohol in the Christmas party punch, and I was the only person not drunk as a skunk playing funk.

- All the stuff about how people put money into a college fund that added up to a number way more than what I earned doing chores.

- The stuff about how they taught me to drive and cook a decent meal and open doors like a gentleman and balance a checkbook and catch a fish and iron a shirt and make an acceptable martini and make refrigerator pickles and remove stains from a tie and other things so I wouldn't be a complete idiot after I left.

- And the stuff about how they created a short-list of schools, watched over my shoulder while I filled out every last blank on the forms, proofread my essays, made sure I didn't miss deadlines, set up meetings with alumni, made sure I didn't look like a slob for the interviews, and then watched the mail for reply letters just as closely as Mr. Herman does when he's expecting a new women's shoe catalog. Delete, delete, delete.

That was all very boring, so I deleted it. That's definitely the reason I deleted it. There is no other reason. The real reason is definitely not that reading it made me sadder than sad. The real reason is definitely not that reading it made me feel lonelier than lonely. And the real reason is definitely not that I don't deserve the parts that are good.

Those chapters were just a snoozefest, so I cut them. End of story.

What? Stop looking at me that way.

Stop it!!

Fine. You win. Here's a chunk I undeleted:

When the last of the letters came back from the schools, the army of little old ladies squeezed in our kitchen and spread them out on the counter. I'm sure Dr. Harry was there in spirit, not wearing pants because pants are stupid. The big 9x12 envelopes were in the middle and the thin regular-sized envelopes were pushed off to the side. I looked at the logos in the corner, then my eyes went to the handle of the sliding door. I couldn't help it. I guess it's in my nature.

"So, then," Miss Elsa said, clapping her hands together like she was going to adjust my spine. "Now we choose, yes?"

You were over on the couch. You weren't crowded around the counter with the rest of us. You were watching the TV, which wasn't on. I leaned to the left to see your face better, looking to see if you had a self-satisfied grin on your face. I squinted my eyes and tried hard to see it, even if it wasn't really there.

I reached down and apparently picked the black envelope.

Black like the TV screen.

Black like under your bed when I am blocked in by my pillow.

Black like the couch at night when the outside bulb is burned out before Jesús comes by, waves, puts in a new bulb, waves, and goes away whistling.

Black like the bruises you had around your nose and eyes.

Black like what I see when things hurt so fudging much.

Back when I was still trying to snap you out of it with swinging zucchinis, etc., I realized I was running out of ideas. Nothing was working, and I was feeling desperate, so I decided to do something crazy—at least crazy for a kid like me who hates communicating like it's costing me $3,773 a second. I stopped the games and spying and traps and vegetable-whacking, and just wrote you a letter:

> *Do you remember the day we met? I didn't know anyone had noticed me there, but you were watching me. It was the sound of the rock that did it, smacking down against the curb to crack the sunflower seeds, but mostly scattering them and making a mess of things. That made you look out the window, and there I was squatting down in my filthy green shirt with the stegosaurus on the front....*

I worked on it for 2 days, rewriting it a half-dozen times to make it match the way it felt to me and the way it probably felt to you that day. When it was done,

I put it on the coffee table in front of you. I straightened everything on the table, making everything 90-degree angles and parallel edges, then blinked my eyes to take a mental picture of it. I went out to do my jobs.

When I came back, the letter wasn't in the same place. I was sure of it. Other people may not have noticed the difference, but I did. It definitely wasn't exactly where it had been.

Maybe.

I stood in the same place where I had taken the mental picture and stared hard at it to be sure. Something was off. The bottom edge wasn't right, I thought. I looked around. The sliding door wasn't open. There was no breeze. The coffee table was pretty far from the couch. You wouldn't have bumped it with your robe if you had gotten up to pee. You must have picked it up. If you picked it up, you must have read it. And if you read it, you may have remembered the dirty kid smashing seeds and the peeking around the drapes and the cookie on the glass of milk. Maybe something sparked inside your brain and made you remember. Or maybe you remembered all along and the letter was a temptation that you couldn't resist. Either way, it didn't matter.

I walked over in front of the TV and folded my arms. You stared through my belly at the screen. The blue light of the TV flashed behind me like I had set a new high score. I tapped my foot and grinned a naughty grin at you.

I cracked my knuckles and got to work. I left you staring at the TV and brought a kitchen chair into your bedroom. I dragged it over to the closet, hopped on top and started pulling down boxes from the top shelf. That's where you had saved mementos from when I started living with you. There were bad drawings, and rocks we had gathered outside, and leaves we had traced to make art, and dumb stories I had written, and other junk like that. I put them all over the apartment like I was setting up for a yard sale. I took mental pictures of exactly where they were, then checked when I came back to see if any of them had moved even a millimeter. I studied it like a crime scene full of clues and ghosts and more clues and more ghosts.

I studied and studied but couldn't know for sure. So I started writing down more of those letters with stories about how you lured me in step by step until I was living here, and how I ran away, and how I came crawling back, and how everything you did to drive me crazy made me stay even longer, and how the more I wanted to get away, the more trapped I got until you got hit in the head and I was completely stuck. Stuck like a duck in the muck who's lost its pluck.

I wrote and wrote and wrote, taping up stories around the apartment in places you would see, like hanging off the bottom of the TV or on the cover of the toilet seat. Whenever I came back from chores, I studied them to see if any of them had moved. Most looked exactly the same, but every once in a while, it looked like a page had moved a millimeter or 2. Just enough to convince me the trap was working.

As I wrote new stories, I pulled down the earlier papers to freshen the bait. I shoved the older pages into a manila folder and that's where this memory book started.

The chapter about you trapping me like an eagle using gross snakes as bait? That was part of my bait for you. Ha!

The chapter about cutting candy bars with forks and knives? Bait.

The chapter about you and me touching a dead guy and giving him a name? Juicy, tasty bait.

I slowed down after a while. Too much homework. Too many *trabajos pequeños*. I stopped seeing the papers move even a nanometer to the left or right. So I shoved everything I had written into a folder and shoved the folder into a box and shoved the box into the back of the closet. Looking at them now, 2 things are clear: I was a terrible speller and I had no clue where, when, or why commas, should, be, used.,

If it weren't for you sitting there like a statue, Mrs. Mary would be the quietest person in the place. You could hear a pin drop or a flea fart when she had me over to do schoolwork while she sipped tea, paying me for every minute I was there even though I was just doing homework, not chores. She wouldn't say more than a dozen words while I was there. She would only say a few things like: "Welcome in, dear," and "Here are your assignments, dear," and "That's the final bell, dear" and not much else. Compared to how the other ladies talked nonstop, nonstop, nonstop, it was a vacation when she was my teacher.

I liked her the best because she left me alone. I could have doodled for hours, and she wouldn't have said a word. I could have made paper footballs and flicked them across the counter hitting her right between the eyes, and she would have sipped her tea and left me alone.

I should have just enjoyed it, but no. I had to open my stupid mouth about it. I asked Dr. Harry about it back when he was still here trying to help me make sense of things that don't make any sense. I asked him, "Why isn't Mrs. Mary as annoying as the other ladies?"

"Annoying? What do you mean?"

"The other ladies never shut up. They ask me 40,000,000,000 questions and they are all trying to fix me . . . like they are robots that Ruth made to drive me crazy until I'm dead."

"You may be on to something there."

"But Mrs. Mary doesn't say anything. She just sips tea." I let that float for a second. "I never see her pee either. She drinks so much tea, but she never pees. That's weird."

"I am confident she is peeing. Some people can hold it, believe it or not. I can't anymore. Getting old ain't fun. But some people can hold their number 1. She probably just waits until you leave."

"It's dumb to wait. You should just pee if you have to pee. Even if you're outside."

"I'll take that under advisement next time my bladder and prostate team up to create a urological emergency."

"Why can't the other ladies be quiet and leave me alone?"

"You're asking the wrong person that. I can't get them to leave me alone either. Mrs. Mary is different, for sure. I bet if we compared notes, she's saved more kids than I did during my doctoring days."

I looked at him like he was an idiot—the same look I gave you at least 30 times a day way back when. "Huh?"

"She has saved a half-dozen kids from drowning. She's pulled kids out of 2 separate burning cars. Maybe it was 3. She ran into traffic to save a kid that was on the highway for some crazy reason. CPR. Heimlich techniques. She even knew when a kid had a tumor in the back of their eye. And there are probably 10 others I'm forgetting. She's like a real-life superhero. Always in the right place at the right time."

"She's probably making all of that up. People lie, you know."

"I am aware of most people's aversion to the truth," he said and looked at me longer than he needed to make his point. "She's not fibbing, though. Some of them come visit her sometimes. She gets cards from all of them. Her mantel at Christmas time is overflowing."

"If she did all those things, why doesn't she brag about it all the time?"

"That's a good question . . . for you to ask her." So I did.

The next time I went over, when I was sitting next to her at the counter, half-focusing on my homework, I waited until she finished adding sugar to a new cup of tea and then asked, "Dr. Harry said you've saved 100 kids from fires and alligators and stuff. That's not real, right?"

Mrs. Mary put down her mug and tilted her head and put her hand on my arm. I thought she was going to talk about how it was no big whoop. How she was just doing what anyone would do. How it's a moral imperative to help your fellow human, blah blah blech. How the reason we're all put on this crazy planet is to help each other, ugg ugger uggest. And how she doesn't deserve any credit because lots of good-hearted people a day do way more in a week than she's done in her lifetime to make the world a better place. Blechety barf.

But that's not what she said. Not even close. She leaned toward me so slowly I didn't know it was happening until we were almost nose-to-nose. And then she opened her mouth but didn't say anything for at least 37 hours. And then, with a voice almost too quiet to hear, she said, "I'm sorry, dear, but it's not possible to save another person." She took her hand off my arm and her eyes drifted away, looking over my shoulder.

I felt a vague nausea start to creep through my body.

She kept looking past me. The nausea started creeping faster. I wished I had never opened my big, fat, stupid mouth. We stayed like that for a long time, and I assumed she wasn't going to say anything else until 1 of us either ran away or died of old age. But then she said more. "You can't do it for them, no matter how much you love them."

She put her hand back on my arm and opened her mouth again, and nothing came out for 37 years. Then she whispered, "Only they can."

She said all of that while looking past me, behind me. Every part of me wanted to turn around and see what she was looking at. 1 side of my neck was straining to try to turn my head to look there, but the other side was straining not to. 1 of my feet was pressing into the floor to spin the stool, while the other was fighting like heck to hold it still. I was afraid of what I would see behind me. Would it be you standing there behind me? Would it be me standing there behind me? Or worst of all, would it be nothing there behind me.

Nothing is the worst of all worsts.

She lifted her hand off my arm, releasing me. "Now, enough of that sad talk. Would you like some tea?" My bladder sent me running to the bathroom, but I didn't have a drop to pee no matter how hard I tried and tried and tried.

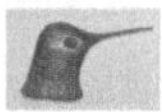

I didn't get much work done at Mrs. Mary's after she said that. I tried to act busy, but I couldn't concentrate. When the time was up, she said, "Take care, dear," and tried to hand me the money. I didn't take it because I was too busy fleeing, leaving a dust outline in the shape of my body like a cartoon character.

When I got to our room, I looked at you on the couch watching TV. You didn't look over at me when I came in. I sat down and looked at the side of your face. I could see all the veins under the skin near your ears and down near the edge of your shirt. I wondered if you were pretty when you were as young as the granddaughters and great-granddaughters that everyone wanted me to meet but that I couldn't look at because it hurt like staring into the sun.

"Ruth." 1 appleorange. 2 appleoranges. "Ruth!" 1 appleorange. 2 appleoranges. "Mrs. Mary said you can't save anyone else, and it's dumb to even try. You probably think she's 500% wrong, huh?"

The light of the commercials reflected off your face.

"Blink if you think she's totally wrong. She's totally wrong, right?"

I waited and waited. And waited. ...and then you finally did.

As I've been packing, I've sorted through lots of old boxes, and I haven't found a single photo of us. None. I don't ever remember posing for a picture with you, so I guess that shouldn't be a surprise. You don't own a camera and I never had a phone with a camera in it, so I guess that explains it. Actually, I don't remember ever seeing people take pictures. After all, who wants to take pictures of old people in an old people's home. Who wants 12 megapixels of sadness?

I could ask a neighbor to take a photo of us now. I could sit on the couch next to you and have them stand in front of the TV so you would be looking at the lens, but it wouldn't be real. I don't want it if it's not real. It has to be the Ruth, the whole Ruth, and nothing but the Ruth.

So no photos to paste here. Instead, I sketched out a little picture of us back during those first weeks together. Can you guess which 1 is me? I'll give you 2 chances to guess it.

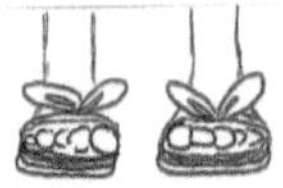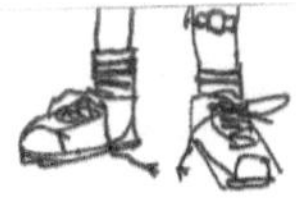

I was supposed to spend today packing, but I finished that yesterday and now I'm agitated because I don't have anything to do until the going-away party that everyone except me is excited about. I knocked on a bunch of doors and offered to help with chores, but nobody would let me. "Don't be silly. Today is your day. You should celebrate and have some fun."

What was there to celebrate? The clock had run out and I hadn't figured out how to get you back to the way you were. I didn't deserve pats on the back, and nobody was going to convince me otherwise. I fidgeted on the couch next to you and wanted time to pass faster or not at all. Maybe we would both drop dead and all our problems would be solved.

A couple of times, I said stuff like, "Do you know what kind of bird is on the feeder?" or "The Mariners won last night," or "Are you going to come to the party tonight?" But you just stared at the set.

I couldn't take it. I got up and left. I walked down to the store. The list of things I needed was short, so I wandered around to kill time. I looked at the toy section, but everything was for little kids. I went to the magazine stand. I started with the baseball magazines, but my stomach made me pick up the cooking magazine with a picture of a cake on the cover. It said "Down-Home Desserts" in cursive letters that looked like icing. I looked at the pictures of cakes and cookies and sherbets and trifles. I had to swallow the spit in my mouth. I looked around me to see if anyone was watching me. Nobody was. I looked at more of the pictures and swallowed more spit.

When I was able to shake myself out of that, I started shopping. I got a bag of brown sugar because we didn't have enough at home. We were fine on flour. I didn't need that. I looked at the chocolate chips. The store brand was on sale and was half as much as the others. I got that kind. I checked the recipe on the back of the bag to see if I was forgetting anything. We had enough eggs. We were out of vanilla, but I would borrow some from a neighbor because it was expensive to get a new bottle. I got a jug of milk. Just a quart. Then I got a new pack of baseball cards and a sudoku book to pass the time on the flight.

I walked back up the street to our building, came in through the front door, nodded at the person at the front desk, and went straight to your room. I said hi. You didn't look over. I put the stuff away and noticed the time. I got dressed in better clothes, came over and sat next to you on the couch. I waited until the clock next to the TV hit the right time, got the wheelchair for you to get into, and rolled you to the party.

It was late when we got back. The party had moved from the dining room to someone's apartment, then to someone else's apartment, then someone else's. There were bottles of alcohol and bowls of hard candy everywhere. People tried to give me sips of whiskey for toasts. I waved them off. Others offered champagne. I waved them off, too. Pretty soon, everyone was tipsy except for me.

They couldn't stop hugging me and wishing me luck and giving me advice and telling me to ignore other people's advice and telling me secrets they may never have told another living soul. With winks and pinches on the cheek, the old ladies put notes into my palm with the names and numbers of granddaughters and grandnieces who were going to school not far from where I was going. With winks and slaps on the back, the old men slipped packets of condoms into my pocket and whispered in my ears to "keep a lid on it" or "don't go out without your raincoat" or "don't go knocking anyone up, champ."

It wasn't all tears and secrets and sex talk, though. They asked me what I would study. They asked me what I would major in. They asked me if I would go to graduate school. They asked about everything except whether I wanted to go. Nobody had ever asked me. It seemed like a pretty important question to me, but I guess it was moot. I guess it had been moot for a while. Probably since you let the boy punch you in the nose and I made my arms go numb hitting the railroad tracks as hard as I could with that metal bar. As moot as a boot trying to blow a flute made of ripe fruit.

Eventually, Miss Elsa rescued me and told everyone it was time for me to get some rest. When we got back to our room, I wheeled you to the bathroom, waited for you to be done, then helped you walk to your bed. I got into my pajamas, brushed my teeth, went into your room, navigated through the boxes on the far side of the room, and crawled into bed with you. The room smelled like lozenges and you started snoring immediately. Lots of things had changed since the first night I stayed with you, but your snoring and your lozenge breath hadn't.

I didn't stay the whole night. I eased out from under the covers, trying not to make the mattress creak, navigated past the boxes, and went out to the living room. I got out my notebook and started writing you a goodbye letter that apologized for not being able to fix you. It was a terrible, dumb letter, so I crumpled it up. I tried several more times and crumpled those, too. I stopped trying. Maybe I would think of what to say once I was on the plane or once I got all the way there. My head would be clearer and I would be able to write it in 5 minutes flat. I was way off. I ended up writing this whole thing for you, and it has taken way longer.

T his is what you might be looking at right now, 3,220 miles away from me:

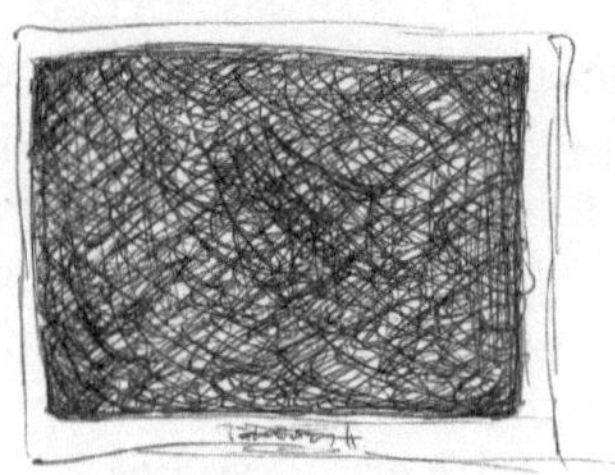

I 'm nervous.

And anxious.

I'm nanxious.

I'm nanxious as heck.

This memory book is almost done. I'm on third base and taking a long lead toward home plate. The pitcher isn't paying any attention to me, and the third baseman is way back on the edge of the left field grass. My lead is 6 feet...8 feet...15 feet. That should feel like a very good thing, but all I feel is nanxious. This is almost ready to send to you. The end is near.

Maybe I shouldn't stop. I should stay on third base forever. If I write just 1 more chapter, will that do the trick?

If I use 2 loops of tape to add 1 more baseball card, will that bring you back?

If I twist the truth enough, will that annoy you enough to end this standoff? What if I go through the Cole Porter songbook and find just the right song?

If I stop writing and send this to you, what will happen?

Will it make a difference?

Or did I miss all these classes and skip all these activities and avoid everything and everyone all for nothing?

Maybe this memory book is a monument to futility. Maybe that's why baseball is such a big part of it. Even the best of the best trudge back to the dugout 70% of the time, and even all-timers who have won a half dozen Cy Young awards are only remembered for the homers they gave up.

But I'm a stubborn so-and-so, as Dr. Harry liked to say about me. So here's 1 more chapter about us fighting. This might be our dumbest fight, which is saying something.

"Look at this lovely card I got!" you said, waving around a card too high and too fast for me to see what it was.

"It's not your birthday."

"Cards aren't just for birthdays," you corrected.

"How much did it cost?"

"It's impolite to look at the price."

"No, it's not. What if they sent you a card that costs 10 cents? That means they don't like you very much."

"Well, that's very superficial. It's the thought that counts," you insisted, but then looked at the back and whistled like you were impressed.

"How much?"

"100 dollars," you said, doing a high whistle and making your eyebrows dance, not quite in synch with each other.

"You're lying."

"See for yourself." You showed me the back of the card with your thumb strategically over the price. I made a face at you.

You opened the card, read it to yourself and slapped your leg laughing. "Oh, I do love a good pun," you said and slapped your leg again.

You handed the card to me. It had a sea lion on the front with a word bubble saying, "Thank you!" while it clapped its flippers. Inside it said, "You get our SEAL of approval!"

I shook my head at you. "That's not a seal."

"What do you mean. Of course, that's a seal."

"That is not a seal. They messed up. And the joke is dumb."

"1st of all, Dear, all puns are funny. Second of all, this is definitely a seal. What do you think it is, a giraffe?"

I felt my ears getting red. I closed my eyes and tried to count to 10, but that is the stupidest thing ever. I only got to 2 and blurted out, "That. Is. Not. A. Seal. That. Is. A. Sea. Lion."

You looked at me confused. You looked at the card confused. You looked back at me. "Those are the same thing. Seal. Sea Lion. Po-tay-to. Po-tah-to."

"Seals and sea lions are different, and this is wrong."

We were at a standoff. You stared down at me with your hands on your hips. I stared up at you with my arms folded tightly enough to turn coal into diamonds. We looked at each other for a while, until you declared war. "Sweetie, let's just agree that we're both right and this is a funny card...................about seals."

"SEA LION," I yelled loud enough to be heard by old people in the retirement home down the street.

"Seal," you said as calm as a cup of chamomile tea. That made me even madder.

"SEA. LION." I spat the words out with a cloud of spit that rose up and engulfed your head.

You slowly wiped half of your face with a sleeve, then wiped the other half with your other sleeve. Then you leaned down, pressed your nose against mine, and, with an "S" that lasted at least 59 seconds, whispered, "Sssssssssssssssssssssssssssssssssssssseal."

I must have blacked out with rage because the next thing I knew I was halfway to the library, which was at least 3 miles away up the big hill toward the high school, then down past the golf course where the rich people plot against everyone else in the world, then down into the old part of town. I was mumbling bad words under my breath the whole way and kicking rocks on the sidewalk like they had tried to feed me cookies with sand-like sprinkles on them. I was gripping the sea lion card so hard, it was soaked with my little-kid sweat.

I marched upstairs to the computers on the 2nd floor, realized I had to pee, went to the bathroom back on the 1st floor, peed, marched back up to the computers, propped up the mangled picture of the sea lion next to the screen, tried to flatten it against my leg, re-propped it next to the screen, and spent no less than 120 minutes forensically comparing it to every species of sea mammal on the planet. I know it was that long because the 30 minute reminder popped up 4 times encouraging me to give other people a chance to use the internet. Other people could go straight to the Aleutian Islands. I was on a mission to prove you wrong.

At the beginning of the 3rd hour, after the library intercom warned they were closing in 15 minutes, I found the match. It was a Steller sea lion, which scientists were studying in Alaska. There were pictures of happy scientists posing near the animals. They were smiling because they were saving the world. They looked smart and happy. I immediately hated them. I started printing pictures.

The librarian came by to make sure I had heard about closing time. I gave her a death stare and she moved on without saying a word.

I grabbed the printouts in a fistful that half-crumpled them, stormed out of the building, walked the 3 miles home, crawled through the bushes, came in through the sliding door, handed the half-crumpled photos to you with shaking hands, and gave you the same death stare that had worked so well on the librarian.

You uncrumpled the photos. You compared it against the card I was aggressively holding up close to your eyes so you could see I was totally, 100%, 1,000%, 1,000,000% right.

And you calmly, crushingly said, "Where did you get such lovely pictures of seals, Dear? I'm going to put these right up on the fridge. Thank you, Pumpkin!"

I was so mad at you, I think I passed out for 48 hours.

Or maybe 84 hours.

Or maybe 4,884 hours.

1 last Ruthism:

The biggest lie you can tell yourself is that you don't deserve love.
Actually, that's the second biggest lie...
...just behind telling yourself you look great in those shorts.

Have I mentioned I hate when you're right?

Not as much as when you're wrong and won't admit it, though. That animal was a sea lion.

There are 2 boxes on my desk. 1 is for you, and 1 is for me.

It's done except for this chapter that I am adding in after I finished everything else. I thought I was done before. I had printed all of it, and taped on the drawings and doodles, and gone down to the post office, and stood in line all the way to the front, but then I realized I was an idiot. If I mailed it to you, it would just end up in your stacks of boxes, unopened, buried in between a set of nonstick frying pans and a box of dicer/slicer/chopper gadgets.

That stumped me, so the boxes have been sitting on my desk waiting for me to come up with a plan. Tick tock, tick tock.

The only thing I was sure of was I wasn't going to deliver it in person. I didn't trust you or myself. If I came back and you were up and about, playing canasta with the ladies like nothing ever happened, I might drop dead on the spot like a bunch of water balloons had just hit my head.

Or, if I came back and you were sitting there on the couch staring at the TV like you were when I left, it would be even worse somehow. Worse than dropping dead.

It's better not to know, like Schrodinger's cat. It's alive and dead, so let's leave it that way.[100] Let's leave it be, then maybe we can both be right and nobody

---

100. Meow?

has to be so wrong—so wrong that our hearts break into 37,000,000,000 pieces smaller than neutrinos.

I won't mail this to you. I will mail it to Miss Elsa and ask her to put this big interdepartmental envelope on your coffee table right where you always put the remote control. It will have the sticky note that says: Read Me.

Actually, I won't put that sticky note. Since you're just like me and always do the opposite, I'll put a different sticky note on the envelope. It will say: Don't Read Me.

Let's hope you won't listen to me.

Not even a little bit.

I didn't go to class today. I filled my bag with some snacks from the dining hall and watched the other students from some bushes near the science building.

Most were looking at their phones while they walked, even when they were walking with someone else. A few people held hands. A girl was reading a book while she walked and kept wandering off the path and almost twisting her ankle. A guy was carrying a lacrosse stick and was spinning it with a ball in the netting. I hated that guy. I don't know why, but I hated that guy as much as anyone I have ever hated. The only way I could have hated him more was if he were shoving nuggets into his face hole.

A boy looked around to make sure nobody was watching and then scratched his crotch. A girl stopped, set her backpack down, let her hair down, put the hair tie on her wrist for safekeeping, arranged her hair, put the hair tie back on, and slid the backpack back over her shoulder—all in slow, slow, slow motion that made my chest hurt, hurt.

I had to look away. But everywhere I looked made my chest hurt.

So I tried to act like they bored me.

And I tried to ignore my bladder.

And I tried to ignore my hungry stomach.

But most of all, I spent a lot of time trying to convince myself I wasn't 1 of them.

Is Ichiro going to stretch a triple into a trip all the way around the bases?

Or will he zoom right through 1st base and keep going, going, going into the sunset?

Itterashhai, number 51!

Sometimes I have trouble sleeping in my bed. It's a good bed with a good mattress, but maybe that's the problem.

When that happens, I get out of bed, go out into the common room—arms full of blankets and pillow—lie down on the couch, fold up my legs so I sort of fit, almost, sort of, but not quite, and I finally feel at home. That always does the trickety trick.

A lot of your Ruthisms are about dying or being dead or being a ghost or something related to being 6 feet under.

Sometimes I worry about you dying. I worry that there's nobody there to check if you are still breathing when you are sleeping.

I worry that you reach for the clicker to switch to a different infomercial and your last act on this earth is to press the channel-up button.

I worry that you are going to kick the bucket before you remember me.

I worry that you will keel over and your wig will fall off and you'll be mad that the last image of you is as a ridiculous woman with an almost-bald head and a wig covering your eye like you are a pirate.

I worry that you were faking, and you will die before I come back and walk in and catch you lying like a stinking lying liar.

I worry that you are not faking, and you will die with me still thinking that this was all an act to make me a better person against my will—against every ounce of my will.

I worry about a lot of things if you haven't noticed.

The biggest thing I worry about is that this all didn't really happen, and I am crazy, and you are not real, and I am not real, and you are a figment of my imagination, and I am a figment of my imagination.

Is there a button I can press to transport myself to cancel all of this out.

Undo it.

Delete it.

Erase it.

Can you tell me how the game ends so I know whether to get my hopes up?
Did Ichiro go 3 for 4 with a stolen base and an assist at 3rd?
   Please tell me.
   Please and thank you and everything else that good boys do.
   Everything else that good boys do.
   Please.

J ust 1 mourning dove:

T he day before I left, I broke our 3rd truism—the biggest, most important,
   most unbreakable truism.
   I sat down next to you, picked up the remote, muted the TV, and told you.
I told you what happened before I met you. Before I was outside your patio
smashing sunflower seeds with a rock. Before you lured me in and trapped me
like a stupid bug in a stupid web.
   I told you everything.
   You stared at the screen.
   I spilled my guts.
   You looked right past them at the ad for razors with 4 blades instead of 3.
   For a half of a half of 1 second, I thought you had finally won.

But I don't give up easily.

I didn't go to classes at all this week.

Or did I?

Would it make you antsy if I hadn't? Would it give you ants in your pants? Would it make you hop on a plane and come out here to set me straight?

Would it make you antsy if I told you I'm trying my best to flunk? Would it make you laugh if I told you I'm terrible at flunking? No more time for questions. Gotta go. It's 4:00 and time for dinner. Maybe I'll have brownies with a brownie salad to make it healthy.

I dried the baking sheet and mixing bowl and spoons and put them away in the cupboard. I wet a paper towel and wiped down the counter. I doublechecked to make sure I had turned off the oven.

I went out into the hall and got the wheelchair. I pushed it up to the couch and set the brake. It wasn't dinner time, but you stood up and sat in the chair like it was. I lowered the footrests and set your feet on them. I straightened your wig. We went for a roll. Out of our room, down the hall, through the lobby and automatic doors that said shooooooosh, across the drop-off area, through the little flower garden, up the sidewalk under the trees, then back to your room, where I parked you in front of the sliding door. I set the brake and fixed your wig again.

I looked into your eyes. One last check to see if you were trying to win. You stared straight ahead, out onto the patio.

I got my bags, brought them outside and dropped them on the other side of the metal railing. I filled up the feeder with fresh seeds, got bread from the cupboard, ripped it up and scattered it on the ground. I went back to the kitchen, filled up a glass with milk and put 2 of the cookies on a small plate. They were still warm. I brought them outside, put the glass on the metal rail, and put the plate next to it.

I slid the screen door closed and pressed my face against it looking at you. You weren't blinking, so I tried not to blink. My eyes started to twitch and itch and water and close. I finally blinked. Maybe you did, too, at the same exact time.

Let's call it a tie.

I climbed over the railing, got down on all 4s, grabbed my bags and scooted across the gap to the bushes. I didn't leave, though. I came crawling back, reached up, and took a treat. Don't worry. I only took 1. I left the other 1 for the next kid.

IT RHYMES WITH TRUTH
Cross out pre
Name
Dept.
until all spaces are uti
Name
Dept.
Name
Dept.
Name
Dept.
Name
Dept.

se repe
Dept.
Name
Dept.
Name
Dept.
Name
Dept.
Nar
De
DON'T
READ
ME
SID

Rich Miller has been a professional writer for more than 25 years. His remark-able debut novel *It Rhymes With Truth* is a tragi-comic tale of an obstreperous elderly woman and even more obstreperous young boy trying to save themselves by attempting to save one another. His upcoming novel, *Love Will Surely Save You, If It Doesn't Kill You First*, will answer the burning question of who is to blame for this colossal mess we humans have gotten ourselves into. Miller wishes he had written *Cat's Cradle*, *Beloved* and *Ubik*, but nobody's perfect. He lives in the Pacific Northwest where the wild things are. For more information visit www.richmillerbooks.com.

Book Club Conversation Starters:

- The narrator speaks directly to Ruth by referring to her as "you" throughout the book. What effect did that use of second person voice have on you as the reader? Did it impact the empathy you felt toward Ruth and the boy?

- The narrator is preoccupied with numbers throughout the book. This manifests with him saying certain numbers repeatedly (e.g. prime numbers), typing number symbols instead of words like "one" and "two," playing sudoku and listing baseball statistics. Why do you think numbers are meaningful to him and what impact did it have on you as the reader?

- Do you agree with the narrator that sprinkle cookies are one of the "worst cookies ever" and that "baby carrots" are all the same size?

- Despite being tormented by thoughts of leaving, the boy only successfully leaves once – briefly. That isn't surprising to Ruth, and she tells him so: "You could have escaped 100 times today if you wanted to. You could have disappeared out the sliding door 1,001 times over the past few weeks, months, however long it's been. But you don't really want to. We both know that." What reasons do you think Ruth has for believing this? What reasons might the narrator actually believe himself? Why?

- Do you think Ruth is on to something when she says the only psychology that matters is reverse psychology?

- Millie is the nemesis of Ruth and the boy during the first half of the book, and the boy's narration paints her as a one-dimensional antagonist with no redeeming qualities. Do you agree with Ruth that asking why Millie is such a bad person who does bad things to them is the wrong question to be asking? What do you think she was trying to get the boy to think about?

- The narrator includes his artwork and other objects in the book to spark Ruth's memory. What objects would you have included in the book if you were the narrator and trying to unlock Ruth's prior personality? What else would you have done to restore Ruth's memory?

- If you were a child, do you think you could successfully hide in a retirement home? And do you think there are enough *trabajos pequeños* that you could support yourself and a hungry older woman who is hiding you in her room?

- Ruth takes increasingly transgressive steps to keep the narrator living with her and protect him from perceived threats. At what point did Ruth's actions cross the line for you? Did your view of Ruth change once she crossed that line?

- Would you be willing to throw ketchup-covered tater tots at noisy people if a loved one was playing "Silent Night" on a violin?

- After Ruth is struck by the boy on the railroad tracks, the narrator debates whether there was ever another boy. Do you believe there was another boy? Do you think the narrator is confused about whether there was another boy?

- Do you believe that the lonely lady, the neglectful husband and the gardener in Ruth's romance novel live happily ever after?

- Late in the book, the narrator describes his discomfort there while watching other students like animals at a zoo. Why is he resistant to seeing himself as one of them? And do you think he will stick with school or run for the hills?

- The narrator leaves cookies on the railing before he leaves for college. What do you think his wish is for Ruth? And what do you think his wish is for himself?

- Do you think Ruth reads the book after the narrator mails it home?